# E B JANES

# Pivotal Darkness

*The Darkness Journals*

# Prologue

**Before...**

Feeble light threw shadows into the corners of her room. She must have fallen asleep without turning off the bedside lamp. She lay on her back, her arms at her side, the bedclothes drawn up over her chest.

She couldn't move.

She could see everything in the room, everything as it should be—the chest of drawers, the bedside cabinet, the book and the alarm clock. All were normal.

But she couldn't move.

She tried to call out for help, but only hoarse breath emerged from between her numbed lips. Conscious but inexplicably paralysed, she lay there, shivering from the fright that spiked her skin.

Seconds masqueraded as minutes as she strove to control her limbs, whilst, in her chest, a cold and hollow fear bloomed. Then basic instinct alerted her to a terrible certainty: she was not alone.

A presence was in the room with her; something that had rendered her immobile and had stolen her voice. Something which meant her harm.

Something *evil*.

She couldn't see or hear anything, yet revulsion crawled through her as fear crystallised into terror.

Then it started. She felt chill hands at the nape of her neck, invisible fingers sliding around her collar to encircle her throat. She could barely swallow; barely breathe.

She couldn't move.

The hands slithered up under her chin and began to squeeze. Insidious fingers gripped tightly, strangling, choking, trapping in dead air and suffocating her.

Something heinous and unseen was trying to kill her.

Frigid with fear, her chest constricted, and she snatched breaths in shallow, panicked sips. When the incremental tightening paused, she maintained consciousness, but the malignant hands remained tightly clamped around her throat, keeping both the pressure and her terror at peak levels. Blood pumped loudly in her ears as her heart punched toxic hysteria through her veins. In silent desperation, she pleaded with anything that might hear her: *don't let the hands squeeze any tighter*.

Then came the pressure on her chest. Something heavy, something solid but unseen, pushed down and squashed her shoulder blades further into the mattress. Like concrete blocks stacked on top of her, the heaviness made it even harder to inhale. Trapped and helpless, her fear-widened eyes dashed frantically from side to side.

But there was no help for her. No escape.

She was going to die.

Utter panic roiled within her, and dread leaked from her pores in a cold sweat. Who was this? *What* was this? Why was this happening to her?

*How can I make it stop?*

Mercifully, then came blackness.

She gasped as she woke in her dark room, her heart pounding, her limbs trembling and her body wet with sweat. She was lying in exactly the same position as moments ago, but this time, she was in darkness.

*Breathe. Breathe again.* Breathe. *Slowly.* Breathe. *Exhale.*

She swallowed down the bile at the back of her throat and coughed to clear her windpipe, then coughed again to free her tightened lungs. She was all right; it had stopped, and she was safe. It was only a dream.

The bedside lamp had been on then, but it wasn't on now. This was reality; the darkness was real, not the light. She was safe, lying in the dark.

Her muscles ached from the rigidity of her limbs, so she forced them to relax by moving her toes, flexing her feet and unlocking her knees. Gradually, she got her body back under control. Her breathing deepened and her heart rate slowed, until the panic receded and the sickness ebbed.

*Breathe.*

She turned onto her side and buried herself beneath the bedclothes, tugging a spare pillow over her head. Inhaling the darkness of the room, she was further soothed by the cool air that reached her nostrils through a small gap between the pillow and the bedspread.

She closed her eyes, screwing them tightly shut, and then prayed as hard as she could that sleep would not drag her back there again.

# 1

# Chapter 1

**The Beginning...**

What is darkness? A mere absence of light or something more? Darkness exists without cause, and it is infinite. Light is transient; eventually, light will always abandon you. Darkness is eternal: a constant, unbound by time or need of source. It is ancient and untamed.

\* \* \*

Ellie sat under the Holm Oak, listening to the sounds of the night. A rustling in the flower border, the calls of a solitary owl, and a dog barking in the distance augmented the soft harmony of the dark garden. The rough bark of the twisted trunk pressed into her back and grounded her in the blackness. She didn't need a light; her eyes could well discern the outlines of trees against the inky sky and the distant hills rounding the horizon. Ellie had always felt comforted by darkness; it wrapped around her like a cloak, hiding her, keeping her safe and minding her secrets.

Relaxing against the old tree, she felt the brush of wings against her cheek as tiny creatures welcomed her into their night-time world. Gazing out to the black woods beyond the garden, Ellie smiled. Even as a child, she had recognised that there was something magical about darkness. At night, the realities of the day faded, and edges became blurred. What appeared one way in the light altered and became unfamiliar in the dark; the ordinary became new and enticingly strange, abundant with endless possibility.

Ellie shivered and gazed upwards towards the stars. It was one of those nights that made her wish she could fly: clear skies inviting her up into the air and very little breeze to chill her skin. She yearned to soar into the blackness and feel the rush of air against her body; to glide effortlessly across hidden landscapes heading towards some strange rendezvous.

As a child, Ellie had liked to put her hand out of the car window when travelling at speed. With her fingers closed together like a paddle, she would surf the rushing wind, relishing the resistance and force of the air. This, she had decided way back then, was what it would feel like to fly.

She let out a deep sigh, releasing the tension of an impossible desire. If only. Maybe in another lifetime.

The evening had grown cold, and Ellie pulled her jacket around herself. Picking up her drink, she rose, dusted crumpled leaf skeletons from the back of her jeans and turned towards the silhouetted house. Its pleasing, granite elevations now disguised, the time-worn farmhouse was a monstrously angular contrast to the natural shadows surrounding her.

Heading inside, she locked the door behind her. But what

was she really keeping at bay? Darkness was already inside the house, as well as outside in the garden. If something strange from the midnight world sought to enter the house, it would not likely be stopped by mere locks and bolts.

Ellie shook herself. *Stop thinking like this.* "Imagination overdrive", her mother would have called it; a malady from which she'd long suffered, according to Grace.

Turning on the kitchen light, Ellie flicked on the kettle. Making herself a hot drink to take to bed was her comfort routine; a tonic to ensure that she fell quickly into a dreamless sleep without any unwelcome diversions en route.

Waiting for the water to boil, Ellie stared at her reflection in the kitchen window. Her features were hidden in the black glass, unless she turned slightly sideways to allow light from behind to illuminate her profile. Again, the known became unfamiliar in the darkness, unless looked at from a different angle. Steam rose from the kettle and it clicked off. She made her hot chocolate and headed upstairs to bed.

Once in her room, Ellie undressed and settled into the sunken comfort of her bed. Sitting propped up, the quilted cover tucked under her chin, she allowed one arm to be outside of her warm tent in order to drink the hot chocolate.

She hadn't pulled the curtains; after all, what was the point? There was no other house for over a mile and small likelihood of passers-by spying on her from the little-used lane meandering past Owl's Ridge. Besides, she liked to look out at the dark landscape and to watch the moths on her window pane, their small furry bodies knocking softly against the glass as dusty wings polished in a flurry of activity that essentially got them nowhere. It almost seemed allegorical.

3

Finishing her drink, Ellie set down her cup and clicked off the bedside light. Rolling onto her side, she snuggled down under the covers. It was her custom to arrange the heavy bedspread to totally envelop her before tucking the edges tightly in. Cocooned in comfort, she was safe. This was how darkness made her feel.

As she slid towards slumber, the blackness behind her eyelids briefly lit to red. Ellie's eyes snapped open.

*What on earth was that? A flash of light from outside?*

There wasn't a thunderstorm, so it wasn't lightning. She clutched the bedclothes more tightly to her throat and held her breath to listen for anomalous noise.

Nothing. She must have imagined it. Ellie exhaled loudly and shut her eyes. Deliberately making her mind blank, she fought her disquiet for sleep.

The bad dreams had started when she'd reached her teenage years. Recurrent still to this day, they had mercifully lessened in frequency over time, yet they had left Ellie with an aversion to anyone touching her neck, particularly from behind.

In the course of her A Level Art studies, Ellie had come across incubi and succubae in nineteenth century paintings. These demonic entities were often pictured crouching on the chests of their sleeping victims; the incubus favouring sexual intercourse with sleeping women while the succubus sought pleasure from sleeping men. The pressure on the victim's chests worryingly paralleled Ellie's own overly realistic nightmares, until she then came across sleep paralysis and night terrors during her wider reading for her Psychology course. Night terrors similar to her own experiences were thought to be caused by the premature release of a hormone which disabled bodily movement during sleep. If the process was triggered before the mind was fully asleep, sensations of paralysis and feeling terrified were reported to occur.

The logical explanation of these findings—and the lack of anything sexual about her own night terrors—led Ellie to conclude that her frightening nocturnal experiences were of a physiological rather than paranormal nature. This lessened her fear of them, and it seemed to follow that their regularity then decreased.

There were still the other nightmares, though. In these, she would wake in bed, suddenly afraid. She would try to switch on the bedside light, but it wouldn't work. This meant that the Evil was coming. She would frantically recite the Lord's Prayer to ward off the approaching terror, but dream-state Ellie could never remember the right order of the words. The prayer was her only defence, her only shield against the approaching Evil, and yet still she couldn't get it right; still couldn't make it work. 'Our Father, who art in heaven, hallowed be thy name, thy kingdom come, thy will be done...' *What was the next bit?* Fear would strip her memory. 'Deliver me from evil, deliver me from evil, deliver me...'

She always awoke from these nightmares in a panicked state, as she did from the night terrors, although perhaps not quite so fear-stricken.

# 2

# Chapter 2

Her eyelids heavy, Ellie rolled out of bed and made her way to the bathroom. The shrill alarm had shocked her out of a dreamless sleep, and several moments had passed before her brain caught up with the rest of her wakened senses. *Today is Monday. Time to get up for college.*

The house was still of activity. Her parents had set off two days ago in her father's cherished Citroën H van for a wellbeing retreat in a neighbouring county. Ellie didn't expect them back for several days yet.

Overnight rain had dampened the lanes, but already the tarmac was drying in the sun. It was going to be a nice day. Driving into the college car park and avoiding the pothole puddles, Ellie carefully manoeuvred her car into a parking space. She drove a Citroën 2CV, which she'd christened Dolly; her father had pronounced it a design classic when buying the car as a reward for Ellie passing her driving test. The car was cream, with deep maroon over her wide wheel arches. Plums and Custard was the model name, but Ellie much preferred Dolly. She checked her watch as she turned off the engine: there was still time to go to the Common Room before first period.

Reaching for her bag in the passenger footwell, she groaned as she lifted it. Inside were two large folders, both heavy with notes she'd made over the last two years. Soon, she would need to revise all those pages in preparation for her final exams in June, which was a disheartening thought. Determinedly, Ellie pushed it to the back of her mind and, after manually locking her car door, set off across the car park, admiring the rainbow-decorated puddles as she went.

Lowford College squatted on the low land at the northern edge of town. Its sprawling campus was a conflict of red brick and concrete buildings, temporary classrooms and more interesting, Lottery-funded, modern architecture. Being the local Sixth Form college to a rural district, it drew post-sixteen students from a wide catchment area.

The student Common Room was housed in a large pre-fabricated hut that sat atop concrete blocks. Wooden steps and a handrail led up to the door. Inside, Flick Sargent, one of Ellie's best friends, was sat with a gang of the usual faces. Like a mob of perched crows, they chatted in "Goth Corner" while sharing headphones, laughing and destroying paper coffee cups.

*He's here*, Ellie noted with satisfaction. She didn't know him well but thought that his long black hair, leather jacket and brooding demeanour made Jacob Tallis pretty much the most fanciable thing at college.

'Hey, Ells!' Flick greeted her warmly. 'What you got first thing?'

Ellie pulled a face. 'Economics.'

'Ouch. Wanna head to town after that to cheer you up?'

Flick asked. She grinned wickedly. 'We could feed the parrot?'

Ellie grinned back. "Feeding the parrot" meant going to the pub near the Art and Design building. The publican owned a pet parrot that lived in a large cage in the Front Bar and enjoyed being fed crisps by the patrons, but Flick had discovered that you could also feed it cider in a long, upturned fingernail. Flick lived with parents who doted on their only child and conveniently turned a blind eye when Flick and her friends came home late at night and smelling of alcohol. But even Flick's folks' lenient attitudes might be stretched to breaking point if faced with the girls rolling in legless on a weekday afternoon.

At five foot, two inches tall and of slim build, Flick was attractive and blessed with long, straight hair which she often dyed purple or red to disguise its natural brunette colouring. Flick's wicked sense of humour could always pull Ellie out of a grump, and when out for the night, Flick could be seriously naughty.

'Nah. I've got to get home to the animals. My folks are away,' Ellie answered.

'Fair do's. We could do the market instead?'

'Sure. Sounds good,' Ellie agreed. 'I'll meet you on the bus.'

Lowford College ran a bus service between the main campus and the Art building in town. It was a very useful way of catching a lift up to town; the driver didn't care whether you were actually going to a class or not.

A collective groan sounded across the Common Room as the lesson bell rang and unenthusiastic students grabbed their bags and filed out. Flick and Ellie headed for their separate classes, Flick happily off to Drama while Ellie dawdled towards the Economics lecture room. It wasn't that she didn't do well in Economics; it was just that Ellie found it uninspiring. Ellie needed subjects which fired her imagination, but learning about market forces and the distribution of wealth simply didn't do that for her. If she achieved a D grade in her final exam, Ellie would be happy, although, personally, she thought that even a D might be aiming too high.

As she passed the Sports Hall, Ellie saw Jacob sauntering towards the car park. He glanced in her direction before crossing the road and, noticing her looking at him, gave her a nod of recognition and twitched his lips in his trademark half-smile.

Ellie grinned to herself as she headed towards Economics. *Not such a bad start to the day after all.*

\* \* \*

The market place was in the old part of town, by Stearn Castle. Standing on a low hill, and more of a ruin now than a habitable building, the twelfth century stronghold still overlooked the town and the age-old trading place along its eastern flank. Every Monday morning, set out across the car parking spaces, a range of stalls drew locals, students and tourists alike. Tucked back against the crumbling castle walls, Delphea's evoked a mild air of mystery with its dark, pointed tent roof and enclosed sides. Invariably bedecked with colourful floaty scarves, ethnic and Goth jewellery, natural crystals and perfumed joss sticks, it was Ellie and Flick's favourite stall.

Today, Mel, the stall holder, had some new rings and

necklaces for sale. Flick immediately pounced upon a silver Celtic cross hung from a black velvet choker, which was very much her style. Ellie more decorously browsed the rings tucked temptingly between velvet-covered foam rolls. One on the tray furthest away from her caught her eye. It was silver and had a curiously-designed spiral engraving upon its highly polished face. Ellie asked if she could have a closer look, so Mel handed her the tray without pausing her discussions with Flick.

Plucking the ring from its slot, Ellie noted its surprising weight and the chill of the metal against her skin as she slid it onto her middle finger. Examining its face, her eye was caught by the rotational design and then drawn to its offset centre, where a deep purple crystal was set like a star. Following the path of the longest spiral arm were five tiny white crystal chips embedded in the metal surface.

Easing the ring from her finger, Ellie turned it over, looking for a price tag. There wasn't one, but she did notice some further engraving on the inside of the ring. The markings were unfamiliar and not in a writing that she recognised. Maybe it was inscribed in one of those languages which didn't use letters like English did?

*English.* She had that after lunch. Checking her watch, Ellie realised they would now need to walk back to college, as they'd missed the return bus. Interrupting Flick to ask the price of the ring, Ellie passed it to Mel, experiencing a palpable sense of loss as she did so.

'I don't remember this one,' said Mel, 'but you can have it at the same price as the rest along that row.'

Ellie nodded and paid for the ring. She slipped it back on her finger, immediately experiencing a feeling of relief.

Smiling, she turned to Flick. 'Come on,' she said. 'We need to get a move on if we're going to make it to English.'

Flick, still stood with a handful of treasures, groaned with indecision. Finally, she settled on the Celtic cross and a scarf with tiny silver crosses dangling from the hem. With a wave to Mel, they walked back across the market to Castle Street, then down past the library on their way back to the college.

\* \* \*

When Ellie got home later that afternoon, she began her usual rounds tending to the animals. The two lambs from the farm down the road were first. One had a slight deformity of the spine that made its back curve to the side, and the other had double-jointed ankles and couldn't walk properly. Ellie was giving them her own version of physiotherapy to straighten and strengthen, which seemed to be working. When she worked with the animals, gently massaging and stretching, Ellie could feel her hands warming and transferring her heat to them. This appeared to calm and soothe the creatures and was especially useful when handling the wild animals outside in the chicken run; occasionally, one actually fell asleep in her hands. Today, however, her animal whispering abilities seemed to be off key, as the pigeons in her wildlife hospital kept away from her, eyeing her suspiciously, and even the ducklings had huddled at the far end of their pen. The family's two rambunctious spaniels, Raff and Chipper, had gone with her parents on their trip, so that concluded her ministrations for the day.

Feeling hungry, Ellie made herself a snack and took a bottle of Diet Coke from the fridge before heading to the back door, collecting her sketch pad and pencil case on the way. She strode to the bottom of the garden and through the gate that led into the field. On the far side of the field, at the furthest point away from her house, was a small wood. A footpath crossed the field in front of the wood and led to an old stile which offered access to the lane.

Ellie crossed the footpath and strolled into the wood. She loved it here. The mature trees screened most of the noise from beyond the wood, and it felt like she was entering another time or realm, where she could no longer hear the cacophony of modern-day life. No wonder the Celts—and many other cultures—thought that dryads or even deities dwelled in trees. The soaring majesty of the trunks and the noises made by their moving branches and leaves would surely give strength to the belief that trees were alive with supernatural energy.

The leaves were still not fully visible yet in the wood; some trees, like the reticent ash, hadn't even bothered partially dressing themselves thus far. Ellie's current Art project was on trees, which was the reason for this afternoon's dalliance into the wood. Her goal was to sketch a tree whilst looking up at it from underneath its canopy. She strolled around the banked edge of the wood, where the trees were more widely spaced and less overrun with brambles, and noted with pleasure the glossy green spears thrusting up through the leaf litter. In May, an abundance of bluebells would embroider the soft, leafy carpet, adding a welcome splash of brightness to the muted, natural palette.

Ellie finally selected a handsome oak tree to study. Balling up her jacket to use as a pillow, she lay down on the moss-covered ground. Above her, the trunk soared impressively upwards, and she noted the fractal-like patterns of the branches at its summit. Standing her sketch pad up on her chest, she began to draw.

As she worked, her mind automatically drew visual parallels with the form of the tree: a ceiling in a cathedral; a spider's web spreading out from the stem at its centre; a net; a natural cage. Her Art tutor had challenged Ellie to draw the energy of a tree, so, while sketching, she pondered how to tackle this more abstract representation. A tree's energy must be in constant motion, she reasoned, drawn from the earth by its roots and then flowing up the trunk to be dispersed through the branches and twigs to the leaves. But, then again, the leaves also generate energy from the light of the sun, which must move back down, too. The bole was like a superhighway of energy, streaming in both directions at once.

Satisfied with her observed drawing, Ellie sat up and turned to a clean page. She marked two bold lines to represent a tree trunk and indicated roots below with a web of tangled line. *The branches have another energy all their own*, she mused. They caught energy from the wind and either stirred or lashed, depending on the amount fed to them. Ellie closed her eyes and brought to mind an image of loose-limbed branches beginning to sway, the movement then intensifying as the wind speed increased. She visualised branches thrashing in gale force winds, blown first one way, then blasted another. In her mind's eye, the frantic branches appeared to spin. An unexpected gust flipped the pages of her sketch pad and blew hair across her face. Sweeping it from her forehead, she opened her eyes and began to draw.

A considerable while later, Ellie paused for a break. Dropping her sketch pad onto the moss beside her, she lay back down and closed her eyes. The soft sounds of a light breeze in the branches, birdsong and the occasional flapping of wings lulled her as she relaxed fully against the ground. If she listened hard enough, Ellie could just about hear the hum of a tractor engine working a few fields away. Settling her shoulders more comfortably, she breathed in deeply the pleasant, earthy aroma of the wood and smelt the fallen, crushed leaves beneath her.

There was a door in a dark, smooth wall. She placed her hand on the wall and felt the cold, perfect surface, similar to glass but with less friction. She knew that the door held something back, kept something hidden; something that once released couldn't be contained again. Even so, she very much wanted to open it. She looked around; there was no one else here, nor were there any sounds. She was in an empty space.

She walked to the door and stood in front of it. There was a presence there. A memory surfaced: it was her mission to guard the door. She had been entrusted with ensuring that it was kept shut. Placing the palm of her hand on the door's surface, she felt smoothness akin to the wall, but here there was also warmth. Her fingertips sensed a faint thrumming in the fabric of the door; a rhythm, a regular beat.

A *heartbeat.*

Ellie woke with a start. Her clothes were damp from the dew, and her back hurt from lying on the uneven ground. It was dusk. She eased herself up and got to her feet. Raising her arms above her head, Ellie stretched the kinks out of her spine and shook some life back into her limbs. She collected her drawing paraphernalia and then, looking about her once more at the beauty of the evenfall wood, made her way out from between the trunks and into the field.

Emerging from the tree line, and for no reason other than instinct, Ellie glanced left towards the stile. There was a tall figure standing there in the lane, about fifty metres away from her. Her attention diverted momentarily from where she was treading, her foot caught in a divot and she stumbled. Regaining her balance, she looked back at the stile, but the figure had gone. A late walker, she assumed. But then, the figure hadn't been walking; they had stood facing into the field.

In the gloaming, Ellie hadn't been able to see their face, but she had the distinct impression they had been watching her. Or even watching *for* her. The unwelcome thought arrived in her mind unbidden. Well, whoever it was, they were gone now. She pushed her disconcerting thoughts from her mind and speedily crossed the field back to the garden gate.

Tonight, Ellie didn't sit outside. She felt unsettled—a little pensive, even—and so preferred to be sheltered inside the house, behind a locked door. Curling up on the end of the sofa, Ellie put the television on for background noise and applied herself to finishing the observed tree drawing from memory.

Completing the piece, she reviewed her work. With the trunk at the centre of the page and the branches and twigs circling it, there was movement implicit in the image that she hadn't noticed before. She turned to the next page and critically assessed her depiction of tree energy, her eyes unfocussed to better follow the movement.

*Wait. What was that?* Had she drawn that? Near the centre

of the windswept branches was a smudge and a dark mark that, together, looked like a small scar on the tree bole. The smudge gave tonal variation suggesting a raised border which circled the dark mark, like a rub-over setting for the polished stone pendants she'd seen at the market, but instead set here in a tree trunk. She didn't remember deliberately drawing it.

Ellie glanced at the ring she'd bought earlier that day, then looked back at her drawing. The purple stone and the tree scar were both fixed points in a swirl of motion, similar even in position. *How odd.* Coincidence, she told herself, or just her mind making connections of pattern. Perhaps the pencil in her hand and her graphite-dusted fingertips had marked the paper just as she'd set aside her sketchpad and fallen asleep.

Ellie took off the ring and put it on the arm of the sofa. Again, she experienced an inexplicable pang of loss. Deliberately moving the ring further away, she placed it on the coffee table and sat back down, daring herself to leave it there. She picked up the pad of paper and turned to a new leaf, then began to sketch the ring's spiral design.

A few minutes later, she scribbled across the page in frustration. It was no good; she needed to look at the design more closely. Retrieving her ring, Ellie peered at it again, noting the purple stone set at the spiral's core and the curve of tiny crystals which led there. Their positioning reminded her of a galaxy of swirling stars.

Now tired of drawing, Ellie laid aside the drawing pad and absentmindedly slipped the ring back on while stretching her legs out across the sofa. Flicking through the television channels, she deliberately challenged her earlier unease by selecting a psychological thriller to watch for the remainder of the evening.

Just before bedtime, her parents phoned. They sent her their love and said that they'd be home by the weekend. Oh, and could she please give the oil company a ring tomorrow and make sure that the tank was filled up? Their supply was running low, and Grace didn't want the Aga to go out.

3

# Chapter 3

Wednesday morning dawned bright, although a heavy mist covered the garden and surrounding fields. As she set off on the drive to college, Ellie turned on Dolly's headlights and fog lights.

The mist was thick in the valleys, but as Dolly climbed to the top of a ridge, they came out of the haze into brilliant sunshine. All around were the grey-green silhouettes of trees and hedges faded to white as they were swallowed by the encroaching mist.

Ellie stopped at the side of the lane and indulged herself by taking a moment to fully delight in the panorama. Getting out of the car, she wrestled her phone from her coat pocket and took a series of photos, but none did justice to the spectacular scenery—basked in sunlight, yet still concealed and mysterious, the ancient landscape was breathtakingly beautiful; magical, almost.

A familiar hunger stirred within her; a pining for something more than the bounds of reality would allow. What could be hidden in those misted valleys? Ellie's imagination thirsted for entrances to other realms or to meet strange peoples from older times. The magic of the night was at work here, too; dressed in brume, the hills and valleys held limitless possibilities, chances for the fantastic to be real, and Ellie felt consumed by a desire to unlock their secrets.

But how could a mere human find the doorways and cloaked avenues that gave access to these unearthly places? Ellie sighed, dragging her mind back to the here and now. She'd dallied for too long and was going to be late.

* * *

Arriving at her Psychology lesson, Ellie excused her tardiness, using the fog as an excuse. Sam Ferrand, the tutor, never made a fuss about the small things, as long as her students got their well written reports in on time.

Recently, the class had moved on to studying Sigmund Freud's model of the mind, and Ellie was finding it fascinating. The illustration in her textbook pictured the human mind as an iceberg. The conscious mind was the smaller section visible above the water, but the larger parts of the mind were hidden below. You could dive down to retrieve memories and knowledge from the subconscious, but further down, too deep to reach, was the dark unconscious. This erratic part of the mind held instincts and impulses like selfish needs, irrational wishes, violent thoughts and unacceptable sexual desires. Some events and desires were just too painful for people to acknowledge, and Freud believed these were kept locked in the unconscious.

Ellie thought of her recurrent nightmares. Had they come from her own dark unconscious? If that were so, did that mean she secretly *wanted* to be held down and terrified out of her mind? That she desired to get close to evil?

*Not bloody likely!* Dreaming about evil petrified her with fear; she certainly had no wish to become better acquainted with it.

The irrational wishes part made slightly more sense, like her desire to soar through the night sky and her longing for experiences of other worlds. She'd always had a keen imagination and an ability to marvel at the natural wonders around her. It wasn't really surprising, therefore, that her untamed unconscious might combine the two and generate a lust for flight and a craving to discover magical secrets.

If she thought of it like that, maybe her mind wasn't that weird, after all.

* * *

Later that day, Ellie sat sketching in the Art studio. Their tutor, Paul Seaton, had tasked the class with drawing the still life arrangement in the centre of the room, and as that required their full attention, they worked in silence. However, having Jacob sitting directly opposite her, and them exchanging small smiles as their glances inevitably met, was adding a sprinkling of titillation for Ellie that made concentration difficult.

At breaktime, most of the students left the studio to sit in the rear courtyard, many stopping at the vending machine as they passed. Perching on old stools relegated to outside seating, they chatted and checked their phones as their hot drinks cooled.

Encouraged by Jacob's mildly flirtatious glances, Ellie

hoped to talk to him during their break. But Jacob was one of the first to leave the studio and was consequently sat surrounded by other students. He also went back inside before the end of the break, so, annoyingly, Ellie had no chance to speak with him.

When the class resumed, Ellie frowned at her work, dissatisfied with the proportions. She picked up her eraser. On the paper underneath, someone had written: *Canteen, lunchtime?*

Ellie's eyes flew to Jacob. He was watching her and smiled lopsidedly before continuing to sketch. Ellie's chest filled with nervous excitement, and throughout the rest of the session, she found herself frequently looking at Jacob. On the few occasions their eyes actually met, they held each other's gaze for seconds at a time fuelling Ellie's delicious anticipation.

As usual, the canteen was packed by lunchtime. Queueing for her coffee, Ellie looked for Jacob and found him sat at a table by the window wall, but he was not alone. Two other Goths—Lily Woods and Pete Saunders—were sat with him.

*Not much of a date, then.*

Having paid, she held her coffee cup by the rim and carefully made her way over to him. Jacob looked up from the castle he'd been constructing from dead paper cups.

'Made it, then,' he greeted.

'Yep, despite missing the bus back.' She had stayed after class to buy supplies from the Art store.

Ellie smiled at Lily and Pete, who nodded in recognition and returned to their low-toned conversation. Pulling out a chair, she sat down next to Jacob and began talking about their artwork.

A short while later, Lily and Pete scraped back their chairs and stood up. They both smiled at Jacob, Lily pouting at him and waving her fingers before walking away.

'Are those two a couple?' Ellie asked, sipping her scalding coffee.

'Yeah, on and off. Right now, they're on.'

Ellie nodded, watching the receding couple. She'd heard that Jacob and Lily had once been an item and hadn't liked the lingering look Lily had just lavished on Jacob. Ellie turned back to him with a bright smile.

'By the way, Flick reckons she's driving to the Spring Thing if you wanted a lift,' Ellie offered.

'Ok. I might make it, then.'

A sudden bang on the window next to Ellie made her jump, and she turned to see Flick and Jaz Tully's gurning faces. Jaz's black hair was spiked particularly high today, and that, combined with their expressions, was borderline disturbing.

'Your friends, right?' Jacob asked with an amused look.

'Yep, afraid so,' joked Ellie. She waved at the gawking pair and signalled for them to come inside, but Flick shook her head, motioning for Ellie to join them instead.

'I gotta go, anyway. Later,' said Jacob, rising from his chair and heading for the exit.

After a moment spent pulling exasperated faces at Flick and Jaz, who responded with theatrically innocent shrugs, Ellie gingerly picked up her still-scalding coffee and left the canteen.

The girls greeted Ellie with ribald shrieks and hugs.

'Hey! Mind the coffee!' said Ellie, grinning regardless.

'You were chatting him up!' accused a delighted Jaz. 'Yay! You finally grew a pair and went in for the kill!'

'We were only *talking*!' Ellie replied.

''Bout bloody time, too!' Flick grinned. 'You've been panting after him for months!'

'Slight over-exaggeration, I think!' objected Ellie, then swiftly changed the subject. 'Anyway, what have you both got this afternoon?'

'Maths,' said Jaz.

'Drama, *dahhlings*,' answered Flick, striking a pose.

'I've got a free period, so I'm going home early to do my psych report and meet the oil delivery guy,' Ellie said. 'I guess I'll see you tomorrow.'

'Sure, see you then,' said Jaz.

'OK, part-timer,' teased Flick. *'Demain matin, mon amie.'*

\* \* \*

When Ellie got to the student car park, she found that her car had been thoughtlessly hemmed in on both sides by two badly-parked rust buckets. She squeezed down the side of Dolly and tried to open the driver-side door. Irritatingly, it only opened a crack, and there was no way even her slim hips were going to fit through that. *Damn.*

The passenger side was the same, so, balancing her coffee cup on the roof, she slithered around to the back of the car and scrambled in through the boot. Sliding down into the driver's seat, she flicked up the half-and-half 2CV window and lifted her coffee from the roof and into the car. Balancing the cup on the narrow passenger-side dashboard shelf, Ellie fished for her car keys, which had fallen down the side of her seat.

As she put the key into the ignition and checked that the peculiar dashboard gear stick was in neutral, her eye caught something on the windscreen. *What the hell was that?* Ellie looked properly. There were marks showing in the patch of condensation caused by her hot drink. She lifted the cup and deliberately steamed up more of the glass. Over the entire windscreen was a swirling pattern drawn in sweeping lines, like a finger drawing on a huffed-upon window, but drawn here with something much finer.

With a shiver of apprehension, Ellie moved the coffee cup from side to side across the centre of the windscreen, half dreading what she instinctively felt would be there. She was right: as the steam swept over the glass, a circular mark offset from the centre of an oval spiral emerged. It was the same image of movement swirling around a single point as on her newly-purchased ring and in her abstract tree drawing. This was now officially weird.

How the hell had someone got into her car and drawn this? She'd had the keys in her bag all day, for Christ's sake!

Suddenly frightened, Ellie needed to get away from the creepy pattern. She opened the car door, forgetting she was boxed in, and Dolly's door bashed into the side of the car next to her.

*Shit!*

Ellie grabbed her jumper from the back seat and wiped furiously at the windscreen instead; she needed to annihilate the markings; to make them never have existed at all. Someone was playing silly buggers, and she was *not* happy about it.

But who? Mel from the market who'd sold her the ring? Flick, even?

*Maybe. But neither of them know about my tree study.*

She yanked the ring off her finger and threw it as hard as

she could from Dolly's small window. It sailed over several cars and bounced off the bonnet of a black Seat Ibiza before disappearing down the far side of the car.

That was *it*. She needed to speak to someone about what was going on in her head; it was getting all too freaky now. She hadn't let her overactive imagination off the leash this time; the markings on the windscreen proved that. But ... Ellie ran her hands through her hair. *No one's going to believe any of this, are they?*

She started Dolly's engine and turned the heater on to full power to demist the windscreen. Easing carefully forwards out of the parking space, she turned towards the exit, but then stopped.

*Was the ring proof?* Switching off the engine, she got out of Dolly and searched the ground between the Seat Ibiza and the car next to it. No luck. Ellie got down on her hands and knees and peered beneath the cars. If anyone saw her, they'd think she'd gone crazy, checking for car bombs or something. An ex-boyfriend of Flick's once had to do just that after carelessly leaving his military identification badge visible on the dashboard of his car.

Nope, no ring in sight. Well, at least she'd managed to get rid of it. Ellie turned back towards Dolly and froze. There, on the ground, right by the driver's door, was something silver.

A shiver ran down her spine. She knew exactly what it was. How had she not seen it when getting out of Dolly? She wasn't that unobservant, surely?

Ellie picked up the ring and again noted its weight and chill. She slid it cautiously onto her finger and was at once transfused with a sense of calm; she felt her shoulders dropping and the stress leaving her.

Maybe she'd just had too many disturbed nights lately. Maybe the lack of refreshing sleep was influencing her perception. Maybe Freud would have something to say about that, too.

\* \* \*

Ellie made it home just in time to meet the oil delivery tanker. The driver was a chatty middle-aged guy, and his jovial normality, along with the late spring sunshine, did much to restore her equilibrium.

After tending to the animals, Ellie made herself a snack and resolved to tackle her Psychology assignment. She unpacked her bag onto the kitchen table, making neat piles of her books and putting her Chromebook on charge. Sitting down, she opened the course textbook to the section they'd been reading in class.

*Freud. Right. Let's hope this doesn't make me feel even more like an unconscious-minded deviant.*

Some time later, Ellie looked up from her reading with a thoughtful frown upon her face. Freud seemed to be saying that dreams were the disguised wish fulfilment of unacceptable desires in the unconscious mind, or, as he had recategorized it, the Id. He thought that dreams presented these forbidden wishes by translating them into a more palatable form, so that the sleeper didn't experience too much anxiety and wake up. But her dreams definitely weren't non-threatening or in an acceptable form; they terrified her to the point that she awoke, traumatised.

*Monsters from the Id.* The phrase slipped into her mind.

26

It was a line from one of her father's favourite movies. She shivered involuntarily; perhaps her dreams couldn't be explained so well by psychological processes, after all. Ellie typed the last few points. She'd finish the report later, but it was essentially all done.

Looking out of the window, she saw that the afternoon was slipping into a beautiful evening. She stretched her arms high and yawned. Time for some fresh air.

She slid the chair back from the table, scraping its pine legs across the quarry tiles. Her mother would have remonstrated with her for that, she thought, experiencing a sudden pang. She was missing her mum; missing *both* of her parents. Still, they would be home soon, and that thought comforted her. Clearly being on her own was giving her a bad case of the heebie-jeebies.

Ellie took her jacket from the coat hooks by the back door. The dog leads were hanging up there, too, and she felt a surge of pleasure at the thought of seeing the spaniels again. They made the house feel so full and alive, and there was nothing quite like the welcome offered by a pet dog when you came home: pure joy and unconditional love.

* * *

It was still warm outside, but being only April, Ellie tied the sleeves of her jacket around her waist, taking it with her as a precaution against a possible evening chill. Crossing the garden, she entered the field. Grass tickled her ankles as she walked, and clouds of midges, brought out by the sunny day, hovered annoyingly at head height. Dodging this way and that to avoid them, Ellie chuckled to herself at the curious picture her sidestepping, head-ducking dance would present to an onlooker. She wandered over towards the lane, intent on a long walk over familiar ground to stretch away the bizarreness of the day and to ease her study-cramped muscles.

The timber stile in the field hedge had weathered pleasingly over time. Ellie ran her finger over the prominent grain of the wood; it felt smooth, doubtless worn so by countless hands and feet levering themselves over the stile. Without thinking, Ellie's fingers began to trace a whorl in the wood. It was satisfying to feel the spiralled woodgrain leading her to its centre knot.

She climbed over the stile and set off along the lane, the low sun making her squint and causing her to shield her eyes with her hand. Swerving to avoid more clouds of midges, she found herself moving from the warm sunlight into the dark shadow of the hedgerow.

Out of nowhere, a blast of wind buffeted her hair back from her face and the stench of decay assaulted her senses. She raised her hand to her face and coughed out the contaminated air she'd just inhaled. Stepping backwards as her lungs heaved, she found herself tucked into a shaded recess in the hedge. As she wiped her watering eyes, her attention was caught by the red brake lights of a grey four-by-four that had stopped just outside her driveway gate. There had been no engine noise to alert her to its presence, and as its rear was facing her, it logically ought to have passed by where she stood, unless it had reversed to Owl's Ridge.

Normally, Ellie would have jogged back down the lane to meet a vehicle stopping at her house, yet something about the situation felt strange and she remained where she was.

After a moment or two, which felt like an age to Ellie, the vehicle drove forwards and vanished from sight around the next bend in the lane.

Waiting a few more moments in the hedge recess for her nerves to settle and to make sure the four-by-four wasn't coming back, Ellie then hastily retraced her steps. She got to the stile and scrambled over.

*Ouch!* She'd caught her finger on a splinter. Ellie looked down to find the rough wood responsible for her injury, mildly surprised that such a time-worn beam would produce splinters.

There, where her fingers had earlier explored what she'd thought was a whorl in the grain, was a spiral engraved into the timber. *Recently* engraved, too, by the look of it, as the pale underwood stood out in stark contrast to the greened, older surface. The spiral itself was perfectly smooth, but across it were two deep rends, the edges of which were rough with splinters.

Fear suddenly gripped her. Ellie raced back across the field and dashed up the garden path. Once inside the house, she bolted the back door and ran to the front door to check that it, too, was secure.

She pulled the thick curtains across and left the lights turned off. No one could see her now. She was safe, hiding here in the darkness.

4

# Chapter 4

Grace and Andy Johnstone returned home, both well balanced and re-energised, to find their only daughter ranting about mysterious patterns appearing everywhere and a grey car that had appeared from nowhere.

Being very broad-minded people, they didn't instantly dismiss Ellie's bizarre claims, as other more mainstream parents might have done. Instead, they discussed with her at length fundamental pattern usage in mythology and the art of ancient cultures. Frustrated at first by their response, Ellie wished that she had more conventional parents who would reassuringly tell her that she was letting her imagination run away with her and seeing things that weren't there. Oh, and would she like a biscuit with her cup of tea?

However, after some thought and a little distance, Ellie decided to do some research into the potential meanings of the mysteriously reoccurring spiral pattern. She began with some Internet research that evening and, in her free period the next morning, paid a visit to the college library. The former hadn't been particularly revealing, and she found the latter to be a rather sterile environment, due to its over-bright strip lighting and white melamine shelving. Moreover, even after a discussion with the bored, gum-chewing librarian, the only reference to spirals that Ellie could find was in books from the Art section.

Disheartened, Ellie went to lunch, making a mental note to continue her online search and to also pay a visit to the library in town as soon as possible.

* * *

Arriving home later that day, Ellie parked Dolly in her usual spot on the gravel drive. It was nice to see her dad's Citroën H van back in its space under the oak trees that lined the road hedge. She'd always thought that the front of the van looked rather like the face of a Saint Bernard's dog, and it did even more so now while sat dozing in the shade. Her mother's car, however, was not in its place, and when Ellie reached the front door, she found it locked. *Damn.* She didn't have her house key with her. Usually, the house was left unlocked when either Andy or Grace were at home, so Ellie didn't often use her own set of keys.

Scrabbling for the spare key under one of the geranium pots to the side of the front door, Ellie caught her finger on something sharp and speedily withdrew her hand. She looked at the line of red seeping from the slice in her skin. It was odd that there should be something sharp where the spare key was hidden.

Looking under and around the plant pots, this time with a great deal of care, Ellie discovered the source of her injury. It was a small broken bottle; one of the charm bottles that her mother created using various plants and tiny objects. Ellie looked up above the window where it had hung, expecting to see a piece of weathered cord but, instead, was surprised to see the neck of the little bottle still dangling there. The bottle had clearly shattered where it hung. *How very odd.* Something must have hit it; perhaps a piece of flying gravel sent up from a spinning car tyre? *Could be*, Ellie supposed. Taking great care not to cut herself again, she collected the shards of the broken bottle.

Peering at them in the palm of her hand, she noticed charred pieces of plant matter clinging to what must have been the inside of the bottle. Could the sun have caused the dried-out leaves to spontaneously combust? Or perhaps that particular bottle had a thickened area of glass which had acted as a lens and focussed the sun's rays? After all, every child knew that you could set fire to dry leaves by concentrating the sun's rays through a magnifying glass, didn't they? In fact, Ellie had once noticed the same effect being caused by a glass paperweight on the surface of a mahogany table. There had been quite deep scorch marks in the wood which, as the only child in the house, Ellie had been called to account for before Andy had realised that the culprits were, in fact, the glass paperweight and the sun.

That must be it. Perhaps the glass bottle had quickly become hot and had shattered, like a cold glass would if exposed to boiling water. Satisfied with her logical, if tenuous, explanation, Ellie retrieved the key and let herself into the house.

Ellie tipped the shards of broken bottle from her hand onto the worn wooden surface of the hall table, intending to leave it there to alert her mother to the unfortunate fate of the

32

charm bottle when she returned home.

On display along the tabletop was the Rogues' Gallery, a term coined by her father for their collection of framed family photographs. From images of Grace and Andy at university through to some taken at the summer equinox last year, her family were all there lined up in smiling, chronological order. Ignoring the ones of herself—she had never liked having her photo taken, even as a small child—Ellie picked up the most recent photo of her mum and dad. It had been taken at a friend's house earlier in the year. Andy and Grace were, of course, smiling for the camera, but their body language gave the impression that they had been interrupted from an intimate conversation for the shot; Grace was leaning towards Andy, his hand resting on her shoulder as if he'd just been whispering into her ear.

Andy was still a good-looking man, Ellie supposed, peering at the photograph objectively. He had good, strong features and still had a full head of floppy sandy hair that naturally fell in a side parting, even if it was not as luxuriant at forty-eight years of age as it had been when he was younger. His clean-shaven face was tanned from the many hours he spent outdoors, and the birth mark on his cheek couldn't be seen in the photo, as his left side was facing away from the camera. Eyes sparkling with laughter from behind his signature rectangular, metal-framed glasses, and with his trim frame hidden under a favourite stripy jumper, Ellie felt that Andy would still be considered quite a catch among his contemporaries.

In this captured moment, Grace had clearly thought so. Her face beamed up at him from the foot stool on which she perched by his chair. She was wearing her long hair loose, and it tumbled down to her shoulder blades, still kept red by the judicious application of henna. The hand resting on Andy's forearm displayed her silver 'pebble rings', as Ellie used to call them. They were polished semi-precious stones held in simple silver rub-over settings: Labradorite, amethyst, tourmaline, onyx, and more.

It was the green and pink watermelon tourmaline that Ellie liked best. Her mother had once explained to her that the pink part of the stone was supposed to relate to love and that the green 'rind' not only symbolised healing of the heart but also represented masculinity. Grace had said it reminded her of Andy. Ellie was too young at the time to register the connection and to wonder why her mother's heart might have needed healing by the masculine presence of her father, but it did occur to her now. Had Grace been unlucky in love before meeting Andy? Perhaps her mother would tell her one day.

In the photo, Grace was wearing her autumnal patchwork skirt and a cheesecloth shirt in complimentary russet tones. Silver pendants dangled down the front of her untied shirt neck on long chains. She looked happy.

Ellie smiled and replaced the frame carefully onto the tabletop. She looked at herself in the mirror hanging on the wall above and asked herself: *do I look like either of my parents?* She had inherited her red hair from her mother, but her wide mouth could only have come from her dad's side of the family; in times past, they had been colloquially known as the "Jolly Johnstones" on account of their generous lips that were frequently to be seen turned up in a smile.

Drawing her mind back to the present, and to the pressing matter of her artwork, Ellie scooped up her backpack from

34

the flagstone floor and headed upstairs with the earnest intention of completing a few hours of uninterrupted sketching in her room.

Yet, despite her best intentions to focus on her artwork, her thoughts kept drifting back to the photo of her parents. Would she ever be as lucky in love as they were? Would she ever find her Mr Right?

5

# Chapter 5

Friday was the day of the much-anticipated Spring Thing. The event was to be held in the large function room of an out-of-town pub and wannabe country club. Its unfavourable geographical location in relation to the main road and the consequential lack of passing trade was the main reason The Sturgeon accepted bookings from the Student Union. Other more frequented and profitable establishments could generally afford greater respect for their carpets.

Throughout the day, not a lot of work was getting done on campus, as the main focus of student attention was fixed on that evening's shindig. Carpools were being sorted and outfits compared, abandoned and reshuffled, and there were many poorly attended lectures that afternoon as students left early to start their preparations for the main event.

Ellie and Jaz were getting ready at Flick's house. All three had bunked off from their last lessons of the day to get a head start on showering and hair-washing before makeup, blow-drying and styling could commence.

Ellie had decided on her outfit weeks ago, as had Flick and

Jaz. She was going to wear a retro dress she'd acquired in a local vintage shop. It had an above knee-length hemline and was made from deep purple crushed velvet, complimented by wide black chiffon shoulder straps. Ellie loved dark greens and purples; they went well with her striking red hair and emphasised her pale complexion.

Flick's mum, Joy, had kindly bought a bottle of Lambrusco to 'get the girls in the party mood'. Whilst Jaz and Ellie sipped the sweet bubbles out of Babycham glasses requisitioned from Joy's drinks cabinet, Flick grumbled jealously about being unable to partake in the predrinks due to her being the evening's designated driver.

'Good move, Mrs. S,' said Jaz happily. 'All the more for me!'

Flick looked at Jaz darkly. 'If I get even an inkling of you being about to throw up in the back of my car on the way home, I'm stopping and kicking you out!'

This was a threat Jaz understood all too well. She had once done pretty much just that to her younger sister Violet on the way back from a rowdy evening at the pub. Jaz had been driving them both home when Vi had suddenly announced that she was going to be sick. Jaz had hastily pulled over to the side of the quiet road, and Vi had opened the door and proceeded to vomit copiously onto the verge. As if this hadn't been unpleasant enough for Vi, Jaz had then unexpectedly popped the catch on Vi's seat belt, causing her to tip headfirst into the mess of her own making. To this day, Jaz claimed that she had been concerned Vi might not be leaning far enough out of the car to miss the doorframe, but Vi maintained Jaz had done it out of malice because she was the one stuck with being the dry driver.

By early evening, all three girls were looking their primped best. Jaz had chosen a dark green velvet jacket which she wore with jeans and strikingly dark makeup, while Flick had opted for her red 'man-grabber' dress—which she emphatically swore had magical powers of attraction—teamed with her newly purchased Scarlet Woman lipstick. The Lambrusco, although not particularly alcoholic, was clearly having an effect, making Ellie and Jaz particularly talkative to the point that Flick's mum could barely get a word in to wish them an enjoyable evening as they paraded through the sitting room and out of the front door. Turning the music up full blast and with the windows down to accommodate Jaz's chain-smoking, they set off for the party.

When Flick pulled into The Sturgeon's car park some fifteen minutes later, flashing disco lights could be seen spilling out into the night from around the edges of the function room's curtained windows. The bass was pounding so intensely that it could be felt through the soles of their shoes—or Flick's 'man-spikes', as she'd christened her new four-inch heels—as they walked up the steps to the decking in front of the planter-sentinelled double doors. Clearly the proprietors hadn't got many overnight guests currently staying at the inn, otherwise Ellie felt sure that the volume wouldn't have been tolerated at such a level. Above the doors hung a banner which had been hastily painted during Ellie's last Art class by almost everyone in the group. Flick nodded towards it as they approached.

'A true work of art. One of yours, I take it?' she asked.

'Naturally,' replied Ellie. 'More fun than still life drawing, any day!'

Met with a blast of sound, light and merriment as they swung through the doors, the three girls strode into the rest of their evening deliciously full of excited anticipation.

Once inside, Jaz immediately headed for the bar and ordered three bottled beers while Ellie and Flick found a prominent section of wall to lounge against, from which they could survey the room. Tables and chairs had been arranged around three sides of the function room, with the disco set up on the fourth, leaving the middle clear for dancing—although, *obviously*, no one was uncool enough to be doing any of that so early in the evening.

As Jaz returned with the drinks, she was met by a stern stare from Flick. 'Don't even *think* about it,' she warned Jaz in a low voice.

'The thought hadn't even crossed my mind,' a falsely innocent Jaz replied.

'Yeah, right—and the Pope's a Hells Angel!' laughed Ellie.

A well-known party trick of Jaz's was to clunk her beer bottle down onto the rim of one being held by someone else, which caused their beer to fizz up over the top. Not only was this frowned upon by her friends as a waste of good beer, but it had also once resulted in a furious Flick going home early with a bleeding lip she'd cut on the resultant chipped glass.

'I'm a reformed character,' Jaz retorted piously.

A short while ago, a new female student had joined Jaz's Chemistry group. Megan Stormand was pretty in a bookish sort of way and, as Jaz herself had declared, was just her type. Since then, Jaz had been at pains to curb her wilder instincts in an effort to make herself appear more mature and responsible and therefore be more appealing to the newcomer.

'Is Meg coming tonight?' Ellie enquired.

Jaz's grin slipped a notch. 'Nah. Her folks have visitors for the weekend and she's on host duty.'

'Well, there's plenty of pretty faces here tonight,' offered a tactless Flick. 'Talking of *pretty*, isn't that Jacob who's just walked in with his mate with all the tattoos?'

Ellie had already noticed Jacob's arrival, but she'd tried to style it out by turning more towards her friends and drinking her beer. With the game up, she subtly shifted position so that she could observe Jacob as he swaggered into the party.

'I *love* a tattooed man,' schmoozed Flick. 'Makes me want to trace all the lines with my finger. I wonder if he's got any below the waist?'

'*Wow*,' said Jaz dryly. 'You never stop.'

'Not from this side of the grave,' Flick threw over her shoulder as she headed to the ladies' room.

Jaz raised her eyebrows and exchanged looks with Ellie. 'Nice to see some things don't change. Show her a pair of trousers and she's off.'

Ellie chuckled. '"Get it while you're young, as you ain't getting it when you're old,"' she parodied, stating a well-known Flickism.

Ellie watched Jacob as he bought drinks at the bar and returned to his friend. Donning black skinny jeans and biker boots, Jacob wore a black shirt with a laced collar under his trademark leather jacket. Around his neck were dog tags and a crucifix on leather thongs. More leather strapping wound around his wrist. Ellie had to admit he was certainly easy on the eye.

Flick returned from her titivations, her lips now exactly matching the colour of her scarlet dress and her naturally-browned arms, legs and cleavage proudly on full display.

'Right, let's get out there,' she said, heading for the dance floor.

A run of their favourite tunes resulted in a prolonged period of dancing as the evening wore on. Shortly after, Ellie slipped outside for a breath of fresh air. People—including Jaz, Ellie noted with a frown—were smoking either side of the double doors, putting their stubs out in the planters. She would have to get back on Jaz's case about the dangers of smoking, although maybe Meg, a non-smoker, would be a good influence on Jaz, particularly if romance blossomed.

Ellie wandered further away from the building. Passing a few discreetly-kissing couples—and one not-so-discreet couple on a picnic bench—she made her way towards the cast-iron seats by the lake. Most of the attendees wouldn't come out this far, and Ellie was glad of the space, as her head was spinning slightly from the loud music and the alcohol she'd consumed. Reaching the deck, she sat down, welcoming the cold iron against her legs and back.

A slight breeze blew, enough to lift the strands of her hair from her damp neck. Wearing her hair up had been a good decision, she thought, particularly as the air passing over her skin felt almost like a lover's breath. Her skin prickled pleasurably at the thought. Maybe Jacob would find her here and do just that? She closed her eyes and let the pleasant tingling sensation in her lower stomach develop.

*Eleanor.*

Her eyes snapped open. *What?* She looked around, but there was no one there. Had she really just heard her name being whispered or was it her imagination? Or even just the wind? No one at college called her by her full name. Maybe it was the drink causing her to hear things. She closed her eyes and relaxed again against the now-warmed iron of the seating.

'*Eleanor*,' a low voice called, gentle as a breath on a window-pane.

She'd certainly heard *that*. 'Who's there?' Ellie answered in a whisper.

There was no reply.

Ellie tried again, this time louder. 'Is anyone there? What do you want?'

Still no answer. *OK. Well, now I must be hearing voices, too.* She made a mental note to add that to the ever-growing list for her clearly not-too-distant-future therapist.

Ellie felt slightly chilled, so she rose and walked back towards the main building. Students in groups and in couples had spilled out onto the grass, and there was only an hour left of the Spring Thing. Too soon, the bar would ring last orders and there'd be only the smoochers left, at which point Ellie felt sure she'd know where to find Flick. Ellie waved at a couple of people she knew and spotted Jaz sitting with a group at a nearby picnic table, so she changed direction and headed over there.

A guy in black jeans and boots going in the opposite direction brushed past her. Her arm made contact with him for only the briefest of moments, but she was hit with a huge shock of static. Glancing up quickly, she saw a broad mouth, a pale, strong chin and, weirdest of all, two tiny sparkling lights in the dark shadow of his hood. It all happened in an instant, but Ellie was left with the impression of him being a tall, broad, attractive male who clearly had a taste for light-up brow piercings, or something along those lines.

'Who was that guy?' she asked, reaching Jaz's table.

'What guy?'

'The one I just bumped into.'

'You walked over here on your own. There was no guy. How much have you been drinking?'

'The guy in the black hoodie? Tall, good-looking?'

'I didn't see any guy. Mind you, if it had been a leggy blonde …' Jaz quipped.

Ellie sighed in exasperation. 'Still reformed then, I see.'

Jaz grinned. 'Reformed, but not dead.'

Ellie frowned in mock censure, then returned Jaz's grin. 'No, thankfully not!' she replied, squeezing Jaz's arm as they both chuckled.

Having cooled down to the extent of now feeling cold, Ellie shivered and rubbed her upper arms. 'I'm going back inside to find Flick,' she told Jaz.

Jaz nodded and took another cigarette from the packet on the table. With a genuine frown this time, Ellie turned towards the building.

As she walked back to the double doors, she looked around for any sign of the guy in the hoodie, but was disappointed to find none.

\* \* \*

Inside, Flick was sat at a table with the tattooed guy, Jacob and some other black-clad individuals including Pete and Lily. Ellie approached the table and caught Flick's eye.

'Here she is!' Flick announced delightedly. 'I told you she'd find her way over here eventually.' She moved over so that there was shared room on her chair for Ellie.

'Here,' said Jacob, pulling a chair over from the table behind him.

43

'Ahh, ain't he the gentleman?' Flick sighed dramatically, clearly channelling Eliza Doolittle.

'The downfalls of a performing arts-based curriculum: she thinks she's going for an Oscar all the time,' Ellie retorted drily as she sat down next to Jacob.

'Drink?' he asked her.

'Great. Beer, thanks.'

Jacob left the table and headed for the bar. Flick winked at Ellie. 'Where have you been?' she said. 'I thought you were going for some air and then coming back in here to collect all the lads stunned by our dancing?'

Overhearing this, Lily rolled her eyes at Pete and returned her gaze to her iPhone.

'*Bitch*,' Flick mouthed to Ellie, tilting her head in the girl's direction.

Jacob returned with Ellie's drink and sat back in his seat. Turning his back on his ex, he slanted his body towards Ellie.

Flick smirked and raised an eyebrow. 'Karma,' she said.

Jacob handed Ellie her beer.

'Thanks,' said Ellie, taking a sip.

''Ya welcome.' Jacob clinked his bottle against the side of hers and took a swig. Taking out his tobacco tin, he began making a roll-up. 'You wanna come outside for a smoke?' he asked Ellie.

'I don't. Smoke, that is,' she replied awkwardly.

Flick rolled her eyes, indicating that she clearly knew what Jacob had meant in asking Ellie outside, and it wasn't smoking.

'OK. Back later.' Jacob licked the paper and gave the roll-up a final twist, then rose from his chair and headed for the exit.

'*Dur!*' mocked Flick. 'When a hot guy asks you to go

44

outside, you *go* with him. Have I taught you nothing, Ms. Johnstone?'

'You know I don't like smoking,' came Ellie's lame reply.

Eventually, the bell rang as the bartender announced last orders, causing a minor stampede of inebriated students towards the bar. Ellie's beer was still full and Flick was driving, so they stayed seated. Jaz appeared from outside and joined the scrum at the bar before emerging triumphant, proudly carrying her beer like a trophy won in battle. She sat down in Jacob's recently vacated chair.

The music changed key, the lighting dimmed, and couples headed for the dance floor. Throughout the rest of the room, not-so-subtle, owl-like head-turning got underway as singles looked for potential dance partners. Chris Tanner, the tattooed guy, stood up and offered his hand to Flick, who smiled demurely and took it, then left with him for the dance floor. Ellie smiled at Jaz and raised her eyebrows. It was well known within their group that any bloke offering Flick a dance was lucky to be able to leave the dance floor without having to pull his top down over his crotch. They watched Flick begin her well-practised routine of grinding and groping. Chris looked mildly surprised, but most definitely not displeased.

'She's pulled. *Again*,' Jaz commented dryly.

Jacob came back into the room and sat down in Flick's chair. 'You wanna?' he said to Ellie, indicating the dancing couples.

'Sure,' Ellie replied with a smile.

The unpopular spot nearest the speakers was the only space free on the dance floor. Arriving there, Jacob put his arms around Ellie's waist and she linked hers around the back of his neck, resting her cheek against the lapels of his patchouli-oil-scented jacket. They stayed swaying together like that for the next couple of songs. Ellie had to admit the experience was not as thrilling as she'd been expecting, but on the grounds that wish fulfilment is generally an infrequent occurrence, she convinced herself she was having a great time.

When the main lights announced the end of the Spring Thing, people collected their coats, bags and insensible friends and made their often-unsteady way out of the building. Flick and Jaz headed to the car park, followed by Ellie, who had Jacob's arm draped over her shoulders. Jaz took the front passenger seat, leaving Ellie and Jacob the privacy of the back of the car.

While Flick drove, she and Jaz laughed uproariously as they recounted the antics of their fellow partygoers. Sitting close to Jacob and feeling that she ought to, Ellie tried to make conversation. After a few inconsequential remarks, to which Jacob responded with either his crooked smile or in monosyllables, he turned his face to Ellie, put his hand around the back of her head and kissed her. Somewhat surprised, Ellie kissed him back.

As kisses go, it was OK. Jacob was clearly good at snogging; he put his hands on either side of her head and directed her face towards his lips—which Ellie and her chums had decreed was the *romantic* way of kissing—and he teased her mouth sensuously with the tip of his tongue rather than sticking it in her mouth and whirling it around à la "washing machine" style.

However, in her slightly drunken state, when she closed her eyes and waited for the kick of excitement, she saw a strong chin and kissable lips protruding from the shadows of a hoodie, and it was that which gave her a fizzing feeling in her belly, instead of Jacob's kiss.

That night, asleep on a put-you-up bed on the floor of Flick's bedroom, Ellie dreamed of startling purple eyes glinting with light and her name being whispered by the wind.

# 6

# Chapter 6

On Tuesday afternoon, Ellie caught the college bus into town.
She hopped off at the usual stop, thanked the driver, and,
turning away from the art building, headed towards the older
part of town.

Halfway down Castle Street, the old Lowford library sat
behind its own entrance courtyard. Its weathered red stone
walls and paler, mullioned sandstone windows with leaded
glass made for an attractive building. The arched entrance
porch led into a high-ceilinged hall that housed the town's
museum. This was a rather forlorn area, with a layer of
dust on the display cases and an impressive collection of
dead flies adorning the windowsills. Ellie found the museum
fascinating and was sorry that there were not more people
who shared her view; the place could use some enthusiastic
volunteers.

The Local Archaeological Finds section was Ellie's
favourite. Eager amateur metal detectorists had unearthed a
fascinating array of Roman coins, beads, medieval jewellery
and other assorted historical treasures. There were even

some very early pottery fragments and other items that had been excavated from the fields surrounding her home.

Owl's Ridge was an ancient dwelling place. Listed in the Doomsday Book as 'Ols Rige', Ellie loved the fact that where she lived, generations of people had dwelled and had worked the land for over a thousand years.

A previous owner of her parent's property had been a keen historian and, along with the local archaeology group, had undertaken several exploratory digs around the farm, donating any finds to the town museum. Owl's Ridge was not actually a farm anymore. The owner prior to the historian had let the land go to weed and then thicket, and the barns had fallen into disrepair. Subsequently, most of the outbuildings had been knocked down and much of the land sold off. Ellie's parents had inherited Owl's Ridge shortly after she was born.

Conscious of the time, Ellie dragged herself away from the display cases and through the high double doors at the back of the museum. Delightfully familiar smells assailed her nostrils as she entered the library. *This is what secrets smell like*, Ellie had decided when she first came here as a small child. Her parents had home-schooled her instead of sending her to the local primary school as they liked to travel and wanted Ellie to share these adventures with them. Formal education—and fines for holidays taken during term-time—did not sit well with the Johnstones' life plan. As a result, Ellie had been taken to many interesting places, retreats and events, where she had played happily with other equally blessed and free-spirited children.

Her education was thorough, but not completed within the usual timescale for GCSEs. Consequently, Ellie had taken those exams just before her eighteenth birthday and was now in her second year of Sixth Form study, aged twenty. Being slightly older than most of the students didn't bother Ellie, who made friends easily based on sharing a similar worldview rather than age, race or gender. Within her close friendship group, Jaz was nineteen and Flick, the baby of the group, was soon to be eighteen. Lowford College was very inclusive and had a fair few more mature students. Indeed, Jacob was one, too.

Ellie wandered over to the library desk, looking for Bertie. The librarian, Bertrand Tanforth, had benevolently bestowed the honour of calling him Bertie on her and her parents, due to their long acquaintance with him and "his books". Bertie considered every tome at the library to be his personal property. A short, dapper man in his mid-sixties, Bertie usually came to work in a three-piece suit and bow tie. He appeared fussy and a little unwelcoming upon first meeting him, but that was only because he didn't like the public upsetting his cataloguing system by putting books back where they had no right to be or damaging the spines of his more delicate charges.

On the desk, a handwritten sign in swirling letters announced that Bertie had *Gone for Lunch*, despite it being virtually mid-afternoon. Happily, Ellie knew her way around the stacks well enough to make a start without Bertie's guidance.

Browsing the shelves, Ellie came to a book titled *Symbolism in Archaeology*. She withdrew it and flicked through its pages. Good, it had lots of pictures. She tucked it under her arm and continued her hunt. *Mythology of Ancient Times*, *Spotting Archaeology* and, fortuitously, a misplaced tome on Occult Symbolism were added to the collection she'd now piled on the floor.

'Is that any way to treat man's finest creation?' an indignant voice demanded from behind her.

Ellie smiled. 'And is that any way to greet an old friend?' she replied, turning around.

'The book is mankind's best friend,' intoned Bertie.

'I thought that was a dog?' Ellie quipped.

Smiling in delight at the unexpected visit from his almost-niece, Bertie embraced Ellie and bestowed a kiss on her cheek. 'So, what particular mission brings you to my dark doors on this disgustingly sun-drenched day?'

Being a faded redhead, his words were not merely flippant. Bertie felt pretty much the same way about the sun as vampires would, and it had a fairly disastrous effect on him, too.

'I need to know about spirals,' Ellie told him. 'In history, ancient cultures, symbolic meanings ... *anything*, really. The college library was pretty useless, and my Internet trawls haven't turned up much of interest, either.'

Bertie nodded in sympathy; he personally preferred books to digital information, but there was a row of computers against one wall for those wishing to scour the Internet.

'Let me see,' he said, tapping his chin in thought. 'Spirals are symbols of perpetual motion—ceaselessly circling and twisting through time' he pronounced precisely, relishing the alliteration. 'But then I expect you've already found that out by looking the word up in a dictionary—online or otherwise,' he added, his eyebrows raised in query.

Ellie's cheeks tinged faintly pink, and she looked down at the books. Reading her slight embarrassment correctly, Bertie sighed dramatically. 'I'll go and get the bible, then,' he said in a resigned voice.

Ellie knew that Bertie's bible was the Oxford English Dictionary; his personal religious text. As he'd instructed Ellie many times, the best way to research a topic was to first discover any other words that it might otherwise be referred to as, described by or connected to. He insisted that setting forth on a quest for knowledge without first referring to the holiest of holies, a dictionary, was to scupper the voyage of discovery before even leaving harbour. A thesaurus, he insisted, should also be an early port of call.

Ellie read from the dictionary that Bertie handed to her. *'Spiral: a twisting, often circular shape. Something moving with a twisting, circular movement.'*

She jotted this centre page on her A4 notepad and proceeded to brainstorm spirals. With Bertie periodically gifting snippets of insight over her shoulder, a few minutes later, her page read:

Universe spiralling out from the Big Bang.

Fleeing from/returning to a centre point.

Speeding up and concentrating near the centre point.

Water flowing into a sinkhole; a whirlpool, eddies.

Spirals in the sky: tornados, cloud form, cyclones.

A mind closing in on itself/expansion of consciousness.

Something in constant motion, never still.

Ellie frowned, dissatisfied. None of these felt likely to offer insight into the peculiar occurrences she'd been experiencing of late. She turned her attention to her book selection and immersed herself, surrounded only by the drowsy quiet of the room and the soft sounds of Bertie working in his office.

*In Tibetan tradition*, she read, *the spiral represents the begin-*

*ning of the universe. But spirals have been used as decorative and spiritual symbols for as long as man has been on the planet. Archaeological finds have shown spirals being used as decoration on Neolithic artefacts and in virtually every age and culture since.*

*Interesting, but not surprising*, thought Ellie, and she read on.

*Spirals can represent eternity, birth, death and rebirth. From universal and galactic spirals, to the smallest structures in nature such as the double helix of DNA, spirals are frequently occurring patterns. They are also seen as symbols of energy and are considered to hold energy like a coiled spring, as well as transporting it into and out of the spiral's centre point. This makes them energy highways*—rather like the tree Ellie had studied in the woods.

'Got another one for you,' Bertie said, interrupting her train of thought. He placed a book carefully on top of her notepad. 'Look up Fibonacci. Two 'c's, by the way, just like glorious Devon.'

Ellie looked at the book: *Mathematics Explained*. This was not her strongest area. She searched the index and found the relevant page.

*Fibonacci*, she read, *was a medieval mathematician. His series of numbers starts with zero and one and proceeds by adding a number and its predecessor to give the next in the sequence, so 0, 1, 1, 2, 3, 5, 8, 13, 21, 34, 55, 89 ad infinitum. If plotted on a graph, these numbers describe a spiral, and Fibonacci spirals can be found on a number of natural objects, such as shells, pine cones and sunflower seed heads.*

That was interesting: numbers as the pattern for nature. Ellie liked that; it seemed to hint that there was a grand design that even nature followed, and if that was so, then perhaps there was such a thing as predestination and everything happening for a reason. She vaguely recalled once reading that scientists study pattern-making in the search for a better understanding of nature, and that pattern-making is also fundamental to mathematics. Some mathematicians speculated that the universe itself could, one day, be described by numbers.

Ellie leaned back in her chair and stretched. She was stiff from sitting in one position for too long, and her neck had a crick in it. She got up and wandered over to Bertie's office door.

'Tea or coffee?' she asked, leaning against the frame.

'Oh, tea, please. Make mine strong and dark, like an attractive man.'

Ellie smiled at the familiar phrase. She stepped forwards to the "Library Restaurant", as Bertie termed the tea-making tray, and switched on the kettle.

Her back to her eccentric friend, she fiddled with the mugs and granulated coffee as she asked, 'Can I ask you something, Bertie? Why might a person keep seeing the same pattern everywhere?'

'That can be nasty,' Bertie replied. 'Happened to me last season, when every gentleman's outfitters I visited wanted to sell me paisley. Finding a plain jacket lining, even if one was prepared to endure a garishly bright colour, was virtually impossible.'

'Be serious, please, Bertie,' Ellie admonished.

Bertie frowned, looking at her back. 'Some cultures and tribes had mystics, witch doctors, wisemen or soothsayers who thought that seeing the same symbol appearing in everyday situations was a portent or message. But whether it was good or bad news depended on the mystic and the cultural beliefs of his people. Some tried to see patterns as pictures, too, like reading tea leaves. Speaking of which, is mine ready yet?'

Ellie shivered involuntarily at his words. Could her experiences be warnings about something? If so, what? According to what she'd just been reading, the spiral-patterned ring catching her eye and its odd similarity to her tree drawing and the image in the windscreen mist, might be suggesting change, an increase or decrease of energy and/or spiritual enhancement.

Placing his tea down on Bertie's desk, she looked up at his face. 'Do you believe there is more to this world than that which we can readily perceive?' she asked.

Bertie looked serious. 'Yes,' he said solemnly, glancing to the wall where a photo of his life partner, Charles, hung in pride of place. 'With every fibre of my being, Ellie. With every particle of my soul.'

Ellie smiled sadly at him. She had never known Charles, as he had died when she was little, but Bertie spoke so frequently of him that Ellie felt that she knew Charles well. Bertie and Charles had met while they were both at Cambridge University. Bertie had been reading English Literature and had met science fanatic Charles when both of them had joined the same rowing club, albeit briefly, in Bertie's case. Bertie claimed that he'd only joined in the first place to meet the gorgeous dark-haired fella with the fabulous legs and, having bagged him, never felt the urge to row again. The two young men had fallen deeply in love and, despite opposition from both their families, had set up home together after graduating.

Charles had returned to the university to undertake a course of post graduate study while Bertie went to work for a publishing company. Bertie and Charles had remained very much in love with each other, and despite Charles' death in his late forties, Bertie often spoke of Charles as if he were still alive. As he'd once explained to Ellie, not only did he feel Charles' presence in their apartment, but he was further comforted by the certain knowledge that in some parallel universe, he and Charles were still happily together, running a bijou literary café in Primrose Hill.

\* \* \*

Having stayed at the library researching and chatting to Bertie for longer than she'd planned, Ellie found herself journeying home later than usual. Driving the long, straight stretch of main road she traversed daily on her way to and from college, Ellie yawned. This particular length of road held morbid notoriety with local people, as there had been several car accidents along it over the last ten years; two of which had been fatal. The danger lay in the hidden dip halfway along. Frustrated motorists, stuck behind a slow-moving vehicle, would see a long, straight road ahead and overtake despite the warning signs, only to collide with an oncoming vehicle emerging from the dip. Sad though it was, it didn't surprise Ellie. In her short driving career, she'd already noticed how many drivers didn't pay heed to what the road signs told them.

Driving into the low sunlight with her visor down, Ellie could clearly see a lorry coming the other way at the far end of the straight as she approached the dip. As Dolly began to descend the slope, the last sight of the road ahead told Ellie that it was clear.

Without warning, a grey car appeared on her side of the road, accelerating towards her. Ellie braked, but there was no chance of either vehicle stopping in time to avoid a collision. Ellie braced herself for impact, her muscles rigid in fear of the trauma of the crash to come.

Suddenly, the steering wheel jerked to the left, swerving Dolly into the end of a layby. Then, almost instantaneously, as the oncoming car flashed past on Ellie's right, it jerked back the other way, sending Dolly careering out onto the road instead of hitting the hedge.

Somehow, she had missed the other car.

Ellie's foot was clamped down on the brake pedal as Dolly shuddered to a stop, her tyres smelling of hot rubber. The approaching lorry had pulled over to the side of the road just beyond the layby, the driver clearly now expecting to have to deal with a bad traffic accident. He climbed down from the cab and crossed the road to Ellie.

'You all right, love? Can you hear me in there?'

He knocked on Dolly's window as Ellie sat there, staring straight ahead in shock. Not getting a response, he knocked more loudly. Ellie slowly emerged from her traumatised tunnel vision and turned her head towards him. She popped the window catch, and the lorry driver lifted up the lower flap of the window to speak to her.

'I ain't never seen anything like it!' he said. 'How the hell did you do that? Bloody amazing driving! I didn't even see that idiot in my mirrors. Mind you, no wonder with him travelling at that speed. First I saw was him beside me and heading straight for you. You've got flipping *lightning* reflexes.

You OK?'

'Yes,' Ellie managed to reply with a rictus smile. Her heart hammered in her chest with the adrenaline rush, and her hands were shaking. 'I'm OK.'

'You'd best get on home then, love. You look as white as a sheet. Here, do you want some coffee? I got some in me Thermos in the truck. Pick you up a bit, before you go on your way?'

Ellie ran her hands up her face and over her head, combing her hair back with her fingers. She was OK. *Breathe*, she told herself. *Everything's OK, and no one was hurt. Time to head on home.*

Ellie took a deep breath. She could do this. 'Thank you, but I really am fine.' To demonstrate, she turned the key in the ignition and Dolly chuntered into life.

'Well, if you're sure. Ta-ta then, love. Take care.'

Looking right and left, the driver crossed the road and climbed back into the lorry cab.

Ellie shook herself and concentrated on her driving. *Mirror, signal, manoeuvre.* She set off on her extremely cautious way home, her speed not exceeding 30mph for the rest of the journey.

When she got home, the house was quiet; her parents were clearly out. Ellie took herself up to her room and lay on the bed. She closed her eyes and breathed deeply. How on earth was she not in a hospital bed right now? Or the morgue, even? The last thing she remembered before the near miss was bracing for impact. She hadn't consciously swerved into the layby; it was almost as if the steering wheel had a mind of its own.

Ellie recalled hearing of people in life-and-death situations suddenly gaining inhuman strength, like the guy in the aeroplane crash at sea who'd ripped the exit door open when it was jammed and no one could escape. Could her subconscious, or even her *unconscious*, have taken control of her body and saved her?

It was possible, she supposed. Settling herself more comfortably against her pillows, her rationale making her feel more at ease, Ellie drifted into a shock-wearied sleep.

* * *

She was in a wood at night-time, humid and airless. Midges buzzed past her hair, making Ellie want to scratch her head. Ahead of her were three paths leading into denser woodland than that in which she stood. She had to decide which path to take.

Unsure of what to do, Ellie stepped into the middle of the clearing where the three paths met. Looking from one to the other, Ellie detected the merest suggestion of light at the furthest visible point of the middle pathway. But the path to the right had a well-trodden look and promised, perhaps, an easier passage than the other two.

Ellie looked over her shoulder, reasoning that she could always go back the way she'd come, wherever that led. But that turned out to be a no-go: trees and dense thicket formed a wall behind her. There was no going back.

The last pathway was darker than the other two, but the leaves on the brambles stirred in a slight breeze. A cool scent reached her nose; it smelt like the first chill Autumn evening. Ellie stepped forwards, feeling the cool air brush pleasantly past her hot skin, then set off down the left-hand pathway.

Now, she was back in the place with the smooth viscous wall. Was it obsidian? Placing her hand on the wall, she again felt the cold, smooth surface; only this time, she could feel the thrumming in the wall itself, rather than just through the door as before. She still had the feeling that she was obligated to keep the door shut, but the urge to open it was even stronger now. Placing both hands flat against the door, Ellie felt both the warmth and the thudding beat.

'*Eleanor*,' a deep voice whispered.

'Eleanor. Ellie!' Her name was called again, but this time in a different voice. 'Ellie, are you up there?'

Ellie woke up. Her mum was calling for her from the bottom of the stairs.

'I'm here,' Ellie called back, stretching her arms behind her head and flexing her legs straight-out, toes pointed.

She felt surprisingly normal, considering the fright she'd had that afternoon. Climbing off the bed, she went downstairs to see her folks. She decided not to tell them about her near-crash experience, as she didn't want to upset them unnecessarily.

After tea, Ellie took the book on the occult from her college bag and headed out of the back door. She hadn't had time to finish reading all the books she'd selected at the library while she'd been there. She'd continued to chat to Bertie in an attempt to pull him out of the sadness that always descended when he spoke of Charles.

Leaving the heavy wooden door ajar so that the spaniels could join her if they wished, Ellie strolled across the lawn to her favourite spot below the big Holm Oak tree. When she was a child, her mother had made up the most fantastic stories for Ellie about the magical folk who apparently lived in the tree. Her favourite image from the tales was of the fairy market which happened each night and was located around the massive roots of the tree. There had been circular marks in the lawn below the tree—with adult understanding, likely the remnants of long-gone trees—and young Ellie had thought them proof of the toadstool rings grown each evening to be used as stalls by the market's fantastical traders. Ellie also thought that the fact the tree didn't lose its leaves in winter, like all the other broad-leafed trees, was further proof of it being magical.

The evening was fine, with the warmth of the afternoon having not yet dissipated. Settling herself down into her usual niche between the buttress roots, Ellie began to read. According to the occult book, spirals were energy vortices which drew power either up from below or down from above, depending on the direction of the spiral. A clockwise spiral drew energy up from the ground and represented man becoming spirit. Ellie pondered that for a moment, supposing that it made sense if you thought of the man as dead and buried and his spirit escaping heavenwards. Anti-clockwise, or left-circling spirals, drew power down from the heavens and represented divine spirit descending into man. Ellie looked at the ring on her hand: the motion of its spiral spun left, which, according to the book, might mean the wearer receiving divine energy. That didn't sound too bad. Ellie flicked further on through the pages.

Spirals also supposedly represented the entrances to life and the route to the afterlife or next plane of existence. Once through the centre point, i.e. death, the spiral arm pathways opened out again with limitless possibility. The author suggested that a visual representation of this was that if you flip a spiral over, it turns in the other direction. Ellie paused her reading to consider this. The depiction of time as a spiral, with human beings moving along it until their point of death at the centre of the spiral. But then what happened? The author suggested that the dynamics of the reversed spiral came into play, so maybe even time worked backwards? Were people young again after their death? Bertie certainly always thought of Charles as the young man he had first met and fallen in love with, rather than the prematurely-aged and ill man he had come to nurse.

*Mankind*, she read, *has long worshipped the sun, and the sun moves clockwise across the sky. Hence, clockwise spirals were often revered by sun-worshipping cultures. Conversely, anticlockwise spirals move against the sun, against the worshipped deity and against the natural order, and so were considered to be bad luck.*

Her ring spiral would be thought to be bad luck, then, as it went against the direction of the sun. Thinking back to her experience that afternoon, her very near scrape with serious injury or death, Ellie certainly did not feel unlucky. Her ring had clearly not brought her bad luck. Could it be that her ring spiral, flowing anticlockwise, therefore symbolised the night?

Further on in the book, she came across a section on witchcraft. Interestingly, widdershins was an old name for anticlockwise. Here, the author described a spell for achieving your goals. The caster should draw a spiral in a tray of sand, then write their goals on nine separate slips of paper and place them at nine points on the spiral, covering each slip with a crystal. As the goals were achieved, the crystals were removed and the paper destroyed to seal the energy at the point of goal fulfilment, preventing it from being drawn backwards through the crystal and undoing what had been achieved.

*Shame they didn't specify which crystal*, Ellie thought. If they had, she might have given the spell a go.

Finally, Ellie read that although some extreme religious groups claim that the spiral is a portal for demons, and that apparently the pattern has been cunningly included in many decorative homeware items to further the progress of evil, this was not actually the case.

Ellie chuckled to herself. Her dad's favourite psychedelic shirt was safe, then; she couldn't imagine him dancing to *The Age of Aquarius* in anything else.

# 7

# Chapter 7

In the college canteen, the usual level of noise, bordering on pain, was pushing new boundaries. Ellie, Flick and Jaz gathered the remainder of their lunch and left for the Common Room in order to actually hear each other speak. Pleased to see that their favourite group of low, armless waiting-room-style chairs was free, they sat down to finish their lunch.

Ellie dumped her pile of books, folders and notes onto the low table before going to the drinks machine for a hot chocolate.

When she returned, Jaz was reading the top page. 'You forgot one,' she said.

'One what?' Ellie asked, sitting down and placing her steaming cup on the coffee table.

'One really cool spiral on your brainstorm. Galactic spirals,' answered Jaz, astrophysicist in the making.

Jaz had an impressive mind, although she often chose to hide that fact. She had once confided to Ellie that her dream job would be at NASA and that she was even considering scuba lessons in accordance with how astronauts at the Johnson Space Center in Houston were trained to deal with space walks.

'Galaxies are littered throughout the universe and come in many different types and sizes—so many they can't be counted. Maybe a hundred billion in the known universe.'

Ellie looked impressed, and Jaz continued.

'They're made up of dust, gas and stars and therefore, obviously, planets.' Jaz paused, looking pointedly at Flick, who was miming a yawn.

'Not to mention containing, and possibly surrounded by, fascinating dark matter. Spiral galaxies rotate, hence the spiral bit in the name, *Flick*, and they usually have two obvious spiral arms. Our own galaxy is a spiral. The Milky Way that smudges across the night sky, that you can't really see unless you're looking directly at it—the bit you said was something on your contact lens, Flick—is a cross-sectional slice of our own galaxy, seen from inside out.'

'So why,' interjected a bored Flick, 'if the universe is packed with star-containing spirals, is the night so flipping dark?'

'That is an unexpectedly relevant and good question.' Flick brightened, but then Jaz continued. 'But it isn't one I intend to waste my words of wisdom on trying to explain to your man-addled brain. If you really want to know, look up Olber's paradox. That is, *if* you can take a moment out from sexting Chris.'

Flick poked her tongue out at Jaz. 'Be careful,' she warned. 'If you're any meaner to me, I will uninvite you, Madam Boffin.'

It was Flick's eighteenth birthday at the weekend, and the trio had planned a night out.

'Knowledge enables man to slip the bonds of stupidity with which he is born,' riposted Jaz. 'And you, Felicity, would do well to examine how to escape bondage. It could come in very handy, considering the company you've been keeping recently.'

Flick, who had been casually seeing Chris, Jacob's tattooed mate, since the Spring Thing, gave a Jaz a salacious grin. 'He likes me for my mind,' she lied.

'Jaz is right, though. Space is fascinating. I read that on a long mission, the weightless environment makes astronauts grow by several centimetres. A career as an astronaut would save you a fortune in heels,' said Ellie, gently teasing Flick.

'Why yes, Ms. Johnstone; space *is* fascinating. In fact, with your apparent superhuman reflexes, you could be up there one day, too, negotiating the asteroid fields,' complimented Jaz.

'I'll run it past the Careers Advisor next time I'm in his office,' quipped Ellie.

She had told her friends about her near-crash. They were both naturally shocked but also impressed that Ellie had managed to avoid the oncoming car. Flick was furious that the driver of the grey car had not bothered to see if Ellie was all right after nearly smashing into her. It was not something Ellie had considered before, but now she thought of it, she couldn't recall seeing the other car again after she'd swerved. It must have been going extremely fast to get clear of the long straight in the moments before Dolly had juddered to a stall and Ellie had looked in her rearview mirror to check that no one was about to crash into the back of her.

'Sooo, have you both decided what you're wearing on Saturday?' asked Flick, bringing the conversation round to their current main subject of discussion. 'I'm still deciding between the red dress I wore to the Spring Thing—Chris won't be coming, so there's no worries about being seen twice in the same outfit—or my blue office siren skirt with an impressively unbuttoned shirt.'

'I'd let the weather decide if I were you,' Ellie offered.

Flick chose this moment to counter with another well-known Flickism. "Rainy days make hair go down and hemlines go up," she said. Her reasoning was that long skirts and trousers get wet on the rain-soaked pavement.

'Working with your logic there, Felicity, I've never under-stood what happens in a flood situation. Would you just be wearing a belt over your knickers at this point?' Jaz sniggered.

'In a flood situation,' replied Flick with a lecherous grin, 'I would be the one being rescued from my bedroom window by hunky fireman, me wearing nothing but my black lacy nightie.'

They all laughed, acknowledging the truth of the statement.

* * *

Although Lowford obviously had its own pubs and bars, the planned outing to commemorate Flick reaching the age of responsibility was to be held in Wester, the county town. It was felt, mostly by Flick, that such a significant event should be marked by all the pomp and ceremony it deserved. It therefore followed that the pubs usually frequented by the trio were just not exciting enough to suitably mark the occasion. Plus, Flick had already worked her way through most of the attractive men to be found in the local watering holes and was looking for fresh prey.

On Saturday night, the three friends once again got ready together at Flick's house. Flick's parents had paid for a taxi to take them out and, more importantly, to bring them safely home again. Ellie was wearing her plum satin dress with its A-line skirt and thin straps. Over this, she wore a black chiffon shirt knotted at the front. She wore her long red curls down tonight, simply dressing them with combs that held back the top and sides and allowed two long tendrils to fall artlessly on either side of her face.

In contrast, Flick had her tresses loosely pinned up in a bun with similarly escaping tendrils. Ellie suspected part of Flick's plan was to let her hair fall loose in front of her chosen victim and toss it mercilessly until he was captivated. Going out with Chris was clearly not going to slow Flick down too much on her eighteenth birthday celebration.

Flick had opted for the office siren look, and Jaz commented dryly that Flick only needed some glasses and a notepad to be the epitome of every pinstripe-suited bosses' wet dream.

Jaz was wearing a silver crushed velvet top with an attractively scooped neckline paired with black tailored trousers and a black bead choker at her throat. Her hair was spiked over to one side, inspiring Flick's retaliatory remark as to whether Jaz thought they were off to a gallery rather than going clubbing, as Jaz had clearly created art instead of a hairstyle.

When the taxi arrived, the ebullient trio clambered into it, taking care not to ladder their sheer stockings nor flatten their hairstyles. Flick commandeered the front seat and stated that as it was her birthday outing, the same worked for both legs of the journey. Jaz and Ellie willingly let her and happily sat themselves in the back.

'The rear seat is a much safer position in frontal car crashes,' Jaz facetiously pointed out to Flick. 'I can always cushion myself against your enormous bouffant upon impact. Plus, there is the bonus that I also don't have to look at your smug self when I'm sat behind you.'

'It's just as well I know and love you, Jazmine Tully, or I might have taken offence at that last part,' Flick retorted, pivoting the passenger sun visor so she could peer menacingly at Jaz in the makeup mirror.

'So, you're OK with the hair jibe? Excellent,' Jaz fired back, grinning.

\* \* \*

To reach the clubs and bars in the city centre took just over half an hour. During this time, the taxi driver was entertained by the nonstop banter between his three passengers. The trading of insults between the bronzed girl in the front and the attractive, dark-haired girl behind her was particularly amusing. Judging by the high spirits of their outward journey, however, he was mildly concerned about the state they'd be in by the time he returned to take them home again later on and so resolved to get the sick bags out of the boot, just in case.

Flick had decided that they should begin their evening at Baubles, a champagne and cocktail bar, followed by clubbing in one of several venues, if not in Baubles' own basement nightclub. Baubles was already busy when they arrived, and the street level bar was adorned with two bouncers guarding the entrance. Eyeing the girls, the bouncers nodded their approval and admitted all three into the old brick building.

'Have a lovely evening, ladies,' one said.

Flick turned and blew him a kiss.

Downstairs was already heaving, but Flick knew it would be less so upstairs, at least until the live music began. They climbed the stairs carefully, Ellie holding the skirt of her dress up in front of her lest she trip and Flick balancing on another pair of man-killers, her pencil skirt so tight that she found it tricky to negotiate the stairs elegantly and without falling over.

The crowding was less around the top floor bar, and they were able to wend their way through the already claimed tables to find an available high-perch table near the French windows at the rear of the room. Flick insisted on having a table as a base from which they could check out the room and to which any smitten men could have bottles of champagne delivered.

One of Baubles' most appealing features was its roof terrace. The cosmopolitan bar had taken over a whole building in a row of nineteenth century shops. Having been built on the side of a steep hill, the row was uneven, in that the street level at the front was much higher than the ground level of the building's rear courtyards. When stood on Baubles' roof terrace, which would only be thought to be at second floor level if viewed from the street, you were actually on the third floor at the back—or indeed the fourth if you included the cellars, parts of which were above ground level sufficiently to merit high level windows. Hence patrons on the popular roof terrace were able to enjoy stunning views over Wester as the ground fell steeply away towards the river.

Having secured their table for the evening, Flick went to

the bar for drinks, ID card at the ready. Flick was known as a barman magnet on account of how speedily she tended to get served. She returned shortly with three luridly-coloured cocktails, mildly disappointed that she hadn't been carded.

'What were you expecting? You've looked twenty-one since you were fifteen and sprouted those two!' Jaz scoffed.

Flick proudly thrust her impressive chest forwards, nearly causing the ogling barman to choke on his iced water.

'They *are* my best assets,' she announced.

Both Ellie and Jaz knew that this was not so; Flick's best asset was her fierce loyalty to her friends, with her sharp sense of humour a close second.

Ellie had once been out for drinks with Flick in a group of female friends when some drunken lads had tried coming on to them rather too strongly. They had not taken it well when given the brush-off by the girls, turning catcalls into jeering, ribald comments. Flick, a non-threatening five feet, two inches plus four inches for her heels, had stormed across to the lads and blasted them with her very pointed views on poorly-endowed, beer-rank oafs inflicting themselves on uninterested women. The stunned silence that billowed across the bar as Flick finished speaking still made Ellie smile when she remembered it.

By mid-evening, the top floor bar was as full as the street level bar had been when they'd arrived. The queue for drinks was three rows deep, and the amps were turned up loud. In a while, the live music act would start their set. Playing tonight were a local all-girl band called Debutee. Jaz knew the lead singer from her Philosophy class; Kaz was another of Lowford College's older students.

Jaz, Ellie and Flick were now on their third round of drinks.

Ellie and Flick were still on cocktails, but Jaz had rebelled at the second round, refusing any more of the "lurid yak piss", and had switched to her preferred bottled beer.

For the next couple of hours while Debutee performed their set, the energy in the top floor bar soared as the packed dance floor heaved and swayed like a single living entity. Ellie, Flick and Jaz became part of that beast, the music so charged that they continued dancing for song after song and caught the attention of a fair few admirers. One guy watched Ellie in particular, and when she next went to the bar for drinks, he positioned himself next to her in the queue.

'Great here, isn't it?' he asked after she had been served and was waiting for her change.

Ellie could barely hear him as the drums crashed in response to the lead guitar solo. She nodded and smiled, then turned to take her money from the barman. Giving the guy another friendly smile, she managed to grasp two cocktail glasses and a bottled beer between her fingers and returned to their table. She was only halfway through her previous drink but had got another round in anyway as the other two were in need of libation.

'Are we staying up here much longer or going down to the club?' Ellie asked after perching herself back on her stool.

'Debutee are only doing another three or four tracks and then that's them done for the night,' Jaz remarked. 'Kaz said she might join us down in Chintz after she finishes playing.'

'Cool. Well, in that case, I'm heading outside to cool off. You coming?' Ellie asked.

'Yeah, I could do with a breath of air,' Flick answered. 'You coming, Jazmine?'

'Nah, I want to hear Kaz and the band. I'm good here.'

Flick nodded and headed towards the French windows that led out to the roof terrace. Just inside the double doors, Flick recognised a girl from one of her classes and stopped to say hello. Ellie, following behind and carrying her full Midnight Kiss cocktail, chose to continue walking outside on her own. She didn't really know Flick's friend, and she was hot and sticky and needed to feel the cool night air. Flick was bound to join her outside eventually.

Ellie walked to the far side of the roof terrace, as it was too crowded by the doors. The paved terrace had a retaining wall around the three open sides and was furnished with chairs and outdoor sofas grouped around coffee tables, as well as high stools around patio heater-tables. The lighting was strung on cables from pole to pole in a criss-cross fashion, making a grid of giant fairy lights to enchant patrons.

At the edge of the roof terrace, the old wall was covered in moss and had small plants growing from its crevices. Ellie imagined it was the original high wall of the building's rear courtyard, or at least if not the original, then built with stones reused from it. She rested her glass on the wall, her hand resting around the stem to stop it from tipping over on the uneven surface. She placed her other hand on the top of the wall, relishing the feel of the old, rough stone, crusty lichen and soft moss beneath her fingers.

Looking out across the city to the river was a delight on a night like this. The evening was dry, with little wind, and the city seemed ready to party. Taxis traversed the streets, collecting and depositing their fares to and from the various pubs and clubs. As she watched, Ellie heard revellers' voices rising from the streets: a single loud voice and retort and the following laughter. Ellie felt as though she was spying on

73

them, and the thought gave her a tiny thrill.

She looked further out towards the rows of Edwardian terrace houses lit by streetlights. In most of the homes, the curtains were drawn, the rooms behind them dark. Light still shone from some upstairs windows, and Ellie imagined the lives and personal dramas going on behind them. It was almost as if she were watching tiny television screens showing different films. All manner of vignettes would no doubt be underway—love stories, tragedies, crime dramas, thrillers—all starring the people who lived there: families, couples and the happily single—or the not-so-happily single. Ellie thought of Bertie. How keenly he must miss Charles when he was all alone at night-time. She imagined looking into one of the lit windows and seeing Bertie and Charles embracing. She fervently hoped that she would one day meet someone with whom she could share such passion. She raised her glass to them in a silent toast and went to sip the cocktail.

A large hand appeared, covering the rim of her glass, and pushed it firmly back down onto the wall. 'Do not drink from that,' a deep male voice ordered.

Ellie started in surprise. She hadn't realised anyone was that close to her. She looked sideways at the man now standing to her left. He was tall, looked like he worked out a lot and wore a black donkey jacket with the hood up, black jeans and chunky boots. Ellie was mildly surprised that he'd been allowed into the bar, given that jeans were against the dress code.

'Why not?' Ellie challenged him.

'Because a man dropped pills into it when you turned to take your money from the bartender,' the deep voice explained.

Removing his hand from her glass, he laid it on top of the wall, matching the position of her free hand.

Raising her glass towards the nearest light source, Ellie peered at the contents. She could just make out some powdery granules sitting at the bottom of the blue liquid. Shocked, Ellie instantly poured her drink out onto the floor and stepped away from it, as if it were still dangerous despite it now seeping into the concrete slab.

'Thank you, I guess,' she said, glancing back at the hooded man. He was facing the short wall overlooking the river and didn't turn his head to her as he spoke. 'You are welcome.'

Ellie leaned slightly forwards to try to see inside his hood. She could see his chin, his generous bottom lip and the smooth skin and philtrum above his top lip as the lights above highlighted the horizontal planes of his face, but his eyes were hidden in shadow. She glanced down at his hand. Was it her imagination, or was there a faint blue glow coming from beneath it? Perhaps he had of those glowing cigarette lighters under his palm.

'Go back to your friends. You will be safer with them than you are out here, alone,' the guy instructed.

'Safer?' said Ellie, confused. What did he mean? She now didn't have a drink that could be spiked, and she was hardly likely to be kidnapped from the roof terrace of Baubles. She wasn't exactly alone out here, either. 'Right. Uh ... OK. I was heading back inside now, anyway.'

She waited for him to look at her or say something more—to justify his remark—but he remained standing there, staring straight ahead. When he continued to offer nothing further, she said, 'OK. So, bye, then. Thanks again,' and turned away from him.

75

'Goodbye, Eleanor,' he replied as she began to walk away.

A memory jangled in her subconscious. *That voice.* Where had she heard it before? It took her several more seconds to register that he'd also felt somehow familiar. Ellie turned back to where they'd been standing moments ago, but the hooded man had already gone. She scanned the roof terrace, looking for him, but there was no sign. Being taller and broader than most of the men at Baubles, he should have been easy to spot.

*He must be a quick mover,* she thought. *Shame.*

Another memory clicked into place: the hooded man outside the Spring Thing. *Was this the same guy?* He was the same size, certainly, and what little she'd seen of their faces tallied, not to mention their shared fondness for hoodies. Could it have been him?

Ellie tried to picture the man she'd briefly bumped into at the Spring Thing. Besides the attraction she'd felt, there was something odd about the memory. Oh yes, that guy had had lights under his hoodie. Tonight's man had had light under his hand. *Weird.* But not as weird as tonight's hero knowing her name. The Spring Thing guy hadn't spoken to her, had he? So how had she recognised the voice tonight?

Annoyingly, that piece of information stayed resolutely locked in her subconscious, and so Ellie walked on back to the French doors, aware that she must have presented an odd spectacle standing there, frozen in thought.

Once inside, she made her way over to their table. Jaz and Kaz were sat there, heads close together as they conversed over the noise of the bar. Flick was on the dance floor, giving her best hip-grinding, arm-waving wiggle, flanked by two men who looked like they'd won the jackpot. Seeing Ellie had returned, Flick sashayed over to their table and lifted her blue cocktail to her lips.

Ellie grabbed her arm. 'Don't,' she insisted. 'Mine was spiked.'

Jaz raised her head, as did Kaz.

Flick looked disbelieving. 'Seriously? How did you know?'

'Yes, I'm serious. Some guy warned me when I was outside, and I saw the dregs of the pills.'

'Christ, what the fuck is going on in here?' Jaz asked rhetorically, her temper rising. 'Freaking perverts all over the place who can't get laid without drugging women. *Fuck*. Are you OK, Ellie? Did you drink any? Flick hasn't drunk hers; she's been getting free drinks off those guys.' Jaz indicated the men looking longingly at Flick from the dance floor.

'No, I'm OK. I didn't drink it. The guy out there stopped me in time.'

'You sure it wasn't him that spiked it in the first place? Maybe he just wanted to appear the hero to get on your good side, then slip another roofie into your drink later on.'

'No, it wasn't like that. *He* wasn't like that.' She couldn't explain why, but Ellie had felt in no danger from the stranger.

'Well, I think it's time to get out of this pervert-infested dive,' declared Jaz. 'Flick, where's the next place on your posh pub crawl? I'll go anywhere as long as it's away from here.'

\* \* \*

By the end of the night—or to be more accurate, by the end of the *very* early morning—the girls had visited two more clubs, happily without incident. Kaz had joined them for the first change of venue but had bowed out for the last, saying she needed to crash as she was knackered from the gig.

The sleepy taxi driver was pleased to see two of his three passengers fall asleep on the drive home. The one in the front, however, gave him an eye-opening, blow-by-blow account of her "fuck-mazing" evening.

Once he'd delivered them safely home, he thought himself lucky that he was no longer a young man having to impress modern girls like her. Some of the opinions his chatty companion had voiced had made him feel old, amused, embarrassed and slightly inadequate.

# 8

# Chapter 8

On Monday morning, with the April showers clearly upping their game, it rained heavily and continued to do so for most of the day. The Common Room was a fug of humid air by lunchtime, where Ellie sat in Goth Corner with Flick, Chris, Jaz and a slightly nervous Meg. Jaz was pursuing her infatuation with "the new girl" and had invited Meg to join her for lunch after their Physics class. Meg looked like she felt a little out of place among the predominantly black-leather-clad gang, but she was admirably trying to make a contribution to the conversation.

'Sounds like you all had a great time,' she said to Flick. 'I wouldn't have made it past midnight, though. How *do* you get the energy to keep partying until 4am?'

'Rocket fuel,' said Jaz. 'In the form of mostly blue, sickly-sweet cocktails that would melt the palate of a discerning connoisseur—or any connoisseur for that matter, even a trainspotter.'

'They were delicious.' Flick licked her lips at the memory. 'Wish I had one now.'

'So do I.' Chris grinned lasciviously 'You get pretty wild under the influence of alcohol, and I could do with cheering up.' With an arm already draped around her shoulders, he pulled Flick in for a kiss, only to be met by her indignant elbow being dug into his ribs.

'Careful, sunshine, or you won't be getting 'cheered up' again anytime soon,' Flick teased, grinning at him. Then, giving lie to her threat, she started kissing him anyway.

'Excuse the on-tap porn show that is Flick,' Jaz apologised to Meg. 'We've become immune to the debauchery, but you might find yourself offended, so feel free to look away.'

Meg, who was doing just that, giggled.

'Give it a rest, Flick, or get a room,' agreed Ellie. 'Either way, take it away from us.'

Flick came up for air and pouted at the other two. 'You two are only jealous because both of you are experiencing a dry spell at the moment,' she said.

'I'm working on that,' replied Jaz, glancing at Meg, who blushed delightfully.

'Hey,' said Jacob, flopping himself down on the vacant chair next to Ellie. 'What you been up to?'

Rather surprised, Ellie answered, 'Not much. Just nearly being drugged, kidnapped and no doubt assaulted. You?'

Jacob raised an eyebrow. 'Seriously?'

'Yep,' confirmed Jaz. 'Turns out Baubles is a nest of limp-dicked wannabe rapists. Who knew?'

'Could have told you that.' Jacob ran his hand through his long hair. 'Any time you want to go somewhere with a normal guy, let me know.'

Ellie smiled at him and looked down at her hands. The ring on her right hand felt cold despite the warmth of the room and the heat of her body.

'Thanks,' she said. 'I'll keep that in mind.'

A few weeks ago, Jacob saying these words to her would have been included in Ellie's perfect fantasy. However, now she didn't feel the flutter of excitement in her chest at Jacob's offer that she would most certainly have done back then.

'Just say the word.' Jacob smiled cockily.

Jaz had been talking quietly to Meg, a small smile frequently playing on her lips. The rest of the Common Room needn't have existed for them; they seemed to be unaware of anything going on outside of their own personal bubble. Ellie smiled as she looked at them. She hoped that Meg would make Jaz happy. Jaz deserved someone who saw her for the amazing person she was.

Jaz had told Ellie and Flick a little of what it had been like coming out as gay at her last college, Turrell's Academy. She had gone public just after her GCSE exams, aged sixteen. Jaz had thought that entering Turrell's Sixth Form as her true self would be fine; some of her friends had gone to other colleges, but plenty of her year group had stayed on to attend the school's own Sixth Form, which was housed on the same site as the school. Sadly, she had overestimated the maturity of many of her fellow pupils.

As the group chatted and complained about the muggy heat, they were joined by Violet Tully, Jaz's sister, who fought her way across the crowded Common Room to Goth Corner.

'Hey, sis,' Vi said. 'Hi, guys.' She flumped down next to Jaz and gave Meg a swift, appraising glance.

Jaz looked up at Vi. 'Hey, squirt.' Turning to Meg, she said, 'This is the curse I was telling you about. The one inflicted upon me for misdemeanours in my past lives.'

'Hi, Violet,' said Meg. 'Great to meet you. Your sister has told me lots about you. Only good things, though.'

'*That,*' replied Vi, liking Meg's earnest response, 'would be very unlike my dear sister. Call me Vi, by the way.'

Vi knew all too well her sister's struggle over acceptance for her sexuality. Jaz had stayed at Turrell's Academy for the first year of A levels, becoming increasingly withdrawn and isolated. Her mother and sister became very worried about Jaz, who now spent most of her time in her room, studying and avoiding social media. Violet, her sister, became extremely upset and angry at comments made about Jaz, especially ones posted online by Jaz's former friends and classmates. This, in turn, had an adverse impact on Vi's own GCSE studies.

Seeing her girls turning into different people before her eyes, Janet Tully made the decision to take them both out of school and move her family to a different part of the country, going back to where she herself had grown up. Vi joined the local school and finished the final year of her GCSEs before signing up to Lowford College, where both girls were now markedly much happier. Jaz was once again her former self—the humorous, irreverent, sparky girl she'd been before bravely coming out—and Vi, although still angry at times and naturally very protective of Jaz, was settling into her first year of her Sixth Form studies.

Having attained her AS levels in Maths, History and Media Studies at her former school, Jaz had decided to change subjects at Lowford and took Chemistry, Physics and Philosophy instead. Vi was younger than Jaz, but because of Jaz effectively doing Year Twelve twice, they were now at Sixth Form college together, which suited them both.

It was clear to all who knew them that Jaz and Vi cared deeply for each other but generally hid this affection behind a screen of mutual point scoring and good-natured squabbling, much like many siblings from very attached and loving families.

'So, Rat Bag, how did the test go?' Jaz asked Vi, who had been grumbling about today's Media Studies assessment at breakfast.

Vi pulled a face. 'I'll have to wait and see next class. At least I wrote more than just my name on the answer sheet this time,' Vi said with a rueful smile.

'Aced it, then! Told you you'd be fine,' Jaz reassured her, illustrating her opinion of the difficulty of the Media Studies course.

Vi relaxed back in her chair. 'It may be easy for you, but some of us are not born geniuses. Some of us have to work at stuff,' she pouted.

Knowing she looked especially attractive when she pouted, Vi was not opposed to letting the guys in her older sister's friendship group get a good look. After all, she had practiced the pout in the bathroom mirror long enough to know it made her full lips even plumper and more enticing. In stark contrast to her big sister's short dark hair, Vi had a cascade of long, enviably straight, pale blonde hair. She generally wore it down so that it could be artlessly tossed over her shoulders or coyly hid behind whenever the occasion demanded. She was usually dressed in shades of blue and preferred long skirts and tie dye; her graceful, willowy frame was well-suited to the hippy look.

The Common Room bell sounded, signalling the end of the lunch break. Jacob looked at Ellie and, while everyone began to gather their belongings, he put his hand on her arm, interrupting her as she tidied up.

'I meant it,' he said, looking pointedly into her eyes.

Ellie just smiled in response and, with a small nod to show she'd understood, finished piling up her folders. Jacob stood up and left, followed by most of their gang.

'Still a spark there on his side,' remarked Jaz, who was more observant that most. 'Maybe rejection is a new and enticing experience for him.'

'I haven't *rejected* him,' Ellie protested.

'But you haven't succumbed to his charms either. Ah well, I suppose there's always next year's intake for the poor lad.'

Jaz had a theory that Jacob was deliberately flunking classes each year in order to stay at college, where the supply of impressionable young women who fell for his dark, mysterious good looks and studied broody demeanour would never run dry. She had him down as a bit of a man-whore. This used to irritate Ellie, who, at the time, was infatuated with Jacob and hence hadn't liked the implication that she was just another one of his sheep. Yet having been close to him at the Spring Thing—having *kissed* him—she could, at last, see Jaz's point. Ellie now thought of his nonchalance as a façade: his "man-of-few-words" act was studied, rehearsed, like he was too cool to talk.

The Monday after the Spring Thing, Jacob had crossed the Common Room to sit with Ellie. However, as she clearly wasn't mooning over him, he hadn't bothered again until today. And Ellie was fine with that. In fact, it was odd that he was having another shot now. Unsurprisingly, Lily, Jacob's number one fan, had broken up with Pete and was now dogging Jacob's steps once again. Maybe he was just trying to shake her off.

Later that afternoon, when Ellie was driving out of the college car park, she saw Meg being given a lift home in Jaz's Ford Focus. A less-than-thrilled Vi had been demoted to the backseat, and she grimaced at Ellie from the rear window as they passed, making a heart shape with both hands.

Ellie smiled to herself. She had high hopes for Meg and Jaz.

9

# Chapter 9

The house was quiet when Ellie got home, so she made her way out to the garden to find her father preparing rows to plant seeds. Andy Johnstone was a keen gardener and relished the fact that he could grow his own food for his family. As well as his vegetable patch, he also had a small polytunnel in which salad crops were grown. His love of gardening didn't extend to the herbaceous borders, however, which he thought a frivolous and unproductive waste of his time; these were Grace and Ellie's domain.

Andy maintained that the flowers could sense his disdain for their existence and that they demonstrated this by failing to thrive whenever he was nagged into weeding the borders. Grace held this to be a flimsy excuse, although, having more respect for her borders than to let Andy decide what was weed or wanted, she could often be found bent double in the flowerbeds, as she was this evening.

'It's the ground ivy,' she announced, straightening up from the large bed by the field gate with a handful of the encroaching creepers. 'Whenever we go away, the stuff seems to take it as a signal to grow rampant, whatever the time of year. I seem to have more ivy in the compost heap than grass cuttings lately, and yes, I realise that the grass has only just started to grow well again. It's all relevant, I'm sure. When we're here, the flowers thrive, but when we head off on our trips, the flowers pine and the ivy flourishes.'

Ellie looked around the garden. The primulas were past their best, but the bluebells were coming out in force on the lawn under the Holm Oak. Soon, there would be a carpet of indigo for Ellie to sit amongst during her evening musings.

'Here, take this please, sweetheart,' said Grace, handing Ellie an armful of ivy. 'Stick it in there for now. Time for a cup of tea, I think.'

Ellie took the weeds and added them to the heap in the wheelbarrow. Grasping and lifting the handles, she wheeled it over to the far side of the lawn where the compost heap lurked by the potting shed. As promised, there was already a large pile of ivy on the heap; clearly Grace had spent most of the afternoon working on its eviction from her cherished beds.

Emptying the waste, Ellie left the wheelbarrow turned up-side down on the compost heap. She knew that composting was an important part of gardening, but she disliked the smell of rot and the rank liquid that seeped into the ground at the base of the heap. It discoloured the earth and made the ground seem poisoned and somehow unstable; she always tried not to step too close to avoid this wet, tainted area.

Entering the kitchen, Ellie crossed to the utility room and took a handful of bird seed from the seed sack. She leaned out of the back door and threw it onto the lawn. A couple of pigeons from her animal hospital had been released and, although now returned to the wild, Ellie was worried that they may have become reliant on her for food. Not wanting them to starve, she'd taken to putting out a little extra food every day.

'I will have a cornfield sprinkled with sunflowers on my lawn come summertime,' her mother commented drily, although actually pleased to see Ellie being so thoughtful. 'You've always been one to take care of injured and poorly creatures, Ellie. I've lost count of the number of baby birds we've housed in winter and small injured creatures that we've had recuperating in cardboard boxes over the years. You even buried the cats' victims in the flowerbeds with small stones as grave markers; sometimes your father or I even had to attend the interments!'

Ellie smiled, too, remembering the animal-obsessed child she had been. Finding the small furry bodies of dead field mice had broken her heart, and although she couldn't help them, she felt she at least ought to mark their existence. She particularly disliked the way cats sadistically played with their victims before executing them. As a child, she'd spent a considerable amount of time stalking the cats and startling them into dropping their prey, which she then rescued and released in a different location.

'Jill is coming for dinner tomorrow, by the way,' Grace announced, ending Ellie's reminiscence. 'I thought we'd have lentil lasagne and banana fritters. What do you think?'

Jill Pengelly was an old friend of her mother's; the pair had met when Ellie was just a baby. Grace and Andy having no siblings had resulted in Ellie collecting aunts and uncles from her parent's friendship group to fill the vacancies, including Bertie and Jill among others. It was very rare to get them all in one place; in fact, Ellie couldn't recall this ever happening, but occasionally one came to visit, and Ellie looked forward to these occasions immensely.

'Sounds great,' said Ellie.

\* \* \*

The next evening, Jill arrived. She lived in the next county, and although her house was not terribly far away from her friends' home as the crow files, it had taken Jill nearly two hours to get to Owl's Ridge. As she explained at length upon her arrival, this was because she had needed to stop en route at a remote village to see a lady who made meditation candles. There was no one like Sherri for making a pure burning candle, apparently.

Ellie loved Jill's visits. Jill was a such a force of nature, and whenever she was in the house, Ellie found the place felt more alive and crowded in an expectant, exciting sort of way, rather than just the obvious physical sense.

No one could gauge what gems of information Jill might choose to impart to Ellie; Jill held *views* on what children ought to be told, and these were essentially that they should be told everything. Adults withholding information from young and enquiring minds because it was "not suitable" or because the child was "too young to know" was one of Jill's pet hates. She maintained that the real world was confusing enough as it was, and one shouldn't add to a child's perplexity by inventing sugar-coated versions of reality. Having said that, Jill was also very open-minded and prepared to accept a variety of alternative cultural, spiritual and religious views—a position shared by Ellie's parents. It was no wonder that they were such close friends.

Jill was a tall, large-boned woman in her fifties who, although not obese, was solidly built and usually wore her wavy hair stuffed haphazardly into a bun at the nape of her neck. Her wrists chimed with an assortment of bangles, and today she wore her favourite necklace: a chain from which silver ears of maize dangled in between green and brown glass beads, their husks peeling back to reveal the plump kernels within. Jill loved it. She felt it epitomised all that was best about nature's bounty and represented a woman as a bringer and nourisher of new life; one of her favourite aphorisms was "women are the only way humans reach earth".

'Ellie!' boomed Jill upon entering the room and seeing that her pseudo-niece was at home. 'Come here, child, and give your favourite visitor a hug! It has been too long.'

Embracing Jill was like being held by Mother Nature herself; Jill radiated comfort and nurture, and her familiar aroma of scented oils and white musk was a balm to Ellie's senses.

'How are you, my darling?' Jill asked.

Ellie laughed with happiness. 'Good, thank you, Jill. Especially now you're here.'

'Something has been bothering you, I can sense it,' said Jill. Lowering her voice for only Ellie to hear, she added, 'We'll talk later.'

Jill proceeded to hug both Grace and Andy in turn and pat each spaniel on the head.

'Right, all well greeted. A blessed reunion. Now, let us waste no time before breaking bread together. I'm famished.'

Sitting down at the head of the kitchen table, Jill helped

herself to a pumpkin seed bread roll. Laughing, Grace began to serve the meal. Having known Jill of old, Grace knew that there was no greater compliment to her cooking than that of having Jill demand to be fed.

The meal was long and relaxed, with much laughter and reminiscing of shared experiences, drawn from the rich tapestry of their near twenty-year friendship.

'Utterly delicious,' pronounced Jill, mopping up the last of the lasagne with some homemade garlic bread. 'I feel my physical batteries recharging already. My spiritual ones are fully charged, so you find me at my best this evening.'

The dessert of banana fritters met with equal praise, and as they sat relaxing around the table and enjoying their choice of the freshly ground coffee or herbal tea on offer, Jill turned the idle chatter to Ellie.

'Now, young lady—to business. There is something changed about you. I can see it in your aura.'

Ellie looked perplexed and cast her eyes towards her father for help. 'You'll have to go from the beginning, Jill,' he said. 'We haven't talked much to Ellie about auras.'

'Goodness be blessed! Why ever not?' exclaimed Jill in surprise. 'Well then, my dear, you'd better pay attention now. Auras are the energy given off by all living things. Some enlightened minds can see these energy auras and also read them, which allows them to determine how that creature currently is physically, mentally and spiritually. Imagine a candle flame, if you will.'

Obligingly, Grace reached for a candle in a squat pottery holder from the sideboard and placed it on the kitchen table before lighting it for all to examine the flame.

'Thank you, dear,' said Jill. 'Now, observe the flame. You

can see that at the centre, next to the wick, is an area of dark light. Expanding out from that is the yellow-white shape of the flame, and at the edge of this, you can see a hazy, indeterminate third layer, usually of red or orange. An aura is like the third layer of the candle flame; sometimes, it is hard to see clearly. The colours of an aura can speak volumes about how a person is, but to the truly enlightened, auras can also be read to predict who the person they surround is *meant* to be.'

Ellie looked puzzled. 'Meant to be?' she queried.

'Sometimes aura colour indicates that a person has a spiritual inclination for a specific role in life—leadership and inspiring others, for example. This we call "the true reading". Yet if that person's current life pathway is not directing them to fulfil their divinely given abilities, they are not taking their intended place in the cosmos and will therefore not be truly happy or fulfilled.'

Ellie peered at the candle flame; it was almost hypnotic, dancing in the slight movements of air across the table.

'Humans, like all creatures, have auras," Jill continued. "When you were a baby, just starting to think about toddling, I met your mother, thanks be, and made a first aura reading for you. Babies are easiest to get a person's true reading from, as at their unadvanced stage of life, there are usually no psychological or physical dimensions impacting on or adding colour to their auras.'

Jill paused. Looking down at the dancing flame, she seemed to be choosing her next words carefully. 'Your aura, Ellie, was unlike any other I have ever seen. It was pure white, with sub-colours of gold and silver shimmering around the edges.'

Grace and Andy were watching Ellie carefully to gauge her

reaction to this information.

After a moment, Ellie spoke. 'You mentioned that auras have meanings?'

'I did. A white aura signifies perfect balance, purity, spiritual truth, divine energy and protection. That is the essential reading for you. The sub-colours are additions which you may already possess, be given, or develop. Gold means angelic guidance, pure knowing intuition and free flowing energy. Silver would suggest that you are predisposed to be very developed psychically, even processing skills such as telekinetic power. Together, these colours are referred to as Royal Hues. It is unusual to see gold as a sub-colour, but more unusual still, I have *never* seen both the regal hues together in any other living being.'

Jill looked determinedly at Grace and Andy. 'It is time she knew what she is—or *could* be.'

Ellie looked disbelieving.

'Auras are like light, Ellie,' Grace added. 'White light can be split by refraction into all colours, but we tend to just recognise the seven: red, orange, yellow, green, blue, indigo and violet.'

'"Richard Of York Gave Battle In Vain,"' whispered Ellie.

'Exactly,' continued her mother. 'Only splitting light into colours means dividing up the energy. Therefore, it stands to reason that white energy is the strongest, as it is whole. Your aura indicates you carry a pure form of energy within you.'

'Grace,' Andy said warningly. He turned to Ellie. 'Don't let them weird you out, Wellie. Having strong spiritual power is something incredible.'

Ellie felt a brief moment of reassurance in her father's use of his childhood nickname for her.

'She *needs* to know,' Jill said firmly, looking directly at Andy.

Andy returned her look and gave a slight shake of his head, then glanced at Grace with a quirked eyebrow. After a long moment exchanging silent views, as only those who have lived together for a long time can, Grace looked across at Jill and gave a faint shake of her head, then looked down at the table. Ellie, meanwhile, had been staring at the candle flame, trying to imagine herself surrounded by a white light with silver and gold smudges and so missed this exchange.

'Very well,' Jill capitulated with a sigh. 'It is your decision. But at least let me give an up-to-date reading.'

Grace nodded, this time giving Andy an overruling stare, and he bent his head in acknowledgement of her wish.

Reaching into her tasselled carpet bag propped against the table leg, Jill withdrew a set of tarot cards. She expertly shuffled them, looking at Ellie as she did so. Ellie recognised the cards; as a child, she used to play with them if her mother and Jill were not paying attention, taking them from Jill's bag and looking at the beautifully drawn pictures. Jill finished shuffling and spread the cards out in a semi-circle.

'Run your right hand over the top of them without touching them, and point out to me the one which calls to you.'

Ellie did as she was asked and tapped a card. Jill withdrew it and placed it face up in front of her. Then she reached across the semi-circle and scooped the cards into a heap in front of Ellie.

'Mix them,' Jill ordered.

Ellie slid them around the tabletop and over and under one another with both hands.

'Now shuffle them back into a deck and hand it to me,' Jill

94

instructed, moving the first card Ellie had chosen into the middle of the table.

Ellie passed her the deck and Jill drew the top card, laying it down slightly overlapping and to the right-hand side of the first card, with both pictures facing up.

'These two cards represent you, the questions you are asking and the answers you are seeking.'

A third card was drawn and laid horizontally across the bottom of the other two.

'This card is linked to the other two. It is about the subject of the question or the person that you are enquiring about.'

Jill continued to draw and place cards until eleven lay face up on the tabletop. She studied the cards for a while, then drew a long breath.

'It is certainly an interesting spread,' she said. 'Although, I have to say, I'm not particularly surprised at this. It is *your* reading, after all.'

Ellie felt slightly uncomfortable about this statement. Why was her reading likely to be unusual?

Jill began to deliver the reading. 'The card you selected was The Star; this is you. The Star is about connecting one's soul with the divine, but it is also known as the Celestial Mandate. Drawing this card means that a person has a role predetermined by divine forces and that if they concentrate less on trying to shape their own destiny, they will become more aware of the divine guidance already around them. The first card I drew from your deck, laid over The Star, is The Hierophant. It signifies a master of natural law and hints towards something or someone that can unravel hidden universal secrets and make links between human existence and the divine. It represents the questions you are asking.'

Ellie pondered this. She had always felt that there was more to be uncovered in this world; things beyond that which we experience as reality. She had frequently yearned to discover what those things might be and the routes taken to reach them.

'The third card is The Citadel, or Broken Tower; its pictogram shows a king falling from his tower. The card represents great change, the destruction of normality, transformation and self-sacrifice,' Jill explained. 'It could be indicating that you are the catalyst for change and, if that is so, that you must manage this change by taking the brunt of its force yourself, so that weaker beings are protected from the turmoil.'

Andy exhaled loudly and glanced sharply at Grace. She made a halting movement with her hand, raising it slightly from the table as if to signal for to him to wait.

'The card to the left of the centre denotes your past, depicted here as The Wheel of Fortune. This means that you were at a safe place at the centre of the wheel, protected and watched over. You followed the flow of events and harmonised with what occurred around you. The card to the right of the centre shows your immediate future. It is The Two of Swords and can mean a conflict between your perceptions and your goals; you may have to wait until more information is given before you can resolve this, as you are not yet fully informed.'

To the right of the cards explained thus far were four other cards arranged in a column. Jill turned her attention to these next. Laying her hand on the card nearest her, she continued.

'This is the place of fears, and you drew Death. That is not uncommon; most humans fear death. But do not think of the Death card as specific to you. It signifies *a* death, but not necessarily that of a person. It might mean, perhaps, the death of an old idea or plan, or maybe of an old relationship or way of thinking.'

Ellie looked relieved.

'Above it, the Seven of Cups sits in your family placing. Interesting.' Jill looked pointedly at Andy and Grace.

'Dreams and visions other than the ones currently surrounding you are desired; a wish to change your path trodden thus far.'

Returning her gaze to the spread before her, Jill continued the reading. 'In the place of hopes sits The Lovers. Not necessarily meaning the obvious—although it may do—but also pertaining to successfully bringing two opposing forces together or risk losing one of them. It may well be indicating both these meanings.

'The final card in the column is The Seven of Wands. This is sat in the position of the Final Outcome. It shows that you must push yourself beyond your limits and reach further than ever before in mind and spirit.'

Jill paused and looked at the final two cards that lay above and below the three centre ones. Placing her finger on the one below, she tapped it twice. 'This is your base card: The Seven of Coins. It means your own energy or power is growing and that others will soon take notice. It may be a warning.'

She gently touched the top card furthest away from her. 'And this last card is The King of Swords. There is masculine energy close to you, hanging over you in this spread. It is the energy of a king, but also that of an adjudicator; it is balanced and even-handed, one uneasily swayed from the centre point. When I first drew it from your deck, I thought it represented your father, but reading it now alongside the rest of the spread, I see that it is *not* him. This energy is as close to you as your past and future are, but is currently mostly hidden from you. It's also possible that you are refusing to recognise it. Beware, it is powerful and may engulf you if your own energy is not a match for it.'

Jill stopped and looked around the table, then, peering over the top of her half-moon spectacles, fixed Ellie with her penetrating brown eyes.

'Ellie, you are on the brink of great change. You may already have begun the transformation without being aware of it. You are important to the grand plan, and you will increase greatly in that importance and in your own power. But your rise will not go unnoticed. There will be others watching. You must seek out and embrace what is coming. To hide behind denial may well place you and others in jeopardy.'

Ellie's hand lay cold in her lap under the table, and Grace gripped and squeezed it twice using their private code to give reassurance. When Ellie had been a small child, she and her mother had developed a coded language they used when holding hands. Two squeezes meant "love you".

Andy scraped his chair back from the table and crossed to the countertop to flick on the kettle, breaking the heavy silence that followed Jill's final pronouncement. He cleared his throat in readiness to speak.

'Well, you've given us all something to think about there, Jill,' he finally managed. 'Thank you. Who would like a hot drink?'

'A spread like this is important, particularly for her,' Jill quietly warned. 'Don't ignore it, Andrew.'

'I think we've all had enough mystery for one evening, Jill.

Ellie, would you like a hot chocolate to take to bed?'

'Yes. Thanks, Dad,' Ellie answered, surfacing from the swell of thoughts in her mind. She turned to Jill. 'So, I have some important role, one I clearly know nothing about or indeed want, and yet I must accept it?'

'If it is your destiny, you have no choice,' Jill answered bluntly.

'I'm not sure I believe that,' said Ellie, feeling her temper starting to rise. 'I think we make our own destiny.'

'You may well be right about that in day-to-day dealings, child. But if we have been given a role in the grand plan, we have no choice but to fulfil it or risk bringing chaos to the cosmos. Your reading warned you against closing your mind. It told you that you may well be the catalyst for the change that is coming. Non-believing isn't a great way of starting down this path.'

'The Two of Swords also indicated that Ellie was not yet fully informed,' Grace interjected before an argument could develop. 'Ideas are conflicting; opposites not meeting. Give her time, Jill. The more Ellie knows, the clearer her path will become.'

'The spread shows it may already be happening,' insisted Jill. 'She may not have much time.'

'Speaking of *time*, I think it's time for bed,' Andy cut in, placing a mug of hot chocolate on the table in front of Ellie. 'There you go, Wellie. Why don't you go on up?' He dropped a kiss onto the top of her head.

Ellie suddenly wished to escape from this closeted room and the unsettling revelations Jill had brought to it. She stood quickly and, clutching the hot mug tightly, said her goodbyes to Jill before heading out of the room.

Pausing on the threshold as a thought occurred to her, she turned back to Jill. 'One more thing. You said that my aura was different. How is it different from before, exactly?'

Glancing at both of Ellie's parents for permission to speak further, and receiving their consent, Jill answered her. 'There is now a purple-and-blue smudge to the centre of your aura. Indigo means highly intuitive, devotion, universal flow and a seeker. Which could be you, but I would suggest that the colour may be linked to this mysterious male energy.'

Jill paused, looking at Grace alone this time before qualifying her remark. 'There were also three sevens in your spread, Ellie. Seven is a number both straight and crooked; neither one thing nor the other, like the King of Swords who sits at the fulcrum, the point of balance. The seventh colour is violet, a purple, shades of which are present in your aura.'

Ellie's eyes widened in surprise. The stone at the centre of her ring was purple; the pivotal point about which all else turned. Jill claimed that Ellie had this important destiny, that she was pivotal to the changes to come. Was this seeming coincidence of colour between the ring, the reading and her aura actually an indication that Jill might just be right?

\* \* \*

That night, Ellie dreamt of the dark corridor again. There was light, as she could clearly see the wall, floor and door, but the source of it was not obvious. The black, glass-like wall seemed endless as it receded into darkness on either side and above of her. Its lack of obvious boundaries gave Ellie the impression that she must be in a cavern or great building with extremely high ceilings. The warm wall was thrumming, and Ellie knelt to feel the floor. There was now a pulse in the stone there, too.

Facing the closed door, she succumbed to her overwhelming desire to discover what had called to her and nervously reached for the doorknob. It looked to be made from black metal and was circular, with seven facets to allow for grip. She touched her fingertips to its surface, then instantly jerked backwards as she received a static-like electric shock. Was this a warning?

Ellie stepped back from the door, reluctant to be near something that might harm her. She sensed a tiny movement on her finger and brought her hand to her face to see what it was. She wore the spiral ring on the third finger of that hand, but all seemed normal under close inspection. Curling her fingers, she brought her knuckles towards her face and touched the ring to her top lip, where her most sensitive skin was. She could feel a tiny, rhythmic beat ticking through the cool metal.

*Seek out and embrace the new.* Ellie heard Jill's words in her mind. *I'm someone who's supposed to be able to uncover secrets*, she told herself. Bracing for another electric shock, Ellie stepped firmly towards the door and grasped and turned the knob.

There was no shock this time, nor any sound, which Ellie thought was odd as every metallic mechanism makes some noise when operated. She pushed the door inwards to open it. Inside the room, even the air was thrumming with the pulse, and all was in darkness. Ellie could hear the sound of wind blowing somewhere in a regular rise and fall, but she felt no movement of air across her face. The space was pleasantly warm, not cold.

With her hand still on the doorknob, Ellie still felt connected to before, not fully in the room, nor able to determine its contents. She made herself let go and took three paces forwards to stand with her feet squarely planted on the ground in an assertive, wide-legged stance. The door swung closed silently behind her, leaving Ellie surrounded by complete darkness.

But she was not afraid.

Darkness was her comfort, not her terror.

She felt herself rise—or the floor drop away, Ellie wasn't sure which—and hung suspended in space, floating in darkness. She lifted her arms away from her sides and spread her fingers to maximise the contact between her skin and the pulsing energy around her. Her body reverberated in tune, and she relished the sensation. It was like being close to huge speakers at a concert and physically feeling the bass notes, but with no sound here to accompany the vibrations. Closing her eyes, Ellie tilted her head upwards and relaxed her mind. The wind sighed in a long exhale, and Ellie curled her lips in a smile.

*'Well done, Eleanor,'* a resonant voice rumbled, sending shivers through her body.

# 10

# Chapter 10

Ellie sat in her English Literature class, reading from a book of works by the poet she'd chosen to study.

The senses folding thick and dark
   About the stifled soul within,
   We guess diviner things beyond,
   And yearn to them with yearning fond;
   We strike out blindly to a mark
   Believed in, but not seen.

Elizabeth Barrett Browning's poem *Human Life's Mystery*, written over one hundred and fifty years ago, resonated with Ellie. She echoed the same yearning for the unknown, which was why she'd chosen to study Browning. *How ironic.* In future, she'd have to be more careful what she wished for, as it seemed possible, according to Jill, that her desire was going to be met, and Ellie wasn't sure she was ready for that.

   Later in the poem, the words seemed eerily pertinent, too:

And sometimes horror chills our blood
  To be so near such mystic Things,
  And we wrap round us for defence
  Our purple manners, moods of sense—
  As angels from the face of God
  Stand hidden in their wings.

Jill clearly felt that this was what Ellie was doing: hiding from her destiny, wrapping normality around herself and avoiding dealing with the abnormal stuff by dismissing odd occurrences with her own patchy logic.

How had she really avoided that car speeding towards her? How had the spiral drawing got inside her car? There were too many weird things happening lately; too big to think about or to begin to try to understand.

Was all that had been happening to her good or bad? Divine guidance was supposed to be helping her on her preordained pathway, which was obviously good, but if that was really the case, then Ellie would have to accept that the flip side also existed: that evil was a part of all of this, too. That was something Ellie didn't even want to begin to think about, particularly in light of her horrific reoccurring nightmares.

Fortuitously, at that moment, the bell signalling the end of lesson rang, effectively putting a stop to Ellie's cogitation. She gathered her books into her bag, shrugged on her jacket and headed out of the portacabin classroom to meet up with her friends.

Jaz and Meg were now officially going out and full couple status looked likely to be adopted relatively soon. Most breaktimes, Ellie and Flick joined Jaz and Meg, but today Meg was not at college due to a tummy bug.

'You sure it wasn't food poisoning from the "special meal" you so lovingly prepared for her the other evening?' joked Flick upon hearing of Meg's indisposition.

'Clearly not, as I'm fine,' replied Jaz in a bored voice, not even looking up from the book she was reading.

'It's movie night at Bertie's next Monday,' announced Ellie. 'Who's turn is it to choose the film?'

The trio had begun the movie night tradition a while ago when Ellie, worried that he was lonely, had decided that Bertie needed keeping an eye on. Initially, they'd met at the local cinema, but Bertie had found the seats uncomfortable and the gentleman's convenience unsanitary, so from then onwards, the girls met at his flat on the first Monday of each month, bringing popcorn, Maltesers and DVDs.

Bertie had naturally complained about the disarray they brought to his immaculate sitting room and the mess on his antique rugs made by the girls vegging out, but only half-heartedly. He actually loved their high-spirited company, filling a hole in his life that he hadn't realised existed before meeting them.

'Mine,' claimed Flick.

'*Mine*, I think you'll find,' disputed Jaz. 'You chose that awful thing with all the half-dressed cowboys last time.'

'Ah, yes, so I did.' Flick smiled in recollection. Defending her film choice, she said, 'Bertie liked it. He said he thought it had "high artistic merit."'

'It was borderline man-on-man soft porn, so no surprise there,' Ellie remarked dryly. 'So, what are we in for then, Jazminda? Art house? Film noir? Thelma and Louise?'

'I haven't decided yet, but it could well be something out of the norm.'

'From you, that doesn't inspire confidence. Every film you choose is abnormal,' complained Flick.

'Well, you'll just have to wait and see,' Jaz answered, turning the page of her book with a malicious grin.

'Are we going to the Heart tomorrow?' Ellie asked, changing the subject. 'I think I deserve a drink after the week I've had.'

The Silver Heart was their regular pub in town. It had an amazing back bar where a talented local artist had muralled the entire room to make it look like the interior of a stone-built tavern in Middle Earth; there were even painted rats running up illusionary timbers.

'Yeah, sure,' Flick answered with enthusiasm. 'Chris reckons his brother's band is playing there, so it'll be good to go and check them out.'

'Them or him?' queried Jaz. 'If I'm not mistaken, Mademoiselle has a penchant for boyfriends' brothers?'

Flick had famously once got off with a previous fella's brother in the bathroom at a party. She'd claimed that she hadn't known they were related, but also felt that no explanation was required for her having cheated on her boyfriend when he was doing the same to her at the time.

'*That* is ancient history,' dismissed Flick. 'Chris and I are together, and he's all I'm interested in.'

'Sure, OK. Until the wind changes.'

'Pack it in, you two.' Ellie found herself suddenly irritated by their sparring. 'Jaz, will Meg and Vi go? Are you driving or do you want to crash at mine?'

'I'll drive, so if you want a lift, I can pick you up. I expect Vi will come; I don't think she's got much else on tomorrow night.'

'Perfect! That would be great. Thanks, Jaz,' replied Ellie.

* * *

Ellie arrived home later that day in a restless mood. She'd planned to stay behind after her last lesson and catch up on some of her poetry essay but had found she couldn't settle. She was fidgety and felt a constant need to move, which was certainly not conducive to working in the college library.

Opening the back door and entering the kitchen, Ellie came across her mother speaking on the telephone. 'No … no … yes, will do. Hang on a minute, she's just walked in. I'll put her on.'

Grace looked up as the door opened. Handing the phone to Ellie, she mouthed, 'Jill'.

Reluctantly, Ellie took the handset; she really didn't need any more of Jill's unsettling forecasts of change and disruption right now. 'Hi, Jill.'

'Ellie. Good. Glad I've caught you. I forgot to ask you about something the other night. When we were eating, I noticed you were wearing an unusual ring. What with the aura and tarot readings, the thought slipped from my mind to ask you about it. Where did you get it from?'

'Delphea's, over at the market.'

'Right. Just a market stall purchase, eh? Describe it to me, please, or better still, snap me a photo and wing it over.'

Ellie did as she was asked and sent Jill a text. She heard Jill's text tone beeping down the line, signalling it had been received.

'Yes, very unusual. Do you know what it represents?' Jill asked.

'I didn't think it represented anything,' replied Ellie. 'I bought it because I liked the design.'

'Hmm. We'll have to see. The stone in the middle of the vortex looks like amethyst. Amethyst is a protection crystal; it defines boundaries and is a powerful aid to creative thought, spiritual wakefulness and healing. It also promotes good dreams—your mother used to put amethyst on your bedroom windowsills when you were little.'

Ellie smiled with recollection; so *that* was what the pretty crystals had been about. She used to wonder why her mother would leave them as presents but then insist that they be left on the windowsills rather than being played with.

*Was she trying to banish my bad dreams?*

It had just occurred to Ellie that she hadn't had one of her horrific nightmares lately, when Jill spoke again. 'The chips look like clear quartz, which is a crystal of very pure light and energy. Did you know the word "crystal" comes from the Greek word for ice? Some people used to think that crystals were water frozen so hard that it would never melt, while others believed that white or clear crystals were the tears of their Gods. Clear crystals amplify power; they open the wearer or carrier's mind to a higher level.'

Jill paused for a moment before continuing.

'You have five clear crystals here. Five is the number of Man, halfway between Earth and Heaven. The whole pattern is a pure energy pathway leading to the awakening amethyst in the centre. A dark purple stone … Ellie, it's *you!*' Jill's voice was suddenly loud.

'What do you mean?' Ellie asked, surprised by the sudden change in Jill's tone from mumbling divination to eureka exclamation. 'What's me?'

'The ring is part of the puzzle, Ellie! Whatever you do, don't lose it or let anyone else have it. Only *you* must be its keeper,' Jill said, excitement evident in her voice. 'Follow the pathway, Ellie. It is leading you to the male energy. Follow the path of stars.'

Ellie felt confused. *What pathway?*

An image from her dream appeared in her mind; the dream in which she'd chosen the pathway in the wood that led back to the dark wall. Then, the other night, she'd dreamt that she had finally gone through the door in that wall; she'd made the choice and walked into the pulsing room and heard the deep male voice. The same voice that had spoken her name in the waking world. Even recalling her dream now, the memory of the intense feeling of energy thrumming against her skin made her shiver.

'Wait a moment.' Jill's voice interrupted Ellie's thoughts. 'When I picture you in my mind, I can still see the purple smudge on your aura, but it's changed now. It's become darker.' There was silence on the phone, then, in a breathy voice, Jill asked, 'Ellie, you've found him, haven't you?'

Ellie ducked her head, making her loose hair fall over the handset pressed to her ear in a curtain that screened her face from the rest of the room.

'Yes,' she whispered. 'I think I may have.'

# 11

# Chapter 11

The horn of Jaz's car sounded impatiently from the lane outside Ellie's house. Shouting goodbye to her parents, Ellie dashed to the front door and out onto the drive. Seeing her emerge from the house, Jaz revved the engine, pretending to be about to leave without her. Ellie ran to the gate, part climbed and part vaulted over, then scrambled into the back of the car. Vi was sitting in the front passenger seat, fiddling with the CD player.

'Made it!' puffed Ellie, grappling for the seat belt.

'Primed and ready to go,' announced Jaz as she pulled away from the gateway.

'I thought you were wearing jeans tonight!' complained Vi, looking accusingly at Ellie's bare legs.

'Laundry malfunction,' Ellie answered. 'I thought Mum was doing the washing and she thought I was. Luckily, I'm not the one who's run out of clean knickers!'

'OK, too much information.'

Vi pulled a face in the vanity mirror where she was trying to touch up her mascara despite Jaz aiming for every pothole in the road ahead. Jaz winked at Ellie in the rearview mirror as she dropped the left front wheel into a particularly deep one.

'*Jeez*! Steady on, Jaz—I look like a panda!' Vi complained.

'Well, you should have got your butt off the sofa and started getting ready sooner, then, shouldn't you?' preached Jaz.

'I was helping Mum,' defended Vi.

'Helping Mum answer questions on TV shows does *not* count as "helping Mum". It counts as being a lazy moo with sticky sofa butt!'

'Again, too much information!' Ellie laughingly objected.

A short while later, Jaz pulled into the car park for The Silver Heart and nudged into a parking space. The original name of the pub, Ellie once reasoned, was probably The Silver Hart and, over time, there had been a corruption of the spelling. Jaz, however, had informed her that it was named after a local lady who, a couple of hundred years ago, had gone around doing good deeds. The lady had earned for herself the name 'She of the Silver Heart' because the locals felt that for her to be so godly, the woman's heart must have been made of the purest silver, like the holy chalices in church.

The Silver Heart sat on the bank of the River Lowes, which flowed through Lowford. Situated at the foot of the road bridge on the lower side, its beer garden looked across the river to where a tall wall stretched up from the water to the garden walls of the terraced properties beyond. The wall was especially high on the far bank because the dropping land sloped down the hill from the centre of town to the river. Because of this, there was no walkway or mooring on the far bank. Ellie had often thought that if someone fell over one of the garden walls, there was no way back up from the sheer drop of about five metres into the water.

The Silver Heart's car park gave direct access to the pub's popular back bar and avoided having to go through the more mainstream front bar from the street entrance.

Flick and Chris were already sat at a table near the dance floor and stage when Ellie, Jaz and Vi stepped into the back bar. Flick waved when she saw the newcomers and Ellie waved back, querying whether Flick needed a drink. Flick shook her head and held up her bottled cider, so Ellie just ordered for Jaz, Vi and herself. They all usually drank the same thing in the Silver Heart; a strong bottled cider called Flash. It was rather too easy to drink and you tended to forget how strong it was until you stood up.

Having been served, Ellie joined the others at the table, and Vi thoughtfully got a stool for her.

'What time's your brother playing?' Ellie asked Chris.

'He's not. The drummer broke his wrist,' he answered.

'Oh, no! I was looking forward to seeing him,' griped Flick while her friends exchanged smirks.

Luckily, Chris hadn't heard of Flick's former exploits with boyfriends' siblings.

'Yeah, they've got a disco in here instead—the good one from last week. But now I've gotta get the car back to my brother as he and his mates are taking the drummer out to drown his sorrows. He can't drink, so they've nominated him the dry driver,' explained Chris.

'Can someone drive with a fractured wrist?' queried Jaz.

'Apparently, the drummer reckons he can. Guess they'll find out later,' Chris replied with a grin.

'You're coming back again, though, right? To walk me

home?' Flick checked, giving Chris a suggestive smile.

'Wouldn't miss it,' he replied with a wink.

'Least there'll still be some music. Means we can still get our groove on later,' Vi enthused. She loved dancing to old skool rock anthems.

'Excellent,' grinned Jaz. 'Flying sweat and dandruff as all the metalheads hit the headbanging riffs. I can't wait.'

'Shut up,' said Vi. 'You're always up there with the rest of them—and you're in no position to complain about anyone's haircare regime.'

There was a collective smirk around the table as the girls registered the hit.

Last year, Jaz had read an article saying that if you didn't wash your hair for sixth months, it would become naturally self-cleaning and be permanently healthy and shiny, and she'd decided she was going to give it a try. She'd lasted nearly three months of head scratching and rain avoidance until the smell finally drove her to the shower with a bottle of shampoo. Having failed in her undertaking, Jaz was remarkably upbeat and virtuously pointed out that all the shampoo she'd not used during those three months had saved both the environment and her some money. Ellie and Flick hadn't noticed any difference in Jaz's hair, as it was usually fairly solid courtesy of all the styling products she used, anyway. They were, however, relieved when normal service resumed, as Flick was certain she'd seen things living in the lab experiment that Jaz's head became.

At nine o'clock, as Jaz had predicted, the floor filled with moshing, headbanging disciples paying homage to vintage Rock. Chris had left a while ago to take his car home, and since then, the trio had been enjoying flinging themselves around the dance floor along with the other punters in the heaving, popular venue.

Jaz returned from her bar run with more bottles of Flash and Diet Coke just as Ellie, Flick and Vi sat down to take a break from their frenzied dancing. The temperature in the back bar was rising as heat from energetic bodies radiated across the room.

Fanning herself with Chris' hat, which he'd plonked on her head earlier in a gesture of farewell, Flick said, 'I need to pee. You coming with?'

'Yeah, I could do with some air,' Ellie answered.

Jaz shook her head, as did Vi. 'We'll guard the table.'

Ellie waited for Flick outside in the dark courtyard, relishing the cool evening air. Flick emerged from the ladies' washroom with freshly applied lipstick and mildly tidier hair. She came to stand with Ellie, who was leaning against the old stone wall and looking towards the far side of the river. On this side, there was a wide concrete walkway a couple of metres below the beer garden wall. It was a popular place for dog walkers, cyclists and pedestrians who preferred to avoid the busy streets. The road bridge over the river narrowed the riverside walkway significantly because of its supporting stone arch, and there was a sign on the wall instructing cyclists to dismount to accommodate the constricted pathway, although many didn't bother.

'What time is Chris coming back?' Ellie asked.

'Not sure. Depends on whether he gets a lift back here or has to walk.'

'You and him seem to be getting along well. I think he may be taming your wild ways.'

'Indeed he might,' grinned Flick.

Ellie grinned. Flick definitely seemed more into Chris than any of her previous boyfriends.

'He's different, you know. He gets me. Not just the extrovert me, but the stuff inside here, too.' Flick tapped her chest. 'I wouldn't say this to Jaz, as she'd take the piss, but I really like him, Ellie. I really don't want to fuck this up.'

Ellie put her arm around Flick's shoulders and gave her a squeeze. 'You're doing just fine. You can see that in his face when he looks at you.'

Flick sniffed indelicately and wiped the corner of her eye, careful not to smudge the black eyeliner that flicked out past the end of her upper lids. 'I love you, you know,' she admitted, the alcohol making her emotional.

'Yeah, me too,' said Ellie, giving her another affectionate squeeze.

'You coming back in?' Flick asked after a few more moments looking down at the river.

'I think I'm going to stay out here for a bit longer. I'm still hot.'

'OK. See you back in there.' Flick turned and walked across the beer garden to the bar doorway.

Ellie leaned back against the wall and continued to gaze at the black river; its unrelenting restlessness was almost mesmerising. She looked downstream towards the far bridge; it was darker there, away from the streetlights of the busy bridge-side pub.

Ellie still felt rather tipsy, so she decided to take a short walk to clear her head. She made her way down from the beer garden and into the car park. From the level of the car park, three wide steps led up to a half landing, followed by five more to the top of the flood defence wall. A flight of steps against the concrete wall led down to the river walkway.

Ellie stood at the top for a minute. Directly in front of the step's exit was a railing by the water's edge, presumably to stop people rushing down the steps and dashing crazily across the walkway into the river. There were some faded plastic flowers tied there, suggesting that someone had once, tragically, done just that.

Ellie descended the steps slowly and began to walk along the embankment towards the dark bridge. The river here was trapped by the town, contained by the concrete. Ellie wondered about the highest point it had ever risen in flood, especially here where it couldn't break its banks and wash across green floodplains. It was fairly deep and already fast-flowing from the recent rains, but it wasn't actually in flood. She strolled nearer to the edge of the concrete to see how far down the water was. Less than a metre, she decided; possible to scramble out of. She noted ropes looped along the drop for probably just that purpose.

Ellie continued to walk towards the second bridge. As she approached it, she saw a cyclist emerging from the gloom underneath its spanning arch. He was headed her way, but there was plenty of room for them to pass; the walkway was at least four metres wide at this point. Ellie continued her leisurely stroll, admiring how the current and eddies made the reflected lights dance on the dark water.

Sensing movement nearby, she quickly looked up. The cyclist was nearly upon her; not over on the other side of the walkway, but heading straight for her. She stepped back as far as she could, but the lip of the drop behind her prevented her from moving any further out of his path.

Instinctively, she turned her body away from the direction

of impact, but the cyclist's shoulder bashed into her arm, pivoting her and leaving her teetering on the edge of the walkway. She saw a face looking sideways at her as she turned. It was blank, the eyes expressionless and pupils nearly all black, the mouth hanging half open despite no words being spoken.

It was Chris.

He carried on cycling away from her as she felt herself falling backwards towards the water.

An arm appeared in her terrified field of vision and a large hand grabbed her outflung arm, jerking her upright and away from the water's edge. Her feet felt firm ground beneath them again, and she was pulled hard against a man's solid chest with the force of the rescue. Her mind still paralysed by the fear of falling into the dark water, Ellie automatically grasped at anything she could. Grabbing handfuls of her rescuer's clothes, she held on tightly, clinging desperately to him.

'He came right at me! He didn't stop. He came right at me!' she repeated, near hysterical.

'You're safe now. Let us move back from the water,' advised a deep male voice.

Ellie was led to a nearby bench, where, detaching her hands from his hooded jacket, her rescuer sat her down and then seated himself beside her, his large form dwarfing hers.

*The voice.* Ellie knew that she had heard it before. Then recognition broke through her adrenaline-fuelled state of shock. 'You!' she said, turning to look at the man next to her.

Turning his body more towards Ellie, he held up his hand, fingers splayed, palm towards her. Not really knowing why, Ellie held up her own hand and pressed it lightly against his. Her thumb relaxed and slid forwards into the space

117

between his index finger and thumb, and he wrapped his thumb around the back of hers, then moved his hand slightly so that their fingers misaligned and slipped between one another's.

'I am Darkall,' he said.

'Ellie,' she stammered.

'I know who you are, Eleanor.'

There seemed to be a faint blue glow coming from between their interlaced hands, but Ellie didn't feel any fear or inclination to remove her hand from his. This felt somehow right; not normal, but natural. He lowered their hands, leaving them linked and resting on his denim-clad thigh.

'You were at Baubles, on the roof terrace,' Ellie stated.

'I was.'

'And you were at the Spring Thing.'

'Yes.'

'And now here. Why?'

'I am here because you are here,' he replied.

Ellie would usually have questioned such a broad statement, but for some reason, it didn't seem to matter. 'Let me see you,' she requested.

He released her hand, put his hands on either side of his hood and lowered it.

Ellie's breath caught in her throat. He was beautiful. His face was large, in keeping with his physique, and he had high slanted cheek bones, a prominent brow and a strong, square jaw. These features were not hidden by hair, as Darkall had a perfectly smooth, hairless scalp which showed off the pleasingly round shape of his skull.

He was facing Ellie but looked downwards, avoiding her eyes. Slowly, he raised his eyes to hers, and Ellie knew at that point, if she hadn't known before, that she was looking into the eyes of someone not entirely human.

Darkall's eyes were the most breathtaking Ellie had ever seen: they were a shade of deep purple, which was peculiar enough in itself, but, around each pupil, small sparks of light actually shone in his eyes, faintly illuminating the smooth skin around them.

'You are not afraid of me?' Darkall questioned, looking into Ellie's eyes.

'No,' she breathed, exhaling slowly. 'I'm amazed. Who are you? Where are you from?'

'I am not like you, Eleanor. I exist everywhere and nowhere,' he replied, not breaking eye contact.

'So, what are you?'

'I am darkness,' he replied.

'You are darkness, like evil?' asked Ellie, becoming wary.

'No. I am neither good nor evil. I just exist. I am darkness.'

He held up his hand once again. This time, Ellie could see that the faint blue glow emanated from a spiral pattern on his palm.

A spiral just like the one engraved onto her ring.

'Ellie? Ellie? Where are you? Ellie!' Jaz's frantic voice called from the beer garden.

'You must go to them,' Darkall's deep voice stated impassively. He stood and offered her his hand. 'I will accompany you to the steps.'

Taking it, Ellie stood up and walked the short distance to the bottom of the steps that led back to the car park.

Ellie turned to face Darkall as they reached the first step. She opened her mouth to speak but stopped herself, not knowing what to say to him, and found herself just looking into his unworldly eyes. Darkall raised her hand and pressed it to his lips in a charmingly old-fashioned salute, then released her fingers, all the while his eyes not leaving her face.

Jaz's voice could be heard, even more urgently, shouting over the beer garden wall. 'Ellie? Where the hell are you? Ellie!'

'Here!' Ellie shouted over her shoulder.

She turned back to say goodbye to Darkall, but he was no longer there. Nor was he to be seen anywhere on the embankment. Ellie crossed her arms over her chest and squeezed her upper arms. *Had that been real?*

'Ellie, there you are!' a cross-sounding Jaz exclaimed from the top of the car park steps. 'For God's sake, Ellie—where *the hell* have you been? All sorts of shit's been going on here, and there's you, missing presumed drowned or kidnapped on top of everything else.'

'Sorry. I'm fine,' said Ellie, running up the steps. 'What's the matter?'

'It's Chris,' Jaz answered. 'He's just ridden a bike full tilt into the bridge wall. Knocked himself clean out. Luckily, some people were leaning on the beer garden wall, watching the river, or he'd be still lying there, or worse, in the river and drowned with no one any the wiser. Flick is frantic; she says he's got amnesia and brain damage as Chris is claiming he doesn't own a push bike and that he set off walking back to the pub. He's in the ambulance now; they're taking him to hospital to get checked out, and Flick's going with him. He can't even remember being on a bike, let alone riding it at speed into a solid stone wall!'

'Or me, then,' Ellie said quietly.

'What? Or you? No, I'll give you a lift home with Vi, then ring Flick to see if she needs a ride back from the hospital. Shit, are our evenings ever going to be drama free? Thank God Meg didn't come along tonight; she'd have been totally freaked out by all this shit. Come on, let's get your stuff.'

At the top of the steps, Ellie turned back once more towards the river walk. It was still deserted; no lone figure haunted the walkway.

Darkall had gone.

# 12

# Chapter 12

*He said that he was darkness. What does that even mean?*

Ellie tried to remember Darkall's words. Something about being everywhere and nowhere—but that didn't make sense. Either you were there, or you weren't. Darkall had also said he was neither good nor evil. What did that make him, then? It seemed to Ellie that being impartial was more or less the same as being untrustworthy. But, then again, he had saved her from falling into the river and he had stopped her from drinking the spiked cocktail. Both of those actions suggested good intentions.

Ellie needed to know more. The Two of Swords in her Tarot reading had indicated that her knowledge was incomplete: ideas are conflicting, opposites not meeting. Ellie decided that she needed to spend more time at Bertie's temple. Inexplicably, she felt it more likely that she would find answers at the old library than searching on the Internet for an unknown subject—or perhaps it was just the library's custodian that she felt might be of help.

Towards the end of the afternoon, Ellie had a free period,

so she walked from college into town and along Castle Street. The weather had been better today, and it was pleasantly warm. As she walked, the thumb of her right hand played with the band of her ring. She often found herself unconsciously toying with it, rubbing the fingers either side against the band or turning it with her thumb. The ring now felt like a link to Darkall, and whenever her thoughts turned to him, her fingers would automatically start to touch the ring.

The library was unexpectedly busy today; a group of tourists were being shown around the museum, and there were several people in the library perusing shelves or sitting at the computer desks and reading tables. From behind his desk, Bertie pulled a face at Ellie as she approached.

'I can barely hear myself think in here today!' he exclaimed in a whisper, looking reproachfully at the members of public. 'Are the gang gracing my humble abode with their presence this evening?'

'As far as I know,' answered Ellie. 'Jaz is bringing the DVD, so we could be literally going anywhere tonight.'

'Ah, good,' said Bertie, elongating the words and raising his eyebrows in approval of a potentially worthy film choice. 'Although I do find that Felicity has an eye for an entertaining movie,' he added, lowering them again.

Ellie grinned, raising her eyebrows at him. She knew exactly which of Flick's recent movie choices he was referring to with that remark.

Choosing a seat away from the library's other patrons, Ellie draped her jacket over the back of the chair. She hooked her bag strap over the top and took out her notepad and pen. Having thus marked her territory, she headed once again into the stacks.

An hour and a half later, Ellie felt frustrated. She had followed and cross-referenced leads and still had not really found any inkling of what Darkall had been telling her. Ellie had found many references to "dark" or "darkness" being used as a synonym for evil, but Darkall had emotionlessly denied that.

The most interesting ideas thus far had come from a compendium of quotes, and Ellie's notepad now read:

How frightening is the dark? And yet, how seductively charged with bewildering secrets.
— Sheila Franks, A Tale of Eternity

When you find light, bear mind it's only there because of it anthesis.
— TF Erics, The Bone Trunk and Other Stories

Darkness is the genesis—always there first, lying in wait for the light.
— Malcom Peters, A Bridge in Time

It was now nearly closing time; Bertie was tidying up books onto a trolley and returning them to their shelves, and the other browsers and readers had already left. Ellie collected the three books that remained on her desk and wandered disconsolately down the aisles to "put them to bed", as Bertie termed it.

She'd liked the first quote the best, as it resonated with her current feelings—scary, confusing but beguilingly mysterious—and she had always been drawn to the esoteric.

The third quote also felt very apt; darkness was always waiting. Darkall had been there in the nick of time to rescue her twice already, after all.

But was it only twice? Had something bad been going to occur at the Spring Thing that his presence had averted? Was Darkall something to do with her car swerving of its own accord to avoid the oncoming vehicle the other week? Following this new track, Ellie thought back to other well-recounted family tales, the ones where she had avoided being harmed by unlikely circumstance.

There was the time on her sixth birthday when she'd been wearing the beautiful princess dress given to her that morning. Ellie had gone upstairs to admire herself in the long mirror in her parents' bedroom. Dancing along the landing, she'd caught her foot in the hem of her skirt and pitched towards the head of the stairs, only to be unexpectedly stopped from tumbling down the flight by an armchair suddenly barring her way. At the time, her relieved parents had said that she must have fallen onto it and that her momentum had sent it skidding across the floorboards before coming to rest at the top of the stairs. But as the chair was too heavy for six-year-old Ellie to move on her own and hence unlikely to be shunted much by her slight weight crashing into it, she had always thought this to be a rather inadequate explanation.

Then there was the time when teenaged Ellie had tripped over a spaniel in the sitting room and fallen towards the fireplace. Her head was saved from hitting the corner of the brass fender by sofa cushions which had conveniently been there to break her fall, despite no one remembering having moved them from the sofa. The spaniels were eventually blamed for the cushion-moving, but now Ellie wondered if Darkall had been her invisible saviour then, too.

'Come, Miss Johnstone. Time has been called, and the house is closing,' Bertie commanded from his office door, nodding pointedly at the clock hanging above his head.

Ellie gathered her belongings and strolled over to him. 'Do you want to get something to eat with me?' Ellie offered. 'It's not really worth me going all the way home and then coming back again for 7pm.'

'A more attractive offer I have not received in weeks! Thank you, my dear; that would be delightful. Which purveyor of fine food shall we deign to grace with our gastronomically-enlightened presence?'

'I was thinking Tesco's café?'

'Perfect! Just the very thing.'

Bertie wrapped his plaid scarf around his throat and switched off the office light before locking the door. He proffered his arm to Ellie, who took it with suitable aplomb, and together they sauntered through the tall double doors into the museum.

Tom, the cleaner, raised his broom in salute as they approached.

'Good evening, Thomas,' Bertie said merrily. 'I'll leave the charges in your capable hands. The windows are closed, and all are tucked up for the night.'

'Right, Bertie. Thanks, then. Goodnight to you.'

With that, Ellie and Bertie paraded out of the main front doors and down the steps into the late afternoon sunshine.

\* \* \*

Tesco's café was not very busy and Ellie and Bertie were able to settle themselves at one of their favourite tables near the big plate glass windows overlooking the car park. Upon first sitting there, Bertie had declared it an excellent location for both people-watching and checking that chavs weren't stealing the car, so it had become their spot. While waiting for the waitress to bring their food order, they caught up with each other's news before the conversation inevitably turned to Ellie's search.

Bertie stirred his coffee with a tinkling of stainless steel on china. 'What were you hoping to find on darkness, my dear?'

Ellie sighed. 'I'm not sure, really. Something about what it is … *who* it is.'

'What an odd notion! Who it is? Darkness is an absence of visible light. We humans can't see colour when there is either too much or too little light. Like at dusk, everything becomes achromatic, and when the light goes, all is black.'

'Yes, that's just about where I've got to. Then full stop. But there is more. I keep finding mentions in poems, even in Shakespeare's writings, but there's nothing definite. It's like a dark secret, often hinted at but never revealed.'

Bertie looked thoughtful. 'Have you ever read about black holes?'

'I have, but not much. I know they happen when stars collapse, but not much more than that.'

'Very odd things, black holes. They're black because they're an area in space where the gravity is so strong that even light can't escape. We see things because light waves bounce off objects and hit our eyes. If there is no light because it's being held captive by intense gravity, then we only see a black patch; hence, black hole. If memory serves, stellar black holes are found in areas where there are stars because they themselves used to be stars. There are small black holes, maybe even as small as one atom in size—which is mildly worrying—as well as supermassive black holes bigger than a million suns put together. The "edge" of a black hole is called the "event horizon", the point at which you could still escape the black hole's gravitational pull if you travelled at the speed of light—as poor Captain Kirk has had to do on several occasions. Inside the event horizon, matter hasn't got a chance; it falls to the centre of the black hole and is squashed to a tiny point of vast density. This point is called "the gravitational singularity", and it's here that the laws of physics break down.'

Ellie looked impressed, and she was also interested in his words; she loved having science explained to her in easy-to-understand language. It made her feel intelligent without the hard work of having to find stuff out for herself. She looked at Bertie expectantly, ready for him to continue.

'My point in all this is not just to show how well read I am, but also to illustrate that there are things we *know* exist in our universe that don't obey the laws of physics; things that won't conform to our accepted version of reality. Scientists have proved this. If you take that as your starting point, then one has to reach the inevitable conclusion that really anything is possible. That which we choose to call reality is, in fact, just a bubble within which we operate daily to protect ourselves from the true weirdness of the universe. Anyway, just a little pointer for your darkness research—and some food for thought. Talking of which, here is food for our bodies.'

The arrival of their meal distracted them from their topic of conversation, forcing their attention away from astrophysics and authors. Laying the plates onto the table with a satisfying clink of heavy china, the waitress bid them to enjoy their meal, and Bertie and Ellie hungrily proceeded to do just that.

\* \* \*

Returning to Bertie's apartment just after half past six that evening, they were in plenty of time to prepare for Bertie's other impending guests.

Bertie lived in a converted red brick woollen mill in the west part of town. The rooms were large and the ceilings high, and his apartment was tastefully decorated in old world splendour and filled with antiques and collectibles. Since childhood, Ellie had enjoyed visiting him there, as Bertie would explain the origin and importance of his treasures. However, she'd always been slightly nervous of accidentally putting her cup down *sans* coaster or spilling tea onto his Chinese silk rugs. Being an excellent host, Bertie would never have made a fuss had she done so, but his wonderous apartment was not somewhere that young Ellie had felt she could relax and so she'd preferred to visit him at the library.

Having become more used to visiting the apartment over the years, and also more comfortable minding his treasures, Ellie now began rearranging the sitting room furniture. The large oxblood leather sofa was pushed back and the two matching armchairs drawn up from the edges of the room to form a snug area. Bertie had previously explained that he didn't normally like the furniture in this configuration as it made him feel as if waiting for other people to fill the empty seats. After repositioning the coffee table, Ellie collected glasses and coasters from the kitchen.

A knock on the door at just after seven o'clock heralded the arrival of Flick and Jaz.

'Enter good friends and true,' trilled Bertie. 'It's on the latch,' he added, making his way to the front door to greet them.

'Good evening, Bertrand,' Jaz greeted him with a hearty handshake.

'Jazmine! A pleasure, as always. Do try the red; it's a rather cheeky Rioja.'

'Hi, Bertie.' Flick gave him a kiss on the cheek and a roguish smile. 'Not going to be *our* sort of an evening, I'm afraid,' she said, pulling a face at Jaz's back.

'There's more to life than biceps and a six pack,' Jaz retorted over her shoulder. 'Minds need feeding as well as libidos, you know.'

Bertie and Flick exchanged disbelieving looks and shrugged their shoulders in exaggerated non-comprehension.

'Yes, well, we must feed our minds, too, of course,' Bertie remarked, and he headed for the kitchen with a wink at Flick.

'I've got the usual and a tempting-looking chili humous for us to try,' he announced, emerging through the kitchen doorway carrying a tray laden with dips, nachos, vegetable sticks and the heralded humous. He set it down onto the coffee table. 'Now, drinky-poos. The usual for you, Flick dear? Ellie, starting with a tipple? Jaz, are you on the red with me?'

Each of them agreed to his suggestions, and in a short while, everyone was comfortably settled and ready for their usual pre-movie chat.

'So, how have you been, Bertie?' enquired Jaz politely.

'Oh, me? Fine, my dear, although I hear there was some excitement last Friday evening for the three of you?'

After recounting the tale of Chris' accident in all its gory detail, Flick concluded with, 'And poor Chris is still in hospital. They think he can come home tomorrow or the next day, though. I'm on standby to go and collect him at any time.'

'Well done you. Just what the poor lad needs: some tender loving care from his beloved. You make sure you take good care of him,' Bertie recommended.

'Oh, I will. As soon as he's strong enough for me to take care of him *properly*, that is,' Flick affirmed with a wanton smile.

'I'm afraid, Bertie, this girl really does have a one-track mind,' Jaz intervened, unable to resist the opportunity to goad her friend. 'Literally, just the one track; nothing else there. The rest is blank. It's all just about men and what she can do with them. Freud would have a field day.'

'I find that rather unfair when clearly your mind would run along similar lines if your switch hadn't been flicked to ladies,' Flick countered.

'We are all at the mercy of our makers in that respect, every one of us,' returned Jaz. 'It's just that *your* switch was turned so far in the male direction that the spring broke and the knob fell off.'

They all sniggered, adding various comments to Jaz's observation along the lines of 'ouch', 'such a shame' and 'now *that's* something I wouldn't want to see', which turned the sniggers into full-blown laughter.

Seeing that the glowering Flick was about to retort to Jaz's jibe, Bertie stepped once more into the breach, as he often did when Flick and Jaz were winding one another up. 'Man to man ill will inflicting, is as a carbuncle on the face of the Lord. Let not thy ugly thought, word or deed deface such divine countenance,' he intoned.

'From scripture, Bertie?' asked Ellie, not recognising the lines but feeling them somewhat familiar.

'No, from yours truly, actually. I wrote them on a placard and placed them in the garden, centre-front and foremost when a plebeian and cretinous neighbour referred to my minimalist front garden design as a carbuncle on the face of the street. I followed the pseudo-quote for several weeks with other scripture-like words along the theme of "loving thy neighbour" and "turning the other cheek". I know for a fact, him being a vainly religious man, that my humbly penned lines caused him great annoyance and resulted in him spending hours and hours searching the Bible trying to identify the passages, which is why I made them up in the first place. Sweet revenge. Charles thought it screamingly funny, but then he also laughed at my garden arrangement. Luckily for him, his secure place in my heart prevented a similar revenge, although I did burn his breakfast muffins for several mornings in a row, just to show that my artistic sensibilities are not to be trifled with.'

'What, dare I ask,' began Ellie, now with a healthy fear of reprisal, 'was your "minimalist front garden design?"'

'Two large round boulders either side of a granite column birdbath,' Bertie replied with a smirk. 'Very expressive, I thought.'

'I have a horrid feeling that your neighbour may have had a point. I'd imagine most people wouldn't want to walk past a stone cock and balls on their way to and from the bus stop every day!' Jaz observed.

The room descended into guffaws and giggles.

'It was *art*,' Bertie defended. 'Which, as you know, is in the eye of the beholder. I can't be held accountable for the depraved mind of the neighbour, which, by merit of them clearly being in a permanent drought state in that department, sees sexual connotation in mere garden ornaments. Now, Jaz dear, let us view your cinematic selection without further ado.'

The movie was a sci-fi that Jaz had read good reviews about. The film's plot seemed surprisingly on topic, based on Ellie and Bertie's earlier conversation. It postulated that black holes led to alternative universes, and Ellie and Bertie enjoyed themselves by objecting throughout about the pseudo-science theories laid on in spades by the moviemakers. Ellie was feeling particularly pleased that she was able to speak from a position of knowledge following her informative dinner with Bertie.

When the film finally finished, even Jaz had to admit that its shaky scientific credentials made it hard for even the basically-educated viewer to suspend their disbelief for the duration of the picture. Flick had dozed off halfway through, so, for pure devilment, Ellie felt it incumbent upon herself to explain to a reluctant Flick the knowledge that Bertie had imparted earlier.

'Dark matter, however, is something else,' Jaz announced, feeling that her pet topic had been hijacked.

'I've heard of anti-matter, but don't know about dark matter,' Ellie said, sipping her Diet Coke.

'Dark matter is one of the current hot topics in astrophysics. It is thought to be another form of matter, possibly consisting of as-yet-undiscovered subatomic particles. The weird thing about dark matter is that it can't be seen, as it doesn't seem to interact with any electromagnetic radiation, like light, and so it can't be observed.'

'Same problem as black holes, then,' remarked Ellie.

'Good point. Same problem for us, the viewers, for sure. Although at least black holes imprison light. Dark matter doesn't seem to give a monkey's about light.'

'But if it can't be seen, how do they even know it exists?' Flick cut to the crux of the matter as per usual.

'Again, an astute observation, Felicity. The existence of dark matter has been identified by observing its effects on astrophysical elements, including gravity, which can't be explained unless there is more matter present than that which we can see.'

Looking at the puzzled faces in front of her, Jaz continued, 'OK. So, for example, imagine our dear Felicity here has got the munchies after pulling a late-nighter. It's the middle of the night, and everyone else in the house is asleep. Flick goes into the tidy kitchen and raids the fridge.'

'Quite likely,' Flick approved with a nod.

'Flick gets out the bread and the cheese and makes herself some melted cheese and ketchup sandwiches.'

'Good choice,' Bertie endorsed.

'While her sarnies are in the microwave, Flick gets the gherkins out of the fridge and munches on a couple. The cheese now suitably melted and stringy, she heads back up to her room with a can of Diet Coke, leaving the kitchen in the usual post-Flick-cuisine mess.'

'Objection,' called Flick.

'Overruled,' Bertie intoned, recalling the state of his own

worktops after Flick had made herself a snack.

'Now, poor Joy comes down in the morning, all ready for her Quaker Oats, to be met with the pickle jar with its lid off, vinegar dripped onto the country pine worktop, ketchup smears, dirty knives, cheese crumbs, the open door of the microwave ... Need I continue?'

'Hey! I'm not *that* untrained.'

'Says you! Anyway, the point is that Mrs. Sargent can see that someone has been there during the night. She can tell that it was likely Flick because of her penchant for late-night cheese, but Joy didn't actually see Flick making the mess.'

'Thankfully,' interjected Flick.

'Dark matter works on the same principle. We know it's there from seeing the effect it has on what's around it, although we can't actually see dark matter itself.'

'That is actually pretty cool. Shame you weren't my Physics teacher.' Flick nodded her approval at Jaz's explanation.

'Astrophysics rocks, baby,' Jaz grinned, chuffed by Flick's compliment.

*The effect it has on what's around it*, thought Ellie, echoing Jaz's words in her mind. Like Ellie's steering wheel veering left and right of its own accord. Like her falling onto cushions that oughtn't to have been there.

Like Darkall.

'I think,' announced Ellie into the silence that followed Jaz's words, 'I'm being haunted.'

'You what?' scoffed Flick, before seeing Ellie's serious, pensive face.

'Things keep happening with no rational explanation. And I think they've happened like that before, ever since I was little.'

Staring in front of her at the cycling menu screen of the movie, Ellie gave them a brief summary of the odd occurrences she'd been involved in.

'You mean there's a guy who appears in the nick of time to save you? That you've got your very own Clark Kent?' Flick asked in amazed disbelief.

Jaz switched off the TV to better hear Ellie's quiet, hesitant voice.

'Not *appears*, as such, although I have seen him and spoken to him, briefly. He's not always there when these weird things happen. It sounds silly, now I come to say it out loud, but it has occurred to me that things seem to happen to me, or *around* me, that defy logical explanation. So, the only conclusion I can draw is that I'm being haunted.'

'If your ghost is looking out for you, as you say, I reckon it's more of a guardian angel,' Flick surmised, serious for once.

'He is dark. He called himself "darkness", and I can't seem to get beyond darkness being bad, so I don't think he can be an angel.'

The friends were quiet, not really knowing what to say. Bertie cleared his throat.

'Darkness is neither good nor evil; in that respect, it has been much maligned by both popular and historic culture. Ellie, there is more to dark matter than Jaz has told you,' he said, all element of flippancy gone. 'Dark matter and black holes, in fact. After the famed Big Bang that started the universe, matter was too hot to coalesce for the first five hundred million years or so. Dark matter, however, was unaffected by the heat because, whatever it actually is, it interacts mostly through gravity. Bunching together through mutual attraction, dark matter supplied the gravitational seed for matter to assemble around, forming the first stars. One astrophysicist suggested that these dark matter seeds could have been black holes. Nothing really dies; we see a star dying and becoming a black hole, but black holes may have given birth to the stars in the first place—darkness creating light and light becoming darkness. It's a circle, a cycle, a spiral neither ending nor beginning.'

'"I am the Alpha and the Omega, the first and the last, the beginning and the end,"' Jaz quoted in a low voice. 'Revelation 22.13.'

'Did you know that if two black holes pass closely enough to one another, they are drawn together by their gravitational fields? Over vast amounts of time, the two black holes spiral towards each other, like a courting couple spinning on the dance floor, before finally merging into one larger black hole. Rather romantic, really.'

Bertie paused to consider his words before continuing.

'I digress, but my point here is as I said before: darkness does not mean evil. Just because something cannot be seen does not mean it doesn't exist, or that it can't have an effect on those around it or be an essential factor. If you have seen this person—and I use the term loosely, for want of a better one—then he *does* exist, although he may not be what we understand the term "person" to mean.'

A solemn silence fell across the trio as each member considered what they'd heard. Then Jaz spoke up.

'I agree, energy never dies; it just changes from one form into another. The conservation of energy principle. Kind of like the wind: energy moves air to blow against the branches of a tree, and those branches then move. The energy or momentum pass from the wind to the tree, from one thing to the other. Lots of people believe that the same happens with the energy within us; our life force, our spirit or whatever you want to call it. Many cultures believe that this energy gets recycled and reused for creating new life, whether staying in the original quantity and configuration it had when inside of a person or merging into a great swell of energy and getting mixed up with everyone else's before being split off and going into a new being. It's one we'll never know for sure in this lifetime. But who's to say what this energy can become? Can it only be a human or a tree or a cow? Of course not! It could be formed into literally anything, including mysterious beings and dark matter. I do accept there are more things on this earth than we can, or will, ever know about.'

'As Willie said, "there are more things in heaven and earth, Horatio, than are dreamt of in your philosophy,"' muttered Bertie.

'Are you seriously suggesting that Ellie's guardian angel is just that—a *dark* angel?' Flick asked Jaz and Bertie incredulously.

'I have known Ellie for a long time. I have never had her pegged as delusional or hysterical. If she says she has spoken to someone or something that has helped her, then I believe her,' Bertie remarked solemnly. 'What he—or *it*—actually is, only Ellie can tell us, and indeed only when she finds out for herself. I, for one, wish her luck in her investigations and remind her that we are here for her when she needs us.'

'Here, here.' Jaz quietly echoed Bertie's sentiment.

'Well, you're not leaving me out,' said Flick. 'If you want to believe in this mystery guy, Ellie, then that's fine by me, too. I just hope he isn't leading you into anything dangerous.'

*Me too*, thought Ellie, as she received a tight hug from Flick.

# 13

# Chapter 13

Over the next few days, things seemed to settle down and return, more or less, to normal. College continued without incident, and Flick was happy, as although Chris had experienced a setback and, at one point, his doctors thought that they might have to operate, he'd recently shown great improvement and was now considered to be out of danger, despite still being kept in hospital.

Ellie spent time at home, enjoying being with the animals in her care who were soon to be returned to the farm. She was in the process of arranging their return with the farmer and saying her goodbyes, so she would soon have no dependents, which was an unusual state of affairs.

Sitting at the kitchen table, rereading her latest essay, a *thunk* against the window pane startled her. There was nothing at the window, but Ellie had a nasty feeling that a bird had just flown into it, so she stood up and went into the garden. A smudge on the exterior window glass confirmed her suspicion, and looking down into the flowerbed below the kitchen window, she saw the tragic, immobile feathered body. Gently, Ellie scooped it up in her hands: a poor sparrow, its eyes closed and its little body floppy.

Ellie's heart broke whenever this happened. The house windows reflected the sky, and a speeding bird could easily get confused and fly straight into the solid glass. It was so sad that the one thing that birds were designed to do—speed through the air being masters of flight—was the thing that killed them when they came too near mankind's booby-trapped creations.

Ellie looked at the tiny creature; it didn't seem to be breathing. Was it stunned or dead? Turning it over gently, she peered closely at its tiny chest and laid a gentle finger there, but could feel no heartbeat. Ellie rolled the sparrow back over onto its front and carefully cupped her other hand over the top of her lower one, making a soft coffin for the unfortunate bird. She walked towards the garden gate, aiming to lay the sparrow's body in the hedge, but stopped as tears blurred her vision.

Diverting from her intended route to lean against the Holm Oak, she allowed herself to weep for the little bird. With eyes closed, she imagined a replay of its last flight. The bird was a bright speck of yellow energy and movement zooming towards the false sky of the window. Then she saw the sudden stop of the collision and the arrested energy falling to the ground. Wait! That meant that it hadn't left the bird! The energy was still there, inside it. So maybe the bird wasn't dead yet?

Maybe she could help it.

Ellie cleared her mind and pictured a vortex of energy turning within her chest; a spiral of bright yellow light spinning with fizzing sparks, like a slow-motion catherine

140

wheel. She visualised an arm of this energy flowing down her own arm and into her lower hand, where the bird lay. Another shoot of yellow light was sent to her top hand, and she watched a golden glow illuminating the sparrow's limp body. Ellie intensified the thought so that the pressure built in her mind. The energy turned from yellow to white, and with a blinding flash on the inside of her eyelids, Ellie sent her energy into the bird.

Having let go of the energy burst, her mind relaxed from the peak of intense concentration and slumped comfortably back into normal thought. Ellie sagged back against the tree, careful to keep her hands gently cupped. She took a deep breath and exhaled long and deep.

There was a flutter of movement against the skin of her palm. Slowly, Ellie tilted her top hand away from the bottom one, like opening a fragile book. Sitting there, in her hand, alert and seemingly unharmed, was the sparrow, its beady black eyes staring up at her, its beak slightly open. Ellie slowly held her cupped hands out in front of her, raising them up and away from her body. The sparrow took to the wing and flew in swoops to the garden hedgerow.

Ellie brought her hands back to her face and peered at them. *Did I really just make that happen?* The little bird had seemed so lifeless, but maybe it was only really stunned.

Ellie had felt angry that the sparrow's life had been stolen and deeply sad, more upset than one would expect over a dead wild bird. She had felt like she'd lost a friend or loved one, and the pain of that had fuelled her anger at the injustice of the situation. It was this wave of emotion that had fuelled her desire to heal the bird and to try using her energy. Yet this was not a new technique for Ellie; she'd tried similar

141

before when nursing injured or sick creatures, visualising passing some of her own energy to them. Never before today, however, had she seen any particularly clear evidence of its success as a healing method; she'd previously accepted that her animal charges might well have got better on their own, anyway.

Grace had explained to Ellie about healing hands when Ellie was little. Her mother had said that it was an ancient form of helping others, also sometimes known as spiritual or energy healing. The Japanese call it Reiki: *rei,* meaning soul or spirit, and *ki,* meaning vital energy. Grace thought it was not uncommon to come across people who'd mastered the ability working with animals. She'd cited horse whisperers and those who animals instinctively liked as examples of people gifted in this manner. This had made little Ellie want to be a vet or work in an animal rescue centre, helping animals with her own healing hands, and she'd then invented her own technique of visualising energy spinning inside her which she could direct to her patients at will. In her head, she'd named it the "healing wheel", although, now she thought about it, the energy was in spiral form as opposed to a circle.

*Spirals again.* Spiral energy. Healing power.

Was the sparrow's revival evidence that her healing skill had developed; that it really worked now? The bird had certainly seemed lifeless. The energy-path picture of the sparrow's flight and collision that had formed in her mind was also new to her; she had not experienced anything like that before. In the vision, every living thing had been outlined with glowing energy; the bird had been a darting yellow, the trees had a rusty orange glow, but the house and its windows had looked more or less the same, just in duller tones than

142

usual. Was an energy picture actually her seeing with her mind?

Ellie sat down against the trunk of the great tree. She hugged her knees to her chest and gazed out over the garden hedge to the hills on the horizon. Her life seemed to be spinning out of control and she had no say in events. She just seemed to be surfing the baffling swell that carried her forwards.

When had all this started? Was it when she'd bought the ring, or had all this been going on long before that, possibly since she was born? According to Jill, Ellie was following a preordained path, and stepping from that path could cause not only cosmic chaos but also harm to those she cared about. Ellie was fiercely loyal to those she loved and would never choose a course that might endanger them.

Who could she talk to about all this? Her mother appeared ready to listen, but her father seemed less so. Would they really give impartial advice, or would they just try to protect Ellie and advise her on choosing the course of least potential danger? Perhaps Ellie needed to talk to Jill on her own, when she couldn't be gagged by either Andy or Grace. Should she arrange a visit, or just turn up at Jill's unannounced? She didn't want her parents to forewarn Jill about what not to tell her; Jill would most likely be more candid if it were just her and Ellie. She didn't like the idea of sneaking around behind her parent's backs, but in this instance, it might be best to just drive over to Jill's place.

* * *

Later that evening, Ellie was in bed, engrossed in a novel by her favourite author, when her mobile phone rang. Looking at the Caller ID, she quickly answered it.

'Ellie?' a small voice queried.

'Yes, it's me. What's up, Flick?'

'It's Chris. He's really sick, Ells. I'm at the hospital now. He started to fit this afternoon and wouldn't stop; they've had to put him into an induced coma.' Flick's voice gave way. 'I'm so scared, Ellie. I think he might be going to die, and I don't know what to do.'

'Do you want me there? I can come straight away.'

'Yes, if that's OK? I feel so alone.'

'I'm leaving now.'

Ellie dressed speedily and popped her head into her parents' room to let them know where she was going. Grabbing her car keys from the bowl on the hall table, she dashed out of the house. With a crunch of wheels spinning on gravel, Dolly pulled out of the driveway and on to the lane.

Thirty minutes later, Ellie walked in through the sliding doors of the Royal City Hospital. Flick had told her which ward Chris was now on: the Intensive Care Unit. Ellie followed the signs, walking down near deserted corridors, until she reached the ward. She buzzed the door and explained to the voice on the intercom who she was and why she was here. The admittance buzzer sounded, and Ellie heaved the door open and fast-walked past locked office doors and dark patient therapy rooms.

Flick was sat alone near the nurses' station on one of a row of moulded plastic chairs. She had clearly been crying, and Ellie sat down next to Flick and held her hand.

'What's happened?'

'He was fine. Just normal Chris; we were joking around

144

and planning what we'd do as soon as they let him out. He said his head was hurting and, soon after, he couldn't see right. Then he started to convulse, they came rushing in, and I was kicked out of the room. The doctors say they think his subdural haematoma has resumed bleeding and is putting pressure on his brain, which is what's causing these new symptoms.'

'Oh, Flick. I'm so sorry.'

'They couldn't make him stop shaking. Then they said they were going to put him in a medically induced coma to help prevent further damage to his brain. Oh, Ellie—what if he doesn't wake up? What if he is brain-damaged? This is all so horrible and so unfair. What the hell was he doing on that bloody bike in the first place?'

Ellie hadn't mentioned the incident with the cyclist on the river walkway to anyone. She didn't know whether to mention it now; maybe Chris had been having some sort of seizure when he'd slammed into her and sent her spinning towards the river. *But then*, she thought, *if you're having a seizure, can you still ride a bike, and fast enough to knock yourself out when crashing into a wall?* It was like Chris had been away with the fairies or temporarily controlled by a schizophrenic second personality when he'd ridden into her.

'Where is he?' Ellie asked.

'In the room behind us. The doctors are in there now with his parents. I think they're discussing surgery. Christ, Ellie, he's only eighteen. He shouldn't be having brain surgery!'

Flick got up and paced about in front of Ellie.

'Here,' said Ellie, handing her a disposable cup of water from the dispenser next to her. 'Drink some. You need it.'

'I guess there's no turning it down if it's from Doctor

Johnstone,' Flick said with a forced grin. Ellie was known as the sensible one when it came to looking after themselves. Ellie would often hand out paracetamol and get a drink of water for the others if they complained of pain in front of her.

'Damn right, lady,' Ellie confirmed.

The door of Chris' room opened and his parents filed out, followed by two doctors. Flick went over to Chris' mother and exchanged a few words with her before receiving a hug from the red-eyed woman and a pat on the shoulder from Chris' father. They offered Ellie a small, weak smile before they both turned and left the ward. Flick stood watching them walk away up the corridor. As the pair rounded the corner, her shoulders slumped, and her hands covered her face for a moment. Then she walked back to Ellie.

'They're going to keep him under tonight and plan to operate tomorrow. They need to drain the subdural blood, but they don't know what he'll be like when he wakes up. The pressure, or even the surgery to release it, may cause additional problems for him.'

Ellie reached out and caught Flick's hand, giving it a squeeze. 'Can we see him?' she asked.

'Yeah, we can go in.' Flick walked to the door of Chris' room. Putting her hand on the brushed steel handle, she looked back at Ellie. 'He's not good, Ellie. He doesn't even really look like himself.'

In the private room, Chris lay in a large bed with fold-down sides. Bleeping machines were plugged into a panel of sockets on the wall behind the headboard, one of which was a drip that continuously fed a trickle of fluid into the back of Chris' hand. He lay very still, his chest rising and falling under the neatly tucked-in sheet. Wires were attached to sticky discs on his chest and temples, and he wore the obligatory patient identification bracelets on both wrists. His skin looked pale and slightly waxy, and there was a dressing on the left side of his head.

The room was dim, lit only by faint light spilling in from the corridor and the glow of the machines' digital displays. Flick sat on the edge of the bed. She picked up Chris' hand and, lifting it to her lips, kissed it before lowering it again. Ellie perched in the high-backed chair beside the bed, looking at them both.

'You're causing a hell of a lot of fuss, Christopher,' Flick admonished. 'About time you stopped arsing around and woke up, I think. How's a girl supposed to chat up her bloke if he lazes around in a coma all the bloody time?'

Ellie smiled at Flick's attempt at lightening the mood. Flick lifted Chris' hand slightly and, letting go, let it fall to her lap.

'He's just not here, is he?' Flick asked rhetorically. 'I suppose there's no point in me being here either, really. Wherever he is right now, he can't hear me or know that I'm here with him.' She paused. 'I guess he's in one of those total blackouts where you don't recall the passing of time.'

'I can give you a lift home, if you want?' Ellie offered gently.

'That's nice of you, but I want to stay here, just in case …'

Flick didn't finish the sentence, but Ellie knew what Flick feared. She also knew that her friend wouldn't forgive herself for being anywhere else if that happened.

Flick stood up and ran her hands through her hair again. 'The nurses said they'd give me some pillows and a blanket so that I could sleep in the chair.' She indicated the vinyl-covered wingback that Ellie was sitting on.

'Do whatever you need to. Would you like me to stay with you?'

'No, you go home and get some sleep, Ells. Thank you for coming. I'm going to go and wash before I curl up on the chair.'

Flick collected her bag from the foot of the bed and headed for the ward's communal bathroom.

Listening to the quiet whir of the machines, Ellie watched Chris. He looked surreal in his comatose state when compared to the laughing, irreverent guy she knew from the Common Room. What had Flick said? A rebleed in his brain? Flick was right; it was not fair that someone so full of vitality and spirit should end up like this after a stupid accident. The sense of injustice infuriated Ellie, and at the same time, she felt a great sorrow for Chris' parents and for Flick. Her hands twitched where they lay loosely in her lap, and a light prickling sensation tickled her palms. Turning her hands over to look at them, she noticed that her palms were red, as if they'd recently been plunged into hot water.

Was this a sign? Was it possible that she could help Chris?

There was little time before Flick would return, so if she was going to try it, she had to do it now.

Ellie stood up and, leaning over the bed, placed a hand on either side of Chris' head, carefully avoiding the wires and the sterile dressing. She felt his cool skin against her hot hands and closed her eyes. *Heat to cold, consciousness to unconscious, light to heal*; she set the vortex spinning inside of her and concentrated. Ellie sent the energy down her arms, envisaging the yellow-white fire filling Chris' head and pushing back the bleed, forcing it to let go of his brain and be washed away by the light. She concentrated on this thought to the exclusion of all else.

'Ellie?' Flick's uncertain voice trembled from the doorway.

Ellie released Chris's face and, opening her eyes, turned to Flick with a self-conscious smile. 'I was sending him good vibes,' she said.

Flick looked at Ellie for a moment. 'Anything anyone can do to help Chris is fine by me.' She paused, then continued in a quieter voice. 'Ellie, I've never said this to you before, but I know you've got something special inside you—something other, beyond normal. A *wisdom* or some shit. I think I've always known it, ever since we first met. If you think you can help Chris in any way, then please do all that you can.'

Ellie walked over to Flick and gave her a hug. 'I will,' she whispered into Flick's hair.

Before she left, Ellie helped Flick to arrange the pillows and blanket as comfortably as they could. While Flick collected the bedding from the nurse's station, Ellie brought in one of the hard-plastic chairs from the corridor for Flick to put her legs across when trying to sleep.

With Flick tucked in as snugly as possible, Ellie withdrew a book from her shoulder bag and handed it to Flick. 'I thought you might need a bit of escapism.'

Flick took the book and read the cover. '*Time's Turning Hours.* Well, I definitely have plenty of those.' She managed a grateful smile.

Ellie leaned down and dropped a kiss on Flick's head, like a mother to her child. No matter how brave and brazen Flick could be, tonight she looked like a scared little girl. Ellie could see that plainly and had acted instinctively.

'I'll see you tomorrow,' Ellie reassured her. 'If there's anything you need, or if you just want to talk, then call me.

Promise?'

'I promise, Doctor Johnstone,' grinned Flick.

Ellie picked up her jacket and turned to leave. As she looked back over her shoulder to give a little wave, Flick called out softly. 'Hey, Ellie? When I was in the bathroom, did a doctor come in to look at Chris?'

'No, it was just me in here,' Ellie replied. 'Why do you ask?'

'Oh, my mistake. It's just that when I came out of the bathroom, I could have sworn there was a light on in here. I thought the docs had come back and turned the lamp on to look at something.'

'No, just Chris and I,' confirmed a surprised Ellie. Then, with a final wave, she left Flick and Chris in their monitored sanctum for the night.

14

# Chapter 14

Ellie had met Jaz and Meg at Tesco's café, where the three girls sat sipping hot chocolate. Jaz was naturally shocked to hear about Chris' rapid decline yesterday evening, and Meg had suggested that they all could do with some chocolate therapy. Tesco had the nearest off-campus café.

'But how did it just rebleed?' Jaz asked. 'He was fine the day before. They were planning to discharge him, as far as I knew.'

'Sometimes a subdural haematoma can rebleed with little or no trauma,' Meg said. 'It's just one of those things, particularly if Chris has an undetected collagen disorder like EDS.' Meg's family were prone to the genetic condition Ehlers-Danlos Syndrome, so she spoke from a position of knowledge when it came to weaker-than-normal vascular tissues—or indeed, any bodily system where collagen was involved, which was pretty much the entirety.

'So, it could just keep rebleeding at any time?'

'I think some subdurals can turn chronic and develop membranes. Then they just rebleed anytime, without needing so much as a bump to start them off. They can be removed, but it's a tricky procedure as the surgeons could end up causing more bleeding. Besides, no one really wants their brain messed around with on the operating table.'

'I can't believe he just rode straight into a wall,' Jaz commented. 'He wasn't even pissed when he left the pub, as he drove his car home. He wouldn't have loitered there either, as Flick's charms were awaiting him at the Heart, so he wouldn't have had lots to drink before coming back. The people who saw him crash said his head was turned towards the water, like he didn't even see the wall. I guess that's why the left side of his head was injured rather than the front.'

'Chris knew the river walk, though, didn't he?' asked Meg.

'Yeah, sure. He walked it to college often enough,' said Jaz.

'Then he knew the bridge wall was there. He would have known the walk narrows under the bridge and should have been looking out for pedestrians,' Meg reasoned. 'How very odd.'

Ellie looked out of the window despondently. Part listening to Meg and Jaz's discussion, she watched the ant-like busyness of the shoppers hoarding their supplies in the boots of their cars. Was Chris looking at her when he'd hit her, or was he looking at the river? She'd been between the water and him, so it was hard to tell. It seemed that whatever he'd been looking at, he'd stayed with his head turned that way as he sped along the river walk, all the way until he crashed into the bridge wall.

Ellie's phone buzzed on the plastic tabletop, the vibrating ringtone making it dance in a curve. 'It's Flick,' she said, picking it up and answering. 'Hey, Flick. How are you?'

'You won't believe this, Ellie, but he's awake!' Flick's excited

152

voice gabbled down the line. 'When I woke up, he was looking at me, and he smiled. The doctors don't know what to make of it—he should still be in zombie-land, but he seems to have shaken off the drugs and is sat up in bed, eating biscuits!'

'Flick, that's amazing!' Ellie enthused. 'Hang on, I'll put you on speakerphone.'

'Hey, Felicity,' called Jaz. 'How you doing?'

'I'm good. I'm better than good. I'm bloody *fantastic*! I can't believe he's come round!'

'Hi, Flick, it's Meg. What did the doctors say?'

'Hey, Meg. They're sending him down for another scan to see what's going on. They seem a bit baffled, as Chris should still be in the medically induced coma right now. He's also not in pain, and his vision is normal.'

There were the muffled sounds of other voices in the background. 'Right, OK,' came Flick's voice, speaking to someone in the hospital room. 'Guys, I've got to go. They're taking him down now. I'll get back to you when I know more. Keep your fingers crossed for us. Love yas! Bye.'

The line went dead.

Meg was the first to comment. 'Wow, that sounds hugely positive!'

'Yes, bloody brilliant. I hope it's all going to be OK now. Sounds like Chris has staged a *pretty* impressive comeback. Good on him,' agreed Jaz.

Ellie could feel herself holding her breath. She didn't even want to think about how Chris had woken up and seemed so well in case the mere thought somehow jinxed it and made it all untrue. She had heard of people briefly coming out of comas, only to fall back into them. Although Chris had woken from a medically induced coma, she didn't want to face the idea that this might only be a temporary reprieve for his symptoms. She kept her fingers crossed under the table, hoping against hope that the scan would not find anything too awful still going on inside Chris' head.

'So, do you want to come with us to the park?' Jaz asked, cutting across Ellie's thoughts. 'We're just going for a walk, but you're welcome to tag along.'

'And play gooseberry? No way! Thanks for the offer, though.' Ellie smiled.

What she really wanted was another few hours of sleep; last night had been a late one by the time she'd finally got back into bed.

That morning, Ellie had told her parents about Chris' condition but had not mentioned her attempt to heal him. It felt like she was fooling herself by even thinking that she had the power to heal, and, anyway, if she didn't—as was most rationally likely—then she risked making herself a laughing stock by bragging about it.

Finishing her hot chocolate, Ellie picked up her bag and keys from the table. She had essays to finish and books to return to the college library, so she said her goodbyes to Meg and Jaz and walked back to campus.

Unusually for him, Jacob was in the library when Ellie got there. After she handed in her books at the desk, she sat down at one of the computer desks to work, and Jacob wandered over to her.

'Hey,' he said.

'Hi,' Ellie smiled.

'I heard about Chris. His bro phoned me. Pretty shitty thing to happen when he was OK to come home.'

'Yeah, poor guy. Flick phoned a while ago; she said Chris

is doing better this morning.'

'Cool, that's good.' There was a pause, then Jacob said, 'So, do you want to get a drink sometime?'

Ellie considered his offer and found that there were no sparks left for Jacob; she owed it to the guy to tell him the truth. 'That's nice of you. Thanks, Jacob. But what with all that's going on, I think we're better off as friends.'

'Right. Cool. We can do that.' He smiled his crooked smile. 'Door's open though, ya know?'

He winked at her and then walked out of the library.

Ellie's phone vibrated in her pocket, causing the librarian to look at her disapprovingly despite it being on silent. Ellie fished it out and answered it in a whisper.

'Ellliieee!' Flick's voice screeched out of the handset. The librarian's frown deepened.

'Hang on a mo,' Ellie said into the phone. 'I've just got to get out of the library.'

Leaving her bag by the desk, Ellie got up and walked out. 'OK, I'm in the corridor now. Fire away.'

'He's fine!' Flick exclaimed. 'The doctors did the scan and there's no sign of the subdural bleed. His brain looks normal, like the injury never happened. I can't believe it. He's going to be all right. And I mean properly all right, like he was before.'

'Oh, Flick, I'm so pleased,' said Ellie, the grin on her face clear in her voice.

'They're keeping him in until tomorrow to monitor him, but if he remains stable, he can come home then. I don't think they really know what's gone on; one doctor mentioned the coma-inducing drugs possibly having unexpectedly bene-ficial side effects, but I don't think they have a clue.' Flick lowered her voice. 'I do though, Ellie, and I won't forget it. Thank you.'

'Hey, I didn't do anything.' Ellie automatically shrugged off the compliment. 'Chris fought it off all on his own. Must have been you there with him that gave him the will to heal himself.'

'Ellie, I know what I saw. You have a gift, and you used it to help Chris. For that, I'm in your debt. I love you, girl. Thank you.'

Smiling, Ellie said goodbye to Flick and hung up. Was it true? Had she helped Chris? Had she made the subdural magically reabsorb? Flick seemed to think so. Perhaps it was time she visited Jill after all.

Ellie returned to her library desk and collected her belongings, then left the library and the campus.

\* \* \*

The drive to Jill's cottage was a pleasant one. Ellie always preferred the old main roads rather than the dual carriageways and motorways. This afternoon's route took her through many rural villages with wonderful names: Middle Hempstead, Charlotte Barton, Under Camel—all places that had been farming settlements since time immemorial where generation after generation had worked the land.

Jill lived on the outskirts of the village of Burrsteignton, in the next county over from Owl's Ridge. Her father, a colonel, and her mother had lived in the manor house in the village, but when they died, Jill had sold the family home and downsized to her cottage. She maintained that she would live perfectly well at Lark's Rest with a good deal less floor space to gather dust, plus she owned the cottage outright and had enough capital investment funds that she didn't need to work for a living. Consequently, Jill had explored a variety of careers, becoming successful in each one before getting bored and moving on to the next. Currently, however, she was taking a break from employment to concentrate on her ceramics.

Ellie hadn't phoned Jill or told her parents where she was going. She knew Jill was not due to depart for one of her tours just yet, as Jill had mentioned so at dinner the other night. Jill periodically set off on a trip lasting several months where she visited old friends all over the country. She referred to these trips as "her jaunts", for which she would pack up to a week's worth of clothes, the contents of the fridge and her cats and set off in her Morris Minor.

Pulling up outside Lark's Rest, Ellie turned off Dolly's engine and listened to it pinging and creaking as it cooled down from the long drive. The downstairs windows were open, indicating that Jill was at home. Ellie got out of Dolly and, opening the little wrought iron gate, approached the front door of the cottage via the brick-edged path. Knocking on the door elicited no response, so Ellie called through the letterbox. Still nothing, save for Stanley the black cat meowing loudly from the sitting room windowsill.

Ellie followed the little path around the lime-rendered walls, pushing back fronds of buddleia and lilac as she went. The rear garden was small and comprised of a handkerchief of lawn surrounded by flourishing flowerbeds. To one side of the lawn was a rather ramshackle garden shed which Jill used as her studio and kiln room. Radio Two could be heard playing in the shed, the drone of the commentator's voice interspersed with Jill's remarks.

'Not if the pound crashes again!' Jill's voice exclaimed from the shed.

Ellie knocked on the door and the noise ceased.

Jill opened the shed door to see her pseudo-niece standing unexpectedly among the lady's mantle. 'Ellie, my darling! What a lovely surprise! What brings you here? Grace and Andy are well, I trust?'

'Yes, Mum and Dad are fine. I just needed to see you on my own, Jill. I need some advice—help I think that only you can give me. I hope it's OK just to turn up like this?'

'Of course, dear child. You know you are welcome to visit anytime. Do your parents know you're here?'

'No, I didn't want them to warn you off speaking openly to me, so I left college early and drove here.'

'Right, I see. Well, I think that you have made a wise choice, although some things are not mine to tell, you must understand. Come on in and we'll put the kettle on.'

Jill put her arm around Ellie's shoulders and led her to the back door of the cottage.

The kitchen was low and rather dark due to having small windows set into the deep cob walls. The lack of light was not helped by the dark-stained beams that crossed the ceiling at regular intervals. In an effort to counteract the gloom, Jill kept the ceiling lights on most of the time and had painted the walls white to reflect as much light as possible. A pine table stood along one wall, and against another sat the Aga, which kept the room warm no matter the season and was great for drying washing; currently, a selection of Jill's clean underwear vied with tea towels for room on its chrome handlebar.

'Sit down, dear. Move that pile off the chair; stick it on the floor,' Jill instructed, pointing at her heap of paper for recycling. 'Tea or coffee?'

Jill lifted a lid on the Aga and set the cast iron kettle on the plate to boil. 'Let's have tea,' she decided for them both.

Jill lifted the tea caddy down from its shelf and measured out two spoons of loose leaves into her favourite teapot, then added the obligatory one for the pot. 'We can always read the leaves if things are looking dicey!' she quipped.

Reading tea leaves was one of the few methods of divination that Jill didn't hold with. She felt that there were limits to the methods with which the powers that be chose to communicate with mere mortals, and that soggy Brooke Bond was going just a step too far—as Jill had told Ellie *many* times before.

When the kettle started to steam, Jill poured in the boiling water, secured the lid and set the tea cosy over the pot while the tea infused.

Making tea was a sacred ritual to Jill, and Ellie knew better than to offer any help, as any variation in the method could have a direct and negative impact on Jill's enjoyment of drinking it. Opening a cupboard above the sink, Jill reached down two cups and saucers from the top shelf and set them on the table in front of Ellie.

'Now then, cake or biscuits? Biscuits, I think.'

Jill placed the biscuit barrel next to the sugar bowl. Judging the tea to have stewed to satisfaction, she poured it into the cups through a strainer, then added a dash of milk to each.

'Lot of old cobblers, reading tea leaves, I've always thought. You don't have sugar, do you? I'm afraid I do. Dreadful habit, but it just doesn't taste right without,' Jill explained, adding two heaped spoons of white granulated to her cup and stirring vigorously. 'Help yourself to the bickies.'

Jill unscrewed the lid of the barrel and selected an oat crunch for herself, then placed one on Ellie's saucer, too.

'You're too thin, you know. Got to keep your strength up with a destiny like yours.'

Jill had meant it as a joke, but seeing Ellie's face, she put her biscuit back down onto her saucer and looked hard at Ellie. 'Tell me, child,' she said.

Ellie didn't know where to begin; the ring, the childhood accidents, the freaky happenings?

'Tell me what has happened since we had dinner together and we'll go from there,' said Jill, seeing Ellie's confusion.

Ellie cast her mind back to the evening of their dinner and all that had happened since. It seemed like ages ago but was only, in fact, a couple of weeks.

'I did meet him—the male energy, I mean. I think it's possible he's been around me my entire life. His name is Darkall, and he's not like other men. He appears out of nowhere when I'm in danger, and he disappears just as seamlessly. I don't really know what to think about him, except that he means me no harm, of that I'm sure, and that he has something to do with spiral energy.'

Ellie proceeded to give Jill an account of the windscreen drawing, the car swerving, her spiked drink at Baubles, the river-walk incident and Chris' subsequent accident.

'These events are not coincidence, Ellie. You are being watched, guarded by this male, although for what reason, we don't yet know. You feel safe with him, you say? Then trust your instincts, for they will rarely lead you wrong. I'm uncomfortable about the riverside accident, both your near miss and the injury suffered by your friend. I agree it appears odd that the lad should not be looking where he was going when riding at speed. You said his eyes looked blank and his mouth was part open when he hit you? Was it too dark to see what colour his eyes were? Yes, I suppose it would have been.'

Jill paused to marshal her thoughts.

'The spiral is a repeating theme. That, I can see. It is leading you into the centre of this—whatever *this* is—and like a spiral arm, the nearer you get to the middle of the vortex, the more intense and convoluted events may become.'

'There's something else,' Ellie said in a quiet voice. 'I think I have the ability to heal.'

She explained to Jill about the sparrow and Chris' subdural.

Jill smiled. 'You have always had the ability to heal, child. That is why animals respond so well to you, particularly wildlife. They recognised your healing energy, even if you didn't! What may be happening now is that your power is growing. Is there a particular method you use? Anything new about it now, compared to before?'

Ellie quietly recounted imagining the energy spiral inside her and the intensity of thought it required. She spoke of the feelings of anger and sorrow that somehow seemed to power it. Finally, she told Jill about the energy picture of the sparrow's flight that she'd seen in her mind.

'Very interesting. Before I make comment, I would warn you not to divulge what you have just told me to another living soul—at least, not one you wouldn't trust with your life. It is your method, your practise, and to explain it may be to reduce its potency and also cause unwanted attention to be drawn to you. The energy map you describe is what

I've heard the vision of a third eye is like; that is, the mind's eye or inner eye. It can allow you to see what is normally hidden from view; to perceive more than can be seen with normal sight. It's possible that you are developing this. In Hinduism, the third eye is the Ajna or brow chakra, and opening it allows you a deeper, more enlightened knowledge of that which surrounds you.'

Jill took a slurp of her tea.

'Your healing power is evolving. Previously, you employed it with good intention and it had a beneficial effect on the creatures you were caring for. Now, it is drawn from intense emotion and is consequently much more powerful. The spiral of energy you set in motion when healing echoes the spiral patterns you are noticing all around you. I cannot say who or what created the one inside your car, but it was clearly a sign; a link to the other spirals. Again, I would keep this information to yourself, or only speak of it to a trusted few. The more that is known about how you are changing, and the more which is known about this Darkall and his interest in you, the greater the risk of you being noticed.'

'Noticed by whom?' asked Ellie. 'You've mentioned this several times, but you haven't explained it at all."

Jill's eyebrows drew together. She cleared her throat, choosing her words carefully. 'There are forces all around us that notice an increase in the power of an individual; things that we might consider supernatural in nature. It is better that they aren't made aware of the changes you are experiencing. Better for you. Better for all of us. I can not say more without telling a tale that is not mine to impart.' Jill looked up, her brow clearing. 'You should talk to your parents about this, Ellie.'

162

Ellie thought for a while. She hadn't liked the sound of this last bit, but she also didn't feel quite so bewildered now that Jill had heard her concerns and had made some sense of them, even though the whole situation was still pretty overwhelming.

Jill clearly sensed Ellie's thoughts. 'You are doing well, Ellie. Just keep heading along your path, and you will understand more with each step. Now, I don't wish to overload you with information, but there is something else you should know of. Have you heard of numerology, child?'

'No. That's a new one on me.'

'It's another way of forecasting one's pathway in this life, like astrology and other forms of divination. Numerology is based on numeric values assigned to the letters of your key words; predominantly the names you were given at birth or the names you are most referred to now. The oldest system of numerology is called the Chaldean Gematria and was used in ancient Babylonia and Egypt, both advanced and ancient cultures. Numerology has also been associated with the occult and the extranormal, although, in fairness, that was more the case years ago and less so nowadays. The Chaldean Gematria also takes account of important dates like your birthday—not the year, but the day.'

Jill paused to see if Ellie was following so far before continuing.

'With Chaldean, there are compound numbers and single numbers. Compound numbers are arrived at by totalling the numeric values of the letters of your key words. Single numbers are arrived at by simplifying the compound numbers, and these solo numbers denote what you appear to be in the eyes of others.'

Ellie was looking rather perplexed, so Jill produced a notebook from her pocket and wrote:

1 = A, I, J, Q, Y
2 = B, K, R
3 = C, G, L, S
4 = D, M, T
5 = E, H, N, X
6 = U, V, W
7 = O, Z
8 = F, P

'Your name "Ellie Johnstone" has the letter values 5, 3, 3, 1, 5 and 1, 7, 5, 5, 3, 4, 7, 5, 5, giving your Christian name a compound vibration of 17 and your surname that of 42'.

'The meaning of life, the universe, and everything?' quipped Ellie, unable to resist.

Jill gave her a rather pointed look before continuing. 'Possibly. Now, as I was saying, 42 has the same meaning as 24, which itself bodes well for future events and suggests an association with the opposite sex. More importantly perhaps, the number 17 in your calculation represents the star of Venus and the Magi, and it is the number of immortality.'

Ellie nodded, an impressed look on her face. Immortality sounded good.

'Your birth date, the 8th of September, also has a compound value of 17, as 8 plus 9 equals 17. Now, to simplify and find your single number vibration, you take the compound value of "Ellie" and add the two digits together: 1 plus 7 equals 8. Then, take the compound vibration of your surname, which was 42, add these together, and you get 6. Add 8 and 6 together and you get 14. Simplify this by adding the digits, and you arrive at a single number of 5. Your numbers of significance are 5 and 17.'

Ellie looked mildly baffled, but, having followed the calculations in general, nodded her understanding. 'But what does that mean?' she asked.

'Patience, child. I was coming to that. As I have said to you before, 5 is the number of Man; man has five senses with which he experiences life. You may have noticed that the Chaldean Gematria has no letters ascribed to the number 9. That is because it is the sacred number; the number of the divine. The number of man is halfway between the Earth at 1 and Heaven at 9. With 5 as your single vibration, you will be naturally curious and feel the need to investigate everything. 5 is the number of the occult pentagram and of a five-pointed star, and like that star, you will point yourself in many directions to find what you are seeking.'

*This doesn't sound too bad*, thought Ellie. The Chaldean Gematria was proving to be fairly accurate so far.

'Now, 17 is a very spiritual number. It suggests that the individual it represents may rise to a higher plain of spirituality, and I can see the beginnings of this in you already.'

Ellie shook her head in denial but then stopped. If she thought about it, what with her healing ability and being in touch with otherworldly beings, she would tend to agree with Jill.

She looked down at her hand, where her restless fingers played with her ring. Jill looked, too, her eyebrows raising slightly.

'Five white quartz chips plotting your course to the centre of the spiral, while you yourself have the single number vibration of 5—it all fits. This is not a pathway you are treading by mere chance, Ellie.'

A thought occurred to Ellie. 'Could I borrow your pen, please?'

Jill handed it to her, along with the notepad. Ellie wrote the numbers:

4, 1, 2, 2, 1, 3, 3 = 16.
  1 + 6 = 7.

The name "Darkall" had the single number vibration of 7.
  She wrote a further set of numbers:

4, 1, 2, 2, 5, 5, 3, 3, = 25.
  2+5 = 7.

The word "darkness" had a single number value of 7.
  *"Darkall" and "darkness" are one and the same.*

Not telling Jill what she had been working out, Ellie asked Jill what the number seven meant.

'7 vibrates to the planet Neptune, which is the planet of mystery and illusion. As I mentioned before, 7 is a number both crooked and straight, and people with this number can see both sides of an argument and are non-judgemental. They can be adjudicators and can be mistakenly considered taciturn, as they carefully consider what they are going to say before they speak. They do not waste words in idle chatter. Sevens are private people. Who are you asking about, Ellie?'

'Darkall,' Ellie said in a quiet voice.

Jill thought for a moment, looking at Ellie's rows of numbers.

'His name has a compound value of 16. Interesting. 16 is the Tower card, or Shattered Citadel, in Tarot. It shows lightning striking a tower and an uncrowned king falling from the burning building. It is the most feared card in the Tarot deck, as many think it predicts chaos, destruction and upheaval. However, the Tower card is not necessarily all negative. As with the Death card, it can have less obvious meanings, like signalling change and the disastrous effects of clinging too tightly to how things currently stand, rather than embracing the new that is coming. You had the Tower in your Tarot spread—one of your centre three, if I remember rightly—and I told you the same then. Now we see that the Tower represents Darkall, too. I think not only is he linked to you, but he is also possibly a catalyst for great change. Together, you may well bring hereto unseen alterations to our world. But then, if he is not human, then who can say whether the cards are capable of representing him at all? His part might be much greater or less than these divinatory systems can detect. He may even *be* the change you are bringing. Only time will tell.'

'It seems to me that there are more links between him and me than coincidence alone can account for,' remarked Ellie, now less easy with what Jill had told her.

'Of that, at least, I am certain,' Jill said. 'You and Darkall are bound together in this. You should speak to him now that you know where you stand. One more thing, Ellie ... The male presence in your Tarot spread was the King of Swords. The word "swords" is 3,6,7,2,4,3, which makes 25. 2 plus 5 is 7. That is thrice the number 7 is significant with him. Three sevens are 21, which gives 3 when the digits are added. 3 is the number of the planet Jupiter, the thinking planet, the

167

guardian of the higher mind, of exploring ideas and seeking insight through knowledge. Because of this, and its place in the night's sky, some describe Jupiter as the light that still burns when all others are dark. Here, contrariwise, darkness brings and upholds enlightenment. Dark as the bringer of light.'

Jill halted for several moments, pursuing her train of thought. In the expectant silence, Ellie fidgeted in her seat, then picked up the pencil and doodled a 5 over the top of a 7.

Jill looked up from the doodle, her eyes meeting Ellie's. 'You know, Ellie,' she said, 'it is possible that he may have been looking for you, too.'

# 15

# Chapter 15

Ellie drove home from Burrsteignton in a contemplative mood. She had phoned her parents to let them know that she'd visited Jill and would be late home. They had not reacted badly, instead seeming surprised, but Ellie expected to face an interrogation when she got home.

The return journey didn't seem to be taking as long as the outward leg, as Ellie had often observed to be the case. Maybe it was because she was thinking about Jill's words as she drove the quiet roads. This preoccupation certainly caused Ellie to pass all four of the petrol stations on the way home before her petrol light caught her attention.

*Bugger.* She'd just have to wing it and fill up in the morning.

Ellie started to watch the petrol gauge anxiously. Being a vintage car, Dolly had no digital readout that indicated how many miles of petrol were left; there was just the hand on the dial creeping ever further into the red reserve segment.

Ellie made it off the main road and was travelling down a serpentine lane along the bottom of a valley, only a couple of miles from home, when Dolly juddered to a halt. Stranded,

169

Ellie tried to call her parents for rescue, but there was no reception down here in the valley; one of the downsides of living amid beautiful but hilly countryside. It was nearly nine o'clock and dark, although the moon did provide a little light.

Andy had instilled in Ellie a need to be prepared when motoring and so she kept a torch and a waterproof jacket in the boot of her car, although sadly not a full petrol can. During the last shuddering lurches of forward momentum, Ellie had managed to tuck Dolly onto the verge opposite a passing place on the narrow lane, enabling other vehicles to pass her stranded Citroën.

Shrugging on the luminous coat over the top of her jacket for added warmth, Ellie grabbed her shoulder bag and, flicking on the torch, set off along the lane. She'd been walking for only five minutes or so when the sound of a car engine broke the quiet of the dark countryside. Her initial thought was of rescue, until her ears and brain registered the speed of the approaching vehicle.

Ellie spun around to be met with a blinding glare of headlights and a car thundering towards her. With no time for her to react, the vehicle was upon her. All she could do was raise her arms in front of her head before impact.

The wrench of arms grabbing her around the waist and heaving her suddenly sideways into a field gateway took her breath away. Her hair having fallen over her face from the swift movement meant that, for a moment, she couldn't see clearly. Shaking her head to dislodge her tresses, Ellie saw red lights disappearing around a bend in the lane and heard the sound of the engine stop; not as if it were preparing to reverse to see if the pedestrian was all right, but as if there were no longer a car there at all.

Darkall still had his arms around Ellie, holding her firmly against his body. She strained against his embrace and he released her, one hand remaining on her elbow to steady her.

'What the hell was that?' she fumed at him. 'And how the hell do you keep doing that?'

Ellie wrenched her elbow from his grasp, her irrational anger born of fear and adrenaline.

'You would prefer that I stop saving your life?' he countered.

'Just leave me alone!' Ellie raged. 'I don't *need* you around me. I just want to be on my own! Get out of my head! Stop following me! I just ….'

Her shock finally found release in the form of great shuddering sobs, and she crumpled against the five-bar gate. Darkall stepped silently up behind her and put his arm around Ellie, turning her to lean against him. His large hand gently cupped the back of her head, drawing it against his shoulder, and his other arm hung at his side, leaving Ellie free to step away from his embrace if she so chose.

'I cannot do that,' he said quietly. 'But I can assure you that you are safe with me.'

Ellie's sobs lessened and she raised her chin, looking up at him. The moonlight caught the planes of his pale face, making him seem like a statue carved from white marble. His arcane eyes looked directly into hers; silver lights dancing against deepest purple. Ellie relaxed against him, the tension leaving her body. With his arm enfolding her, she felt shielded and safe; a sense of absolute security washed over Ellie and swept away much of her panic.

Not wanting to move but feeling that she ought to, Ellie slowly pulled away from Darkall. 'I'm OK now,' she said.

'You'd think those bloody idiots would have seen me in this luminous jacket, at least.'

'They saw you,' Darkall responded, letting his arm drop.

'You're saying that they *deliberately* tried to run me over?' Ellie exclaimed.

'Yes,' he answered, his reply concise and unnerving.

Ellie felt herself starting to tremble. 'Why? I don't even know who they were! Why would they want to hurt me?'

'Because you are light.'

Feeling her panic rising and a fresh surge of adrenaline kickstarting her muscles, Ellie turned and strode away from him down the lane.

'Eleanor, wait.' Darkall was suddenly in front of her, without seeming to have had the time to move. 'It is not safe for you to walk alone. You must go back to your car.'

'I can't drive it. It's out of petrol,' she snapped.

Promptly, his arms wrapped around her and drew her to him. His hand on the back of her head pressed her face into the lapel of his coat, and the meagre light cast by the moon vanished momentarily. Angrily, Ellie pulled back away from him.

'You can continue your journey,' he said, releasing her from his embrace.

Light and engine noise immediately flooded her senses. She was standing in front of Dolly, in the beam of the dipped headlights. Dolly's engine was running, and the driver's door was open.

'Get in, Eleanor, and drive straight to your home,' Darkall's voice commanded from somewhere behind her.

Ellie turned towards him, but there was no one there. She looked from left to right, then all around her, but she was alone in the dark lane. Getting quickly into the car, Ellie clicked the door locks forwards on all four doors, crunched Dolly into gear and drove home as quickly as was safe. Every fibre of her being needed the security of the thick stone walls of Owl's Ridge, with its stout door locked against the weirdness she'd just experienced.

Her father was in the kitchen when Ellie burst through the door.

'Woah there! What's the rush?' Andy asked.

Ellie didn't know what to say or how to put what she was feeling into words. 'Dad, I ….' She started to cry.

Stepping quickly towards her, Andy hugged his daughter. 'Shush, it's OK. Shush, Wellie.' He stroked her hair back from her wet face and ran his hand down its length, just as he'd done since she was a child. 'It's fine that you went to see Jill. You have every right to see whoever you want and talk about what you like. You're an adult. You needn't have kept your mum and me in the dark; we wouldn't have stopped you,' he soothed, misconstruing the reason for her distress.

'No, Dad, it's not that. I ran out of petrol and then a car nearly hit me, and then … then ….'

A fresh wave of tears stole the rest of her sentence. But then, what was she going to say, anyway? Was she ready to tell her father about Darkall? She didn't really know anything about him to tell, except that he was different.

*Not human.*

'It doesn't matter—you're home now, safe with us, and we can sort out whatever else needs dealing with in the morning. Hush, now. Everything's OK; no harm done,' Andy said.

Her face buried in the folds of her father's chunky woollen jumper, Ellie wished more than anything that his words were true.

But she wasn't sure she fully believed that.

# 16

# Chapter 16

Flick was in high spirits when Ellie next saw her in the Common Room. Chris was being discharged from hospital that afternoon, and Flick was planning to miss her last class of the day in order to collect him and drive him home. Chris' parents were so delighted with his rapid recovery that they were more than happy to let Flick perform this task; his mother had even invited her to dinner with the family that evening as part of Chris' "welcome home" celebrations.

Jaz and Meg had been spending more and more time together lately and were rarely seen apart anymore. They'd stayed at Meg's parents' holiday home in Cornwall for the weekend and were in glowing spirits upon their return, having spent the two days as a 'proper grown-up couple,' as Meg had put it.

Jaz was Meg's first same sex partner. She said that she wasn't gay or straight but had just recognised the soul she was meant to be with in Jaz. Traditional concepts of male/female relationships held no sway with Meg, as she believed everyone had a soulmate and the difficulty was in finding them rather than concerning yourself with what gender they were. Ellie and Flick were very impressed with this enlightened pansexual thinking and had warmed to Meg even more. Jaz had looked at Meg in wonder, as if she'd just opened a Wonka bar and found the Golden Ticket under its wrapper. It was good to see that after all Jaz had been through at Turrell's Academy, she had found somewhere and someone with whom she could be truly happy. Vi approved of Meg, too, and was delighted to see her sister so happy.

Seeing the pair of turtle doves, as Vi's mother had named the couple, Vi left her group of friends and joined her sister and Meg.

'Hey you,' Vi said, sitting down beside Meg. 'Are you round ours tonight? I could do with your thoughts on my Physics paper.'

'Yes, I'll be over later. But you could always ask your sister for help; she knows just as much as I do.'

'Nah, she'd likely give me the wrong advice just to teach me the importance of finding out stuff for myself.'

'Yes, that I would, you lazy mare. You are not to use Meg as your proofreader.'

'It's fine. I don't mind helping Vi,' said Meg.

'OK then, but don't let her take advantage,' Jaz said with a glare at her little sister, who simply leaned forwards to see around Meg better, then poked out her tongue out in response.

'Juvenile brat,' remarked Jaz. Turning to Ellie on the seat next to her, she lowered her voice and said, 'I hear from Flick that you helped Chris?'

Ellie thought for a moment, not wanting to answer the question directly. 'I tried to help, but I don't know if anything

I did actually made a difference.'

Looking around to check who might overhear their conversation, Jaz dropped her voice still further. 'Bit of a coincidence, wouldn't you say? One minute, he's out for the count, the next he's back to his old self and being discharged. What changed, if it wasn't your help? People have believed in radiant healing and healing thoughts for centuries—longer, even. Think of a tribal medicine man, or even Voodoo. If evil thoughts and black magic can harm, then healing thoughts and good magic can help. You can buy talismans protecting you from the Evil Eye on eBay, for heaven's sake! If *that* can exist—or, at least, enough people believe it does to the extent they need to ward it off with glass eyes—then the flip side of telepathic healing seems equally likely.'

Ellie smiled at Jaz, grateful for her friend's support.

'Meg's aunt is a spiritual healer. Maybe you should meet her and have a chat? She also does crystal therapy and herbal remedies among other stuff. She would no doubt have been burnt at the stake in the Middle Ages,' Jaz said with a frown.

'What are you two whispering about? It's rude, don't ya know?'

Flick, having finished her latest text to Chris, looked up at Ellie and Jaz accusingly.

'Holistic healing,' Jaz replied with a meaningful look at Flick, who demonstrated she understood the reason for their hushed voices with an exaggerated "*oh*" of her lips.

\* \* \*

Jaz and Flick had actually had a long conversation about what had happened in hospital. Flick had been so relieved after all the tension that she'd needed to talk it through before there was any likelihood of her being able to rest and relax. She'd driven from the hospital directly to Jaz's house, where, conveniently, she had found Jaz alone. Flick had explained how ill Chris had been, and Jaz had held her as Flick cried.

'Ellie came to be with me at the hospital,' she'd said when her tears abated. 'I didn't call you as I knew you were with Meg and I didn't want to interrupt you guys.'

'You can call me anytime. You know that.'

'I do, but I just wanted to let you guys be together. It looks like what you've got is the real deal, and I didn't want to mess anything up by dragging you away.' Flick had paused to regain her thread. 'Anyway, we were sitting with Chris. He was looking really bad, totally out of it and half dead already. I remember being angry that he'd had such a stupid accident. Why the hell hadn't he been looking where he was going? Anyway, me and Ellie planned to make up a bed on the chair and then I went to the bathroom to wash. When I came out, I saw a light in Chris' room, but as I walked down the corridor, it seemed to fade out. I thought I'd imagined it. When I got to the door, Ellie was standing over Chris, her hands touching his head and her eyes closed like she was praying. She didn't hear me, so I called her name. At first, she looked at me blankly, like she didn't know who I was or where she was. It was like she was coming out of a trance or something. Then she came to, let go of Chris and stepped back. She said she was sending him good vibes, and I thought that was nice of her. But then with what happened, how he was suddenly OK and with no sign of the bleed in his head, I'm a bit fazed. I mean, did *she* really heal him?'

Jaz had thought for a while before answering. 'I think Ellie

178

is going through some stuff that we can't really understand. But, as her friends, we're just going to have to be there for her, even if she can't tell us what it is.'

'I will stand by Ellie. You know that. She's one of us.'

'I know,' Jaz had affirmed, 'and in answer to your question, yes, I *do* think Ellie had something to do with Chris' recovery. I don't know how or what she did and I'm not going to question her about it, but Ellie has some sort of special gift for healing. She's always bringing half-dead wildlife home and making them better, for a start. Most people who try to do that end up with a little corpse in a few days, but our Ellie is the Florence Nightingale for anything small, feathery or fluffy.'

'Yes, she is, and she's a really good person, too. But I'm worried about the strangeness she's getting into. At Bertie's, Ellie said she'd seen a bloke who wasn't real or wasn't there. A bloke who told her he was darkness. If that's not creepy, I don't know what is. And now she can heal people? What if this guy is evil? Evil won't like her going around stopping people from suffering. Is it going to be coming after Ellie?'

'I don't know. I don't know what this is all about, and I don't think Ellie does either—*yet*. She'll find out in her own time. All we can do is let her know that we don't think she's crazy, and that, despite all the freaky stuff going on around her, we aren't going anywhere. If she needs us to know more, then she'll tell us. She *trusts* us. It's not like she's keeping secrets. I just think she hasn't figured out what the hell is going on herself yet. But maybe when she does, it might be better for us *not* to know. It's hard being in the dark, but sometimes friends have just got to accept it. Us being weird about her private stuff is not going to help her.'

179

'Preaching to the converted, sister,' Flick had said with a smile. 'I'm always here for both of you; it goes without saying. Wherever Ellie needs to go, or whatever she needs to be, that's OK by me. I just hope we can keep her safe.'

'Me too,' Jaz had replied. 'And she'll be having the same thoughts about us, too. You can be sure of that.'

\* \* \*

Jaz's sentiments were right; Ellie *was* thinking about her friends. She was deeply worried about what she was dragging them all into. Chris' accident really didn't add up. Nor did the grey vehicles that had tried to crash into her car and run her over. It seemed that there was a sinister undercurrent flowing beneath everything that had happened lately; speeding cars appearing and disappearing and accidents that didn't feel accidental. Whatever was taking place clearly had an element of danger; in fact, more than that, it was actually *dangerous*. But if she stopped, if she did an about-turn and refused to see anything beyond the normal, would it all go away? Or was the only way out of this to go forwards towards whatever destiny had in store for her? Jill had said that to ignore the changes coming might well be dangerous, but was that more perilous than whatever was looming ahead of her? Again, it was obvious that she needed more information and, this time, she wasn't going to get the answers she needed out of a book.

She needed to talk to Darkall.

\* \* \*

At home that evening, Ellie waited until the sun had fallen behind the hills. The evening breeze would make sitting outside without a jacket uncomfortable, so Ellie wrapped her warm coat around herself, put on her cycle helmet and headed out into the dusk. She walked to her favourite spot under the Holm Oak and then stepped to the far side of the tree to avoid being seen from the house.

Ellie stood still and listened to the leaves rustling above her head. She didn't know if this would work—didn't wholeheartedly believe it was *possible*—but without any defined way of contacting him, it was worth a try.

Turning to face the trunk, she placed her foot on a bulbous buttress root and started to climb. Just how many times she'd taken this route up into the boughs she couldn't say; maybe fifty, a hundred even, maybe more. It had been her treehouse, climbing tree and best hiding place: an important part of her childhood. She reached for the broken branch, still firm near the trunk, and hefted herself up to her favourite perch, where a wide bough divided near the trunk. But this wasn't high enough, so she continued to weave herself up through the branches.

Here was where her lookout had been. In daylight, she could see the end of the lane from up here, where it turned the corner and disappeared out of sight. Ellie looked down; would this do? Much higher and she wouldn't have a strong enough bough to ease herself out along. She climbed another couple of feet to a fairly horizontal branch that reached out towards the field and away from the house. Sitting astride it, Ellie began to shuffle along its diminishing girth.

Judging herself to be clear of most of the lower branches, she paused for a moment, gripping the bough tightly with

181

her thighs. Was she really going to do this? What if it didn't work? The ground was a long way down from here, and she'd be lucky to avoid broken bones. Would she be able to heal herself?

Thinking too much was going to zap her courage and so she swung one leg over the branch, leaving herself perched sideways. She closed her eyes, took a deep breath, leaned forwards and left herself fall. A rush of air, a plummeting sensation, twigs scratching at her limbs and face—

And then the impact of being caught by two strong arms.

Her heart racing, Ellie opened her eyes and looked into his. The silver lights were glaringly bright, the deep purple almost black.

'That was unwise, Eleanor. You do not need to test me.'

'It wasn't a test. I needed to talk to you.'

'And you believed that throwing yourself out of a tree was the best way to attract my attention? Putting yourself in danger was not a rational response. You could have just called for me.'

'What, like calling your name?'

'Yes.'

'Oh. Well, in that case, you can put me down now, thank you.'

He lowered her to the ground, and she stood up straight, unstrapping her safety helmet.

Darkall appeared even more eldritch when seen in her own familiar surroundings. He was taller than Ellie, who, at five foot eight, was not short herself. Darkall had to be at least six foot four, Ellie estimated, perhaps taller. He was powerfully built, like the gym bros at nightclubs who thought they were God's gift to women in their tight, bicep-advertising shirts.

But Darkall carried his physique without their arrogance and need for recognition. His was a quiet, almost sombre air of utter self-assurance, like he was aware that he was far, far superior to those around him without displaying a need to advertise the fact.

'You wanted to speak with me?' Darkall prompted after a few moments of silence.

'Yes, but let's walk away from the house a bit.'

Ellie suddenly wanted to distance her home and her parents from the otherworldly being in front of her. She led him to the garden gate and through into the field. The light was leeching out of the sky, but there was just enough to see their way across the grass. Ellie stopped at the stile that led to the lane and turned back towards Darkall, leaning against the weathered timbers.

'I have so many questions, but I don't know where to start,' she said, her eyes searching his face.

Darkall waited patiently, at ease under her scrutiny.

'Was it you … has it always been you, saving me? I've had so many accidents where I should have been hurt, or worse, and I wasn't.'

'Mostly it was me.'

'Are you always watching me?' Ellie asked, naively hoping he would dispel her beliefs.

'Yes, but not in the way you are thinking.'

'How, then?'

'It is hard to explain. I am everywhere.'

'You are darkness?'

'Yes.'

'So, how can you be there when it's daylight?'

'Darkness exists in the light. It is just you cannot see it,

Eleanor.'

'You are there, everywhere, all the time?'

'I can be.'

'And you watch me?'

'I can desist if you'd prefer.'

Ellie paused to think. 'No, I have always felt safe in the dark. Now I know why. Because *you* were there. I guess I'm safer *with* you than without.'

Darkall nodded in recognition of her decision.

'But why are you interested in me?'

'Because you are light.'

'Light? You said this the other night, too, when the morons in that car nearly ran me down. I am just a human being. One of billions on the planet. Nothing special. Just a person minding their own business.'

'Others would disagree.'

'What others?'

Darkall sighed and stepping forwards, turned to lean his back against the stile beside Ellie. 'Eleanor, there are things you do not know. Things that you may prefer *not* to know. However, they know of you. And they have been watching you for a long time.'

His words made Ellie shiver, and she wrapped her coat more tightly around herself.

'Things like you?' she asked hesitantly.

'No, they are not like me. I am unique. I am impartial. The things I speak of have needs and desires, and they will act to satisfy them.'

Ellie was turning her ring on her finger, and noticing this, Darkall gently took her hand and lifted it up in front of her face. 'What do you see here, Eleanor?'

'A pattern. A spiral with a deep purple centre and a pathway of stars leading to it.'

Darkall smiled slightly and nodded. He held up his hand so that Ellie could see his palm. There was a faint blue glow emanating from the spiral tattoo across it—if it *was* a tattoo. Perhaps it was a scar or a birthmark, but Ellie couldn't tell for sure. Either way, his spiral was a mirror image of the one on her ring, but without the path of stars. Although slight, the blue glow was brightest in the centre where it surrounded the dark core. It was too dark to see, but Ellie had a hunch that core would be purple.

'This symbol is my ward. Where you see it, my protection extends, and these creatures will not harm you.'

Ellie thought of the times she'd seen the spiral pattern: on the ring, in her drawing, her car windscreen, the stile. Ellie reached her free hand back to find the stile carving with her fingers. She identified it by the deep lines gouged across it.

'It was challenged, yet still it holds,' Darkall remarked, understanding what she had sought and found.

'You're protecting me from these things. But why are they after me?'

'Because you, too, are unique, Eleanor. In all time, there has never been one such as you. This is why I am here. You draw me to you.'

Ellie still did not feel satisfied with his answer; although it had the tang of truth about it, she still felt he was withholding information.

'I am fascinated by you.'

Bowing his head, Darkall lifted the hand he was holding to his lips and kissed her fingers on either side of the ring. Ellie felt the ring vibrate and suddenly grow warm.

'Do not take this off,' he said. 'No matter the reason.'

His unnatural eyes looked into hers from his slightly bowed position, and Ellie felt a fizz of excitement plummet in her belly. The silver lights in his eyes danced, softly illuminating his face in the darkness surrounding them.

'If I need you …' she began.

'I will come. You may call my name to summon me,' Darkall interrupted, pre-empting her question. 'No more risking your life to get my attention, Eleanor, if you please,' he added, with a smile that confirmed he was *the* most stunning man Ellie had ever seen.

'Promise,' Ellie said, flushing slightly and returning his smile with a grin.

'Ellie? You out here?' Her father's voice called from the back garden.

Ellie looked at Darkall, who gave a slight shrug.

'Coming, Dad!' she called back.

She pushed herself away from the stile as if to walk off, but then turned back to face Darkall. She placed her right hand on his shoulder, and Darkall turned his head slightly to look at it, an eyebrow lifted in query. Ellie quickly leaned forwards and kissed him lightly on his exposed left cheek.

'Thank you for saving me. *Again*,' she breathed against his skin.

Darkall's eyes flashed silver, and his hands cupped her face. Standing up straight, he looked down at her. 'You are most welcome,' he replied, dropping a kiss onto her hairline.

Ellie closed her eyes, savouring the sensation, then opened them, looking up into his face and wanting more.

'Ellie! For Heaven's sake, get a move on! The hot chocolate your mother's made for you is going cold!' Andy's voice carried clearly on the night air.

Darkall reluctantly released Ellie. 'You must go to your father.'

Ellie turned to look at the house. 'But I still have questions …'

'All in good time, Eleanor. Now go to the house.' Darkall's voice sounded somehow close and yet inescapably distant.

Sensing a movement in the air behind her, Ellie turned back to Darkall, but he was no longer there.

Instead, there was only darkness.

# 17

# Chapter 17

Ellie couldn't get to sleep that night, kept awake by envisioning a pair of unearthly eyes staring at her from below a heavy brow.

*'I am fascinated by you … You draw me to you.'*

Darkall's words had to be just about the sexiest thing a guy had ever said to Ellie. Plus, when delivered by an extremely handsome supernatural being whose hobby was apparently saving her life, what girl could resist? Ellie now understood Lois Lane's predicament all too well.

The next morning, surprisingly, Ellie wasn't tired, despite having been awake for half the night thinking of Darkall. She seemed to be running on an excited, nervous energy which suppressed her appetite as well as causing her every thought to turn to him. She revelled in the knowledge that she could simply summon him; she wanted to try it out so many times during the day but somehow resisted. Her plan was to meet him again that evening in the garden or field, and she hoped that the weather would stay dry and mild so that they could continue their ethereal conversation.

Jaz and Meg noticed Ellie was rather distracted as they watched her gaze out of the canteen window after lunch. Flick, however, had thoughts only of Chris, who was now home and delighted to be so. As soon as the last lesson of the day was over, Flick intended to rush off to Chris' place to see how her beau was doing. Ellie, fresh from her late night liaison with Darkall, now understood Flick's need to see him. She wondered what it would be like to kiss Darkall's lips and unconsciously smiled a small, secret smile to herself.

Meg noticed and nudged Jaz.

'She's thinking of *him*,' Meg whispered.

'What? How do you know?'

'Because that's the same smile I get thinking about you.'

In response, Jaz leant forwards and kissed her.

'Oi! Get a room!' Flick hollered delightedly, most pleased that, for once, she could turn the tables on Jaz and grumble about her public displays of affection.

Hearing Flick's loud voice, Ellie snapped out of her day-dreaming and re-joined the conversation. 'So, anyone up for going on this Student Union trip thing?'

'More information needed. Does not compute,' remarked Flick in a robotic monotone.

'There was a poster up about it outside the library. The Student Union guys have organised a coach to take us to London for the Climate Change protest on Tuesday the week after next,' Ellie explained. 'We'd have to sleep in the Common Room and leave at about 4am to get there in time, though. What do you reckon? I thought I might go.'

'Sounds like a laugh,' said Flick. 'As long as Chris is OK. He might actually be able to make it, which would be cool.'

'I'm in. I actually meant to mention it to you guys, but I

189

wasn't sure if it'd be your thing. It's such an important issue and, besides, there's no point moaning thirty years from now that the planet is dying when it's too late to do anything about it. We need to speak out *now*. It's us that are going to have to live on a poisoned planet and deal with the mess our parents and grandparents created,' opined Meg, who was hot on environmental issues.

'I agree,' Jaz declared. 'I'm in, too.'

'I'll pick us all up some forms when I'm in the library later,' promised Meg. 'But you need to get them in quickly, as the deadline is Friday.'

'Cheers, Meg,' Flick said. 'But you might need to nag me hourly until I hand the damn thing in. My memory is shot at the moment.'

'You've had a lot on your mind lately,' Meg responded kindly.

\* \* \*

Ellie floated through the rest of the afternoon feeling detached from the events happening around her. It was like she was a spectator, watching herself going about her usual routine rather than actually being involved in it herself; like seeing a movie of her life, as opposed to living it.

At the end of the afternoon Ellie drove herself home. Her parents were out for the day and had told Ellie not to expect them home before she'd gone to bed, which was perfect timing as far as Ellie was concerned; she could talk to Darkall without worrying about her parents looking out of the window and seeing her talking to a strange man. Mind you, would they see him or did he just make himself visible to her? She'd have to ask him.

Maybe she ought to make a list of all the questions that had popped into her head during the day? But, then again, if she badgered him with her thirst for knowledge, maybe he wouldn't answer. He was fairly reticent with his words, and she didn't want to put him off her by being too inquisitive.

Was his interest in her romantic, though? She was nothing special; although pretty, Ellie harboured no illusions that she was a great beauty. In fact, if Darkall were a normal guy in a club, Ellie would not have felt brave enough to chat him up, instead believing him to be far out of her league. It was flattering but fairly unbelievable that, for some reason, she'd drawn his fancy.

Ellie made herself scrambled eggs on toast for tea. It was possibly the laziest hot meal she knew. Ellie was not particularly interested in cooking, as it seemed to her to be a great waste of time. Three hours spent slaving in the kitchen to make a Sunday roast and then it was all gone in twenty minutes. What was the point?

*What does Darkall eat? Does he even eat at all?* Somehow, she couldn't imagine him sitting at the kitchen table, drinking tea and eating cake with her, Grace and Andy. What would they make of him? He was so large and otherworldly that he would surely look like a giant in the confines of the farmhouse kitchen. That would be a *seriously* weird meeting.

*Darkall, these are my parents, Grace and Andy. Mum, Dad, this is Darkall. He's a ...*

A what? *What* was he? A being other than human. A *god*?

*Didn't the Ancient Egyptians believe that some of their gods were the personifications of astral bodies like the sun? Yes, Ra, who was also in charge of creation—and then there was the moon*

191

*god Khonsu.* Someone claiming to be darkness would fit right in with that bunch.

She'd read theories that the Ancient Egyptian gods were actually aliens, believed by some on account of the seeming impossibility of building such fantastic structures as the pyramids without any modern-day machinery.

Darkall had said that he was everywhere and nowhere, which seemed to suggest to Ellie a being who was unaffected by the constraints of a three-dimensional universe. Of course, time was generally considered to be the fourth dimension. If Darkall existed outside of the known dimensions of the universe, then there was no limit to what he might be able to do. When looked at from the human perspective, he would be considered a god. Perhaps the Egyptian gods were indeed aliens—ones like him.

Ellie went upstairs to her bedroom. Looking in the full-length mirror stuck to the front of her wardrobe door, she frowned: tomato ketchup down her jumper was not a good look. She'd have to change. But what to wear? It wasn't like she was going on a date—or then again, maybe it was. She certainly felt excited and nervous, and she'd been thinking about him somewhat obsessively for nearly twenty-four hours.

So, what should she wear? Something sexy, something black? Rather unsurprisingly, he always wore black. He'd said that she was light, so why try to hide that by mimicking his signature colour?

The evenings were still not terribly warm, so perhaps she'd go for sexy and snuggly in tight trousers and an oversized jumper. Ellie smiled to herself in the mirror; she had problems putting the word "snuggly" next to Darkall. It just wasn't him.

Maybe he would take her somewhere with him? He had magicked her back to her car after her near miss the other night. Perhaps he would show her something of where he lived, or existed, or whatever.

Could humans travel outside of their three dimensions, or would they just explode or disintegrate?

Pulling out a pair of skinny jeans and her new slip-shoulder purple jumper, Ellie got changed and brushed her hair so that it fell in a copper waterfall down her back. She added silver stud earrings and a locket chain around her neck. Was perfume going too far? Heck, why not? The scent would likely be blown away in the breeze, anyway.

She crossed the hall to the bathroom, where the mirror had a strip of light running down either side and was consequently the best one in the house for doing makeup. Peering critically, Ellie assessed her face. Two eyes, widely spaced and green, stared back at her, surrounded by brown eyelashes and eyebrows. Pale skin with a sprinkling of freckles across her slightly upturned nose and below her eyes. Good cheekbones led down to a determined chin with the hint of a dimple, and, above that, her mouth was wide with a generous bottom lip and a pronounced Cupid's bow. Her hairline was high and her jaw strong. It was an attractive, symmetrical face, which Ellie had read somewhere was a requirement for beauty in both males and females. Darkall's face was perfectly symmetrical, with no blemishes and, now she came to think of it, no shaving stubble or rash. He didn't even have freckles or moles; just unnaturally perfect skin. But then, that likely went with the whole "being non-human" thing.

Ellie applied some cover-up to her freckles and dusted her face with powder. She carefully applied some eyeliner above her top lashes, taking care to make the extended points even on both eyelids, then flicked her lashes with mascara. She wasn't going out for the evening and so avoided the whole eyeshadow and blusher shebang. After all, she didn't want to look like she had gone to too much effort; she just wanted to look good. A lick of tinted lip gloss, and she was done. Now the face looking back at her in the bathroom mirror was slightly more sophisticated, with smoky lashes and a pouting mouth.

Ellie checked her watch. Sunset wasn't for another hour or so. Darkall had said that he was present in the light, too, but would she be able to see him in daylight? Ellie went downstairs and let the spaniels out into the back garden to stretch their legs. She followed their exuberant zigzagging down the path that led to the field. Ellie leaned on the gate and looked towards the wood. The bluebells would be out by now, and she'd always loved the carpet of blue that appeared each year under the canopy of beech.

On a whim, Ellie opened the gate and whistled to the spaniels to come to heel. Both dogs dashed to her, and then, seeing the open gate, tore through it and out across the wide expanse of grass, sending winged creatures flying up in startled response to their passing. Ellie strolled directly across the middle of the field to the wood, entering underneath its branches. There, bobbing around the feet of the trees, were what she had come to see. Bluebells curved their silvery stalks as the flowerheads danced in the breeze, guarded by the dark green spikes of their leaves. The dappled sunlight cast shadows on the leafy moss carpet of the wood, and the bluebells highlighted by shafts of light were a startling indigo-blue.

Ellie crouched down to smell them; she could just detect a hint of perfume rather like hyacinths. That made sense to Ellie, as the six-petalled flowers on the bluebells made her think of the hyacinths that her mother grew in glass vases each Spring. Their heavy scent gloriously perfumed the downstairs of the house for a week or so each year and reminded them all that winter was passing, even though the sky outside was grey.

The spaniels started barking, their uproar coming from the field, so Ellie whistled for them. Chipper came running, crushing bluebells in his eagerness to please, but dominant-dog Raff stood his ground and continued to bark.

Ellie marched out of the wood towards the noise, irritated that the dog had disobeyed her. Raff was standing by the stile, one paw on the first step and barking non-stop at something he'd sensed in the road. Ellie felt unaccountably reluctant to go over to the stile to see what that might be. She called Raff by name and, finally responding to the irritation in her voice, he came bounding over to her. Grabbing both dogs by their collars, Ellie marched half-bent back to the garden gate and, closing it behind her, took the dogs back into the house.

Returning to the garden gate alone, she looked across to the stile. Nothing was there, but she thought she could detect a faint haze in the air, like dust thrown up by a vehicle pulling away in a hurry from the dry mud of the verge. Or, then again, she could have been imagining it.

Turning her thoughts back to Darkall, she checked her watch: still half an hour until she would be with him again. The thought sent a shiver of anticipation down her spine, and her stomach fluttered in excitement. Was her heart beating faster, too? Honestly, her body was behaving like one of the excited spaniels every time she thought of him. Maybe she needed something to settle her nerves.

Back in the kitchen, Ellie opened the fridge and assessed the contents with dissatisfaction. Only her father's cans of Stella were cooling in the drawer; no bottles of wine open or otherwise. Closing the door, a flash of colour in the door shelves caught her eye: a can of dry cider. *Result.*

Rinsing the top under the kitchen tap and drying it on a tea towel—as her mother insisted she do to avoid the risk of leptospirosis—Ellie shrugged on her long coat and took the can outside with her. She crossed to her spot under the Holm Oak, settled herself comfortably on the cushion of grass and moss and leaned against the trunk. She popped the ring pull on the can and took a long swig of the golden liquid. *Does Darkall drink?* Probably not. He probably didn't approve of her drinking, either, as she might be more likely to put herself in dangerous situations when under the influence of alcohol. Just as well he wasn't here yet, and that she only had the one can.

Ellie leaned her head back against the gnarled trunk of the tree and looked up. She hadn't really noticed before how the grain of the bark twisted around the trunk as the tree grew taller. It was like the top of the tree had been rotating incredibly slowly all the time it had been growing. She supposed if you could look down on the tree from above, seeing through the evergreen leaves, it might look rather like a spiral, with branches leading the eye in towards the central, twisting trunk.

Ellie took another swig of cider. The sun was heading

for the horizon and the sky was decorated with orange-bottomed cloud. In another twenty minutes or so, it would set. Ellie felt a nervous flutter in her stomach, and she took another sip. That was enough for now; she didn't want to be babbling when Darkall appeared. She closed her eyes and deliberately slowed her breathing.

What if he didn't come when she called to him? Perhaps he'd thought better of the whole thing? Maybe jumping out of the tree had been a bad move and now he thought that she was reckless with the life he'd been at pains to preserve for years.

'Oh, Darkall.' Ellie breathed out in a long sigh. 'You're driving me crazy. Too scared to summon you, but I can't stop thinking about you,' she admitted aloud.

*Sitting here beneath a tree, waiting for darkness to fall so that I can talk to a supernatural being and question him about the impossible.*

Why was she doing this to herself? Was this really a good idea? Ellie started to get cold feet. Perhaps it would be better if she forgot the whole thing and went back inside to bed. After all, she could always change her mind and summon him tomorrow, couldn't she? Yes, she'd thought about him all day, but then, what girl wouldn't? A gorgeous guy interested in her, and one with extra powers like Thor or someone was pretty mind-blowing. But was that actually someone you could get involved with? Maybe she'd be better off hanging out with a normal guy.

'Maybe I should give Jacob another chance,' she murmured to herself.

'I would prefer that you did not,' Darkall said.

Ellie's eyes snapped open. There, crouched in front of her,

197

his elbows resting on his thighs, his left foot flat to the ground and his right bearing his weight on the ball of the foot, was Darkall. He was perfectly balanced and still, his body not wobbling like hers would have if she had to hold that position for any length of time.

'How long have you been there?' Ellie asked in shocked surprise.

'Ever since you called to me.'

'But I didn't call for you—not yet. I was waiting until after sunset.'

'You did. I could sense you calling to me all day. But I would not be so thoughtless as to interrupt your interactions with others.'

'You mean, you can hear me thinking about you?' Ellie blushed.

'Yes, in a manner of speaking. But I waited until you were ready to see me before coming to you.'

'You heard me talking aloud to myself?'

'Yes.' Darkall smiled.

'Oh.' Ellie's blush deepened as she realised the extent of what he'd overheard.

'Eleanor, I cannot tell what you were thinking; just that I was in your thoughts. I hope that helps to ease your discomfort.'

Ellie nearly sighed in relief; some of what she had been thinking about him was for her imagination only. *At least for now, anyway.*

'It's not dark yet.' Ellie tried to change the subject.

'I am darkness, yet I do not necessarily have to be in pitch-black,' he responded. 'In bright light, I may not be visible, but in less luminous situations, I can be seen. Think of shadows.

They are there despite the light. I am the same.'

'Shadows are there *because* of the light, I always thought.'

Darkall smiled and looked down at the ground before glancing back up at her. 'As am I,' he said, his silver eye-lights flaring briefly.

Ellie felt herself start to blush again. Thank goodness for the cover of the fading light.

'Shadows are dark. Night is dark. My realm is darkness.'

'You said before that you're not evil. But your realm is darkness?'

'That is correct. I am neither good nor evil. I just am.'

'But you've been saving my life? Doesn't that make you good?'

'That would depend on the perspective of those examining my actions. I have kept you from harm for my own purpose, not for one side or the other.'

'But you can do good?'

'Actions that you would consider as such, yes. If I so chose.'

'Then surely you ought to do so?' said Ellie, warming to her theme. 'If you have the opportunity to do good, and you are not bound by the laws of my reality, then you could do a great deal of good. Surely that puts you under obligation to do just that?'

'No. It does not.'

'You are saying you *choose* not to do good? Doesn't that make you evil?'

'No. It does not.'

Ellie was getting cross at his absolutist stance. She let out an irritated tut and looked away towards the horizon.

'I maintain balance. I am on neither side. I just am.' Darkall repeated his statement of a moment ago.

'Yeah, I get it. You sit on the fence.'

'No. For me, there is no fence. Balance must be maintained or chaos ensues. If I should choose a side, be it good or evil, think for a moment what would happen. One side would conquer the other, millions of lives would be lost, and good or evil would rule supreme over this planet. But how long would that state last? Dissatisfaction enters surreptitiously, eventually the dominant rule would be overthrown and millions more would die. Nothing remains in its changed state forever. The pendulum always swings back in the other direction eventually. Maintaining the balance is the least destructive option.'

'I hear what you're saying, but there are so many things that you could help with or prevent. It seems wrong to me that you don't.'

'I am what I am,' Darkall replied.

Ellie dropped her chin onto her arms, still not looking at Darkall. 'The same could be said of all of us. But some of us try to be more than we are.'

'You have the option to pursue this course. Others do not.'

Ellie didn't answer him. She spent several minutes continuing to look at the darkening horizon. When she finally did look back at him, he was no longer there.

Ellie started, looking around her. She stood up and turned around. *No!* She had driven him away with her criticism. What if he had heard enough and decided not to come back again? What a fool she had been.

'Darkall?' Ellie called urgently.

'Yes?' his deep voice whispered against her ear, his breath stirring the hairs that fell against her cheek.

She leaned back against him in relief. 'I thought you'd gone.'

200

'Not until I have done this,' he said, wrapping his arms around her from behind and drawing her against his body.

Once again, Ellie felt the sensation of being totally shielded and safe. She tilted her head to the side and looked up at his jawline. 'I am glad,' she said.

Darkall looked down at her, his face centimetres from hers. 'As am I,' he said, and, lowering his head, he gently pressed his lips to hers.

The sensation that coursed through Ellie the moment their lips touched was unlike anything she'd experienced before. It was like an electric current flowing through her into the ground, like a bolt of non-lethal lightning. It made every muscle and sinew tense and feel more alive than ever before and set her every nerve end tingling. Ellie raised her arm and, placing her palm against his cheek, held him there against her lips.

'I was right,' said Darkall in a low voice.

'About what?' asked Ellie, still reeling from his kiss.

'That you were the one. My inverse.'

'I don't understand.'

'I will explain more to you in time. For now, just know that you have me.'

A car engine was approaching along the lane. Darkall looked up quickly, his arms tightening around Ellie as he assessed the situation.

'It is your parents,' he told her as he relaxed his embrace. 'It is time for you to go.'

'No,' she objected. 'I still have so many questions I want to ask you.'

'We have time. Your questions can be addressed on another occasion.'

'*You* may have time,' Ellie grumbled, sensing a fob-off. 'But I am impatient.'

Darkall chuckled; a deep rumbling in his chest. 'I might command time, but I can see that you are going to be much more difficult to manage.' He dropped a kiss on the top of her head and inhaled the scent of her hair. 'Goodnight, Eleanor.'

'Goodnight,' she sighed.

Feeling him release her from his arms and step back away from her, Ellie knew that there was no point in turning around; he would already be gone.

She stooped to pick up the spilt can of cider, and, emptying the remainder of its contents onto the grass, she walked around the side of the house to greet her parents and help them to unload the car.

# 18

# Chapter 18

For the next couple of days, Ellie was kept extremely busy completing coursework and managing her obligations at home. She tried not to think too much about Darkall, not because she didn't want to, but because he could sense when she was thinking of him and she didn't want him to know just how into him she really was. At the end of the day, however, Ellie had completed all her work and found herself able to take a moment to process. She wandered out of the front door and across the gravel driveway.

Ellie leaned against the wooden five-bar gate that separated the drive from the lane. The sky was painted with streaks of pink that stretched to the horizon, yet despite her artistic leanings, Ellie paid scant attention to the brilliant, painterly sunset. The minor argument with Darkall still rankled, making her feel irritable and unsure of him despite the security she felt in his arms and that amazing kiss.

The front door of the house opened and the spaniels raced out of the porch, barking in excited rivalry.

'Pointless discourse!' her father's voice called after them.

Andy stood on the threshold, admiring the evening's display. Seeing Ellie, he strolled over to join her at the gate. 'Deep thoughts, Wellie?'

Ellie sighed. 'I'm OK.' She paused, wondering whether to unburden herself on him. 'Why can't things be better? Why can't good beat back evil into non-existence? Shouldn't everyone be striving for good to win?'

'Ah, one of the good ones,' said Andy. 'What's brought this on? I thought you were taking Psychology, not Philosophy."

"It's just … something I've been thinking about lately," she replied.

Andy nodded and took a moment to think. 'Balance, Ellie,' he eventually said. 'There must always be *balance*. Life and death. Good and evil. Light and dark.'

'But why does there have to be evil? Why can't only good exist?' Ellie asked, knowing that she sounded like a petulant child.

Andy considered the question. 'The old order changeth yielding place to new, and old worlds must die so new ones are born,' he quoted, splicing Tennyson with an essence of Dutschke.

'Look out there.' He indicated the evening landscape with an expansive sweep of his arm. 'What do you see?'

'Trees. Hills. Hedges. Fields. Animals.'

'What would happen if the trees never died? If they just carried on growing upwards? If leaves never fell? If fields and hedges weren't chopped down? If no animals died?'

'A forest. A scrubland.'

'Not just that. Monstrous towering trees; matted branches; colossal leaves obscuring the sky. The land choked by impenetrable thickets; billions of creatures crammed together,

204

crushing, tearing, bleeding. In short, carnage and chaos. There has to be a balance between life and death to maintain order, and I guess it's the same with good and evil.'

Ellie mulled over his words, not wanting to accept the truth of them.

'Most humans are both good *and* evil, Ellie, usually to varying degrees of one or the other. We are none of us pure enough to cast the first stone,' he said, sensing that her thoughts were born of a deeper lack of acceptance.

'But can someone ever be entirely neutral? Can they choose to stand between both sides? And assuming they can, doesn't that make their stance automatically bad from the perspective of the good?'

'I don't believe a mere human would be capable of fulfilling that position. We are too involved in what happens around us as we go about the daily job of living. To be totally impartial, someone would have to be totally detached; divorced from that which goes on around them. Maybe a god could do it; someone outside of this reality.'

'But definitely not a human? Is that what you're saying? So, if someone claimed to be neither good nor evil, they would either be beyond mortal or lying?'

'You look at every situation in black and white, and you always have done. But there are many shades of grey in between those two opposites. Don't close your mind, Ellie, or you'll let your practicality blind you.' He looked at her frowning face. 'Our reality is bound by what we know exists, but we don't know everything. The more we find out, the more we realise how little we actually know of our universe and beyond.'

She looked up at him, his face in shadowed contrast to the

brilliance of the sky behind his head. Ellie squinted into the last rays of the evening sun. Bertie's words from their last movie night suddenly rang in her ears, and she said, "'There are more things in heaven and earth", you mean?'

'Shakespeare was a wise man. His much-quoted "The fault, dear Brutus, is not in our stars, but in ourselves, that we are underlings" springs to mind, but merits a little updating for the purposes our point here. More like, "but in ourselves, that we are persistently blinded." He dropped a kiss on the top of her head. 'Be great, Ellie, and open your eyes.'

Giving her another squeeze, Andy headed back towards the house, pausing halfway across the dusty drive as another thought struck him.

'If you really need any more proof that the impossible exists, go check out the Many-Worlds Theory. You'll find it if you have a rummage around in quantum mechanics.'

\* \* \*

A couple of days later, Ellie took the opportunity to quiz Jaz and Meg on their science knowledge when she caught up with them in town. The friends were having lunch in Mags, one of their favourite haunts. Flick was at Chris' house, so it was just the three of them.

'My father said I should take a look at the Many-Worlds Theory if I needed proof that the impossible exists. He mentioned quantum mechanics? Would this be something either of you know much about?' Ellie asked the pair of them.

Jaz looked at Meg. 'You want to field this one?'

'Sure,' replied Meg. 'Quantum physics is more my jam than Jaz's. I'll have a go at explaining it to you, although please bear in mind I'm not a teacher.' Meg smiled at Ellie. 'You know how atoms consist of a nucleus made of protons and neutrons and that electrons orbit this nucleus?'

Ellie nodded.

'The speed of the orbiting electrons can be altered by adding more energy, maybe in the form of a beam of light or something. The amount of energy needed to make the electrons change from one speed to the other is called a "quant", hence the term *quantum* mechanics. Ignore the advertising rubbish everywhere like the power of quantum cleaning or quantum health supplements. That's just companies jumping on the quantum "it-word" bandwagon.'

Following Meg's explanation so far, Ellie nodded for her to continue.

'The idea of quantum computing is that two different speeds of electrons whizzing around the nucleus might be used to store information in the binary format currently used by computers. The fast speed might represent 1 and the slow speed could mean 0, for example.'

Meg looked at Ellie, who nodded again.

'What's weird about the two speeds of the electrons is that they can be in both states at once. It is not something we can picture in our imaginations; a thing can't be going both fast and slow at the same time, but quantum mechanics says it can. This has given rise to speculation that this is an indication of parallel universes overlapping; the electron is going fast in one and slow in another. But as the worlds overlap, we see both effects here in ours. That is a very simplified version of the Many-Worlds Interpretation, although that's an older phrase. It's more commonly known as "The Multiverse" in today's science. It shows us that the impossible exists here in our universe.'

'Wow, that's so cool,' Ellie commented, thoroughly impressed.

Still trying to picture an electron going both fast and slow at the same time, all Ellie was managing was a kangaroo-hopping sort of orbit for the unlucky electron.

Jaz recognised the puzzled look on her face. 'Give it up, Johnstone,' she recommended cheerfully. 'You can't do it.'

'So, Dad was right. The impossible *does* exist.'

'According to quantum physics, yes, it does,' Meg answered her. 'Quantum theory has a lot of weird stuff in it that is difficult for our every-day imaginations to grasp. The maths of quantum physics is strange in what it seems to be telling us about the universe.'

'The impossible has *always* existed. Think about extrasensory perception, telekinesis, telepathy, levitation, the paranormal?' interjected Jaz.

'Physics says they don't exist,' countered Meg.

'No, physics, as you've just proved, says that weird stuff does exist, so why not these? People have witnessed these happening for thousands of years, but still their existence is denied. Then along comes Einstein and Co. and suddenly freaky parallel universes popping up all over the place are entirely acceptable given that *mathematics* say that they're possible. Wise women throughout the ages, many of whom were burned alive in witch trials, could have told that! Typical men! Turning up late to the party and claiming the glory for themselves!'

Ellie and Meg exchanged glances; Jaz was working up to one of her anti-men rants. Meg quickly changed the subject. 'So, have you handed your form in for the protest trip yet?'

'Yes, this morning. I gave in Flick's form at the same time, so we're all set. I do need to have a rummage in the loft for my sleeping bag, though. Are we changing into pyjamas to sleep in the Common Room? I don't know how much stuff to bring,' said Ellie.

'I vote a lock-in at the Heart to party our way through until the wee small hours, then stumble back to the Common Room in time for an hour's snooze on uncomfortable chairs. We can continue sleeping once we're on board the coach. Then we wake up in London, ready to protest, all bright-eyed and bushy-tailed,' Jaz said, successfully distracted by the new topic.

'You don't think drinking will more likely result in us being hungover and queasy?' Ellie queried.

'Nah, not if we drink lots of water.' Looking at Ellie's sceptically raised eyebrows, Jaz added, 'There is a loo on the coach, you know.'

'I hope so. If you're being social secretary for the pre-protest event, it looks like we're going to need it,' Ellie responded cynically.

'I'm in,' said Meg. She hadn't often been to the Silver Heart and was beginning to enjoy the atmosphere and ambiance of the place. She also loved the murals, which made her feel like she was on a quest in one of the online fantasy role-playing games she so enjoyed.

'OK,' Ellie agreed reluctantly. 'Me too, although I'm sticking to Diet Coke the whole evening.'

'Right, and the Pope's popping down the pub with us for a swift half!' Jaz laughed disbelievingly.

'Did Flick say whether Chris could make the trip?' Meg enquired.

209

'No, I don't think he can. He's fine, but his parents are watching him closely, half expecting the subdural bleed to reoccur. They want to keep a close eye on him for the time being.'

'I can understand that,' said Ellie. The responsibility of looking after her animals made her feel like a mother sometimes. To be a parent and come close to losing your child, even when they are an adult, must be the worst experience in the world for anyone to have to go through. That aside, Ellie supposed that Chris' surveillance by his parents would wear off after a while, or, more likely, Chris would soon get sick of the restrictions and his confinement and kick over the traces. She could only put up with a couple of days of being cooped up and cosseted herself. Although Chris, being male, could likely go for several weeks of being spoilt and waited on hand and foot before itching for something different in his routine, possibly even longer.

*Who looks after Darkall?* Ellie found herself wondering. Would he have servants at his palace—or wherever a Lord of Darkness chose to abide?

Did multi-dimensional beings even *have* dwellings?

19

# Chapter 19

When Ellie arrived home, she found a parcel waiting for her on the kitchen table.

'It came this morning,' Grace informed her while making chutney from the last of the store apples.

The strong smell of vinegar and spices wafted through the whole of downstairs. Ellie quite liked the smell, but Andy found it too much and, as an escape, was consequently digging over a corner of the vegetable patch to plant beetroot.

Ellie picked up the parcel and looked at the postmark; it was from Jill. She collected a can of Diet Coke from the fridge and took the parcel with her into the sitting room. Curling her legs up under her on the sofa, Ellie tore open the brown paper wrapping. Inside was a small blue box and a folded note. Unfolding the thick paper, Ellie read the missive.

Jill's wrote that she had been 'checking in' on Ellie and had seen the purple smudge in her aura growing darker still, from which she had deduced that Ellie was now consorting with the male energy. Jill also mentioned having conducted another reading for Ellie, but she wrote that she wouldn't go into detail in this note. Instead, she had a gift for Ellie. It had been made by Sherri—the meditation candle maker—and Jill entreated Ellie to wear it at all times.

Lifting the lid from the box and unfolding the silver tissue paper, Ellie found a bracelet made of semi-precious stones and uncut crystals caught in silver wire settings. She held the bracelet up in front of her face and examined the crystals. Seven stones hung suspended from a silver chain; each wire setting had been cleverly twisted around the individual forms of the particular crystal, holding it firmly so that it could be attached to the bracelet.

Inside the box lay a piece of card upon which the crystal's properties were listed:

Protection Crystals

Black obsidian. Good for breaking curses and defending against evil energy.

Blue kyanite. Helps you to stay focussed. Very good against psychic attack.

Hematite. Dissolves negative energy around your aura. Reduces fear of failure.

Labradorite. Defends against psychic attack and those trying to diminish your energy.

Staurolite. Essential when astral journeying as it protects against unwanted influences.

Cactus Quartz. Lessens the influence of fear and helps to maintain normal thinking.

Fluorite. Cloaks your energy and aura to foil negative attacks.

On the bottom of the card, Jill had scribbled:

*Some crystals are good for blocking negative energy or cloaking yours so that deliberate attacks miss their target. Others will keep your energy strong and turn away thrusts intended to confuse or manipulate you. Several crystals can deflect and alter the energy around you so that it becomes harmless.*

*These seven stones cover all bases. Make sure you wear it.*

*J x*

Laying the bracelet over her wrist, Ellie fastened it securely and then held her forearm up in front of the window to admire the play of light on the stones. The labradorite was the most beautiful, with a magical opalescence within it. The staurolite was perhaps the least attractive as it was brown in colour, but then it did have the shape of a cross in its crystal formation pattern to add interest. Ellie had not encountered cactus quartz before; it had the expected point at one end of the crystal wand, but all down the length of its shaft were small points of crystal poking out. The fluorite Ellie had seen before; she remembered the pretty mauves and blues swirling within the clear crystal sections. Black obsidian looked as its name suggested, and the kyanite was a deep blue; was that where the colour for cyan paint originated? Hematite was a beautiful dark silver; wasn't it magnetic, too? Ellie was sure she used to have a set of three hematite stones that would cling together.

The weight of the bracelet felt odd on her wrist, but that and the stones banging against her skin was something she'd just have to get used to. It was interesting that the stones were left in their natural state rather than being polished like the magnetic hematite she'd had as a child. Maybe they were more powerful in their unrefined state.

Ellie considered why Jill had chosen to send the bracelet. The stones had been selected for their protective properties, so Jill was obviously expecting Ellie to be attacked—and her note with the bracelet suggested as much. Aside from that, the fluorite crystal was meant to cloak her aura. When Jill had come to Owl's Ridge for dinner, she'd said that Ellie's aura was unusual and unlike any she'd seen before. Later on, Darkall had said that Ellie was light, which, at the time, made her think he could see her white aura, too. He'd also mentioned others noticing her; "creatures", he'd called them. To have had the bracelet made and sent to her now, Jill was obviously concerned for Ellie's safety. Was it linked to these creatures?

Well, at least her timing proved that Jill was very accurate in her forecasting. Ellie had already been attacked: a car had tried to run her down; a zombielike Chris had nearly shoved her into the river; and her near miss car accident now seemed less like a piece of reckless driving and more like a deliberate act of aggression.

But the protection offered by Jill's gift was against *supernatural* abilities—negative energy and psychic attacks draining her own energy and so on. Had there been any of this happening besides the more obvious natural stuff? Could she really consider the threats she'd already faced as *natural*?

From now on, she would see if she felt more in control and energised. Ellie thought she could do with another trinket that stabilised her fear, too. Maybe she needed two cactus quartz crystals? It was fear that floored her and froze her mind, preventing it from extricating itself from dangerous situations, like at the river. Instead of just spinning at the edge, she should have thrown herself flat on her belly or something—*anything*, really—other than twirling off the edge of the concrete.

*Hang on a minute. Could that be it?* Was zombified Chris actually being controlled by something else when he'd bashed into her and then gone full tilt into the bridge wall? That would certainly explain how he didn't know why he was on a bike or where he'd got it from. Everyone had assumed that it was the concussion talking when Chris had said this immediately after his accident, but maybe it wasn't. Maybe he couldn't recall these things because he had not been in control of his own body when they happened. He would also have no memory of knocking into Ellie, either, if he'd been enthralled by some mystical entity. It might well be the reason he hadn't stopped or swerved to avoid hitting the wall.

*Enthralled.* Was that the word? Or did she mean "enchanted" or "possessed"? Either way, it could well be an example of the psychic attacks Jill had been warning her about.

Ellie made a mental note to insist that her friends urgently got some protection crystals to keep about their persons. If whatever was after her could affect them, too, then they needed protecting just as much as she did. Her parents and Bertie, too.

Jill was likely already well covered in that department, but Ellie would phone her just to make sure. She could get Sherri's number from Jill at the same time and then contact her about making some more protection bracelets.

Ellie left the sitting room, walked upstairs to her room and called Jill on her mobile phone.

'Hello, Ellie. Did you get my present?'

'Yes, I did. It's lovely, thank you. I was thinking, I might want to get some for my friends, too.' Ellie dropped her voice. 'I think Flick's fella, Chris, was being controlled the other night when he nearly knocked me into the river.'

'Goodness be! Then the cards were right! They said that you had recently encountered personal danger. Psychic attack can come in many forms; possession is just one of them. You could find yourself feeling down and demotivated and all "what is the point of it all, anyway?" and not realise that others are taking your energy or directing black magic spells and curses at you. Wear the bracelet, Ellie; it will deflect a lot and keep you grounded. I can get some made for your friends, too, although they may do well with just one or two crystals as they are not the focus of the attacks.'

'Who do you think is attacking me?' Ellie asked in a quiet voice.

'I'm not sure. The cards just indicate that you are being attacked, but not by whom or what. I will try another reading later and get back to you if I gain any insight. If I had to guess, I would say you are being targeted by something that objects to the growth of your spirit energy. That would then logically lead one to the conclusion that your attacker represents the opposite of white energy and, hence, is an evil power. I won't say *dark*, as that means something different entirely for you. I trust you are keeping an open mind with your dark king of swords? Remember, he is tied to your own path.'

'I am.' The smile in Ellie's voice was obvious to Jill. 'He's ... very interesting.'

Ellie wondered whether to ask Jill's opinion about Darkall's impartiality. She took a deep breath.

'He claims to be impartial when it comes to good and evil,

and I'm having trouble understanding it. He won't come down on either side, and I can't help feeling that with his powers and abilities, he ought to be on the side of good. My dad said I have black-and-white thinking.'

'Andy is quite right; you do. The problem you have is getting beyond that. Does this male do good for you?'

'He has saved my life twice. I think he's done more than that, too. I think it's possible he's been saving me *my whole life*.'

'Then he is good for you, Ellie. He is *right* for you.'

Ellie felt a surge of relief at Jill's words. It was like she had been given official permission to like Darkall. 'But he's not someone I could ever bring home to meet my parents,' she said.

'Often the most exciting ones aren't, dear!' Jill joked. 'Now then, I must get off the line and talk to Sherri about making those protection charms for your friends. How many do you need?'

'Five. Oh—and one each for Mum, Dad and Bertie.'

'You don't need to worry about Andy, Grace and Bertie; they will be well protected already. And if they aren't, then they deserve all the negative arrows that are fired at them.'

Ellie briefly wondered why her parents would already be protected and reasoned that maybe it had something to do with their New Age beliefs. 'OK. Thank you, Jill,' she said.

'You're welcome, my dear. Don't worry, and leave the bracelets to me. I'll have them with you as soon as possible. I never could stand the devious ways others try to harm with psychic attack, so it's a pleasure to further flout the schemes of anything using such underhand methods.'

Jill rang off and Ellie lay back on her bed, placing her mobile phone on the bedside cabinet. She closed her eyes. She'd opened her bedroom window that morning as her room had been overly hot and stuffy due to the sun streaming in through her cotton curtains. Now, it allowed Ellie to hear the lawnmower and smell the sweet scent of freshly cut grass; Andy had obviously finished digging in the beetroot bed and had moved onto mowing to avoid Grace's chutney-making pong. Ellie inhaled deeply and relaxed, letting the familiar sound and smells lull her. Within minutes, she was asleep.

\* \* \*

She was floating in dark, still water. Darkness was all around her, but she sensed she was surrounded by far-reaching space, like she was floating in the underground lake of a gigantic cavern.

She felt peaceful.

Pleasantly cool rather than freezing as one might expect, the water supported her supine body. Ellie lay perfectly still, with only her breathing making small ripples in the shiny black surface. Relaxing and allowing her body to sag, she dropped beneath the surface of the water.

Ellie sank slowly through the darkness, unafraid. This was a familiar environment, and she was totally comfortable with sinking towards the bottom of the lake, however far down that was. Impossibly, Ellie could still breathe underwater, and there were no unpleasant feelings of pressure as she dropped deeper. Eventually, she gently touched down on the bottom of the lake, felt hard rock against her back, and swam slightly upwards to turn over onto her front.

Ahead of her was a speck of light; a tiny yellow-white

beacon in the darkness. Curious, Ellie swam forwards. As she approached, she could see a beam of light projecting upwards through the depths. Reaching the source, she found it to be no bigger than her fist. She moved some rocks to increase the aperture and, consequently, the brightness of the light spilling from it. Courtesy of her persistence, the hole eventually became large enough for her to swim through. Propelling herself forwards by pushing off the rocks with her hands and then her feet, she passed into the hole.

Ellie now stood in brilliant daylight. When her eyes adjusted, she saw that she was standing on the edge of a very high cliff; so high, in fact, that the landscape far below was in miniature. The ground where she stood was covered with close-cropped grass, sparse heathers and the occasional boulder; it reminded her of the moors. Ellie felt no fear of the drop; she felt as comfortable here as she had done in the dark lake.

Stepping towards the edge of the precipice, Ellie felt a strong rush of air blowing up the face of the cliff: a thermal ready to bear her aloft. Spreading her arms wide and closing her eyes, she let herself tip forwards into the updraft.

Cushioning her body and pushing against her skin as it took her weight, the thermal carried her up into the sky.

And with that, she was flying.

# 20

# Chapter 20

The following Monday was the day of the college sleepover. All day, there was an excited buzz in the Common Room, as the students taking part in the protest anticipated a fun twenty-four hours with their fellow students. The four girls were all going on the march, as was Jacob and some of his crowd. Even though Chris wasn't attending the protest, he was still going to the Silver Heart with them that evening as a halfway measure.

After their last classes of the day, Ellie and Flick set up camp in the Common Room, reserving Goth Corner with sleeping bags and rucksacks and saving comfy chairs for the other two to sleep on later. Meg and Jaz drove to Meg's house to collect her gear and the banner she'd made for the protest.

Meg was pleased with the result of her efforts; she had painted a sheet which they could all hold and walk behind. Her slogan of choice was *"Global warming: Global warning!"* As well as that, she'd also painted *"Climate Change. Going, going, gone."* onto one of her father's extra-large T-shirts, which she intended to slip on over her own clothes when they got to London.

Jaz was impressed with the handiwork; her own efforts to personalise the back of a school shirt with puffy paint had pretty much resembled a patch of colourful vomit. Not disheartened by this result, Jaz had written *"Rebuke and I'll Puke"* in permanent marker over the dry paint. She'd proudly worn the shirt for several weeks until forgetting about her custom paint job and removing her blazer in a Food Design and Technology lesson. Unfortunately for Jaz, the teacher was one of the Deputy Heads and, consequently, that episode of teenage rebellion had ended in after-school detentions and a stern letter home.

When Meg and Jaz got back to the college, they dumped their kit in the Common Room and set off walking with Ellie and Flick through the afternoon drizzle. The plan was to walk up to town, drop in on Bertie, and then get something to eat before heading for the pub.

Bertie was on his own in the library.

'I've discovered it's all because of the rain, you know,' he announced in a scholarly tone, gesturing towards the empty space. 'Water vapour gets in through the ears and chills the brain, making it less able to absorb written information. I've observed the phenomenon over many years.'

'Or could it be that they just don't want to get their purple perms wet?' teased Flick, in a jibe aimed at Bertie's new Internet taster sessions for silver surfers.

'Did you say something, Felicity dear?' Bertie queried archly, pretending not to have heard her.

Flick grinned and wandered away to browse the stacks along with Meg and Jaz. There was still half an hour until the library closed and they had time to kill.

Ellie stepped up close to Bertie. 'Can we have a quick chat?' she asked in a low voice.

Indicating his office with a nod of his head, he checked that the others were suitably occupied before following her in and quietly closing the door behind them. Sitting down in his leather swivel chair, he leaned back and placed his arms on the rests.

'What can I do for you, Ellie?' Bertie said in his more serious voice; one without the usual dramatic flair and tuneful intonation.

Ellie held up her arm so that the cuff of her sleeve fell back to reveal her crystal bracelet. Bertie sat forwards in his chair to see it more clearly.

'I'm afraid I can't take it off for you to have a look at,' Ellie explained. 'Jill was most definite about me wearing it at all times.'

Bertie peered at the crystals through his half-round spectacles. 'I can see why. That is a powerful set of stones you have there. Jill gave it to you, you say? In that case, I would *most definitely* not take it off. That woman knows what she's doing when it comes to protection crystals.'

'Bertie, I was worried about you. I appear to be under attack, in the physical sense as well as psychically, as do the people around me.' She briefly shared her thoughts on Chris' possession. 'And I wanted to make sure that you're safe from whatever is fixated on me,' she finished.

'Sweet girl, of course you did. But then, it is ever your nature to protect those you care about. But you needn't have worried; I have my own means of protection. And I also have the added bonus of this.'

Bertie pulled at the side of his shirt collar and leaned his neck away from his finger. Ellie could see a mark that started at the bottom of his neck and disappeared under his shirt. *The top of a glyph, maybe, or a tattoo?*

'It's a sigil,' he said. 'And a powerful one at that. It wards off evil influence. I received it many years ago.'

For a moment, his eyes unfocussed and he seemed to be seeing a different time, then, with a small shake of his head, he pulled himself back into the room with Ellie.

'Now, I am not suggesting that you go and get yourself tattooed all over, but I find it suits me well as I don't have to worry about losing it. It also makes me look rather dashingly butch, don't you think?'

Ellie smiled.

'I do have a pair of rather attractive black onyx cufflinks that dear Jilly Dilly once gave me, but they don't go with this suit.' Seeing Ellie's still uncertain face, he added reassuringly, 'I am well covered, Ellie. There's really no need to worry.'

A sudden rapping on the glass of the office door interrupted their conversation.

'What are you two up to in there? Snaffling all the biscuits, I suppose. Come on, Bertie, shut up early so we can go for tea. I'm starving!' Flick demanded.

'Whatever the lady wants, the lady gets,' declared Bertie resignedly, and he reached for his coat from the hook by the door as he ushered Ellie out of the office.

'Well, ladies,' he said, locking the office door, 'shall we adjourn to The Parlour for our late afternoon repast?'

Jaz and Meg eagerly headed for the exit while Ellie, Flick and Bertie brought up the rear.

'Goodnight, my charges,' Bertie called to the empty library before quietly closing the door.

The five friends walked at a leisurely pace along Castle Street, past its namesake, and into the top end of Lowford High Street. The Parlour was a snug tea room in an old stone building. The owners—Sandra and Tim Blenfield—had earned a good reputation for home-cooked vegan food. They valued their customers, encouraged them to dawdle over coffee, and perhaps to select something to read from the bookshelves lining an entire wall of the comfortable upstairs tearoom.

A bell rang as Bertie opened the door from the street, and a delicious waft of savoury aromas greeted them. Sandra immediately bustled forwards, smiling at Bertie and welcoming him back. She then launched into a description of which of today's dishes Bertie would most enjoy before also warmly greeting his companions.

'Ellie and her friends are all ravenous, Sandra dear,' Bertie announced. 'I do hope you've got a large pan on the stove with enough to feed us all.'

Once they were all comfortably seated at a table towards the rear of the room, Sandra brought over a tabletop chalkboard listing today's menu. She left them to consider the mouth-watering choices, before returning a few minutes later with a note pad and pen.

'What can I get you?' she asked with a smile.

'As always, I am in a quandary. Too many lovely choices and a lack of decision,' lamented Bertie. 'Ladies, you order first, please, and then I'll know which meal to order to prevent it from feeling unloved.'

Having made a speedy note of their order, Sandra delivered it to Tim in the kitchen. Moments later, she returned with a jug of iced water and glasses, before slipping away to tend to her other customers.

'So, my young anarchists, are you all set to storm the Bastille tomorrow? Invade the echoing halls of Westminster? March upon the country's leaders and demand they act to save our world before it is too late?'

'Yes,' answered Meg plainly. Not knowing Bertie as well as the others, she thought that he might be making fun of them. 'We are all prepared and willing to make our voices heard,' she added.

'Excellent, my dear.' Bertie smiled and nodded in approval. 'It is about time that people stand up and be counted on climate change. It's all very well avoiding one's own respon- sibilities by saying "Oh well, what's the point when China are vast polluters and America allows everyone to drive around in gas guzzlers?" but change is like an avalanche or landslide. Once you get a few pebbles rolling, the rest will eventually follow behind. Lead by example; *that* is what the people of this country have always been good at.'

Meg relaxed and blushed slightly pink with pleasure at his approval. 'I've made a banner and a T-shirt,' she said.

Bertie smiled in delight and clapped his hands. 'Clever girl! I shall look out for you on BBC News tomorrow.'

Bertie and Meg then settled into a conversation on the various ways in which mankind's stupidity was killing their own planet. During this exchange, Flick and Jaz had been speaking in low voices while Ellie gazed across the room and out of the café windows.

'Penny for them,' said Jaz, seeing that Ellie's thoughts were clearly elsewhere.

Ellie smiled. 'I don't think they're worth that much.'

'Nice bracelet, by the way,' said Flick, noticing the trinket on Ellie's arm.

'Actually, I wanted to talk to you about that,' said Ellie, clearing her throat. 'Jill had this made for me. All the crystals are intended to protect me in various ways from psychic attack.'

'Once more, in English?' asked Flick.

'Negative energy, curses, black magic. Others trying to drain your energy. Manipulation, possession ...'

'*Jeez*. Do you actually need protecting from all that?' asked Flick.

'Yes—and not just me. You do, too.'

In a quiet voice, Ellie then explained her theory about Chris' accident.

At first, Flick looked incredulous, but, as Ellie quietly stated the facts, her expression changed to thoughtfulness. 'You're saying that *any of us* could be the next targets?' she asked.

'I'm not sure. I don't know why Chris was chosen, or whether some of us are more susceptible to psychic suggestion than others. Jill believes that whatever is after me is evil, which could be why it had no qualms about crashing Chris head first into a stone wall. I don't really know what's going on, just that things are changing and I'm mixed up in the middle of it. I'm groping around in the dark and I can't give you the answers you need, as I don't have them myself. But I'm certain I don't want to take risks with your safety, so I've asked Jill to get some more crystal protection jewellery made. I'd like each of you to wear your piece at all times. And yes,' Ellie nodded at Flick, seeing the query in her face, 'I have asked for some for Chris, too. And for Vi.'

Jaz nodded seriously. 'It would be foolish *not* to wear it, even if you don't believe you'll be under attack from whatever it is that's out there. Thank you for thinking of us, Ellie.'

'How could I not?' Ellie replied. 'You guys are like family to me.'

Just then, the kitchen door opened and Sandra emerged, carrying a tray bearing their starters. The conversation ceased, to be replaced with delighted sounds of approval and declarations of thanks.

The meal was delicious and pleasantly light on the stomach, as it contained no meat. Having cleared their plates thoroughly, they sat back replete and in good spirits.

Flick's mood had lightened following their earlier discussion. She had been brooding on Ellie's theory about Chris' accident and had come to the conclusion that it made more sense than Chris having had some kind of blackout. Flick was naturally scared that this indicated there were forces able to take control of the human mind, but that fear was tempered by the knowledge that this could be prevented from happening.

'Do you think Chris was particularly susceptible?' Flick asked Ellie, breaking the companionable silence.

'I'm sorry, I don't know. Possibly. Why else would he have been chosen and not some other bloke?' Ellie thought for a moment., 'Bertie, Chris likes tattoos. Perhaps you could have a chat with Flick about sigils? It might be wise for Chris to add another tattoo to his collection.'

'Delighted to,' Bertie said helpfully.

Sandra arrived at the table to clear their plates and to ask if anyone would like a dessert.

'I am replete, thank you, my dear, but the ladies might have a corner left unfilled?' Bertie looked at the girls, but they all shook their heads.

'No, thank you,' Flick said politely, adding quietly to the rest of them once Sandra had left to prepare their bill, 'need to keep some free space for alcohol.'

'And there's me thinking we're staying teetotal tonight to be wide awake and enthusiastic at the protest march?' Ellie looked at her in mock surprise.

'I think you'll find I can be enthusiastic on very little sleep,' replied Flick.

'And I'm sure Chris could confirm that for us, were he here,' Jaz remarked cheekily.

They all smiled except Flick, who, fixing Jaz with a hard stare, said, 'I think, Jazmine, that you had better save your smutty remarks for a more suitable venue. Ladies, shall we head to the pub?'

'Good idea,' said Bertie. 'I, too, have an appointment and so must not dally any longer. I wish you all the best and shall bid you *adieu*. Sandra will put this on my tab as my treat, and I shall count myself privileged to have been responsible for supplying the fearless protesters with sufficient nourishment to sustain them on the morrow.'

Bertie stood and wrapped himself in his long coat. He gave a final wave and left amid a chorus of thanks, the bell on the door musically marking his departure.

'Well, ladies, we have some drinking to be doing, so let's get cracking,' said Flick, heading for the door.

\* \* \*

The Silver Heart was fairly quiet, which wasn't uncustomary for a Monday evening, but already there were several faces from the Common Room propping up the bar when the girls

228

arrived. Ellie went to the bar to buy the first round while the others chose their base for the evening.

'What's with the student invasion, then?' asked Col, the barman. 'We don't usually see you lot until Thursday's live music or Friday's disco.'

'There's a climate change protest in London tomorrow and a group of us are going up on a coach. Basically, it's an excuse for a crash-over party in the Common Room and a jolly up to London. Of course, we're all very concerned about global warming, too,' Ellie added, not wishing to sound too flaky.

Col grinned. 'Sure you are. Very worried indeed. So, what'll it be?'

'Three bottles of Becks and a pint of blackcurrant and soda, please, Col.'

'Coming right up.'

Delivering the drinks to their table, Ellie pulled up a chair and sat down. The others were talking eagerly about their extended trip to London. They had decided as a group that, having taken the time and trouble to get themselves up to the capital, it was worth staying there for a short while to make all those travel miles worthwhile. Pursuing this train of thought to its logical conclusion, they reasoned that the best thing to do to mitigate their carbon footprint would be to stay over and enjoy the next day exploring the capital, before taking the train home later that afternoon.

To this end, Ellie had called in a favour from one of her father's old friends; an erudite sixty-year-old called Charles Thomas Mackworth, or Titch for short. Titch had been more than happy to oblige Ellie; assuring them that his three-bedroom maisonette in Notting Hill could comfortably accommodate them all. He'd even offered to take them all out to dinner on Tuesday evening at one of his favourite restaurants.

'I can't wait to get there and do some shopping,' declared Flick. 'I want to check out Portobello Market. I know it's not the antique one until Saturday, but Monday to Wednesday is fashion, bric-a-brac and fruit and veg.'

'Glad to see you're paying attention to your five-a-day consumption,' remarked Jaz.

'Well, of course,' replied Flick sweetly, 'and while doing so, I shall be fulfilling my wardrobe needs, too.'

'I'm really excited to see the museum,' Meg enthused. Titch worked at the British Museum and had promised to show the girls the behind-the-scenes world of his department on Wednesday. 'You do know some very cool people, Ellie, I have to say.'

Ellie grinned. 'I do—and I'm looking at three of them.' She raised her glass and took a drink of the blackcurrant and soda.

'Aww, you'll make us blush,' said Flick as she and the other two smiled.

'I wonder which is Titch's favourite restaurant?' pondered Meg. 'I haven't packed anything posh, so I hope it's not too upmarket.'

'Don't worry,' soothed Flick. 'The scruffier you look in posh restaurants, the better they treat you, as they think you're probably an incognito A-lister. Pick up some shades from a street stall and you're all set. *Fact.*'

'I can do that,' grinned Meg.

'I can do aloof and condescending, which seems to be the stat persona of a bona fide A-lister,' Jaz said with her usual cynicism.

'We're all sorted, then. Look out, London—here we come!'

'I'll drink to that!'

They raised their drinks and clinked glasses together before taking a swig.

'Mine's going down rather fast. Anyone up for Round Two?' Jaz asked.

'Said the vicar to the tart,' laughed Flick. 'But yes, please, missus, I'm in for seconds. Ellie, you sure you won't have just one? It'll help you sleep on the coach, you know.'

'Well, if you put it like that, then I'd better. A beer please, Jaz, but purely for medicinal purposes, of course. I have been known to suffer from coach-induced insomnia,' she added with a wink.

'And I may get a lack-of-alcohol-induced travel sickness, so mine's another Beck's, please, babe,' added Meg.

'Just call me Dr Beer,' grinned Jaz, getting up and heading for the bar.

It was slightly busier in the back bar now that several other groups of students had arrived, plus there were some regulars also now at the bar. A delighted shriek from Flick alerted Ellie to the arrival of Chris and his brother, Tom. Flick stood up and waved unnecessarily at Chris, who was already making his way over to their table.

'Hey, gorgeous,' he said to Flick, putting his arm around her waist and kissing her.

Flick reached up with her hand and cupped the side of his face as their kiss deepened.

'OK, Time Out!' announced Jaz, returning with the drinks and looking distastefully at the snogging couple. 'Chris, what are you having?'

'I'm cool, thanks; my bro has funds tonight. Mum actually

gave us forty quid to get out of the house and enjoy ourselves, so we're all good.'

Chris drew up a chair and sat next to Flick, draping his arm around her shoulders.

'It's good to see you back to your normal self,' Ellie said, smiling at the pair of them.

Tom brought drinks over to their table and placed one in front of Chris. 'There you go, bro. Mater's round. Enjoy.'

'Cheers, man. You know Ellie, Jaz and Meg, right?'

'I know *of* them, sure. You helped my brother,' Tom said, specifically addressing his words to Ellie. 'If you ever need anything, just ask.'

'Thanks. I will.' Ellie blushed slightly and smiled at Tom, who nodded and turned away to join his friends at another table. There was a short silence, broken by Chris clearing his throat.

'Ellie, Flick said you helped my recovery in some way; that without you, I wouldn't be here having a pint but still in hospital after having had my head opened up on the operating table. I don't know exactly what you did, but thank you.'

Ellie smiled, blushing even more, and looked down at the table.

'What do you remember about the accident, Chris?' Meg asked.

'Not that much, really. I remember being in the pub with you guys, then driving the car back to mine and throwing the keys to Tom. I started walking back to the pub, but from then onwards, I can't remember much else until coming round covered in blood and my head hurting like hell. I have some pretty impressive bruises, but I don't actually know what caused them, other than through other people telling me I

232

hit a wall.'

'Do you remember seeing me?' Ellie asked in a small voice.

Chris thought for a moment and looked down at his pint, rather embarrassed. Flick nudged him gently, and when he looked at her, she gave him a reassuring nod. Chris cleared his throat again.

'I think so. It's the only memory I've got from between me heading back to the pub and the pain and blood bit. But it's a bit weird, though. Maybe more of a dream, really.'

He coughed again, clearly uncomfortable. Ellie waited for him to continue.

'You were there, all lit up, like an angel on top of a Christmas tree. You were spinning, and there was all this light around you. You were sort of blurred by light.'

Jaz looked puzzled, but Meg said, 'How do you mean "blurred?"'

'I can't really describe it. I knew it was you, Ellie, but you didn't look … normal. You were kinda giving off a bright light, with an outline of you in there somewhere.'

Chris stopped speaking. He looked back down at his pint, and Flick put her hand over his.

'I told Chris he needed to tell you,' Flick said. 'I thought it might be important to … you know, the *weird* stuff?'

Ellie gave a small smile. 'Maybe. Thanks for telling me, Chris.'

'There was one more thing, Ellie. It sounds stupid, but when I think of the picture of light-up you, I get a memory of fear. I've no idea why, but then I've no idea why I seem to have a memory of you lit up, either.'

'I told him it is *not* OK to be thinking of other girls, but if you scare him, I guess it's OK, after all,' Flick joked, trying to make Chris less uncomfortable. She gave his hand a squeeze as Meg exchanged a knowing look with Jaz.

'Right,' said Jaz. 'Anyone up for a game of pool? I'll take on all challengers.'

'Me,' said Chris, gladly accepting Jaz's challenge.

'Cool. Game on,' Jaz replied, and she and Chris left for the pool room.

When they had gone, Ellie looked at Flick and Meg before speaking. 'That's the third time someone has connected me to light. I don't get what that means, exactly, but it seems to be a reoccurring theme.'

'I'm sure my aunt would have some thoughts on this,' said Meg.

'Who else told you that you were light?' Flick asked.

'Jill was the first, from an aura reading she did when I was a baby. The second was …' Ellie paused, deliberating over how much to tell her friends. 'The second was the guy I mentioned at Bertie's the other night; the one who's been saving my life. His name is Darkall, and he's always there to stop me from coming to harm.'

She looked at the other two to gauge their reactions.

'This is the mystery guy, right? Clark Kent?'

Elie nodded.

'Phew,' Flick exhaled loudly. 'This is some pretty big shit then, I guess.'

Ellie nodded again and gave Flick a rueful look. 'That's one way of putting it.'

'I missed something here,' Meg complained. 'Clark Kent?'

'Because he keeps saving me. It's Flick's nickname for Darkall.'

'So he's not a normal guy, then? He's someone with

extranormal abilities?' Meg clarified.

'Yes, that's a fair description, I suppose,' Ellie agreed with a wry smile.

'Sounds to me like you've got your own guardian spirit or spirit guide.'

'What's that?' Flick looked at Meg.

'As my aunt explained it to me, guardian spirits are meant to protect you. They can keep you from harm, even if that harm is physical in nature. Some think they can actually put a shield of energy around you and stop you from getting into dangerous situations.'

Ellie's interest was piqued.

'What about controlling a car? Do you think a spirit guide could do that?'

'It's possible, I suppose.'

'I told you that you had a guardian angel!' Flick said smugly. 'Do you have anything else, Meg?'

'Well, there are other types of spirit guide—*many* others, according to some. There are messenger guides, who might turn up when your life's changing direction and you need help making the right choices. They communicate their guidance through dreams, symbols and patterns. Besides those, there are also gatekeeper guides, who help you to pass to the next life after you die, but they're also around in this life if you need them. They'll show you the doors between realms and can protect you from negative forces when passing through these portals or travelling psychically, like in astral projection. Then there are healing guides and teaching guides. Their names are kind of self-explanatory, but healer guides can also be useful when you're healing others. This seems particularly relevant to you, Ellie'—Meg

235

lowered her voice—'after what you did for Chris.'

'Anything else?' queried an eager Flick.

'Teacher guides will introduce you to people who can teach you whatever you need to know to face a given situation. It is their responsibility that you learn what you're supposed to.'

Taking a sip of her drink, Ellie considered Darkall. 'I think he might be all of those things,' she said.

Meg looked thoughtful. 'In that case, he's obviously very important to you. The question is, why has he arrived in your life now?'

'I think he's always been there, Meg. I just didn't see it.'

'Then that makes him even more important to you—and *for* you, I would think.'

'He is,' said Ellie with a small smile.

'Well, who knew? It only took Superman for this chick to fall in love!' said Flick, lightening the atmosphere.

The three girls smiled at the truth in her statement as Jaz returned to the table, just in time to hear the end of Flick's remark.

'Finally fessed up, has she? Good. In that case, when do we get to meet this tall, dark and handsome guy? I'm assuming he *is* tall, dark and handsome?'

'Amazingly so,' grinned Ellie.

# 21

# Chapter 21

The Common Room housed a mixed batch of sleepers and rioters when the girls returned from the Silver Heart. Not wanting to join in with the drunken antics of some of their classmates, the four friends settled themselves in their pre-arranged corner. Ellie handed out small bottles of water and insisted that everyone drank all of theirs before allowing themselves to fall asleep.

'Yes, Mum, or should that be Doctor Johnstone?' Flick teased, before realising the startling truth in that nickname and looking uncomfortable. 'Sorry. I didn't mean to make a jibe.'

'You didn't. You've always called me that, and I don't expect you to stop now. I don't want you to change towards me at all. Any of you.' Ellie looked around at her friends. 'You, Bertie and Jill are the ones keeping me sane at the moment. If it weren't for you, I would have had myself committed by now.'

'And your folks?' asked Jaz quietly, looking up at Ellie from the book she'd just opened.

Ellie looked uncomfortable. 'I can't tell them. Not yet. I know they're open-minded and New Age and stuff, but *this*? And happening to their only daughter? My dad would *freak*. I'll get around to talking it over with them soon, but I'm just not ready. I need to know more myself before I can face answering their inevitable barrage of questions. You guys just accept what is happening and don't make me feel like I have to justify myself all the time. But it won't be the same from them, and I couldn't stand the disappointed, confused, disbelieving looks my folks would give me if I laid all this on them right now.'

'You are protecting them, when they would argue that it is their job to protect *you*,' Meg ventured.

'But that's the point. They can't protect me from whatever this is. I have to protect them.'

'Your parents are long-time friends of Bertie and Jill; think about that for a moment. I think you might be underestimating them, Ellie,' surmised Jaz. 'If you were my child, I would want to know about something as huge as this.'

Ellie shook her head slightly, her mind lost in thought. Maybe she *had* been underestimating her parents. Perhaps she ought to open up to them when she got back from London.

A while later, all was quiet in the Common Room, save for the sound of deep breathing and gentle snoring. All too soon, the brash lesson bell sounded their wake-up call, shocking the roomful of sleeping students into sudden wakefulness.

'*Bloody hell!*' shouted Flick as the bell sounded. 'I've gone deaf.'

When the bell stopped, an overly bright and lively Student Union officer addressed the stirring, grumbling room. 'OK.

Loos for poos, people! You don't want to have to use a Portaloo in London, and we definitely don't want you having to go on the coach!'

In just three quarters of an hour, everyone going on the trip was on the moving bus and trying to get themselves comfy enough to go back to sleep, which was no mean feat when the legroom was budget and the seats were not designed for lolling heads. Ellie and her friends, however, did manage to fall sleep after a while, and the coach carried its slumbering cargo on through the night.

Ellie, who was sitting between a dribbling Flick and the window, took longer to nod off than the others. She was thinking over what had been said at the pub about spirit guides. It made sense for Darkall to be a guardian, as he had saved her from harm many times. The theory also explained the swerving car, if she considered him to be one of these types of spirit guides. But then, according to Meg's list, he was also a messenger spirit guide who had repeatedly communicated the pattern of his spiral ward to her. He could also be a gatekeeper, too, ready to show her the doors between worlds.

In fact, the more Ellie thought about it, the more he might well have many wonderfully strange things to teach her.

Was Meg right? Did Darkall have a hand in the increase in potency and the effectiveness of her healing ability? What was it that Meg had said? Something about healing spirit guides being by your side while you're healing others. Maybe Darkall had been involved in Chris' miraculous recovery.

*But then, Darkall doesn't follow either good or evil. Surely healing someone can only be a good deed?*

Maybe there was another entity present when she was

239

healing, something other than Darkall?

There were the dreams, too. Meg had said that messenger spirit guides use dreams to communicate with their charge. Ellie had certainly dreamt some weirdly real and portent-like dreams lately. First, the corridor with the immense smooth black wall and its single door, then the path in the wood that led back to the corridor. The third dream in the sequence had involved her opening the door and entering the room, with the heartbeat thrumming through the very air. More recently, she'd dreamt of the still, black lake and the high clifftop. On reflection, it seemed that these dreams had been leading her to Darkall, but having reached him, were they now possibly trying to tell her of her next step? Could a messenger spirit guide be putting them into her head? If so, maybe the messenger guide wasn't Darkall, either. Maybe there were several other spirit guides involved in guiding her down her preordained path.

Ellie stared at the dark window glass, looking out onto the early twilight motorway. For a split second, two silver-purple eyes looked back at her. Involuntarily, her hand rose to touch the cool glass, but the eyes vanished virtually as soon as they had appeared and she couldn't make contact with them. Darkall was simply letting her know that he was with her.

Smiling to herself and feeling comfortingly safe, Ellie pulled her blanket up over her shoulder, tucked it in around her back and neck and settled into sleep.

* * *

When morning arrived, the coach pulled into a motorway

service station. Yawning, bleary-eyed students disembarked, carrying rucksacks containing makeup and washbags—or, at least, those conscious of their appearance and dental hygiene were. Others headed straight for McDonalds, Costa or Greggs. After refreshing themselves in the Ladies, the four friends wandered into McDonalds and found a free table.

'OK, so is it McMuffins all round, or is anyone crazily heading off in a hotcake and maple syrup direction?' asked Jaz.

'Guilty as charged,' answered Flick. 'I'm having the hot-cakes and sausage.'

'Call me boring but I'm having the fruit and maple oatmeal. My tummy just doesn't like anything too exciting when I'm travelling.'

'Cool, I'll go and order, and you can give me the cash when I get back.'

Jaz went over to a self-order kiosk.

'She's very overbearing, you know,' Flick confided to Meg. 'Don't let Miss Bossy Britches walk all over you.'

Meg smiled. 'I think she's met her match in me. I don't take orders easily either.'

Flick realised that this was actually quite true; quiet, thoughtful Meg was no one's fool. She listened to and considered what was being said before passing comment and her remarks were always pertinent and delivered in a calm manner. She was very good for the sometimes rather self-opinionated Jaz.

Making idle conversation, they watched the big screen above the serving counter until their order number changed from "preparing" to "ready". Jaz got back up to collect the trays and Meg went with her.

'I do like Meg,' Flick said quietly to Ellie.

'Yes, me too. She's just slotted right in, as if she's always been part of our gang.'

'Heads up! Move the purses, please,' said Jaz, returning with the trays of food. She put her full tray down onto the tabletop, and Meg set a second one down beside it.

'Ok, now I want hotcakes,' complained Meg, having seen Flick's meal.

'I'll let you have a taste if you're good and eat up all your porridge.' Flick winked.

Jaz pulled a face at Meg's oatmeal. 'If you'd chosen anything other than that, I'd have swapped with you, but frankly—*yuck.*'

'Wow, true love at its finest,' teased Ellie with a grin.

'Talking of which, isn't that Jacob with Lily draped all over him in the corner by the window?'

They all turned to look. Sensing that he was the focus of attention, Jacob looked up and then waved at Ellie. Lily, however, cast a hard look towards Ellie's table and, grabbing Jacob's upraised hand in her own, leaned in towards him for a snog.

'And that is a prime example of persistence finally paying off,' Jaz commented drily.

'And also a prime example of why one should always carry a protection talisman against the Evil Eye,' added Meg. 'Anyone got an Eye of Horus on them? No? Well, we could be in deep trouble here, judging by the look that's just scorched Ellie's skin!'

Smiling, they returned to their meals. After finishing, they put their waste into the recycling bins and wandered out of the restaurant to browse around the service's shop. Ellie always felt tempted to buy one of the large cardboard trays of Krispy Kreme doughnuts which looked so temptingly American and delicious, but she couldn't justify buying twelve of them for herself and was sure she wouldn't want to share them. The bus was due to leave in twenty minutes, so Ellie returned to the restroom for a final freshen-up. Meg opted to go with her while the others remained in the shopping area.

As the pair retraced their steps back past McDonalds, a group of men walked towards them. The men were loud and leery and looked like a stag party or a group of football fans. They had clearly been drinking despite the early hour or were perhaps still drinking from the night before. Ellie and Meg walked towards the side of the corridor to avoid the group. As the men passed, making unwanted offers of their company to the girls, Ellie recoiled from the haze of stale beer and cigarette smoke that surrounded them.

A late-middle-aged man at the back of the group, a whisky drinker judging from the fumes coming off him and his unsteady gait, lurched towards the girls. 'It's you, ain't it? The shiny one. All glittery and delicious,' he said, squinting at Ellie.

'Leave the nice young ladies alone now, Matt.' His mate grabbed his arm and forcibly led him up the corridor away from Ellie and Meg.

'All shiny light. They're going to love you, they are!' the whisky drinker called back to Ellie before his mate's suggestion to have another swig took his attention away from the girls.

'Why are there always drunk people that think it's OK to accost perfect strangers with irrelevant babble and general bollocks wherever I go?' Meg asked in an exasperated voice.

Ellie, however, was quiet. She had a nasty feeling that what she'd just heard was very relevant to her and also likely connected with her fate: it had almost felt prophetic. Did being drunk make you easier to manipulate and control psychically? She thought so; it seemed logical that if being inebriated made you less inhibited, then your barriers were down, so to speak, and you would, therefore, be more open to attack.

On the coach, everyone settled back into their seats bar two missing people. The Student Union representative stood agitatedly at the front of the coach with clipboard in hand, glancing frequently at her watch. Some ten minutes later, Jacob and Lily came running across the car park. Lily was giggling and was rather pink in the face, and Jacob had the label sticking out of his T-shirt. They made their way down the coach aisle to their seats at the back, both grinning.

'Three guesses what held them up,' said Jaz, leaning across the aisle and speaking in a low voice to Ellie and Flick.

'Going on reputation, I'd imagine it was the cubicle wall and her foot on the toilet seat that held her up. That, and Jacob's tent pole,' sniggered Flick.

'I was told that engaging in that sort of activity made your hair curly,' added Ellie in an innocent voice.

'If that were the case, Lily over there would be styling tight ringlets by now.'

Flick's remark made Ellie snigger.

'Hey, your hair's curly—what have you been up to, Miss Johnstone?' Flick demanded as Ellie tossed her loose red curls over her shoulder. 'Have you seen more of this mystery man of yours than you're letting on—and, by more, I mean literally *more,* in the physical sense of his delectable body?'

'Not yet, but there's still hope,' Ellie giggled.

'Hoisted by your own petard there, Ellie,' said Jaz with a smile.

'She definitely appears blown away by this guy's petard,' Flick remarked, giving Ellie a wink and a thumbs up.

# 22

# Chapter 22

Central London was always congested, but as over two hundred coaches from all corners of the land brought protesters to the city, it was even more so today. Ellie's coach joined a line of others crawling along the top of Hyde Park, each depositing its human cargo before preparing to move as instructed by the traffic stewards in luminous march tabards.

The march was due to begin mid-morning, and the Student Union rep had told them to be ready to start walking as soon as they arrived. Beginning in Park Lane, the protest march would end up outside the Houses of Parliament, where there would be speeches in Parliament Square before everyone disbursed. The route itself was under two miles, but at the pace the march would be moving, it was expected to take several hours. Taking into account time for the speeches and an hour or so to get out of what by then would be a very overcrowded part of London, Ellie and her friends expected to be free to pursue their own plans somewhere around two or three o'clock that afternoon.

Everyone on Ellie's coach was in high spirits as they finally filed off. Just to be part of something so huge and involving so many like-minded people was very energising. Hefting their backpacks onto their shoulders, the students of Lowford College joined the flow of humanity walking towards Park Lane. Ellie could already hear whistles blowing and drums being beaten up ahead. Skirting the edge of the park, they cut off Speaker's Corner and arrived in Park Lane by the Animals in War memorial.

This particular memorial always made Ellie feel so sad. The soldiers had gone bravely to war arguably conscious of at least some of the horrors they were likely to face, but the animals had had no say, just like now. Mankind seemed to greedily use its fellow creatures for its own means regardless of the pain, suffering and terror caused to them. Sometimes, Ellie felt that the best course of action for this planet would be for mankind to be wiped out entirely. Then the planet might have a chance to recover and another species could have a shot at being the dominant one—maybe the insects.

But, then again, amid all this hateful treatment of animals, there were still some people who were outstanding defenders and protectors of the natural world; people who risked their own lives to stop the cruelty and to rescue animals. Nothing important was ever that clear-cut; there were always shades of grey that prevented any logical argument from reaching a definite conclusion. Ellie supposed she had just summed herself up, in a way. She wanted black and white, wanted there to be a good guy and a bad guy and for the bad guy to get stopped and punished, but life was never going to be that simple—and certainly not for *her*, if events of late were anything to go by.

The march organisers, as well as the protesters themselves,

were intensifying the energy levels of the crowd all around them. Ellie could almost feel an electrical current running along the street, through the air and under her feet; the energy in the area was virtually tangible.

Looking around at other protesters and listening to the accents of the voices around them, it was clear that people from all over the country and of all classes and ages had descended on London to make their voices heard. Numerous people sported green hats, hair dyed green or green face paint. Others were dressed entirely in green or even in fancy dress; Ellie saw an orangutan, a horse and a tree in the first twenty minutes alone.

The general air was one of a carnival, but there was also an undercurrent of anger and injustice. One group of protesters had an enormous inflatable banana and were chanting as loudly as they could:

'Where do we stick Banana?
   Up pollution's arse!
   Which way? This way!
   How far? All the way!'

Periodically, the chant would substitute the word "pollution" for a politician or country's name, and several superpowers were featured deservedly heavily. Many members of the crowd around the "Banana" group joined in the chant, and fists were punched into the air in time with the shouted refrain.

Meg dropped her backpack to the ground and unpacked her tightly-rolled banner and T-shirt. Putting the latter on over her outer clothes, she grinned and got Jaz to hold one

248

end of the painted sheet. Meg had made four padded handles along the top of the sheet to enable them to hold it more comfortably for a prolonged period. The sheet was hemmed, too, turned over two or three times so that the folded fabric made the sheet slightly stiffer around the edges and less floppy.

'I'm very impressed, Meg,' complimented Ellie sincerely. 'This banner is very well made.'

'She put a lot of time into it,' Jaz reported proudly.

Meg blushed and grinned 'Ellie, swap with Jaz, please, so that she's on the end and you're on one of the middle handles. I've given Jaz a lecture about how best to hold it so the words stand out well,' she explained.

Taking up the handle Jaz had recently vacated, Ellie smelled a faint waft of lavender and something else vaguely familiar. *Rosemary?* Maybe it was Meg's mum's washing powder or flowery fabric conditioner.

Just before the off, organisers in luminous jackets began shouting final instructions down megaphones, informing the crowd that the march would soon be underway and to please keep an eye on children. Also, they advised, that if there was a medical emergency, attendees were to approach a march organiser or one of the police officers lining the route.

'Pay attention, please, Flick,' joked Jaz. 'We don't want a little lost Felicity before the end of the day, now do we?'

'I'll try my best not to get lost, *Mum*,' replied Flick in a childish voice, putting her thumb in her mouth.

'Here,' said Jaz, shepherding Flick to the middle of the banner next to Ellie. 'You'd better go in between Mummy and Mummy so we can keep an eye on you.' Jaz looked at Meg with a grin.

'Kids these days,' remarked Meg with a resigned sigh. 'She clearly takes after you, dear.'

'Christ, now there's a thought!' said Jaz. 'If we do have kids one day, they'd better have your genes. If my kids are going to turn out like Flick, then they'd be better off staying as a twinkle in their mummy's eye!'

'*That*, I take personal offense to,' said Flick.

'OK, that's enough, you two,' Ellie grumbled. 'I'm not spending the next few hours stuck behind a sheet with the pair of you tearing strips off one another the whole time!'

Jaz caught Flick's eye, and they both sniggered.

'Better behind it than *under* it!' said Flick provocatively.

'Keep your mind on the march, please, ladies,' said Meg, lifting her chin with a prudish air.

'Sorry, dear,' Jaz replied meekly.

Meg grinned at her. 'You can come under *my* sheet anytime,' she offered with a quietly suggestive smile.

'Now there's an offer I can't refuse.' Jaz grinned.

An air horn sounded, and the noise of the march increased. They were off, but not in any real sense because the protesters in Ellie's segment had to wait for those ahead of them to move off first. This took quite some time. Ellie imagined that from the air, there must have been a pleasing ripple effect to be seen, like cars pulling away from a hold-up on the motorway.

Finally, the wave of motion reached them, and they were off with the tide. The noise was intense; marching drums were vigorously beaten, and protesters were shouting slogans and waving placards. Ellie read "Change politicians, NOT the climate", "Stop it, Sort it, Save it" and "Fossil Fuels my Anger", along with many other slogans, all painted or written on cardboard, plywood and fabric. Somewhere, there was a bass drum being played as its deep percussive beat was the most noticeable, the whole procession imitating a living creature with the bass as its thumping heartbeat.

After an hour or so of walking, the crowd thickened as more people joined the procession from connecting side streets. A sudden surge of bodies from the right jostled the four friends behind their sheet banner. Jaz must have moved quickly out of the way to avoid being bumped into, as suddenly she was standing behind them with Meg, making the sheet wrap around all four of them. The surge moved on, passing them, and Meg and Jaz returned to their previous positions at opposite ends of the banner, unwrapping the other two.

'You nearly had me over, then,' grumbled Flick.

'Sorry, I was jostled,' came Jaz's brief reply.

Their section of the march was now entering Whitehall, having already passed Charing Cross roundabout with the statue of Charles I on horseback at its centre. Flick, who was getting hungry, suggested popping into McDonalds as they passed, but Meg was insistent that they stay behind the banner and complete the route before stopping for lunch. On down Westminster they walked, past the Women of World War II memorial, until, ahead of them, they could see the Cenotaph.

Ellie's feet were falling in time with the beat of a nearby drum, the banner held tautly to either side of her by Flick and Meg acting as a guide for her forward motion. Ellie closed her eyes and breathed in the smells of the city: exhaust fumes; cooked food; a hint of refuse; human bodies and the chemical fragrances sprayed on them.

On the inside of her eyelids, a picture formed. It was the

street, but not as it was normally seen. The shapes of the buildings appeared shadowy and portrayed in subdued hues. In contrast, the huge swell of bright yellow energy coming from the protesters lit the street. This portrayal reminded Ellie of the image that had formed in her mind of the bird's flight before it had crashed into the window at Owl's Ridge. Yet the image she was looking at now was in real time, rather than a replay of something that had already occurred.

*Interesting*, thought Ellie. *Could it be possible to use this method to observe an energy picture of the future, too?*

Amid the vast flow of moving yellow energy forms was an occasional smudge of another colour: off to the right was a green patch, and ahead and to the left was a large area of red. Perhaps this bigger area of dissimilar energy came from several beings, or, more fantastically still, maybe colours different to the predominant yellow were from creatures other than humans. Intriguing as this thought was, Ellie didn't want to open her eyes to find out and risk losing the energy image, so she kept them closed.

Ahead of her, she could see the Cenotaph, but unlike the other concrete structures around her, it was not in subdued grey tones but coloured a vivid blue, which seemed to darken towards the top. She focussed her attention on the Cenotaph, and the image enlarged. She could see that the darker top was actually caused by loads of black specks peppering the highest point of the memorial, and as Ellie watched, some of the specks detached from the stone and fell down onto the people below.

*What on earth are they?*

Some of the human energy forms showed a partial colour change as they passed the Cenotaph, going from bright yellow

252

to having patches of dull blue or grey. Ellie speculated that she might be seeing people's auras; they were supposed to change colour depending on the psychic, physical and emotional wellbeing of the individual, weren't they? Maybe the subdued patches were sadness, caused by the marchers thinking of what the Cenotaph commemorated?

As she walked nearer, Ellie could see that the black specks were falling from the top of the monument and landing on the miscoloured patches on individual energy forms. Were the specks causing the colour change, she wondered, or were they falling onto the patches of darker energy because they were attracted to them in some way?

Tripping on the raised tarmac around a manhole, Ellie stumbled slightly, causing her to automatically open her eyes. Blinking as they adjusted to the light, the sights and sounds of the march crashed back in on her consciousness, making her realise that while she had been focussing on the energy picture, there had been no sound. It seemed she was able to totally dissociate herself from her surroundings in order to concentrate on reading the energy of those around her. Ellie closed her eyes again to recapture the energy image, but it was gone, and she couldn't turn off the intrusive, noisy flow of information from her surroundings.

Huge wrought iron entrance gates marked the mouth of Downing Street, and the protesters' chants turned to shouts as they passed. A little further down the street, the flow of protesters was passing either side of the Cenotaph. Ellie looked up to its summit, but there was no noticeable change in colour at the top of the monument apparent to her normal vision.

She looked around her. Some faces were looking at the

monument, a few looked solemn, a few heads were bowed, but most were looking ahead, fully engaged in the march and where it was heading. Wanting to observe the dark specks at close quarters, Ellie shut her eyes again, but the energy picture still would not form. Frustrated, she returned her attention to the march. Soon they would reach Parliament Square and hear the speeches that marked the end of the protest.

Eventually, Big Ben loomed overhead and the Houses of Parliament lined the river, stretching southwards. The spires of Westminster Abbey were ahead and to their right. Thousands of protesters now spread out across the grass of Parliament Square, but Ellie and her friends stayed back, close to the statue of Gandhi, to avoid getting lost. They also wanted to get away speedily and so didn't want to be trapped at the front of the crowd.

Over on the east side of the square, a stage had been set up in front of a key entrance to the Palace of Westminster, and loudspeakers were arranged around the edges of Parliament Square's grassy lawn. *A far cry*, thought Ellie, *from times past, when those objecting to government action or inaction would have had to use a megaphone or even just stand and shout.*

The first speaker was angry at the governments of all countries, but particularly those in the West, who seemed, he said, to be utterly delusional in maintaining that global warming was not happening. He also lambasted the governments of developing countries, who paid no heed to how their growing economies consumed the planet's resources and how much pollution they generated; the race for cash paid no heed to ecological destruction.

The second speaker reported environmental tragedies

from Borneo's destroyed rainforests and starving orangutans to pack ice melting and starving polar bears. She touched on many well-reported environmental disasters and concluded by speaking of the plastic-choked oceans. This speaker made Ellie once again think that mankind really needed exterminating for the sake of the rest of planet.

The last speaker urged governments, local councils and individuals to act. He maintained that despite big economies polluting so massively, the stance that individual efforts wouldn't make a difference was just an excuse for inaction. He urged everyone to start right now with the small things: pick up litter; drive less; grow wild flowers for bees; plant trees; buy food without plastic packaging; shop locally.

Ellie felt that each speaker had made their points well, the last guy in particular. Change had to start with the little things, as well as tackling the huge stuff. As Bertie had said, change was like an avalanche.

The speeches now having concluded, the march organisers thanked the protesters for an orderly and incident-free event and then issued instructions on crowd dispersal. The other students from their college were heading back along the march route to catch the coach home, but sticking to their plans to further enjoy their time in the capital, Ellie and her friends made their way to St James's Park Underground Station.

It was not the nearest Tube stop to Parliament Square, but as Meg had pointed out, the closest would likely be totally overrun with departing protesters, so there was merit in walking a little further away. Happily—for Flick, in particular—their route passed many food vendors, so the friends stopped at a street kiosk to buy huge slices of hot, greasy pizza and cans of diet soda. Perching on a convenient wall to eat their lunch, they discussed where to go next.

'I want to check out Portobello Market, please,' said Flick. 'Especially if we're going somewhere fancy to eat tonight. I haven't got anything suitable to wear.'

'Even though your rucksack is of large, if not gargantuan, proportions?' queried Jaz.

Flick fired a dark look at Jaz.

'Good idea,' Meg said, seconding Flick's suggestion. 'As I said before, I don't have anything smart enough, either.'

'I think we might all benefit from a wardrobe refresh,' agreed Ellie.

'Ok, then. Portobello it is,' proclaimed Jaz.

\* \* \*

The Tube was crowded despite it being early afternoon, as other protesters obviously had the same idea as Meg. On the Circle Line, they had to stand up along the middle of the carriage and hold on to the overhead handles, much to Ellie's dislike; she felt that she was likely to fall onto some stranger's lap if the train suddenly braked. Conversely, the Hammersmith & City Line was a lot less busy and the friends were able to sit down, being accompanied by only six other passengers in their carriage.

The train set off from Paddington and made stops at Royal Oak and Westbourne Park. Just before the doors slid shut at the latter, an unkempt, middle-aged man got on board and sat at the far end of the carriage, on the opposite side to Ellie. He took a swig from the bottle in his hand and glanced morosely around the carriage. Upon seeing Ellie, he did a double take, squinting at her as if to be certain of what he was seeing. Raising the bottle to his lips, he took another gulp, his eyes still fixed on her.

Noticing his scrutiny, Ellie became slightly uncomfortable. Her eyes met those of Jaz, who indicated to ignore the guy with a slight shake of her head. Ellie closed her eyes to shut out the man's invasive surveillance.

At once, an energy picture formed in her mind. She could clearly see the bright energy of the other passengers, including Flick, Jaz, and Meg, against their dull surroundings. She turned her attention to the man staring at her. His energy was more muted, with only an area of bright yellow near his centre. Interestingly, he was decorated with black specs akin to those she'd witnessed falling onto people from the Cenotaph. This man, however, also had a black patch in his cranial energy, and it seemed to be expanding.

Startled, Ellie opened her eyes and looked directly at the man. He was still staring at her, but his eyes looked blank, the pupils fully dilated, and his mouth hung half open.

Suddenly, the lights on the train went out, leaving the carriage in pitch-blackness. Seconds later, they came back on, but only for a few moments before all was dark again. They then began to flicker on and off, making any movement within the carriage appear juddering and disjointed.

The scruffy man rose to his feet and began making his way towards Ellie in unbalanced lurches. Intermittently, she could see him getting nearer and nearer, and she could smell the stench of stale urine and his unwashed body. Ellie felt panic rising in her chest. Zombielike, the man raised his arm in slow motion, and Ellie swung her bag up in front of her, ready to block an attack.

It was then that she noticed the blue glow surrounding the third finger of her right hand. Her ring! *Of course! Darkall's protection ward.* Ellie twisted the ring around on her finger so that the spiral was on the inside of her hand and held up her palm, fingers splayed, towards the approaching man. The glow swiftly increased in intensity, then a blue flash lit the carriage interior like tame lightning or sparking electricity on the Tube tunnel wall.

The lights came back on fully as a voice from the speakers announced Ladbroke Grove as the next stop. Ellie leapt up and made for the door at her end of the carriage. Looking behind her as the train began to brake, she was surprised to see the man was now lying on the bench seat a little way down from where she had sat, his eyes closed and his mouth gaping as he snored. Ellie grabbed Flick's arm and quickly exited the train, Jaz and Meg in her wake.

'Did you see that?' she asked the others in a breathless voice, her heart pounding.

'What?' asked Jaz.

'That homeless guy! He came at me with his arm raised to strike!'

'He did? I didn't see, but then I was already at the door.' Jaz exchanged a concerned look with Meg.

'I thought he was just pissed,' said Flick. 'And I didn't notice his arm was raised, but then the lights were on and off. To be honest, I was focussed on getting off the train.'

'Well, he was.'

'Weird. But you're OK? He didn't touch you?'

'No, I'm good. Just a bit freaked out, that's all.'

'OK, well, he's gone now. Let's get out of here,' said Jaz.

Emerging from the Tube station, Ellie felt a wash of relief

to be above ground and in the open air again, even if it was tainted with exhaust fumes. She'd always thought that she was slightly claustrophobic, and being underground invariably made her twitchy. But whatever had happened on the Tube, she was away from it now and she was determined to enjoy her afternoon.

Turning left out of the station, they walked past the estate agents and the fish bar before crossing the street and heading for Portobello Road. They'd agreed that if nothing suitable to wear could be found, then they'd embrace the capsule-wardrobe concept and invest in colourful, floaty scarves to dress up their unprepossessing outfits. Jaz had already declared the scarf option was for her, as she then didn't have to worry about finding a "frock" to wear.

They needn't have worried, however, as upon reaching Portobello Road, a myriad of street stalls, boutiques and vintage clothes shops stretched out before them. Flick let out a squeal of delight and launched herself at the nearest stall. Ellie suggested to Meg and Jaz that they split up and meet back here in an hour. Nodding gratefully, Jaz led Meg off by the hand towards a coffee shop. Clearly, they were going to have a rest before tackling the market. Ellie, however, wouldn't be so lucky; she was now the eager Flick's designated chaperone.

With three purchases made within the first twenty minutes, Ellie insisted that she and Flick stop for a quick coffee. Claiming her feet were in need of a rest, which was true enough, Ellie was also mildly concerned about how Flick was going to fit all her new gear into her rucksack to take on the train home. Flick had bought a vintage green tea dress, matching 1940s-style louis heel shoes and a faux fur stole.

259

She only needed a fascinator and she'd be all set to play an extra in a World War II movie.

Titch had said that he would be taking them to his favourite restaurant. Knowing Titch as Ellie did, that would be somewhere fairly posh, as he was a foodie. He loved city life and relished the fantastic restaurants, theatres and nightlife on offer. Titch was intentionally single, but he invariably appeared with a beautiful woman on his arm if he so desired or needed a plus one to accompany him to a specific occasion.

Post their re-energising coffee, only another fifteen minutes of searching passed before Ellie found her perfect dress. She also splashed out on a pair of strappy silver high heels to wear with it, as the flat shoes she currently wore just would not do the dress justice.

Feeling happy, the two friends headed back up the road to meet Meg and Jaz. To their surprise, Jaz was carrying a shopping bag, too.

'You were tempted then, Jazmine?' asked Flick.

'*More* than tempted. I fell in love.' Jaz grinned ruefully. 'But you will have to wait until tonight to see what I've chosen to wear for our dinner extraordinaire.'

'Hmm, mysterious! In that case, I think it's something totally out of character. A pink ballgown, I reckon,' teased Flick.

'Or lederhosen,' chimed in Ellie.

'Could be, could be,' replied an evasive Jaz. 'Patience is a virtue.'

'I'll give you a clue,' offered Meg. 'It's rather sexier than Jaz's usual choices—but then, we *are* in the big city!' she finished with a wink.

Exchanging rather shocked looks, Ellie and Flick were not

260

only mystified but genuinely agog to see what Jaz would be wearing that evening.

'What about you, Meg? Did you find something you liked?' Ellie asked.

'I found hundreds of things I liked. My problem was narrowing it down to just *a few*! But I'm going to be secretive, too, and say you'll have to wait until tonight to see what I've selected.'

'Fair enough. Let's have the grand reveal at seven o'clock in the living room of Titch's apartment. He said he'll meet us at the restaurant at eight; we're to let ourselves in and make ourselves at home in the meantime. I don't know about you guys, but I'm pretty whacked and could do with a shower and a rest before tonight. I vote we head over to Titch's place next.'

'Hear, hear,' said Meg, who had not slept well on the coach and was consequently flagging, but didn't want to let the side down by complaining.

'Excellent. We'll call it a day, then, and have some down-time,' said Jaz.

Flick looked regretfully towards the market stalls, but as her feet were beginning to ache, she agreed to the plan without protest.

Ellie checked the map application on her smartphone and got her bearings. They were less than a ten-minute walk from Titch's place, so Ellie led the way.

23

# Chapter 23

Built in the 1860s, Elgin Crescent is both architecturally attractive and a very desirable residential street, and Titch owned the top two floors of one of its gorgeous stucco-clad houses. On the end of a row, the building benefited from light and air from three elevations, rather than two like the other houses in the terrace. It also had the luxury of access to the private communal gardens behind the row of houses.

'Your sort-of-uncle is seriously loaded, then,' remarked Jaz as Ellie pointed out Titch's house.

'I've never thought to ask,' replied Ellie. 'But living here, I guess he must be.'

'He's not married, though?' queried Flick, mentally assessing the gold-digging potential.

'Nope. Single unless escorting beautiful women, as far as I know,' Ellie replied.

Looking up at the house, Ellie had to admit it was beautiful—likely Victorian, she guessed, judging by the windows. There was a stone balustrade around the plot boundary and similar around the perimeter of a first-floor roof terrace and the edge of the roof. Lines in the stucco of the ground floor simulated finely-dressed stonework, and elaborate windowsills and pediments embellished the rendered elevations. The exterior was painted in the palest shade of grey, with all the decorative features highlighted in white. Ellie had once read that the end of a terrace was often the builder's own house and so was frequently rather more elaborate than the other properties in the row. This was certainly the case here; the bay windows alone made it stand out from its adjoining property.

Ellie unlatched the wrought iron gate and crossed the paved area to the stone steps and porticoed front entrance. The heavy, four panelled-door was painted in gloss black and ornamented with large brass door furniture. To the right-hand side of it was a keyless entry pad. Ellie entered the six-digit code Titch had furnished her with, and a buzzing sound issued from behind the door. Ellie pushed it open.

The hallway was spacious, with pistachio green walls and decorative white plasterwork. A graceful staircase rose from the checkerboard floor, its curvaceous, mahogany banister triggering a childish urge within Ellie to slide down it. The four girls began to climb, keeping their footsteps light; the hallway had the high-ceilinged, echoing silence of a library and they didn't dare speak except in whispers. Reaching Titch's front door at the end of the last turn, they found another keyless entry pad.

Ellie entered the second sequence of numbers she'd stored on her phone's note-taking app and stepped into Titch's apartment, closely followed by her rather overawed companions.

The wide hallway led past a well-fitted kitchen, utility room and study to a beautifully light sitting room furnished in simple but exquisite taste. The sitting room's pale walls were ornamented by large, gold-framed paintings, and antique feature pieces and sculptures sat on the highly polished surfaces of the cabinets and tables gracing the perimeter of the room.

Meg perched on the edge of one of the soft leather sofas. 'I feel like I'm in a five-star hotel,' she said in a disbelieving voice. 'Are we *really* allowed to stay here?'

'Yes, of course! Come on, I'll show you your rooms.' Ellie grinned at her friend's wonderment and led the way upstairs.

The upper landing was just as high-ceilinged as the entrance corridor below and created a feeling of airy space. Three bedrooms led off the upstairs hallway, each with its own well-appointed en suite bathroom.

Ellie led Jaz and Meg to the second-best bedroom, which overlooked the rear courtyard and private gardens behind the property. The room was large, with two full-height windows in the south wall; one of which gave access to the balustraded roof of the bay window below. Meg opened the door and stepped out to enjoy the view.

The communal garden was like a mini-park, existing specifically for the enjoyment of those who lived in the properties backing on to it. The only access to the garden was through the private homes or via the locked gates in the high wrought iron railings along the side streets.

Meg turned back into the room with a smile of delight on her face. 'This is just *so* amazing,' she said.

'Come and see the bathroom,' Jaz's voice called from the adjoining room. 'There's so much marble, I'm surprised the floor joists can take it!'

Laughing, Ellie left them to it and led Flick along the corridor to the room they were sharing. It was next to Meg and Jaz's room but was on the corner of the building and so had windows in two adjacent walls. It, too, had access to the outside, onto the roof terrace above the sitting room, where a couple of chairs were arranged invitingly.

'I guess there isn't much in this place that isn't an antique?' Flick queried.

'Maybe in the kitchen, but that's about it, I should think.' Ellie smiled back at her. 'I could use a drink. How about you?'

'No, thanks, I'm good. I'll just have a quick lie-down here and admire my palatial surroundings,' Flick replied.

'Sure thing. See you in a bit.'

Ellie left their room and padded down the corridor. Titch's suite was on her left; he preferred the front of the house to the quieter rear. Ellie knocked on the door to Meg and Jaz's room and asked if they wanted a drink, but as there was no answer, she left them in peace and made her way back downstairs to the kitchen.

Opening the chiller cabinet, Ellie selected a Diet Pepsi from the array of cold drinks on offer. Titch certainly didn't skimp on provisions for his guests; there was everything from Cristal and Bollinger to carbonated drinks and juice on offer.

Looking in the fridge, she noted with pleasure that it was similarly well stocked with delights from the deli as well as her personal favourites, cheese triangles. Knowing Ellie well, Titch had also provided a good hoard of chocolate.

Titch had a serious demeanour upon first meeting him, but as you got to know him better, you understood his very dry sense of humour and got to recognise the twinkle in his eye. He was a very intelligent man. Initially educated at Oxford, he had accrued many subsequent post- graduate qualifications, including a Doctor of Philosophy from Cambridge. Titch had flatteringly old-fashioned manners; which was probably one of the reasons why he always seemed to be surrounded by beautiful, well-educated women. Ellie recalled her father mentioning that Titch had a flat in the Barbican, too, although that seemed rather unnecessary to her when looking around this fabulous home. *He most definitely has a cleaner*, she thought, noticing the cobweb-and-dust-free decorative coving and smudge-free high-gloss kitchen cupboard doors.

Titch was tall, perhaps six foot two, and somewhere in his early sixties. He had a shock of floppy, bob-length silver hair that he usually wore pulled back in a bun on the crown of his head, and he kept his grey-white beard close-cropped. Titch favoured casual suit jackets over loosely buttoned shirts with a T-shirt underneath. His trousers were mostly of the canvas jeans type, unless he was having to present a talk, which merited a suit, or attend an evening event, where he invariably stole the attention of the room the moment he entered in full black tie.

When you spoke to Titch, you always got the impression he was listening very carefully to you; he would steeple his hands and observe your delivery, taking note of the things your body language told him, as well as your words. He would nod in encouragement or pull the corners of his mouth down in consideration or disbelief. When he spoke to you, it was evident that he had considered his words carefully, delivering each sentence with an economy of language. He didn't have an accent, neither regional nor class-related, but spoke exceptionally clearly, his deep voice rumbling out words of wisdom.

Ellie had known Titch her whole life and trusted him implicitly, as she did Bertie and Jill. He was one of her parent's gang who'd adopted her as a niece and treated her as such. Titch had always seemed to carry chocolate eclair sweets in his pockets and would secretively pass one to Ellie under the table at dinner—particularly if she was being reprimanded by her parents for some misdemeanour—while maintaining a guile-free countenance. Ellie thought this calm, serious giant a truly wonderful person and admired him greatly for his intelligence and his unspoken kindness.

Titch was a man of great taste, and Ellie knew the restaurants he frequented would be nothing short of exceptional. Tonight's dinner venue was to be Mario's, which—as the name would suggest—was an Italian restaurant, located in the vicinity of Fleet Street. A pre-arranged taxi was due to take them to meet Titch for eight o'clock, and Ellie casually wondered whether Titch had gone to the trouble of organising the booking himself or whether he'd got one of his adoring assistants to step in. With a half-smile, she suspected the latter.

Carrying her can of Diet Pepsi and a bar of milk chocolate into the sitting room, Ellie curled herself up on one end of the deeply comfortable sofa and wiggled her toes under the seat cushion next to her. *Bliss.* Carefully placing her can on a coaster, Ellie broke off a row of chocolate chunks and munched happily.

She re-ran the events of the day through her mind: the early start and Darkall's eyes briefly appearing in the coach

267

window; the march and the energy picture she'd seen of the Cenotaph; the scary vagrant on the Tube and her ring's flash of light stunning him. She recalled the energy picture showing an expanding blackness in the region of his head. *Could this have been him being controlled by something else? Maybe being possessed?* It was possible, she supposed.

Then there had been the odd black specks that had fallen from the top of the Cenotaph—were those things possessing the people below? But, then again, no one had tried to harm her during the actual march, had they? The specks must have been something else, although they did seem to be attracted to, or possibly cause, the grey-blue smudges in the protesters' energy forms.

Ellie raised her arm to look at her ring and the bracelet dangling from her wrist. When she'd repelled the man, it had been this hand she'd held out, so maybe both the ring's spiral ward and the protection crystals had worked to keep him away.

The flickering blackouts on the Tube had prevented Ellie from seeing exactly what had happened to the drunk man. One moment, he had been approaching her with his arm raised, threatening attack, and the next, when the lights came back on, he was fast asleep on the seat.

The blue light that had emanated from the ring confirmed that Darkall's protection ward had been at work; of that, Ellie was certain. His own palm spiral emitted the same blue glow.

Taking another sip of her drink, and once again being very careful where she set it down, Ellie relaxed into the sofa's expensive softness and closed her eyes.

* * *

Ellie was flying, soaring high above the clifftop where she'd just stood. The thermals supported her weight, and she could sweep in wide circles to ride them higher and higher. The layout of the land below was virtually impossible to see from this height. She felt no cold; only a glorious elation and the rushing of air around her.

Looking west, she altered her direction and started to speed towards the sun that, although hidden behind clouds, was just visible. Light streaked in long yellow-white lines as she flew faster and faster, reminding her of film imagery of spaceships travelling at the speed of light. She was virtually travelling in a tunnel of light herself now.

Ellie had once been on a skiing trip with her parents. She'd been riding a chairlift up the mountain through thick mist, the sun directly ahead of her. The mist had hid its orb, creating a diffuse glow to light her surroundings. As the chair had neared the top of the mountain, the mist had thinned and the rays of the sun could clearly be seen. This, as well as the silence of the mountain all around her, had made Ellie feel as if she were taking a chairlift up to Heaven.

She experienced a similar sensation now, coupled with a sense of heading exactly where she was meant to be going and a certain knowledge that it would be truly wonderful once she arrived.

The background colour to the light streaks surrounding her became pinkish, as if it were sunset. The further and the faster she flew, the deeper the background colour became, passing through mauve, purple and indigo and finally reaching a deep blue-black. Ellie slowed her speed, and the streaks around her resolved into points of light. Looking about her, she saw she was now hovering in space and that the points of light were, in fact, stars.

Ellie looked down. Below her was a huge spiral galaxy, its seemingly infinite long arms reaching out across space. Within the dusty swirls were countless stars and solar systems, and at its very core, a supermassive black hole.

Feeling the attraction of the black hole pull at her, she began to drop. Joyfully, she pivoted her body and stretched out in a dive, straight towards its centre. The certain knowledge she would not be met with crushing gravity but by something marvellous, combined with an intense sense of safety and of coming home, made her will her body to fall ever faster.

Ellie smiled, experiencing something akin to rapture as she sped towards the darkness.

\* \* \*

Ellie awoke to Flick's voice shouting at her from the upstairs landing. '*Oi!* Lazy bird! Wake up or you'll make us late!'

Groggily, Ellie peeled herself off the sofa and made her way to the sitting room door. 'I'm coming,' she called to Flick.

At the top of the stairs, Ellie trod barefoot along the corridor, relishing the feeling of her toes sinking into the deep pile carpet. The heavily-framed oil paintings and regency mirror all looked to be originals, but then, what else would one expect in Titch's home? As she reached Meg and Jaz's room, Ellie paused to knock on the door and make sure they were awake, but realised there was no need when she heard a hairdryer being used within.

'What time is it?' Ellie asked Flick, entering their room.

'Five past six—and you've got to have a shower yet.' Flick was sat on her bed, wrapped in an enormous white towelling robe. She noticed Ellie looking at it. 'I must remember to compliment the management on their excellent customer care, as well as the most comfortable beds. I was out like a light after you left.'

'I'm sure Titch will be delighted,' Ellie said with a smile, heading into the en suite.

By twenty past seven, Flick and Ellie were both ready and waiting in the sitting room for Jaz and Meg's big reveal. Flick's green vintage dress had puff sleeves and a tight bodice above a flared skirt that came to just below her knees. With matching shoes and her hair carefully waved and pinned-up, Flick looked like a 1940s siren. Ellie was wearing her newly purchased purple dress. It was in a wrapover style with a belted waist and tulip petal short sleeves dropping from lightly padded shoulders. She, too, had dressed her hair in a style sympathetic to the period of her dress, with two Victory Rolls on top of her head and her long tresses confined in a hairnet at the back. It really was amazing how well equipped Titch's guestrooms were for the purposes of dressing ladies' hair. He'd obviously welcomed many female guests here in the past.

Ellie passed Flick a flute of champagne, and they both sipped the golden bubbles whilst being careful not to smudge their lipstick.

'OK all below? We're ready for the fashion show,' Meg's voice called from upstairs.

'Come on down, ladies!' Flick called back.

The sound of heels on the stairs heralded Meg's arrival at the door of the sitting room. She swirled into the room, beaming, and spinning out the flared skirt of her red and white polka dot dress. It was sleeveless and suited Meg, who'd styled her naturally wavy blonde hair into a large bun on the crown of her head to show off her slender neck. She wore large red circular earrings and a chunky necklace and looked beautiful. Ellie and Flick clapped as Meg strolled up and down in front of them, smiling delightedly.

'Ready for the main event!' Meg called up to Jaz. 'Drumroll, please, ladies.'

Flick and Ellie obliged by speedily slapping their knees.

'Ta dah!'

Jaz appeared in the doorway. She looked utterly sensational in a blue satin jacket with tails and matching shorts. The fitted jacket emphasised her waist, and beneath it, she wore a gold silk corset. Her dark hair was slicked back, and over it, a bright blue bowler hat tilted forwards towards her left eye. With carefully applied dark makeup, she looked like a cross between a cast member of *A Clockwork Orange* and Frankie from *The Rocky Horror Picture Show*.

Flick wolf-whistled. 'Wow! You both look *gorgeous*.'

'You, too,' replied a delighted Jaz. 'I think Titch is going to be the envy of all the men in the restaurant tonight—and the women, too, for that matter.'

'Damn right he is!' exclaimed Flick, standing up and parading her outfit for them all to see.

Ellie poured two more glasses of champagne. 'Here, ladies. Bottoms up!' she said, handing them to Meg and Jaz, who clinked glasses while parroting the toast.

'By the way, Ellie, did you notice the parcel addressed to you on the hall table?' asked Meg.

'No. What parcel?'

Meg slipped out of the room to collect it, handing it to Ellie when she returned. Ellie looked at the package. It was addressed to her at Titch's apartment in Jill's handwriting. Peeling off the wrapping paper, she found five small, blue-lidded cardboard boxes inside.

'These are for you,' Ellie said, opening the first.

Inside was a bracelet made of uncut crystals dangling from a silver chain, similarly to Ellie's own protection bracelet. Ellie set it down on the marble-topped coffee table. Opening the rest, she lined them up next to the first. The last box contained a leather thong necklace with three stones hanging from it. The card inside this box read:

*Labradorite - Shields against psychic attack.*
  *Black Onyx - Absorbs negative energy.*
  *Black Obsidian - Protects from sorcery & manipulation.*

'This is for Chris,' Ellie said, passing the box to Flick. 'And this is for you,' she added, passing Flick one of the four identical bracelet boxes.

Handing Jaz and Meg a box each, Ellie then passed a second box to Jaz. 'For Vi,' she said.

Her friends each took their bracelets out of the boxes and looked at them. They were attractive pieces of jewellery in their own right, as well as being protection talismans.

'Please wear them at all times, and ask Chris and Vi to do the same. I don't know whether you might become the focus of some kind of psychic attack from the entities focussing on me, but I want you to be protected from them, just in case.'

No words were necessary. Ellie's demonstration of how much she cared about them spoke volumes to her friends. They each fastened their bracelets around their wrists and then automatically moved towards each other for a group hug.

'Be safe,' breathed Ellie.

'You, too,' said Jaz.

After a moment, they broke apart, all smiling at one another.

'Let's finish up this cheeky little Bollinger,' Flick suggested, squinting at the label in an impressed fashion, 'and then show this town what it's been missing.'

'Hear, hear.'

They lifted their glasses and tilted them towards each other in another toast, all cherishing the precious happiness and mutual affection of the moment, then swigged the effervescent amber liquid.

24

# Chapter 24

Mario's was one of those places that only people in the know knew about; its reputation for excellence meant it didn't have to advertise. Two twisted bay trees stood in hammered metal pots either side of the entrance, lit from above by a picture light over a discreet sign, and heavy maroon drapes could just be seen through the tinted glass of the large windows, giving the restaurant a very understated aspect from the street. The restaurant was downstairs, with just the reception and bar at street level.

Entering the building, the four friends were met by a diligent maître d', who politely informed them that *monsieur* awaited them in the bar. He clicked his fingers, and a lackey in a black bow tie and waistcoat over his immaculate white shirt offered to take the *mademoiselles'* coats. Relinquishing their outerwear, they were ushered through into the bar area.

Ellie spotted Titch immediately, and her heart lifted. He was perched on a high seat at the bar, reading a newspaper while swirling the ice cubes in his cut glass whisky tumbler. One long leg was stretched leisurely to the floor while the heel of his other foot was propped on a rung of the chair.

The maître d' gave a discreet signal to the barman, who, leaning over the bar, quietly informed Titch of their presence. He looked towards the door, a smile spreading across his distinguished face, and, setting down his glass, walked towards them with arms outstretched.

'Ellie, you look even more lovely than the last time we met,' his delighted, deep voice rumbled.

Ellie trotted forwards to be met with an all-engulfing bear hug. 'I've missed you, Uncle Tiny,' she said into his lapel, using her childhood nickname for him.

'You too, squirt,' he replied, giving her an extra squeeze and bending his neck to place a gentle kiss on her cheek. Releasing her from the embrace but keeping his arm around her shoulders, he turned towards Ellie's friends. 'Why don't you introduce me to your beautiful companions?'

'Titch, this is Flick, Jaz and Meg.'

He shook each of their hands in turn. 'Enchanted. Charles Mackworth, at your service—but feel free to call me Titch.'

'Thank you for allowing us free reign of your gorgeous apartment,' said Meg politely.

'Any friends of Ellie's are always most welcome.' Titch brushed off the thanks with a smile. 'Now, would you care for a drink up here before going down to dinner?'

'Yes, please,' Flick responded eagerly on behalf of all of them.

'Champagne?' Titch quirked an eyebrow in query, a slight

smile playing around his generous mouth.

'May as well continue as we've begun.' Jaz looked to the others for approval. Receiving nods of agreement, she answered for them all. 'That would be great, thank you, Titch.'

'Let us make ourselves comfortable,' he suggested, gesturing towards a group of chairs around a low table.

Adjusting the chairs to ensure the girls were comfortable, Titch then sat in an armchair and spread both arms along the rollback in a relaxed and somewhat proprietorial fashion. Clearly, he came to Mario's often, as he relaxed as readily into the furniture and surroundings of the restaurant as he would into those at his club or own home.

Titch was wearing a charcoal suit and a matching shirt. He didn't wear a tie; instead, the open neck of his shirt hinted at a black T-shirt beneath. His shoes were black and polished, although more ankle boot in design that dress shoes. Titch always slightly reminded Ellie of Sean Connery, only taller and with a more generous upper lip. His eyes were the piercing blue of a summer's sky and sparkled with lively intelligence under still dark eyebrows that contrasted with his silvered beard.

He steepled his hands and looked around at the young, attractive faces in front of him. 'So, tell me, how was your protest march?'

'Tiring on the feet,' Flick responded, with a slight frown followed by a smile.

Titch grinned. 'The pavement is hard here in London.'

'I enjoyed it,' Meg said. 'There was a wonderful feeling of solidarity and proactivity. It actually went by much quicker than I'd expected.'

'I felt the same. It felt good to be doing something rather than just sitting at home, grumbling,' Jaz remarked. 'Having said that, we all have to up our game on the recycling, zero plastic packaging and reduced energy consumption front if we are to have any chance of making a difference. Not to mention refusing to buy products not ethically produced and anything containing palm oil.'

Titch nodded his head.

'It's hard, though, particularly when you're forced to grab the cheapest products out there as you're on a small budget,' Flick said. 'Free range meat is often the most expensive.'

'That's because farming methods need to change,' Meg replied. 'Free range needs to be the norm and not the exception or the 'exclusive' choice. It's like with eggs. A few years ago, free range eggs were a fair bit more expensive than barn eggs, but, over time, their prices have become much more comparable and barn eggs are in the minority on the supermarket shelves. There's also many more local people selling free range eggs by the side of the road. Public awareness, progress and change for the better needs to happen across all areas of food production.'

'That's reliant on responsible sourcing by the supermarkets,' Jaz commented.

Titch watched them, his eyes switching between the faces of the four girls. He gave an occasional nod of agreement as the discussion continued or a slight tilt of the head and twist of his lips in response to a point he felt less affiliation with. When the conversation reached a natural pause, he glanced towards Ellie, who had not yet spoken. 'What was your experience of the march, Ellie?' he said, making direct eye contact with her.

Ellie looked down at her hands. She wasn't sure whether she ought to explain the energy pictures or her "other" experiences. She looked around at her friends and then returned her gaze to his. 'Different to what you'd expect,' she said casually.

The others looked at Ellie curiously.

'Did something else happen other than that guy on the Tube?' Jaz asked.

Ellie looked around the plush room, where several couples and a group of men in suits sipped their drinks and talked. 'I think it's something that needs a more private location for me to explain,' she replied.

Titch nodded at Ellie, understanding immediately. 'Then we will not talk of it tonight. Tonight is for enjoyment, good food and good company,' he said. 'Other matters can wait for tomorrow.'

Ellie visibly relaxed and smiled at him. Jaz nodded and glanced at Meg, who gave a very slight shrug in return, followed by a smile.

A waiter approached, bringing menus. He handed them courteously to the ladies before passing a menu and the wine list to Titch. 'For when *monsieur* is ready to order,' he said amenably, before leaving to escort other diners down to the restaurant.

The menu was filled with foodie terminology that only a MasterChef contestant would be familiar with. Ellie, who was definitely of the non-foodie club, required a lot of interpretation, which Jaz and Titch were happy to provide.

Having finally made their selections, Titch raised his hand to summon a waiter. He relayed their choices, adding his own and ordering a wine to accompany the starters and another for the main course. The waiter disappeared through a door on the opposite side of the bar, while another approached, picked up the champagne bottle from the silver cooler bucket and refilled the *mademoiselles'* glasses.

Ellie took a sip from her glass, relishing the feel of the bubbles on her tongue. She glanced around the now near-empty room and, making a snap decision, began to speak in a low voice.

'There is something I need to talk to you about, Titch, and I don't think it can wait until tomorrow. I've been going through some changes recently—or changes have been happening *around* me. I'm not even sure if it isn't a little of both. The point is that my perspective on reality has shifted, and I'm left feeling rather off balance.'

Titch merely nodded, looking at her to continue.

Ellie cleared her throat. 'Flick, Jaz and Meg are all on this rollercoaster ride with me—or, more accurately, I'm dragging them along.'

Jaz frowned and Flick shook her head. Ellie gave a them small, apologetic smile.

'There are things happening that are dangerous, things that are unexplainable. Things that, at first, I wanted to deny, as they seemed totally impossible. But the truth is, they're not. They're entirely *possible*.' She paused. 'Does that sound crazy to you?'

'No,' he said concisely. 'In my experience, the impossible happens a lot more frequently than you might think. Why don't you tell me what's been going on?'

For the next twenty minutes, Ellie explained much of what had been happening to her and her friends, with interjections from the others when they felt she'd missed a point. Titch was a very trusted old friend of her parents and Ellie had known him all of her life; she had no compunction about quietly telling him of her potentially developing healing ability. Titch listened attentively throughout her account and nodded in encouragement and understanding.

'It is an unusual tale, but not one I would discount as fiction,' he said, once she'd finished speaking. 'I have known you a long time, Ellie, and I've known your parents even longer. Have you spoken to them about this?'

Ellie bowed her head. 'No, I haven't. I didn't want to upset them or make them think I'm going crazy.'

'They will certainly *not* think that,' he said. 'But you *do* need to talk to them. You will be surprised, I think, at just how understanding they will be.'

Ellie shrugged. She knew that her parents would be understanding, at least to her face. Whether they then called the men in white coats as soon as she'd gone to bed was another matter.

'Don't underestimate your parents,' Titch said more sternly, as if he could read her mind. 'They are more aware and accepting than you think.'

Ellie, slightly chastened, smiled apologetically.

Titch returned her smile. 'I see that you're all wearing similar bracelets. Jill's handiwork, by the look of them,' he said.

Ellie nodded.

'Good. It would be wise for you not to take them off as the current situation develops,' Titch advised, then, glancing at the approaching maître d', he said in a louder voice, 'Excellent! I believe they are ready for us downstairs.'

The dining room was lit by subtle wall lighting and candles

in glass bowls set on the pristine tablecloths; there were no overhead lights to cast unflatteringly harsh light on the faces of the expensively-clad diners. Their group was shown to a circular table and waiters appeared as if from nowhere to usher them into their seats. Heavy napkins were whipped from plates, shaken with a flourish and laid on their laps. Water was offered and poured before those waiters departed and two more arrived bearing small plates.

'*Amuse-bouche*,' said Jaz. 'Nice. It means to amuse your mouth, the idea being that they will stimulate your appetite ready for your meal.'

'Nice,' agreed Flick. 'Kinda like sipping the curry sauce before your pour it over your chips and scoff them.'

Jaz gave her a long look and raised an eyebrow. 'Do you think you could elevate your culinary commentary to match the level of your surroundings and, indeed, your outfit? Just for this evening?'

'I might.' Flick grinned, adding in a little girl voice, 'If I'm allowed chocolate sauce with my gelato.'

Titch chuckled at the sparring pair. 'I can see why Ellie likes you,' he remarked.

The meal was utterly delicious, and as dessert plates were cleared and the tablecloth tidied by a keen waiter with a crumb tray and brush, Titch leaned back in his chair to survey the group. They were an engaging bunch and clearly devoted to each other, which he was pleased to see; Ellie would need good friends around her as she faced what he feared lay ahead.

'That was the most delicious meal I've ever eaten,' said Meg. 'Thank you for bringing us here, Titch.'

'You are more than welcome. It has been a most enjoyable

evening, and I am certain that I have been the envy of everyone in the restaurant to be sat with such attractive and entertaining young companions.'

The girls smiled at his compliment, and Meg's cheeks tinged pink with pleasure.

'We aim to please,' said Flick, yawning discreetly behind her purse. She'd lost count of how many glasses of wine she'd drunk, courtesy of her glass being continually refilled by the ever-solicitous waiters.

After the coffees had been drunk, Titch signalled to the waiter to bring the bill, and when it arrived, he merely dropped his credit card onto the brown leather folder without looking at the total. 'Add the usual,' he told the waiter.

'*Grazie signore.*'

The waiter handed him a card reader and, with payment having been made, departed to organise the taxi requested by Titch.

'The one true Italian waiter at Mario's. All the others are French.'

'True!' said Meg delightedly. 'I was wondering why we were "*mademoiselle*" instead of "*signorina*."'

'You are very perceptive,' Titch complimented her.

Jaz smiled at Meg lovingly, if slightly drunkenly. She took Meg's hand and kissed her fingers. Noticing the small gesture, Titch smiled to himself before suggesting that they make their way upstairs and wait for the taxi outside to get some fresh air. In the entrance lobby, they were helped into their coats and the doors were held open for them to step out onto the street.

Night had fallen while they'd been eating, and Ellie looked at her watch to discover that it was past eleven o'clock. Titch took a packet of slim cigars from his inside jacket pocket and lit one. The smoke circled around them as they stood on the pavement, surrounded by the lights and noise of the city at night. A waiter stood a little way away from them, ready to meet the ordered taxi.

'This is where I must say goodnight, ladies. I have another engagement this evening and won't come back to the apartment tonight and disturb you all from your sleep. I will see you tomorrow at the museum. Let's make it early afternoon,' Titch suggested, grinning at the tipsy, tired-looking faces around him.

The waiter raised his arm and indicated the waiting group to the approaching taxi as it drew up at the kerb. Titch opened the door for the sleepy friends, then offered his address to the driver through the front window. He also paid the fare in advance, adding a healthy tip to allow for any hold-ups, which they both knew there wouldn't be at that time of night.

'Farewell and sleep well,' Titch said, closing the taxi door.

'Thank you for a lovely evening, Titch,' they chorused, more or less in unison, waving as the taxi pulled away.

'What a nice guy,' said Jaz, a yawn attacking her sentence halfway through.

'He really is,' Ellie confirmed proudly. 'Which is probably why his other engagement this evening is eagerly awaiting him, dripping in poised mid-life beauty. I hear he has several stunning forty-somethings after him at the moment.'

'No surprise there,' said Flick mischievously. 'He's fit!'

The journey to Elgin Crescent took over half an hour, and when they finally drove down the quiet street, the taxi slowed, looking for their building. Only Ellie and Flick were left awake, mostly because if they'd fallen asleep on their fold-down seats, they would likely have fallen off them.

'It's just ahead on the left,' Ellie informed the driver.

Unexpectedly, the taxi suddenly surged forwards, making them both nearly slip from their seats.

'Hey, you've missed it!' declared Ellie in surprise.

The driver made no remark, and the noise of the engine increased to a whine before the automatic transmission changed up a gear.

'Hey! Stop!' exclaimed Flick. 'Let us out!'

Again, there was no response from the driver as the vehicle continued to accelerate. It sped out of Elgin Crescent and into Clarendon Road without stopping at the "Give way" sign, but thankfully there were no other vehicles at the junction.

'Christ! Stop the bloody car!' Flick shouted at the driver.

Her raised voice woke Jaz and Meg, who blinked, bleary-eyed, for a moment before realising their predicament. Jaz leaned forwards, her arm across Meg's body and her hand grasping the door bar.

'Slow down, mister, and stop the taxi!' she said in a loud, commanding voice, obviously using hostage negotiation tactics gleaned from the movies she enjoyed.

Her ploy failed, however, and the car continued to raced forwards. Ellie looked at the rearview mirror for a glimpse of the taxi driver's face. He was staring blankly forwards, his pupils large and dilated, his mouth sagging open.

Ellie reached her arm through the sliding screen and shook his shoulder. 'Wake up! *Stop* the car!' she shouted at him in an authoritative voice.

The driver's head snapped around with inhuman speed,

making Ellie snatch her arm back as if avoiding a strike from a snake. A hissing noise emerged from his open mouth, but, most disturbingly, his head stayed turned backwards at the maximum rotation of his neck. The road ahead was straight, but the speedometer read forty miles per hour and rising.

Ahead was the junction where Ladbroke Walk met Clarendon Road. Luckily, the one-way system was currently with them, but soon there would be the traffic-directing measure to contend with. If they made it over the raised pavement without turning over, they'd eventually reach the T junction where there was no road ahead. If the vehicle carried on straight at this point, they would crash into the garden walls and trees of the houses on the other side of the avenue. But to even get that far was assuming that nothing met them coming from the other direction or pulled out in front of them beforehand. Ellie prayed that no pedestrians would attempt to cross the road. Thank God it was late at night and the likelihood of children being outside was minimal.

Meg was sobbing in fright and Flick repeatedly shouted for the seemingly senseless driver to stop.

'Brace yourselves as best you can. He's not going to stop!' said Jaz, wedging her foot against the rear of the front seats between Ellie and Flick.

Ellie felt her finger becoming warmer and glanced at her glowing ring. She held her hand up in front of the sliding screen.

'Stop now!' she commanded.

The hissing noise grew louder, but the driver still did not slow, nor did he turn his head to look where he was driving—although, with such blank eyes, it seemed unlikely that he could see, anyway.

Panic filled Ellie's chest and she fought it down, knowing it would cloud her thoughts. She took a deep breath. 'We're going to have to jump out,' she told the others, their faces white.

'At this speed, we'll be killed by the impact with the road or by hitting a tree or something,' cried Flick.

Out of ideas, Ellie looked ahead to the approaching junction. 'Hang on to something!' she shouted.

The taxi hit the low central island with one wheel while the other slipped through the lowered cyclists' section, the driver's side door scraping the signpost. The girls were thrown up from their seats by the impact and then dumped back down, hitting heads against windows and elbows on doors, but the taxi made it and sped ahead, travelling the wrong way along a one-way street.

There was no course of action Ellie could think of to stop the driver. She closed her eyes and thought of the one person who could help.

Darkall.

Opening her eyes, she looked ahead through the front windscreen. Further on down the road stood a figure, his feet widely spaced and planted firmly on the road, his hood up to hide his face. His hands were clasped in front of his chest, his elbows out to the side. A blue glow radiated from his linked hands and spread swiftly outwards, obscuring the middle of his body. The taxi sped towards the figure, only seconds away from collision.

'It's him!' gasped Ellie in breathless relief.

The others looked up just as blue light flashed in a blaze towards the taxi. The engine noise immediately changed: they were no longer accelerating.

The vehicle slowed and eventually rolled to a stop, wheels grinding along the kerb and the driver slumped forwards onto the steering wheel. Jaz opened the door, and she and Meg all but fell out onto the road. Flick scrambled after them, as did Ellie.

She stared down the road, looking for Darkall, but there was no sign of him. Her ring was warm against her finger, and she felt a slight tremor running through it as she spun it with her thumb. He was still with her, but unseen.

'Thank you,' she whispered.

She felt the pressure of unseen lips brush her cheek and heard him whisper on the very cusp of hearing, 'You are welcome, as ever.' A tingling sensation raced down her spine.

Flick and Jaz were supporting Meg. The four friends hugged one another and checked for serious injuries. Happily, they'd all got away with just some bumps and bruises. Ellie walked around to the driver's side of the cab and tentatively knocked on the window. The driver raised his head and shook himself as if waking from a sleep. He buzzed down the window, looking at her in confusion. Ellie saw that his eyes had returned to normal and he was back in control of his facial features.

'Are you OK?' she asked.

'I … I … why are we here? Why aren't you in the back?'

'I think you've had some sort of blackout,' she replied. 'Or you fell asleep.'

'Twenty-two years behind the wheel and I've never fallen asleep.' He rubbed his eyes. 'You and the other ladies all OK, are you?'

'Yes,' Ellie replied. 'Just a little shaken up. We'll walk back from here.'

'Right. Righty-ho. Well then, there's no charge; all settled already.'

'I should *bloody well* think not!' Flick muttered darkly.

Ellie gave her a quietening look. Flick might not have realised what had just happened, but Ellie certainly did and she would not have the innocent driver blamed.

'Right. Well. You sure you don't want a lift back up to your doorstep?'

Ellie looked at the others. They were in rather a shocked state, their pale faces drawn, and Meg was trembling while being held by Jaz. She'd hit her head the hardest on the glass of the side window when the taxi hit the kerb, and a bump was already forming.

'Well?' Ellie whispered, still feeling the ring on her finger vibrating.

'You will be safe,' Darkall answered, his breath tickling her ear.

'OK, that would be great, thanks,' Ellie told the driver.

'You're not serious?' argued Flick.

Ellie looked her directly in the eyes, and Jaz and Meg, too. 'It's safe. We're being … *accompanied*.'

She turned around and got back into the taxi. Meg was the first to step forwards out of the other three, and leading Jaz by the hand, she climbed back in, too. Flick hesitated and looked as if she was about to insist on walking back. However, she eventually walked around to the other side of the taxi and, opening the front passenger door, got in.

'I'll sit here, to make sure you're OK,' she said to the driver.

As a precaution, her right hand hovered over the handbrake for the whole of the brief journey back to Titch's building.

The taxi pulled up to the kerb outside, and they got

out. Ellie thanked the driver before the weary friends let themselves into the entrance hall and climbed the stairs to the apartment. Not wishing to discuss their recent terror, they exchanged hugs, wished one another goodnight and went to their rooms. Explanations and discussions could wait for the morning; it was late and they were all exhausted from the combination of a long day, a big meal, plenty of wine and the trauma of what had just happened.

Ellie wanted to apologise for her friends being in danger, but she read in their faces and subdued manner that they couldn't take any more tonight; they'd had enough and needed sleep, not discussion. She was also scared. No matter how well she knew them and believed their promises of support, she was afraid that, after tonight, they might decide being her friend was just not worth the associated risks.

# 25

# Chapter 25

Ellie stayed downstairs for a while after the others had gone to bed. Her thoughts wouldn't allow her to relax just yet; they were far too disturbing. Clearly tonight had been another attempt by "them" to get rid of her. Had they intended kidnap or just death in an accident? Either way, they meant serious harm and were not bothered who they hurt or killed alongside her.

She looked down at her ring. It hadn't worked. On the Tube, it had deflected the drunkard's attack, but in the taxi, nothing had happened. Why?

She needed to speak to Darkall.

Quietly climbing the stairs, she crept to the end of the landing and opened the door. Behind it, a narrow staircase led to the roof access. Ellie tiptoed up the stairs, not wanting to make any noise that might disturb the others.

The building's roof was an unusual design. There was the roof proper, which was slate, but instead of overhanging the walls as one might expect, its steep slope met a flat strip of lead roof about a meter wide. This allowed a walkway bounded by stone balustrade to run around the three unattached sides of the building.

Ellie walked around the roof until she overlooked the gardens at the rear of the property. 'Are you here?' Ellie asked into the darkness.

Darkall's arms slipped around her waist, and he rested his chin briefly on the top of her head before dropping his lips to her ear. 'Always.'

Ellie relaxed back against him. He felt so solid—so powerful—and he provided a feeling of total safety, especially when she was in his arms. They stood like that for a while, not needing to speak, Ellie just drawing strength and comfort from his presence and bodily contact.

Eventually, she broke the silence. 'What happened?' she asked.

'It was an attempt to remove you.'

'That's an odd choice of words. To *remove* me. Why not just say "kill" me?'

'The outcome would be the same. You would have been removed from the destiny mapped for you, and that would please those opposed to your ascension.'

'I appear to be following a dangerous path—and one not of my choosing.'

'Yes,' Darkall replied.

Ellie waited to see if he was going to elaborate. When he didn't say anything further, she stepped away and turned to face him. Again, she was caught by the beauty of the face in front of her. He was a Greek sculpture come to life—over-large proportions and perfect features. This evening, he wore a black sweater, matching trousers and the usual boots, but even these normal clothes couldn't mask his otherworldliness. And nothing could disguise those eyes.

'OK, you're going to have to give me something here. What exactly is after me? What do they want? How do I stop them?'

Darkall looked at her for a moment, considering his reply. 'To answer, I would have to offer some background detail first,' he said.

'I am all ears. Go for it.'

'Then let us go somewhere warmer.'

Darkall stepped forwards and took her in his arms. Just as she was about to protest, she felt a sense of movement and then the noise of cars passing. She looked around her and was surprised to see that they were in the bar of a closed pub. The exit sign above the door and the streetlights shining through the curtained windows were all that illuminated the room.

'Woah! You need to give me warning before doing that next time.'

'I am sorry if you were startled,' he replied calmly. 'Let us sit down.'

He indicated to some seating in a bay window overlooking the shadowy street. Ellie sat down, and Darkall perched on the arm of the sofa opposite her. His hands were clasped loosely on his thighs, his head slightly bowed so that he looked at them rather than her.

'OK,' she said. 'Tell me.'

Darkall said nothing.

Ellie was just about to ask him again for an explanation when he finally spoke. 'Do you remember your nightmares, Eleanor?' he asked, his eyes looking up at her.

She shivered. Of course she remembered them. They were not something she could likely forget without some serious therapy. Ellie nodded.

'It was your terror that they required.'

'What?'

'There are beings who share this world with mankind which cannot be detected in your reality. Nevertheless, the creatures do exist. Some of these creatures are nourished by, and therefore feed on, negative energy. A vast source of this is your human race.'

'You mean like devils making people's lives hell for their own enjoyment?'

'Some of your religions have simplified the other beings as such, certainly. It is a crude analogy but useful, if it helps you to understand. Your nightmares were not just dreams, Eleanor. They were real experiences. The terror you felt was manna to the creatures inducing it. You were a particularly rich source of nourishment for them.'

'They fed off ... my terror?' Ellie asked, almost dumbstruck with horror and revulsion.

'Certainly.'

Ellie couldn't believe what she was hearing. This was impossible, surely? Dreams were just that: *dreams*. The "royal road to the unconscious", Freud had said. Nightmares were just her unconscious processing her fears, experiences and desires that hadn't been dealt with and which her conscious mind had tried to bury. They weren't real.

She looked at Darkall's face, hoping to read something there, but it was placid; expressionless.

'So, you're saying there really was evil in my room? That I was actually paralysed and throttled and crushed? All to feed demons with my terror?'

'Essentially, yes.'

'If that's true, why would it always stop? Why didn't these beings continue to torture me all night long, if I was such a good meal? In my nightmares, I always managed to escape into darkness before I was actually strangled or suffocated.'

'That was me.'

'You?'

'Yes. I pulled you to me, took you from them, but not in this form. I had not yet taken this shape.'

'And it's these things that want me out of the way now?'

'Some of them do, certainly. Although their intention may not be to kill you. You are valuable to them.'

'As a meal?'

'Yes.'

'*Jeez*. What kind of freaky, sick things are they?'

'They are not unusual in their desires, Eleanor. All things feed.'

Ellie looked at him in distaste. 'And this is OK with you, is it?'

He took a moment before answering. 'No. Not when it involves you.'

'But these creatures causing negative emotion in other humans, making people's lives hell just to feed off their misery … that's fine with you, is it?'

'It is their nature. All creatures seek that which nourishes them.' Darkall paused for a moment, looking at her before continuing. 'I have observed a wasp build a nest of mud and lay eggs on a caterpillar that it then seals inside. When the wasp's offspring hatch, they devour the trapped creature alive. This would appear to be a worse fate than a human being milked of negative energy, yet this is acceptable to human beings because it is nature. The nature of the creatures of which I speak is to feed on negative energy, and they will farm and harvest it to sustain themselves.'

'But no one can see these things feeding on them, so you can't fight them off. That seems very unfair; you ought to be able to at least see your attacker, to have a chance of defending yourself, or even a choice of whether you want to be fed from or not.'

'Do humans give animals a choice? Does the cow get asked if it wants to be milked?'

'At least the cow can see the farmer and gets grass or feed to eat. What do people get?'

'They get to live, as long as they are a valuable resource. There are worse things than the feeders of energy.'

Ellie crossed her arms in front of herself, her legs already crossed. Her body was drawing away from him in a physical echo of her thoughts.

Sensing her disbelief and abhorrence of the world he presented, Darkall stood up and looked out of the window. 'Join me,' he said.

Ellie got up from her chair and stood next to him, careful to keep her distance.

'Look across this street. What do you see?'

'Buildings. A road. Parked cars.'

'Specifically, in the doorway opposite.'

Ellie peered. 'A huddled figure sat on the doorstep, head bowed onto their knees.'

'Look at him and tell me what you see.'

'Just a homeless guy in the doorway.'

'No. *Really* look.'

'I don't understand.'

'Look at his energy.'

*Ah, an energy picture.* Ellie was unsure whether she could call them to order. She closed her eyes and concentrated, but no image formed in her mind.

'Sorry, nothing happening,' she said, opening her eyes.

Darkall raised his hand slowly and pressed his palm to her forehead. Ellie could feel a tingling sensation and saw a blue glow on the inside of her eyelids.

'Read the energy from here,' Darkall instructed her, removing his hand.

She closed her eyes and imagined looking out from her mind, from the forehead chakra; her third eye. The buildings across the street came into focus, emerging from the darkness behind her eyelids in tones of dull grey. She could see the guy in the doorway, his energy yellow-green and darker around his head. Or was it?

She focussed more specifically on his head, and the image zoomed in. *Eugh, what is that?* There seemed to be insect-like creatures on his head, flapping their ragged wings slowly. They were like ugly butterflies with wings ending in sharp points. Their movements were either in slow time or oddly fast, like a sped-up film, and they ranged in colour from deep blue to black.

'Malaflies,' Darkall said. 'They are feeding.'

Ellie took an involuntary step backwards, repulsed by what she saw; yet she felt compelled to watch. 'They are eating him?'

She shuddered at the thought.

'No, merely consuming his negative energy. The man may well feel more positive when he awakens—or perhaps not if the Malaflies are being herded.'

'I'm almost too disgusted to ask, but what do you mean by

297

"herded?"'

'The creatures you see feeding, if left to function via their instincts, would feed from the negative energy until the supply exhausts, then move on to find another source. Having done so, there would be less negative energy around the human. The man would feel drained of energy and so would likely sleep, but when he awakens, he may well feel more positive than he did before.

'However, if Malaflies are being farmed, the Herders will ensure the negative energy supply continues, as opposed to moving the flock to another source.'

'You're saying that these Herders make the man suffer to continue harvesting negative energy for food? What will they do to him?'

'Anything that achieves the desired result.'

'Like what? Cause him pain? Illness? Misery?'

'Yes. And worse.'

'That's horrible! It's *disgusting!*' Ellie shuddered again. 'What are these Herders like?'

'Small bipeds, able to fly by riding Malaflies. Some have rudimentary wings, hence the ability to fly themselves.'

'They sound like bad fairies!'

'Possibly, but they are not. Should they feel under attack, Herders are able to fuse together to create larger creatures that are more capable of fighting. They merge with their Malaflies, too, so that the large creature possesses the Malafly energy with which to fell a foe. But they do not do this lightly, as it destroys the Malaflies.'

Ellie thought for a moment. 'Are there Herders over there, around that poor guy?' she asked in a small voice.

'No.'

She sighed. 'This is not what I wanted. I don't want any of this. I want my world back, the old one—the one without this strange, freaky stuff in it.' Ellie paused, then turning to look at Darkall, she added, 'Except for *you*, that is.'

'Unfortunately, Eleanor, knowledge cannot be unlearnt. But even if it could, you would still be in the same position you are now, if not a worse one. With knowledge, you can understand, you can plan and you can act. Without knowledge, you are helpless, at the mercy of those who possess it.'

Ellie looked away from him and out of the window at the hunched figure across the street. She shook her head. This was more than she'd bargained for. This was serious, frightening and repugnant. There was a whole other world out there that no one could see—no human, that is. She exhaled a long breath. He was right; she couldn't go back now.

'So, is that what's after me? A morphed being of Herders and Malaflies?'

'No. They are insignificant, minor beings. You have caught the attention of others.'

'Who?'

'In all things, there is order. Hierarchy; leaders; power struggles; allegiances. Those watching you are near the top of the social order. You have drawn their attention, as you have drawn mine.'

'These things that are after me—do they always possess people in order to attack?'

'No.'

'Great,' she said, disheartened. 'So there's even weirder stuff to come, then.'

'I'm afraid there is no doubt.'

Ellie continued to look towards the window, this time seeing her own pale, frightened face reflected in the glass. Her thumb circled the ring around her finger; it buzzed a gentle vibration against her skin, as it always did whenever Darkall was near. A thought occurred to her.

'The taxi driver. When I tried to use my ring on him, it didn't work, but it worked with the drunk guy on the Tube. Why was that? Why didn't it work?'

'The spiral ward on your ring will deflect an attack against you. The taxi driver was not attacking you directly. These others I have spoken of have realised that you have protection and so have tried a different tactic.'

'You stopped the taxi. I saw you standing in the road.'

'Indeed. The spiral linking of hands you witnessed forms a focal point for energy release. I will show you.'

Darkall curled his left hand into a fist, his thumb encircling his coiled index finger. Then he pressed the tip of his right thumb to his left and wrapped his right hand around his left fist. Looking down from the top, his curled fingers and thumbs formed a spiral.

'Learn this. It is a method for energy focus.'

She formed her hands into the same shape as his and pressed them to her chest, the spiral shape facing upwards. Feeling nothing, she let them go.

'I can't do what you can, Darkall. I'm only human,' she exclaimed, exasperated.

'No, you cannot do what I do. But you are incorrect about only being human. You are unique, and you have already demonstrated considerable power.'

'But I can only heal with my power. I can't fight off an

attack with it.'

'In that, you are wrong.'

'How can I use healing to fight?'

'You need to understand your power to be able to utilise it in other forms. To begin understanding, you must first fully accept that it exists. Energy such as yours can be used as you determine: to fight; to heal; to protect.'

'But I can't do any of those! At least, not well,' she whined.

'Then improve.'

Ellie felt frustrated. It was all very well for Mr. Superpowers to tell her to improve. She was only human, and not like him. Not like the "others" he spoke of. Not magical or able to feed from energy.

'I'm tired,' she said, turning away from him, her irritation evident in her voice.

'Then we will return.'

Darkall stepped up behind Ellie and wrapped her in his arms. She didn't lean back against him, but dropped her head forwards and closed her eyes. When she opened them, they were once again standing on the roof of Titch's apartment.

The wind had increased and her hair whipped around her face, but she left it unchecked, utilising her tresses as a shield for her mixed emotions.

Darkall pulled her back against him, pivoting them both so that his body shielded her from the wind. He lowered his head to the side of hers. 'You have great power, Eleanor. You will discover the ways to use it, given time.'

Ellie sighed again. 'I hope I have time.'

He dropped a kiss on the top of her head. 'There is always time,' he said. 'Now, you must rest.'

Ellie felt his arms drop away from her, and she knew he was

about to leave. A sudden need for physical comfort overtook her. She spun around and caught hold of his shoulders to stop him from disappearing, before flinging her arms around his neck and clinging to him. 'I'm afraid,' she said.

'I know,' he replied. 'But I am here for you. Remember that.'

She looked up at his face, staring directly into his silver-lit eyes. 'Promise me?'

In answer, he slowly lowered his head and kissed her. His lips were dry and warm, and Ellie felt her own tingle as tiny electric shocks danced along them. Shivering slightly, she returned the pressure of his kiss and felt his hands slide up from her back to hold her head. Looking into his eyes, she saw the silver lights sparking with increasing intensity, and this discernible effect of her kiss fuelled her own desire. Pressing herself against Darkall, Ellie closed her eyes and surrendered to her senses. Every point of contact with him generated a delicious prickle of electricity, and she crushed herself against him to intensify the feelings.

Darkall pulled back from the kiss, drawing a deep breath. His virtually pure silver eyes stared into hers for a long moment. As she watched, the purple gradually resurfaced, the fire of sparks separating into individual stars once again. 'You must go now. You need to rest,' he said.

Reluctantly, Ellie nodded in agreement, afraid to speak in case her swollen, fizzing lips lost this tantalising new sensation.

Darkall placed a final kiss on her forehead before releasing her face from between his hands. 'Goodnight, Eleanor,' he said with a smile.

Ellie turned away from him and walked towards the roof

access door. Closing it behind her and turning the key, she made her way back down the narrow staircase, her head spinning from the kiss. To say that she'd never been kissed like that before would be far too much of an understatement. *No one* had ever been kissed like that, she was sure. Nothing had ever set her senses alight quite like that; her whole body was still effervescing.

Quietly, Ellie passed through the doorway at the bottom of the stairs and closed it as silently as she could. The thick carpet muffled her footsteps as she trod carefully along the landing. Her breathing still disordered, she tried to breathe more quietly through her nose, but found that to actually be louder, with the slight whistling sound it generated.

Passing Jaz and Meg's room, she put her hand gently on the handle and carefully opened the door a crack. Hearing the sounds of deep breathing, she opened the door a little further so that she could see for herself they were safe.

Meg and Jaz lay in each other's arms under the covers, Meg's head tucked under Jaz's chin. Meg's banner had been draped across the counterpane as another blanket; perhaps they were still cold from the shock of recent events.

A warm feeling of deep affection for these two women suffused Ellie as she stood there and she smiled in the dark, but worry tainted the positive feeling. Ellie gently closed the door and continued along the corridor to her room. Flick was asleep in her bed, making no noise; she was curled in a ball, her back to Ellie's bed. She looked small and vulnerable. Ellie again felt guilty that she was endangering her dearest friends as she became further enmeshed in the bizarre and the uncanny.

As quietly as she could, Ellie undressed and slipped into

bed. She exhaled, only then realising that she'd been repeatedly holding her breath since entering the room to avoid disturbing Flick. Lying on her back under the covers, Ellie stretched her legs and pointed her toes. Next, she elongated her neck and pushed her head back into the pillows in a full body stretch. The tension of the stretch was gradually released as she relaxed every muscle group in turn, starting with her toes. It was something she'd done since childhood, particularly when trying to regroup from the nightmares and allow herself to unwind for normal sleep. Finally untensing her arms, fingers and neck, she exhaled a long breath and lay silent and loose limbed.

'I'm still here for you,' Flick said quietly, her voice slightly muffled by her duvet. 'If you need me. I'm not going anywhere. Sleep well, Ells.'

'I love you, Flick,' Ellie whispered, a smile in her voice. 'Sleep well, too.'

Ellie felt as if a weight had been lifted from her mind, but, at the same time, she also felt like crying. Whatever had she done in this life—or a previous one, perhaps—to deserve such loyalty, love and friendship?

26

# Chapter 26

Ellie woke early the next morning. She had slept deeply and without dreaming, as far as she could remember. Daylight illuminated the edges of the thick velvet curtains, and Ellie observed the pattern of corrugated light on the wall above. Not eager to begin a day in which she could potentially have to face the loss of some of her most cherished friends, or at least a reduction in their support, she lay still in her bed and tried to make herself fall back to sleep. But with her mind having already raised her major concern, however, there was no chance of revisiting that cherished state of oblivion.

Malaflies. Disgusting, abhorrent, invisible things that fed on negative energy; that sought out and feasted on the misery of people. And, presumably, not just misery, but grief, fear, hate, despair: indeed, all kinds of negative emotions were likely to be fodder for them. Worse still, the Herders deliberately stimulated these feelings in humans for their flocks to feed on. Ellie was glad she hadn't seen one of those, as the jagged-winged, insectoid Malaflies had been disturbing enough.

Was it these things she'd seen on the top of the Cenotaph, flying down to alight on passing protesters? Perhaps they'd been targeting those feeling sorrow or grief for the fallen soldiers represented by the memorial and relishing in their unhappiness. If so, it would make sense, according to Darkall's account. It followed, then, that the drunkard on the Tube had also been infested with these parasites, as Ellie had observed his dull-coloured energy being peppered with dark specks.

Ellie sighed. It was all too fantastical, too much to take on board and process, or even believe in.

But it was true.

She'd seen these things in her own energy vision. This other world, hidden from human reality, really did exist. Moreover, she'd only just lifted the corner of the lid on it and its nightmarish denizens, or the *Others,* as she'd mentally labelled the things pursuing her and those she'd witnessed.

Was it too late to put the lid back down? Could she go back to just being normal and living her life as she'd previously imagined she would without any of this scary and unwanted knowledge? She would lose *him,* of course, but before him, she'd been happy with normal guys like Jacob.

She had asked for this, though, hadn't she? She'd yearned to find the secrets she felt were just out of reach; the mysteries lying there, just waiting to be discovered. Ellie remembered the morning when the vales had been swathed in mist and recalled her yearning for the magical and the unknown. Isn't this what she had wished for?

No. This was way more frightening. Much more than she'd ever bargained for.

But, then again, would she really want to go back to a state

306

of ignorance? Beyond being frightening, this hidden world was hers alone to explore. Had any other humans ever been in the position she now found herself, poised at the very doorway of accepted reality?

There were also the new powers she'd developed to consider. Going back to being as she was before would mean giving them up. Darkall had said she would be able to use her energy in different ways; maybe she could learn to protect herself and those she loved from harm by the Others. But who could teach her those abilities? Mastering extranormal capabilities was not something you could simply learn at college.

Jill had predicted this. She'd read in the Tarot cards that change was coming; change that Ellie had to face or risk harming those around her. Harm had definitely arrived: she'd nearly got all four of them killed last night through her meddling in otherworldly matters. It was her role, her path to follow, not her friends', and by dragging them along with her, Ellie knew she was needlessly endangering some of the people she loved most.

As she reached this conclusion, a hollowness grew in her chest. The only logical option henceforth was to proceed on her own; keeping them close was clearly going to put their lives in jeopardy. The same applied to her parents. Ellie didn't want them involved in whatever was coming, either. Perhaps it would be better if she left home and went into self-imposed exile somewhere, away from everyone she cared about. At least that way, they couldn't be dragged into this bizarre future of hers.

A tear rolled down her cheek, wetting the cotton pillowcase. She sniffed, fighting back further tears, feeling alone and frightened. Having opened this Pandora's box, Ellie was now committed to playing out the hand she'd dealt herself. At least she would have Darkall. He was her rock; immovable, solid, something to cling on to amid the turmoil. He provided assurance and ease like no one else could.

*Wait a minute. When had Darkall become all of those things?*

Realisation dawned, and she now saw him as a feature of her life: always there to rescue her, to comfort her with his strength and to guide her through what lay ahead. At some point, Darkall had transformed from being a mysterious guy she was intrigued by, to being essential to Ellie—and she hadn't even noticed the change.

Ellie could hear noises downstairs in the kitchen. *The others must be up.* Coffee was what she needed to face her friends.

Ellie quietly got out of bed and slipped from the room, grabbing a jumper off the balloon-backed chair. Shrugging on the jumper, she went downstairs to the kitchen.

Leaning against the doorframe, she watched Jaz and Meg exploring Titch's cupboards and fridge.

'Lime, thickly cut orange or Harrod's own?' asked Jaz, whose head was virtually inside the fridge.

'Jam, treacle or honey for me, please. I can't stand peel in things.' Meg reached up and extracted two mugs from a wall cupboard.

'Really? You only mention this now? It's almost as big of a relationship wrecker as a love of ironing or not liking Marmite!'

Meg nudged Jaz's bottom with her hip as she passed, making Jaz's nose bump the butter dish. 'Ouch!' complained Jaz. 'That was cold!'

Smiling at their interaction, Ellie cleared her throat. 'Good morning.'

Jaz's head whipped up out of the fridge. 'Hi, Ellie,' she said. 'Sleep well?'

'Yes and no. Are you OK?' Ellie asked nervously.

Meg was leaning against the worktop, chewing her bottom lip and clutching the mugs to her chest. She turned and placed them carefully down on the marble worktop, then, crossing the space between them in three strides, she hugged Ellie. 'We're fine,' Meg reassured her.

Ellie felt tears running down her cheeks. She looked up at Jaz over Meg's shoulder, and Jaz nodded and smiled.

'We're fine. Still Team Ellie,' Jaz reaffirmed. 'I know you'll have been stewing about it all night, so don't even try to deny it. We came along on this trip by choice. You didn't *make* us do anything.'

'But you didn't know what you were getting yourselves into when you chose to stay over in London with me.'

'Neither did you,' Jaz replied.

'We knew there was something strange going on, and that it centred on you, Ellie,' said Meg. 'But we stayed with you because we're your friends and friends support each other, especially when one is in need. You've not chosen what has happened to you. You haven't had a choice at all, as far as I can see. Whatever is going on, it's not your fault.'

'But I think it is. I wished for this. Well, not *this*, exactly, but something other; something more than I had already. I wanted greater knowledge; to know mysterious secrets. *Magic*, even …' Ellie's voice tailed off, and she hung her head. 'I even chose him. I could have ignored him.'

'Not if he's been there your whole life, Ellie. You didn't ask for his help; it was given. You didn't appoint him as your bodyguard. Your destiny is something you can't control or avoid. You're a good person; this is not bad karma coming back on you—at least, not unless you were totally awful in a former life, and that I won't accept about someone who has the power to heal. This is not a mess of your making, but it is something that you'll have to go through and sort out, and we're planning on being right here with you, if you need us,' Meg assured Ellie.

'Hear, hear.' Flick's voice came from behind Ellie as she stepped into the kitchen, rubbing her eyes. 'Did you put the kettle on, Meg?'

'Yes, I'm on it,' said Meg, turning towards the kettle and flicking it on. She also reached up for two more mugs from the cupboard.

'Are you all sure?' asked a disbelieving Ellie, looking around at the earnest faces of her friends.

'As sure as you are that this is real and something you have to get through,' said Flick, opening the biscuit barrel and munching on a chocolate chip cookie. 'I'm not going to abandon you to those … whatever they are that are trying to get you.'

'The Others,' said Ellie in a small voice. 'It's what I call them.'

'Fine. "The Others". I'm not going to leave you on your own to face them.'

'And we can't, either,' Meg said, smiling.

Ellie wiped her tears with the sleeve of her nightshirt. 'I can't tell you what's going to happen. We'll get no warning of whatever is coming. You'll be safer away from me.'

'And we would be ashamed, too. Running away and leaving you to face all this on your own is *not* part of the plan,' Jaz replied.

'I just wish I knew what the plan was,' sighed Ellie.

'You'll find out. No. *We'll* find out,' answered Meg.

'Thank you, *all* of you. I don't deserve friends like you.'

'But that's just the point, Ells—you do,' said Flick.

The kettle started to whistle.

'Now, who's for tea and who's for coffee?'

'Brandy might be more appropriate, judging by Ellie's face,' suggested Flick.

'No, I'm fine,' she said, rubbing her eyes vigorously and managing a watery smile. 'I just don't know what to say. You're amazing. All of you.'

'And you've only just realised this now?' said Jaz with a wide grin.

\* \* \*

Having showered and dressed, the friends gathered in the luxurious sitting room and made their plans for the day. They were due to meet Titch at the museum at 2pm, and their train home left Paddington Station just after four. Other than that, they had the day to themselves.

Flick and Meg were keen to do some sightseeing, so Jaz agreed to accompany them around the tourist trail for the morning. Ellie declined to go with them, despite Meg's entreaties, because she claimed she had a headache and wanted to sleep it off before meeting Titch later on. In truth, Ellie was not unwell but wanted some time to herself to consider what to do next. She also felt that she ought to stay away from her friends where possible until she had more of a plan and more control over her power.

311

Having decided upon their course of action for the morning, Jaz and Meg popped back upstairs to collect their bags and jackets while Ellie and Flick remained in the sitting room. Flick glanced behind her to check they were alone before clearing her throat.

'I heard him, you know,' she said, looking seriously at Ellie. 'When you didn't come to bed, I wondered if you were OK, so I went downstairs to find you. I couldn't, obviously, so I returned to our room and opened the window for some air. I was just wondering where you were and whether I should wake the other two when I heard your voice—and his.'

Ellie just gave Flick a slight nod.

'I didn't eavesdrop on you; I couldn't hear what was being said. I just heard your voice and a deep male one. I figured you were with him, so I didn't panic. It was him, wasn't it?'

'Yes, it was Darkall,' answered Ellie.

'*Wow.* So, it really is all true; him, you, everything.'

Ellie nodded, and Flick exhaled a long breath. 'I just wanted you to know that I believe you.'

Ellie smiled at her friend. 'Thank you, Flick.'

'He sounds very sexy, by the way.'

Ellie grinned. 'He is.'

Meg and Jaz came back into the sitting room at that point, so their conversation on Darkall's finer points was curtailed before it really began. The adventurous trio left the apartment in good spirits, and upon hearing the front door of the house close, Ellie relaxed back on the sofa with her lukewarm coffee.

She swung her legs up and pivoted herself around, then wiggled down to rest her head on the arm. Peace. Stillness. She closed her eyes and breathed slowly, letting her anxiety wash from her mind. The trick was not to let anything else back in.

She concentrated on a blank white screen on the inside of her eyelids and held that state of detachment, not allowing any thoughts to permeate the white. Ellie could only hold this for a few seconds before her mind forced thoughts back across her consciousness. It was always a battle: defending the borders of the white screen from invading thoughts pressing in around its edges. It was like maintaining balance with her mind. Ellie's mother had taught her to do this; Grace had said that it created a meditative state which was important for Ellie to be able to achieve.

Ellie tried again. This time, she allowed the white screen to be the warm yellow of the energy she saw in her mind's eye; not a swirl, just a flat colour. She held the balance point for longer this time, although the yellow would not stay flat, instead pulsing across the screen behind her eyelids. Ellie ignored the movement, however, and did not allow her mind to think about it or anything else.

She tried a third time. After fifteen seconds, a tingle began at the back of her head. She ignored it and continued to breathe deeply. The longer she held the balance, the greater the tingle grew, until it filled her head and made the back of her eyes ache slightly. It was a building, tickling, shivering, near orgasmic sensation, but it all took place inside her head, rather than her body. Still, she held the balance point. Ellie's hands began to tingle with pins and needles, and her arms felt tiny pinpricks of invisible electricity dancing along them. Still clasped around her mug of coffee, her hands were getting warm. No, they were getting hot. *Very* hot.

Ellie's eyes flew open, and she swiftly grasped the handle

313

of the mug. Releasing the bowl from her painfully hot hands, she looked at the brown liquid in disbelief.

It was boiling.

Putting the mug swiftly down on the side table, Ellie drew back from it, fearing what she had just witnessed. She rubbed her stinging hands together; the boiling hot cup had not scalded them, but her palms were red. Steam rose from her mug as she watched in disbelief. Had she just done that? She must have, unless the Others' new plan was to attack her with small amounts of scalding liquid.

Ellie lifted the corner of her mouth in a wry smile at the unlikelihood of this last thought; if only their offensive deeds were that minor. It was her. It *had* to be her. Her energy had made the cold coffee boil. Darkall had said she had power which could be used how she saw fit. But she hadn't registered a desire for hot coffee. Perhaps that had been just a by-product of her summoning the energy in her head.

The first stage in controlling her power was to accept that it existed, Darkall had told her. Well, this was it. Picking up the mug by the handle, she brought it to her lips, blowing on the hot liquid before taking a careful sip. It was piping hot and as delicious as a fresh cup.

She had power. Fact.

Ellie smiled. *Stage one: check.*

'Well done, Eleanor.' Darkall's voice sounded very close.

'I can do this!' she said, her confidence leaping at the proof of her power.

'You can indeed.'

She looked up at him standing behind the sofa in the shadow thrown by the one still-closed curtain. His hands dropped onto her shoulders, and he began to massage the back of her neck. Ellie tensed; she hated anyone touching her neck due to the strangling fingers in her nightmares—although now she supposed she'd have to think of them as *attacks* rather than nightmares.

Darkall's hands stilled, then slid down her arms as he crouched down behind the low-backed sofa. His chin replaced his hand on her shoulder and he began to kiss her neck, leaving a trail of tingling, excited skin. Ellie tilted her head and stretched her neck to grant his lips further access to her skin. He took the mug from her hand and placed it on the side table, then softly touched the skin of her upper arms and trailed his fingers down to the backs of her hands. Ellie gasped at the electricity stinging her skin at his touch. It was as if he were setting her on fire.

Linking his fingers with hers, he brought her hands up to her face. 'Look at them,' Darkhall said, holding her palms inwards. 'Here is where you direct your power.'

Ellie looked at her hands, but her mind wasn't concentrating on his words, only her need for him to continue touching her. He chuckled as if reading her mind. 'Perhaps another time may be more appropriate to discuss your power.'

Ellie closed her fingers around his and pulled his arms tightly against her torso. He rose to his feet, lifting her easily as he did so. Ellie was now standing on the sofa, facing away from him. She wriggled around inside the circle of his arms and knelt on the rolled sofa back, facing him, her lips level with his chin. Reaching up, she held his face and brought his lips down to meet hers. She relished his solidity; his sheer physical size, combined with the taunt muscles of his arms and torso pressed against her, was overwhelmingly erotic. His hands lowered to the back of her thighs as if about to

315

lift her legs around him, but then stayed and returned to her back. She made a small mew of discontent, and he chuckled.

'We have time, Eleanor,' he said, gently brushing the hair back from her flushed face.

'I always think there's no time like the present,' she replied with a coy smile.

His lips spread in a wide smile, and he laughed. 'That is undoubtably true, and very welcome to hear.' He looked down into her eyes and said in a more serious tone of voice, 'Should we take this further, it will be when we have *plenty* of time.'

Ellie nodded, rather disappointed. It seemed to her that there was plenty of time now, but she supposed that Flick, Jaz and Meg would be back for lunch in due course.

Darkall picked her up, one arm around her back and the other under her knees. He carried her around to the front of the sofa and lightly set her down in her former repose. 'Now,' he said, 'you need to speak to someone, I believe.'

'I do?' asked Ellie.

On the side table, her mobile phone started to ring. She glanced automatically at it before looking back up to him, but he was gone. With a regretful sigh, Ellie picked up her phone and answered the call.

'Ellie! Thank goodness! Are you safe, child? I have made a most disturbing reading and was worried you had been attacked again.'

'You were right; we were attacked. But I'm OK. In fact, very much so, at the moment.' Ellie grinned to herself.

'Ah, I am *so* relieved,' replied Jill, not picking up on the last part of the sentence. 'How were you attacked?'

Ellie proceeded to explain the events of the previous

evening.

'You have seen him since?' Jill asked.

'Yes.' Ellie grinned again, 'I have.' Then, bringing her full attention to the conversation, she added, 'He's told me some amazingly strange things—the stuff of fairy tales or nightmares— but I believe him. I've seen some for myself.'

'Seen with your own eyes?'

'No. Seen with my mind's eye, as an energy picture.'

'Ah! Then you can rely on that. Sometimes what we see with our eyes can be manipulated, but what you see with your third eye cannot be falsified.'

'I've also proved to myself beyond any doubt that I do have power … energy abilities … or whatever they're called.'

'Mercy be! I'm so glad you've finally accepted what you are capable of. So many people refuse to believe what they witness or experience due to it being "impossible". They deny their own abilities and those of others because their closed minds don't allow them to consider that there is more to this world than can be seen or touched. That way often leads to wasted lives, unachieved potentials, and a constant feeling of dissatisfaction.'

'I don't really know what I'm capable of. Darkall tells me I can use my power to heal, to protect, to attack and defend—pretty much anything I need it to do. But I've no idea how I'm going to learn to do so, or who could teach me.'

'I don't think there is a teacher capable of teaching you, child. But there may be some who can advise or point you in the right direction with tips and suggestions. I will have a think about it.'

Ellie's confidence slightly deflated at the truth in Jill's words. This was not going to be easy; she was going to have to feel her way forwards in the dark in terms of developing her powers.

'This Darkall is likely to be the one who can guide you best,' Jill said, breaking into Ellie's dispiriting speculation.

A thought occurred to Ellie. 'Speaking of *guiding*, Meg was telling me about spirit guides. She thought Darkall might be one. Have you come across them before?'

'Yes. Or, at least, I know there are different types that are thought to guide us on our journey through life; to keep us on our intended path.'

'Have you ever come across one, or found any evidence of them? Have you ever been helped by one?'

Jill thought for a moment. 'Possibly, although mine have been more subtle than yours if your Darkall is indeed a guide. Mind you, his role appears to be much more than one of guidance.'

Ellie grinned to herself again. She really hoped so.

'Was that a smirk I could detect, Ellie dear?' queried Jill, amusement in her voice.

Ellie wondered how the woman had sensed her grinning. But if Ellie accepted that she herself had extranormal powers, then why shouldn't others have them, too?

'Quite right, dear,' said Jill, in an uncanny response to Ellie's thoughts. She cleared her throat. 'I was once in the presence of a guardian spirit,' she began. 'When I was many years younger, I was walking on the Quantock Hills in Somerset in a guided group with some friends. These are ancient lands with high-heath-covered summits and deep, wooded valleys. The rolling farmland is sprinkled with small villages clinging to the sides of the hills. It is a very dramatic place and full of age-old mystery.'

Jill paused for a moment to marshal her memories.

'We were following a ley line to the top of a particular hill. Around the summit was an ancient grove of trees that was to be our destination. As we approached the top of the hill, we all felt something immense and powerful stirring ahead of us within the trees. The hairs on our arms stood up, and we all sensed imminent danger. As we stood there, frightened and not knowing what to do, a great energy surged through all of us, rushing down the ley line towards the trees. Our group leader and guide, a local wisewoman, told us that we needed to leave immediately, as there were matters beyond our comprehension being resolved at the brow of the hill. She insisted we turn around and walk away without looking backwards. We did as we were bid, of course, and made our way back down the hill. Some of the group departed as soon as they reached the car park, clearly having been spooked by the experience and keen to get away. Others, including myself, my friends and our guide, retired to the local pub for a quick drink to steady our nerves.'

Ellie felt the skin on her arms prickle at the unsettling tale. She waited silently for Jill to continue.

'Well, when we were all settled around a table with our cider and ale, we began to speak quietly about what we'd jointly experienced. I could only testify to a feeling of terror and helplessness and the rush of energy that passed through me. It blew my hair and my clothes as it passed, as it did for the others in the line. A friend of mine spoke up then. He said he had seen a vision, an outline of a horse-backed rider speeding towards the brow of the hill with sword outstretched. He had been at the front of the line of walkers, and as we'd turned to retrace our steps, he found himself at the rear. He said

319

he had turned for a final look at the summit, despite being instructed not to by our guide, and had seen the trees in the circle thrashing in an unfelt and unheard gale. Our guide had said nothing during his account, merely raising her eyebrows when he admitted to not having followed her instructions. "You are blessed in seeing the guardian of the ley line," she said. "Had you seen more than that when you turned around, you may not be here with us now. I would suggest you keep this experience to yourselves. It was not meant for us to see or witness." With that, she stood up, nodded at each of us in turn and left the pub. Well, I haven't spoken of the experience to many, but I share it with you now as an assurance that I do believe what you've told me. I have witnessed beings from outside our realm myself.'

'Thank you for telling me,' said Ellie. 'So, that was a guardian of the ley line. Well, if he exists, then there are no reasons why other guardians shouldn't also.'

'My thoughts exactly,' said Jill. 'One other point. When you get back, I might be able to help you with your protective energy. There is a visualisation technique you may find helpful.'

'I don't think I can wait until I get back. If you have something that might help, then I need to know now. We are already under attack."

'Very well, child. But an explanation over the phone only goes so far. You previously entrusted me with a description of how you raised your healing energy. I remember you saying that you envisaged a spiral of yellow-white fire inside you. The formation of protection energy is all about creating a shell. Try it for yourself, at first. Imagine seeing inside yourself a wall around your core being, like an eggshell but impervious and made of pure energy. Sometimes it helps if you see a miniature version of yourself inside the energy shell to represent your core being. Now, see all the arrows of psychic attack, not necessarily from these creatures but from human negative attack, too; things such as jealousy, ill will, nastiness and so on. Visualise the arrows being turned aside, points blunted and bent from impact with the energy shell. They don't even leave a mark. Nothing can get through to you; your core is protected, the shell totally impenetrable. When you have mastered this for your inner self, then develop the technique and expand the shell to surround your actual physical being. Following that, you might explore expanding it further to encompass those around you. Eventually, you may even be able to project it to protect someone further away. It is not a tried and tested method, at least not beyond protecting one's own inner self from psychic attack, but it seems to me that it might be a way for you to develop a protection power. When I was thinking of your healing method, it came to me. Because you visualise your energy, this method just might work for you.'

'Wow. I think I understand. I'll have to try it.'

'Yes, make sure that you do. It sounds like you are going to need it.'

'There's something else, too.' Ellie recounted the boiling coffee incident.

'Amazing! You truly are blessed, Ellie. Having taken on board what you have just imparted, I feel even more strongly that the method I've just outlined might really work well for you.'

'Thanks, Jill. I really do appreciate all your help.'

'Nonsense, child! We are family, of a sort. Family looks

after one another.'

'My friends have said pretty much the same thing.'

'Glad to hear it. You will need all the support you can get. None of this is easy, nor, I am sorry to say, do I think it will get any easier without becoming much more difficult first. Have you spoken to your parents yet?'

Ellie hesitated. 'No. No, I haven't. I still don't want to drag them into this.'

'They are your parents, Ellie; they are already involved in this in more ways than you think. But I will say no more; it is your decision. Take care, Ellie. I will be watching out for you.'

'Bye, Jill,' Ellie said, just before the line went dead. Jill didn't like goodbyes.

Ellie felt reassured; she did have friends and family that could help her. Maybe she ought to speak to her parents now and explain what she'd been going through. At least that way, they'd be aware of any weird stuff going on around them, or even weird stuff happening to her. Worse-case scenario, they would be more prepared for news of her death.

Ellie relaxed back into the sofa and closed her eyes, but the bright sunlight made the room too light. Ellie flung her arm over her eyes to block out the light and tutted in dissatisfaction. Without any evident cause, the curtains slid smoothly across the windows, shutting the sun's rays from the room. Ellie felt warm lips press against her forehead; she smiled and drifted off into restful sleep.

# 27

# Chapter 27

'Wake up, lazy bones!' Flick's voice called from across the room. 'Look what I've bought!'

Ellie blinked at the sudden light flooding the room as Jaz pulled the curtains open.

'How's your head?' Meg asked solicitously, perching on the end of the sofa upon which Ellie lay.

'Much better, thank you,' Ellie answered honestly, although not making reference to her fabricated headache.

Flick dumped a London Dungeon paper bag onto Ellie's stomach, making her flinch. Inside was a resin model of three severed heads on spikes, all with appropriate amounts of modelled gore spilling from their gaping necks.

Ellie pulled a face. 'Seriously?! What goes on in your head, Felicity?'

'It's for Chris. He'll love it,' Flick replied with a confident smile.

'In that case, if I were you, I'd be rather concerned that my boyfriend is potentially an axe murderer,' remarked Jaz darkly.

'He's a pussycat,' Flick tossed back.

'OK, well, we warned you. At least the press can't say we didn't try when parts of your dismembered body are found across three different counties.'

'Never going to happen,' replied Flick. 'He worships the ground I walk on.'

'I'm surprised you don't float, you're so self-inflated,' Jaz retorted.

'Enough!' snapped the usually mild Meg. 'They have been like this all morning! I couldn't wait to get back here and have some normal conversation with you, Ellie.'

Jaz looked contrite. 'Sorry, Meg. We just do it for fun, you know.'

'I know. It may be fun for the both of you, but it's very trying for the spectator, especially after a couple of hours of it.'

'Sorry, Meg,' said Flick repentantly. 'We'll play nice now, promise.' She winked at Jaz.

'I'm glad to see you've had a sleep, Ellie,' Meg remarked. 'You look a better colour now than when we left.'

Ellie almost blushed thinking about what may have heightened her colour that morning. 'I had a chat with Jill,' she said, to cover her thoughts. 'She advised me on some prevention tactics.'

'Great. It might not be an easy path you're on, but as long as you have your back up team, you'll be OK,' said Jaz with an encouraging grin and a double thumbs up.

Ellie had a hunch that her friends just might have had a conversation during their sightseeing trip along the lines of how to keep Ellie's spirits up. Ellie smiled and felt a grateful rush of love towards the three women in the room with her.

'Let's raid Titch's kitchen once more for lunch and then get all packed up ready for the museum,' she suggested.

'Plan!' declared Flick.

Their lunch was a delicious buffet of olives, cured meats, salad, cheeses and fresh bread cooked from the par-baked baguettes Jaz found in the freezer.

'Do you think we ought to leave some money for Titch to restock his fridge, or even pop out and buy replacements? I wouldn't want to leave him short,' Meg asked amid mouthfuls of pesto and herb-drenched macaroni.

'No,' said Ellie. 'He wouldn't want us to do that. Titch is incredibly generous and likes to provide all he can think of for his guests. He wouldn't accept our money. Besides, he rarely eats here as he's out for most of his meals.'

'In that case, maybe he wouldn't mind us packing up a snack for the train journey home?' Flick suggested, an eyebrow raised in query.

Ellie laughed. 'No, not at all. In fact, he would be delighted we'd enjoyed the food so much that we wanted to take it home with us,' she answered with a confident smile.

'Excellent!' declared Jaz. 'Then you can get your paws off the humous; it's *mine*,' she said, lunging for the lidded pot.

After a lunch enjoyable not only in its cuisine but also in its light-hearted companionship, Ellie and the others gathered their belongings and packed their bags. After seeing Titch, and depending on the amount of time they had left before needing to be at the station, they had various ideas of how to spend the remainder of their London excursion. These included a quick mooch around the shops (Flick), people-watching while sipping coffee at an outside café table (Meg) and wandering around the British Museum exhibits and shop

(Jaz). Ellie was not fussed what she did.

Having stripped the beds and tidied the apartment, they regretfully closed the front door on Titch's home and descended the stairs to the entrance hallway.

'Ooo, wait! My thank you card,' said Meg.

'Post it in the box outside,' recommended Jaz.

Exiting the building, Meg peered at the labels on the metal postbox to the right of the front door. 'Funny to think of Titch as Charles Mackworth,' she said. 'He's always going to be Titch in my head.'

'It suits him to have a nickname,' said Jaz. 'He's a genuinely nice guy.'

Leaving Elgin Crescent, they unhurriedly made their way towards the Tube station. Ellie's backpack felt uncomfortably heavy and full due to her new clothes and the weighty package she carried within it.

Ladbroke Grove Tube station was not busy in the early afternoon, so they didn't have to shuffle along cramped platforms or stand up on the train; as is the usual case anywhere near rush hour. Ellie was understandably nervous about going on the Tube; her claustrophobic tendencies combined with yesterday's experience put her on edge and ever vigilant for a possible source of attack.

'It's OK,' said Jaz, seeing her unease and squeezing Ellie's hand, which lay clenched on her thigh. 'We're all together. We can take down another crazy drunk, no problem.'

Ellie smiled, but it came out as more of a grimace.

Ladbroke Grove was on the Hammersmith & City line. They'd have to change at King's Cross St. Pancras on their journey to the museum. As the train pulled away from the station, Ellie experienced a niggling anxiety. She withdrew her smartphone from her pocket and examined the Tube map she'd downloaded. Looking at the spaghetti-like tangle of stations, her gaze kept returning to King's Cross St. Pancras. Here, six Underground lines interchanged, as well as the two mainline stations. There would be literally thousands of people milling about; all too easy to find susceptible minds.

The more she looked at the map, the greater her unease grew. Was this her instincts sending her a message? A precognitive warning? Or was it just fear making her unnecessarily cautious? Realising quickly that it didn't matter either way, and that anything which might possibly be dangerous needed avoiding, Ellie stood up as the train pulled into Edgware Road.

'We need to get off,' she told the other three.

They each looked confused. Jaz had decided upon their route as their designated "Tube Planner". For one moment, she looked as though she might argue with Ellie's instruction, but after Meg elbowed her in the ribs, she stood up and stepped off the train with the rest of them. Huddling against the wall as other passengers headed for the exit, they all looked to Ellie for an explanation of the sudden change in travel plans.

'I just got this feeling that something bad was likely to happen at King's Cross,' she said. 'So many people there; so many minds to control.'

'It's OK,' Meg said. 'We trust you.'

Flick looked pointedly at Jaz with a raised eyebrow.

'Well, of course we do. You're the one with the connection to this weird stuff, after all.'

327

Jaz took Ellie's smartphone and looked at the map. She pointed out an alternative route to Ellie. Having followed Jaz's finger, Ellie nodded; her instincts told her that this was safer. They made their way over to the westbound platform, and after a brief wait, a rush of air signalled the arrival of the next train.

As soon as the doors slid open, the friends stepped aboard, Jaz in front of Ellie and Meg and Flick behind her. On the long side seats, her friends sat either side of and directly across from her, and Ellie realised that they were forming a protective circle around her.

The change at Notting Hill Gate was incident-free, and Ellie's nervousness began to lessen. She felt her shoulders relax, and some of the tension left her face. Jaz smiled at her from across the aisle, clearly noticing Ellie's reduced anxiety. Ellie looked up at the route map on the wall above Jaz's head; only two stops away from the museum station. Not long to go now.

The train rocked unexpectedly from side to side, and the carriage lights briefly flickered. Ellie held her breath, then exhaled. *It's OK*, she told herself, *it's just an electrical glitch. It happens all the time on Tube trains.* The train rocked again, more forcefully this time, and Ellie swayed with the movement. Suddenly, the lights went out, plunging the carriage into pitch black as the train slowed to a stop.

Ellie tensed and looked pointlessly up and down the carriage, unable to see anything. *Stupid*, she admonished herself. Feeling Meg's hand on her arm giving a squeeze of reassurance, Ellie closed her eyes. She concentrated on the point where Darkall had pressed his palm to her forehead, and an energy picture formed in her mind, showing the passengers in the carriage. Ellie scanned all seventeen energy forms; they each showed different colours along with the usual yellow energy, but none of them had the blooming blackness in the area of their heads. Interestingly, a few had Malaflies on them, but not in great numbers. She relaxed and opened her eyes.

'It's OK,' she said aloud to the others. 'Nothing weird.'

'Phew,' Flicks voice replied from Ellie's right.

Staring ahead of her into the blackness, Elie glimpsed two purple and silver points flash briefly in the glass of the window opposite just before the carriage lights came back on. Seconds later, the train juddered forwards and picked up speed with its familiar rising whine. Ellie pressed her thumb to the ring on her third finger and felt a very faint vibration running through the warm metal. It was barely noticeable and became fainter still, until the metal was free from all tremorous sensation.

Darkall had been there. Maybe he had prevented something from happening, or maybe nothing was going to happen and he was just reassuring her. Either way, it felt good to know that he'd been looking out for her. The tension left her now that she knew he was around to deal with anything bad, and she allowed her mind to recall the brief meeting with Darkall that morning.

'I'm coming to recognise that expression, Ellie Johnstone,' Jaz said, looking at Ellie's slightly distracted but smiling face.

'Yeah, she gets it when she's thinking of Mr Dark N' Mysterious,' said Flick.

Ellie grinned; they were right.

The train eventually slowed into Tottenham Court Road Station, and the four friends got off and followed the overhead signs to the exit. The British Museum was only five minutes' walk from here.

Emerging from the station building, Ellie felt relieved. Open spaces were her natural environment—even if they were crowded with buildings, cars and people, they were more familiar and less threatening than being underground.

Strolling along Great Russell Street, the four girls saw the high, metal railings which guarded the museum's grounds on the opposite side of the road. It was a truly magnificent building. The entrance pavilion was flanked by two grand wings reaching forwards, and in front of it, an open area of grass separated the museum from the busy street.

Ellie watched the comparatively tiny people swarming in and out of the building. They reminded her bees entering and leaving the hives in Jill's garden. Perhaps knowledge was hoarded in the museum like honey in the hive? The building dwarfed the humans and instilled a sense of awe and wonder in the visitor while, at the same time, highlighting their own transient insignificance—which was no doubt the intention of the architect.

The girls crossed the road opposite a gate in the railings. Entering the British Museum site, they followed the pathway heading for the entrance marquee, where their bags would be searched.

'Wait a minute,' said Ellie. 'We should get a picture here. Go and stand together so I can take one of you guys.'

Grumbling mildly but good-naturedly, Flick, Jaz and Meg obliged by standing in a line with the museum's porticoed entrance behind them. Ellie had snapped several shots before a grey-haired Oriental gentleman approached her and offered, through the language of hand signals, to take

330

a photo of all four of them. Ellie thanked him and went to stand with the other three.

Having taken several photos, the gentleman gave a thumbs up and Ellie walked back to him to retrieve her phone and thank him for his kindness. The man spoke to her in Japanese, repeating the same phrases several times accompanied by hand signals, but Ellie couldn't understand either. She shrugged helplessly and shook her head, indicating her incomprehension.

The man turned and called to a group of Japanese people, and a girl of about Ellie's age detached herself from the group and walked over. Reaching them, she stood to her elder's left and bent her head to speak with him. After several nods, she looked back to Ellie and relayed his message.

'My grandfather says you and your friends are like the four elements. He says you are Fire.' She ran her hands down her own long hair and indicated Ellie's tresses. 'You are Fire here.' She pointed at Ellie's hair and then at her heart. 'Your friends are Earth, Water and Wind.' She pointed at Flick, Jaz and Meg in turn. 'Grandfather says you are the four elements. You are …'

She turned back to the man and they exchanged further words.

'He says you are strong when you are together, but Fire will always be the element with the most power. It is given by the sun goddess Amaterasu.'

'Thank you,' said Ellie, 'and please pass my thanks to your grandfather.'

They bowed to each other, and Ellie returned to her friends as the pair linked arms and walked back to their group.

'You're always getting waylaid by strangers! If there's some oddball out there, then it's Ellie they make a beeline for,' Flick remarked.

'Not fair. That guy was just trying to help me; he was sweet. His granddaughter told me we are the four elements: Jaz is Water, Meg is Wind, and you're Earth. We're apparently powerful when we're together.'

'I don't know about powerful. More like powerfully annoying, when these two get together,' Meg remarked cynically.

'Objection!' Flick intoned.

'Sustained,' chimed Jaz sonorously.

'Anyway, why do I get to be Earth?'

'I'm guessing because your hair is currently brown,' said Jaz. 'That would make me deep, black water, if we're going by hair colours.'

Flick eyed Jaz with an assessing gaze. 'You're definitely dark. And kind of scary.'

'I don't mind being Wind,' interrupted Meg in a timely fashion. 'I like the idea of being light and floaty.'

'Or farty and smelly,' added Flick in an undertone, with a wicked grin.

Meg and Ellie laughed. Jaz grimaced.

'People, please,' begged Jaz dramatically. 'We are standing in front of a temple to mankind's culture, art, history and life—and you're laughing at fart jokes? Am I the only one who sees anything wrong here?'

Ellie, Flick and Meg exchanged conspiratorial grins before turning and walking to the bag checking marquee.

28

# Chapter 28

Although rather gloomy on first impression, having stepped from sunlight into the shade of the building's interior, Ellie thought the high Entrance Hall of the British Museum was even more impressive than its exterior. Mighty square columns held up the gridded stone ceiling many metres above their heads, and they craned their necks to take in the impressive dimensions of the room, until they were forced to keep moving with the press of visitors.

To their left, the imperial staircase was guarded either side by stone lions. At the half landing, it split right and left to return back on itself and reach the floor above. Directly ahead of them, light spilled into the lobby from the vast, bright interior of the Great Court.

The pull of the light, as well as a desire to get away from the crush of bodies, drew them into the vast space.

'*Wow!* That roof is immense,' remarked Jaz. She arched her neck to take in the full splendour of the framed glass roof enclosing the entire internal courtyard.

'I wouldn't want to clean it,' commented Flick.

Ellie looked up and admired the architecture. Steel beams looped out in massive curves from the base of the Reading Room dome to meet the roof edges of the courtyard buildings. The whole glass roof curved vertically, dissected by its beams curving in the horizontal plane. It took her breath away to think of the logistics of designing such a roof. She supposed computer modelling had played a large part, otherwise it would surely stretch a designer's mind to distraction to compute the loads, spans and stresses of such a huge structure. The curves of the roof steels running in one direction were crossed with arcs going in the other direction. The whole effect was of two huge spirals turning against each other, one on top of the other, but also impossibly interwoven at the same time.

Jaz acquired a leaflet from a nearby stand and held it open for them to view the museum map. 'I would like to see the Egyptian rooms,' she said.

'It's half past one now, and I want to check out the Chinese Tomb guardians and the Sutton Hoo exhibition, so why don't we split up as we've only got half an hour before meeting Titch?' suggested Ellie.

'Where are we meeting him?' asked Meg.

'He said to go to the information desk in the Great Court and ask them to call him.'

Flick acquired three more leaflets and handed them out. 'Right, now we can all go our own separate ways and meet back here in half an hour,' she said.

Meg glanced at Ellie nervously. 'Ellie, will it be safe splitting up?'

Ellie was about to nod and reassure her, but then took a moment to wonder why she was so ready to send all of them off alone throughout the building. She realised that she felt a great sense of calm here; all the anxiety of the Underground had entirely left her, and she felt safe. Was it because she thought Darkall was watching her, ready to protect her? No, that wasn't it. She didn't actually know that for a fact, and even if it were so, attacks could still happen, as the last twenty-four hours had proved.

She looked up again at the massive spirals frozen in motion above her head. Perhaps that was it; here was a space protected by the spiral symbol, and her own experience had taught her it was therefore likely to be safe.

'Yes, we're OK here,' she said, smiling reassuringly at Meg.

Jaz looked like she was going to intervene, but Meg took her arm and led her away towards the Egyptian galleries.

'Enjoy the head space,' said Flick, before turning and heading towards the Enlightenment Galleries.

Ellie looked around her, suddenly feeling rather vulnerable in such a huge public space. Yet the anxiety she had experienced on the Tube did not return, and she squared her shoulders and walked purposely around the curve of the Reading Room building towards the galleries at the rear. She walked quickly, conscious that she had little time and that her chosen galleries were not particularly close to one another.

Reaching the Chinese Tomb Guardian gallery, she slowed her pace dramatically and strolled towards a large, centrally located glass display case. Here, arranged in a parade, were the tomb guardians of the Tang Dynasty. Maybe they would have filled a corridor that led to the actual tomb.

The front two were rather demonic-looking, with ferocious faces, wings and cloven hooves. One figure had a green-glazed face and was rather dragon-like while the other's face was the pale biscuit colour of the fired clay. Behind these two were a pair of scary, more human-like beings with faces set in smiling grimaces, and behind them were two humans supposed to be a pair of civil servants. At the rear were two horses, two camels and three grooms. This ruler was well guarded in the afterlife and would certainly have been so during his lifetime, too. Ellie found herself ruefully wishing she had such a back-up team.

But, then again, she did, didn't she? Her loyal friends, Jill, Bertie, Titch, her parents—all of them were on her side. Ellie smiled to herself at the comforting realisation. Then there was Darkall, too, of course. Ellie's smile widened. Grinning to herself, she left the guardians to their vigil and retraced her steps towards her next stop, the Sutton Hoo room.

Taking a shortcut up the stairs of the Grand Court and through the restaurant, Ellie turned right into the Gems of Ur gallery. At the end of the wing, she turned right again and headed past the beautiful gold pieces of the Oxus Treasure.

As Ellie hurried along, a particularly ornate armlet caught her attention. She stopped and walked back to its cabinet. There was something odd about it; she felt almost as if it were calling to her. Looking closer, Ellie saw an intricate gold arm bracelet with two griffins facing each other across a small gap; the claws on their paws nearly touching. Horns curved up and back over their heads, their wings were raised high above their backs, beaks open as if facing off for a fight. It was one of a pair of armlets and, according to their information card, they would originally have been enamelled and had precious stones set into the gold.

Ellie concentrated on the artefact. She felt, rather than heard, a slow thrumming coming from the piece. She closed her eyes and opened her mind's eye. Sure enough, the armlet was pulsing with a purple-red energy. Ellie wished she could touch it to further explore the source and type of energy, but the item was sealed in a glass case, so she had to make do with placing her palm on the glass directly in front of it. Her skin could feel the energy coming off it in waves, one every few seconds.

She opened her eyes. No one had noticed her stood there with her eyes shut, except a rather sticky-looking child. Ellie removed her hand from the glass and gave it a guilty polish with the sleeve of her jacket. Winking at the child, she moved on.

So, objects as well as living things could have energy, too. Or maybe they could at least collect and store it. How long had that armlet been pulsing energy? The items here were from the First Persian Empire, dating back more than 2500 years ago. Could it have been pulsing all that time? If so, Ellie couldn't imagine just how much energy it would have had originally. It must have been an extremely powerful object—and there were a pair of them.

Ellie checked her watch: only ten minutes until she had to meet back up with the others. She hurried through the rest of the rooms until she came to Room 41. This exhibition, she was really keen to see: it was the Sutton Hoo gallery and inside were some of the amazing ship burial finds excavated from a grave mound in Suffolk.

Wandering around the display, Ellie felt that one of most impressive things about the whole find was that the Anglo Saxons had dragged an entire ship up from the river, dug out enough ground to sink it so that only its keel and bow stood up from the ground and then, after placing fabulous treasure and their dead king in the centre, mounded earth over the whole lot.

The second most amazing thing was how internationally connected the Anglo Saxons appeared to have been. Treasures found in the ship came from Europe and beyond and included precious metal items, arms and armour such as the famous Sutton Hoo helmet: a crested, full face mask with deep cheek pieces and beautifully intricate decoration chased into the tinned bronze. Here were the belongings of a great man whose people valued him highly enough to ensure he was well provided for in the afterlife. The replica of the reconstructed helmet was a marvel of detailed ornamentation, but it was too perfect and somehow felt dead and sterile. Ellie thought the fragments of the original helmet had more awe about them; it was they that had once rested on the ancient monarch's head.

Ellie drew her hair to one side as she leaned in to read the information card for the silver dining bowls and spoons. Sensing a tingling on the back of her neck, she straightened up and turned around. Behind her was a display case containing the remains of a purse and the Great Buckle made of gold, among other pieces. It was the Buckle; she was sure of it. Just like the Persian armlet in the previous gallery, the Buckle had power. She closed her eyes and concentrated. Sure enough, the Buckle was surrounded by sparkling gold energy; not coming off in waves as before, but hanging in the air as a glinting mist.

Moving, pulsing energy; static, shimmering energy; her own energy which she could set spinning and then fire off into another person—clearly, energy came in many forms and, indeed, colours. Ellie wondered what the significance of the colour was; could it be to do with the level of energy or the different types such as healing or harming; good or bad? No, that didn't seem right; energy was surely just energy. It was the user that decreed what it did. She wondered if energy could be charged with, or tainted by, intent long term? She would have to have a conversation with Jill on the subject, or maybe Darkall, if he felt like being slightly less enigmatic than usual.

Becoming aware of her frowning reflection in the glass of the display case, Ellie drew her thoughts back to the room with a slight shake of her head. *Titch.* She looked at her watch: she was already seven minutes late to meet back up with the others.

Turning abruptly and startling a woman behind her who'd been reading the display case information over Ellie's shoulder, Ellie swiftly made her way out of the gallery. She skirted the crowd in the Lewis Chessmen gallery and glimpsed many fabulous Medieval treasures as she somewhat guiltily sped through rooms towards the main staircase.

The sticky child was suddenly in front of her, swinging on the arm of a tired looking mother. 'Look, Mummy! Mummy! Mummy! Sparkly lady!'

The child pointed up at Ellie. His mother smiled at Ellie in an apologetic manner and lifted the child up into her arms, telling him it was not polite to point. As Ellie moved forwards again, regaining her momentum, she could hear the child's voice replying to its mother. 'But she's sparkly, like the gold bucket.'

Ellie smiled to herself; flattering to be likened to a bucket, but then maybe not so bad if it were a gold one.

Back in the Great Court, her friends were waiting for her.

'And what time do you call this?' asked Flick in an officious tone.

'Sorry, I got lost in the Sutton Hoo exhibit.'

'Sutton who?' asked Flick, unable to resist.

'*Hoo*,' replied Ellie with a grin.

'Who's Hoo?'

'Don't think they'll sell it here,' said Jaz. 'More of a Waterstones type book, I should think.'

'Stop it. We're late,' Meg interrupted in a firm voice.

Walking across the pale stone floor to the Information Desk, they joined the back of the queue. Happily, the queue moved swiftly, and within minutes, they were in front of the attractive, smiling desk attendant, who politely enquired how she could be of help.

'We're here to see Charles Mackworth. The Department of Britain, Europe and Prehistory,' answered Ellie.

'We have a two-thirty appointment, but we're late,' added Meg helpfully.

'Just one moment, please' the attendant said, reaching for the phone. She pressed a couple of buttons and, after a moment, relayed the message. 'Professor Mackworth's 2.30pm visitors are here at Court Info,' she said, eyeing the four friends slightly disbelievingly, and possibly with just a little envy.

'Yes, certainly,' she answered the invisible speaker and replaced the handset. 'If you'd care to wait to one side, he will come up and meet you,' she said brightly, involuntarily smoothing her already immaculate bun with her hand.

Ellie and the other three shuffled to the side, allowing the next person in the queue to take their place. Ellie slipped the straps of her backpack from her aching shoulders and lowered it gently to the floor.

The security guards in the entrance marquee had taken a good look at her bag but were clearly expecting a visitor to be carrying a parcel for Professor Mackworth, as they didn't insist on unwrapping it at the security desk. They merely scanned it and nodded her through. The pass card that Titch had left in the apartment for her had obviously identified Ellie as a non-threat. She would be glad to get rid of the package her father had sent to Titch as it took up space and made her backpack heavy and ungainly.

Jaz started humming tunelessly, and Meg took a leaflet from the selection at the desk and began reading. 'Did you know that the British Museum opened in 1753 and was the only free museum in the world at the time?' she said. 'Apparently, it contains a collection of over eight million objects from all over the world. *Eight million!* That's an incredible amount. It would take you a couple of years just to count them!

'Imagine dusting them,' said Flick, who'd once had a Saturday job cleaning holiday cottages.

Ellie let their idle chatter wash over her as she gazed vacantly across the concourse. Her gaze came to rest on a tall figure striding towards them, his silvering hair pulled back in a man bun and a broad smile surrounded by a neatly trimmed grey beard. She stepped forwards into Titch's arms for a bear hug.

Warmly shaking hands with Flick, Meg and Jaz, Titch asked about the comfort of their stay in his flat and of their enjoyment of the day so far.

'It was wonderful. Thank you for letting us stay,' Meg answered for them all. 'And we've had a lovely morning poking around the tourist trail.'

'Not so great after we left you last night, though,' said Jaz.

Ellie cast her a warning glance.

'We can discuss everything in my office. Follow me, ladies.'

Titch turned to personally thank the desk attendant, Ursula, who blushed and followed the receding figures walking away with Titch with definite envy.

'She likes you,' Jaz said to Titch.

'Possibly a little too much,' answered Titch. 'Too much for me to make her one of my dinner companions, anyway.'

'The more I know of him, the more I like,' whispered Flick to Ellie in an undertone.

Titch, who had excellent hearing, smiled to himself as he took the stairs to the lower ground floor.

# Chapter 29

The Sainsbury's Africa gallery had a very different feel to the massive, open space Ellie had just left. The lighting was subdued, and the ceiling height was much lower than in the galleries on the upper and ground floors. There was a certain smell, maybe of old animal material, that added to the sense of secrecy and mystery of the artefacts on display.

Ellie felt the tingle of energy from several directions but deliberately kept her gaze on the floor in front of her. This more enclosed, darker space reminded her of her recent experiences on the Tube; consequently, she felt mildly anxious and disinclined to use her ability to witness other strange, energy-charged objects.

Titch led them to a door disguised by the panelling of the room. He swiped his security card against a discreet reader on the wall and pushed the section of panelling outlined as a door. It swung noiselessly inwards, and Titch ushered them through into the corridor beyond. The door closed behind them and settled into its frame with an audible click and slight hiss.

Ellie raised an eyebrow. 'Swipe entry and air sealed?' she asked in surprise.

'Staff only areas are all swipe entry. Some are air locked, and some have other measures, too, as you'll see in a short while.'

Ellie pulled an impressed face at Jaz, then followed Titch along the corridor behind Flick and Meg. On either side of them were closed doors displaying name cards in small framed holders, but they continued to walk by them all. The corridor was very long and must have stretched for most of the length of the building, if not beyond it into tunnels under the grounds. Ahead, there was another swipe entry door, but behind it a staircase led downwards, instead of into a room like Ellie had been expecting.

'Don't they believe in lifts or something?' moaned Flick. 'I thought there'd been a great amount of remodelling. Surely someone could have thought of fitting a lift or two?'

Titch smiled. 'We have lifts,' he said, 'but I prefer to walk. Besides, the lifts have monitors, and the security would expect to see visitor passes hung around each of your necks.'

'Why don't we have visitor passes?' asked Meg, worriedly concluding that they might be in the wrong from a security guard's perspective.

'Because you're with me,' was Titch's uninformative reply.

'And you're so important around here that your guests don't need to abide by the rules?' Jaz asked incredulously, picking up on Meg's unease.

'Something like that,' answered Titch with an amused grin, and he started down the stairs at a brisk pace.

To Ellie's surprise when she looked over the bannister, she found that the stairwell appeared to be at least five floors

344

deep. She'd assumed that the museum had a basement, maybe even a sub-basement, but she hadn't expected it to extend that far below ground.

Descending only two flights, Titch swiped open the landing exit door and led them into a surprisingly light corridor. A series of rectangular light panels, each about a foot wide and three feet long, were set into the corridor ceiling and gave off a glow akin to daylight. Glancing up at one of these as she walked below it, Ellie could have sworn she saw the dark shape of a bird swoop in and out of view behind the frosted glass. She stopped and peered more closely. Smudgy areas on the panel could almost make one think that clouds were moving behind it, which there obviously couldn't be as they were underground at least three stories.

'This way, please, Ellie,' Titch called from further along the corridor.

With a last puzzled look at the light panel, Ellie hurried on to catch up with the others.

The corridor turned a corner and ended abruptly at a door marked "Department of Britain, Europe and Prehistory", and under that, a sub title proclaiming "Recondite Esoterica Division". Titch paused at the door and looked around at the four friends, as if checking they were all there.

'Step closely towards the door, please,' Titch instructed.

They shuffled closer together in front of the door. He swiped his card against the panel on the doorframe, which caused a low humming sound and a brief sweep of warm, golden light to pass over them. The humming rose in pitch and then stopped abruptly as the door slid open.

'Security,' Titch said to the four mildly puzzled faces looking at him.

'Some of the other measures you spoke of earlier?' Ellie queried.

'Yes,' Titch replied, volunteering no further information.

On the other side of the door was a sizeable lobby. At a reception desk sat a woman in a black suit, her blonde hair perfectly coiffured in a chignon. She looked to be in her early forties, but was of that beautifully made-up and immaculately presented variety of woman which can be anywhere from mid-thirties to late-fifties.

'Professor.' She greeted Titch, looking up from her typing.

'Veronica, these ladies are my personal guests.'

'Of course,' she replied. She looked at each of them in turn, blinking, before moving from one face to the next. Ellie and Meg glanced at each other; Ellie felt like she had just been scanned again.

'More security measures?' Ellie muttered to Titch as they moved across the lobby towards double doors on the far side.

'In a way,' Titch answered. 'Veronica has a photographic memory. She will now remember you as my guests and treat you accordingly.'

'What does that mean?' asked Jaz. 'That we'll get the chocolate digestives instead of plain?'

Titch chuckled. 'Most likely,' he evaded with a smile.

'Why do I get the feeling we're being humoured like children and only told what the grown-ups think we ought to hear?' Jaz whispered to Meg.

'Probably because to him, we are children; in both age and knowledge. Recondite Esoterica, remember? And he's the head honcho, by the look of it.'

'So, he's in charge of an underground department—guarded by some serious security—which studies cryptic and demonically difficult to understand knowledge, meant only for the select few?'

'Sounds about right,' agreed Meg. 'Although I'm hoping we can leave out the "demonic" and settle for just "seriously arcane and ancient artefacts."'

'Or maybe,' added Flick, catching the end of their whispered conversation as she shuffled around them in the doorway, 'we could just settle for freaky, old, secret stuff.'

The double doors led into an open office space where desks and work areas were divided by privacy screens covered in hundreds of notes and pinned newspaper articles. Ellie estimated it was a workspace for about twenty people, although there were only three currently sat at the desks, peering at books and computer screens.

'Late lunch?' she asked Titch.

'Our staff are often away from their desks, working in the stores or out in the field.' He paused, then added with a smile, 'But, yes—right now, I'd say late lunch.'

One of the people at the desks was a man in his fifties with balding grey hair and a knitted waistcoat over his shirt and tie. His tweed jacket was slung over the back of his swivel chair. He looked up at them and nodded cheerfully.

'She had it in one!' he said with a smile. Then, looking directly at Titch, he added, 'I've got those papers now, Professor.'

'Thank you, Albert. I will look at them shortly,' Titch replied, turning to lead the group across the room.

\* \* \*

The wall on the far side of the open space was made of glass,

347

and through it could be seen three rooms. The two smaller rooms were clearly offices and were on either side of the largest, which was set out as a meeting room with a large table and twenty or more chairs around it.

Titch led them to the larger of the two offices and ushered them into the room. In the corner was a sofa capable of seating eight and a steel-and-smoked-glass coffee table upon which sat a jug of water and five glasses. The jug of water had still-moving ice cubes that tinkled as they collided with each other and the side of the vessel.

Ellie wondered whether Veronica had put it there when she knew that Titch was returning. But then, like he had said earlier, there were no security cameras except for in the lifts—so how would Veronica know to put the fresh water out mere moments before they walked into the near-deserted department? It must have been literally only seconds before, too, as otherwise the ice cubes would be still. How odd.

Titch indicated that they were to make themselves comfortable on the sofa, inviting them to sit down with a sweep of his arm. Walking behind his desk, he tapped at a digital panel set into the smooth surface. The glass walls between Titch's office, the meeting room and the open plan office went suddenly opaque, obscuring their view of both.

'Very James Bond,' remarked Flick, trying to lighten the rather serious mood the journey to Titch's office had engendered.

Titch smiled. 'Would you like something to drink?' he enquired solicitously, then tapped their requests into the panel.

'So,' said Meg, determined not to be overawed, 'three stories below ground and you've got pretty advanced security measures. What does it take to get into the department at the bottom of the stairs?'

'There isn't a department down there,' Titch answered her. 'In fact, the bottom floors are all one storage area.'

'Woah! That must be *huge!*' Jaz quickly estimated the size of the storage area from what they'd seen and traversed so far.

'It is quite substantial,' Titch replied.

The door of Titch's office opened and Veronica entered, carrying a tray bearing their drinks. She set it down precisely, avoiding any spillages, and accepted their thanks with a nod and a professional smile.

'If there is anything else, Professor, do ask.' She smiled more genuinely at Titch as she left the room.

'Another dinner date?' Jaz enquired of Titch with a raised eyebrow.

He smiled ruefully. 'No, Veronica wouldn't have me. She is only interested in *very* intelligent men.'

'Seriously?' said Flick. 'What are you in her eyes, then? Pre-service?'

Jaz sniggered. There was a long-standing joke at college about how many pre-service course students it took to change a light bulb, and it was not very flattering to their intelligence. Meg frowned at her.

Titch ignored the remark and perched on the front of his desk, his legs extended, arms and ankles crossed.

'Now,' he began in an authoritative manner, 'tell me what happened last night.'

As the friends recounted their terrifying experience in the runaway taxi, Titch's face grew increasingly grave. When they finished speaking, he looked directly at Ellie. 'It is possible that you all are targets for these attacks, although it may simply have been that you were with Ellie at the time. Have any of you experienced something similar when on your own, without Ellie?'

Flick, Jaz and Meg all shook their heads.

'Apart from Chris, who we now think was being controlled, nothing has happened without Ellie being present,' Jaz replied. 'And we can't say for certain that Chris wasn't behaving normally until he came within striking distance of Ellie.'

Ellie told Titch about the experiences she'd had on the Tube; how she'd felt that danger was ahead and so had trusted her instincts and changed routes.

'That was a wise move. Whether intuition or just caution, you made the right choice in avoiding something that didn't feel one hundred percent safe.'

'Can I ask something?' enquired Flick, who had been fairly quiet up to this point.

Titch nodded. 'Of course.'

'Why did these things choose to control Chris? Why him and not someone else at the pub that night?'

'I can't say for sure. It seems most likely that he was simply in the right place at the right time. As to why he was able to be controlled, I think it might be easier to control the young than the old. Younger minds are easier prey, as the young tend to see more in absolutes. Similarly, minds clouded by drink, drugs or illness might be more easily influenced, as there are less barriers to get past.'

'For example?' challenged Jaz, in defence of her allegedly black-and-white-thinking generation.

'A young woman saying that when she has children, she will

350

never let them play with guns and swords. Then that same woman, maybe ten years later, staying up late into the night to finish the knight's costume, complete with foil-wrapped cardboard sword, that her child wants to wear for World Book Day in the morning. It's easy to be idealistic when you're young, before many of the harsh realities of life have soiled your quixotic vision of how things should be. Look at how easily young minds can be corrupted and controlled by twisted religious ideologies.'

'I like to think I'm not *that* unrealistically utopian,' Jaz replied.

'You, Jaz—indeed, all of you sat here—are rather an exception to the vast majority. You think and you question, but also, unlike many older minds, you are not closed to the possibility that what we think we know as fact may be proved wrong through experience. An older mind may try to dismiss what it has actually experienced and attempt to find logical explanations for seemingly illogical happenings. You don't. You call it as you see it— or at least you are starting to. Ellie, you have come a long way along this particular path already. I have to say, I am impressed. Now, I believe you have something for me?' Titch said, abruptly changing the subject.

Ellie lifted her backpack from the floor and, opening it, eased out the box her father had given her. She carefully handed it to Titch, who, taking care to keep the package horizontal, walked around his desk and laid the box on the uncluttered surface. He tapped the control panel set into the desk, and the colour of the obscured glass walls changed from white to pale amber.

'A precaution,' he said. 'Although I am sure, most likely,

unnecessary.'

Removing the bindings and placing his fingers on either end of the box, Titch eased off the lid. Inside were Styrofoam packing chips which he removed and deposited neatly onto his desk. Underneath the packaging was a silver metal container. Titch took it out and carefully set it upright. He flicked up the catches on the cannister lid, and a small hissing sound escaped.

'Vacuum sealed?' asked Jaz.

'Should you be opening that in here, in front of us?' Flick queried, only half joking.

'Relax, it's from Dad,' said Ellie.

'It is perfectly safe to you,' replied Titch. 'Possibly less so were you currently being "controlled", as you termed it earlier.'

Titch eased the contents from the container, and the four friends leaned forwards to see what it was.

Titch stood a small jade figure up on the desk. It was about six inches tall by two inches wide and was a squat, fat figure of a man in a semi-crouch, his arms at his sides and his tongue thrust out and down in a grimace.

'What is it?' asked Meg.

'A house guardian, I think,' replied Titch. 'But I have not seen one made from jade before. One would usually find such figures carved into the main pole supporting the roofs of meeting houses. Small, freestanding stone versions are often grave guardians, but this one is more in the style of a house guardian.'

There was a note folded up in the bottom of the container, which Titch tipped out onto the desk. He unfolded the paper and read Andy's scrawled handwriting. Chuckling to himself, he fed the paper into a slot on the surface of his desk, and a whirring noise suggested that the note had just been shredded. The four friends looked at him expectantly.

'I will look into this. Your father said he unearthed it when digging in the beetroot patch, and he has asked me several questions about it to which I currently don't have any answers. Please let him know I will get back to him shortly.'

Acting on impulse, and with her recent discoveries made in the galleries above still fresh in her mind, Ellie closed her eyes and looked at the desk. The energy of the small figure was clear to be seen; white-gold and sparkling around it in a halo.

'It is still full of energy,' she said, opening her eyes and pointing at the figure.

Titch raised his eyebrows. 'One of the questions your father has asked of me,' he said. 'Can you tell what sort of energy?'

'I'm not sure. I don't know how to define colours yet, but the feel of it suggests to me there is nothing negative about it. It's protective, if anything.'

'Very interesting.' Titch put his hand in his trouser pocket and pulled out a small object before sitting down in his high-backed swivel chair. He placed a glass orb carefully on the desk. It was about the size of a large egg and was cloudy with hints of a reflective surface inside, like a polished labradorite stone. 'What can you tell me about this?' he asked.

Ellie closed her eyes and concentrated. Sat on the dull-coloured desk, the orb came into focus, but there was no energy in it; it was just dark. However, faint yellowish strands of energy appeared to be being sucked into it before disappearing, like matter and light drawn into the black holes Bertie had described.

353

Ellie looked at Titch with her mind's eye and was disturbed to see him appear to have no energy, either; his form was as dull and subdued as the chair he sat on. Ellie's eyes snapped open in alarm.

'Don't worry,' said Titch quickly, placing the orb in the cannister and closing the lid. 'Now, take another look.'

Ellie did as he asked and, with a deep breath, closed her eyes to again summon the energy picture. This time, Titch could clearly be seen by his energy, as well as the sparkling energy of the statue on the desk. Ellie opened her eyes in relief. For one panicked moment, she had thought that Titch was something wrong.

Something like the Others.

'It's the orb,' Titch explained. 'It is an energy shield.'

'But I saw energy disappearing into it,' said Ellie.

'A small amount does. Call it a trade-off for the shielding effect it provides. Consequently, it is wise not to forget you've put it in your pocket.'

'Or you'll die?' said Meg in alarm.

Titch chuckled. 'It's more likely you wouldn't have the energy to make it to the opera that evening. It's not that much of a drain.'

Ellie relaxed. She hadn't liked the idea of Titch having his energy drained. A thought occurred suddenly to her.

'So why were you shielding our energy as we entered the staff only areas?'

'Ah, a pertinent question. The orb not only shields energy but also disrupts the imagery of moving objects if viewed on digital cameras like CCTV, hence no lifts and no standing still.'

'But why? Why are the guards not supposed to know we're

here?' interrupted Flick.

'The reason your presence was not made official—if that term can be used in this context—is that there are rules and regulations here at the British Museum of which certain departments and staff need take no notice, but by which the majority of the museum is run. We are one such department. However, it is better for all those following the rules not to know there are others who don't. Let's just say that we in this department might bring objects into and out of the museum by different means and under other permissions than the normal objects' triple-stamped paper trail route. Not because we are underhand, I should add, but out of necessity and safety.'

'So, you deal in unusual or strange objects?' asked Jaz.

'In a nutshell, yes. Mostly. Like this little fellow here,' Titch said, indicating the jade figure on the desk.

Ellie took a deep breath and blew out slowly. 'Are you saying that some of the things here are somewhat otherworldly. Magical, even?' she asked.

'To put it crudely, yes. Although many things might seem magical before how they operate is understood.'

'Give me an example.'

'You noticed some yourself on our way in. The light panels in the corridor. Tell me your thoughts on those.'

'Well, I thought they looked remarkably like daylight, which I knew was impossible as we are several floors below ground. Yet, when I looked at them for a moment, I thought there might be the suggestion of clouds moving behind the frosted glass and a bird swooping across the pane.'

'Bravo!' exclaimed Titch. 'Well observed. However, the "impossible" remark is unworthy of you, particularly in light of your current predicament.'

'Then it was the sky? But how?'

'The panels behind the frosted covers are the partners of several pairs of mirrors. Very peculiar mirrors, whose idiosyncrasy is to reflect what the other one sees. They were discovered in Asia in 1902 and brought here under a special licence. They were even used for Allied communications during both World Wars, I believe. Now, however, they have been made somewhat obsolete by modern communication methods, so Albert came up with the idea of installing their partners on the dome of the great courtyard to allow us down here in the bowels of the museum to have some daylight. They work remarkably well, don't they?'

'And the gold light that scanned us before we entered the department, and the amber lighting of these glass walls, they're something magical, too?' enquired Ellie.

'You could say that. The golden light was an energy screen. It would have detected if one of you was being influenced or controlled. It would sense the negative energy. Equally well, it would have contained it here in this room if the artefact Andy had sent to me was similarly charged.'

'*Wow*. I feel like I'm in *Warehouse 13*,' said Flick.

'Where do you think the idea for the show came from?' joked Jaz.

'You're not too far off, actually,' Titch remarked.

'Just one question,' interjected Flick. 'What would have happened if the light had detected something it didn't like?'

'The subject would have been removed.'

'From the person or from the building?' Flick queried.

'It depends. Possibly from existence entirely,' Titch answered.

'You must have been very sure of us, then,' said Jaz.

'Ellie trusts you, and I know Ellie. There was nothing to be concerned about.'

Ellie smiled at the compliment and at his faith in her; he'd spoken in such a matter of fact tone that she knew his remarks weren't just idle compliments.

Titch tapped at the control panel again, and a desk drawer slid open at the same time as the frosted effect and colour disappeared from the glass walls of his office. He placed the jade figure and the metal cannister in the drawer and it slid closed. With another tap on the tablet, a different drawer opened, and Titch took out two small boxes, one the size of a large matchbox and the other larger.

'Before you go, I have two things for you, Ellie. The first is something I would like you to return to your father, please,' Titch said, sliding the larger box across the desk towards her.

Ellie picked it up and carefully stowed it in her backpack, then slid the zipper up to the top to make sure that nothing could possibly fall out.

'The second is for you and your friends.'

Titch picked up the small box and opened the lid. He tipped the contents into his palm and then laid them on his desk. There were four small silver discs; possibly old coins, Ellie thought. Each one had a square hole in the middle, and tiny markings crowded across the remaining metal.

'They are amulets. Recovered from a dig near Woodbridge in Suffolk,' Titch explained.

A bell rang in Ellie's mind. 'Sutton Hoo?' she asked in disbelief.

Titch smiled at the evidence of her knowledge in subjects close to his own interests. 'Again, well done. Yes. Close to

357

the site of the famous ship burial, the hoard from which these came was found recently by a metal detectorist. You won't have heard of it on the news, though,' he added, looking at Meg's thoughtful face. 'It was rather a surprise discovery—for the detectorist, in particular.'

'Why?' asked Flick.

'Because some of the items that were buried were still remarkably potent when unearthed, and with the incantations of their burial broken, they sent forth such a shockwave of energy that he was blown off his feet and into a nearby tree.'

The friends looked suspiciously at the four items of treasure on the desk.

'Suffice to say that after he called the police, assuming he had inadvertently triggered a buried hand grenade or similar, we were called to the scene. It took quite some time to stabilise the items before they could be moved, due to the way in which they had been set into the ground and the vestiges of their decaying enchantments. These four have been thoroughly examined, however, and they are protection amulets. There is one here for each of you to attach to the bracelets Jill had made for you. Please remember to wear them at all times.'

He gave them each a meaningful, almost stern look to emphasise his request.

'They will afford you a measure of individual protection, although they do seem to be more potent when in close proximity to one another, as the somewhat unfortunate metal detectorist discovered. Their purpose in being buried as they were, appears to have been to protect the other more important items buried with them. Which, at this point, I am not at liberty to divulge details of,' he added as an afterthought, upon seeing the question poised on Jaz's lips.

Jaz exhaled audibly, and Titch smiled and nodded in approval of her questioning mind. He tapped at the screen in the desk, and a moment later, the door of his office swung open and a man stood there. The girls were all surprised, as they hadn't seen him approaching Titch's office through the now clear-glass office walls.

Titch welcomed him into the office. 'Joe, do come in and meet my young friends.'

'This is Ellie, Flick, Jaz and Meg. They are wearing the bracelets.'

Joe entered the room. He was dressed in brown cords and a brown shirt with a headband visor. Around his waist was a tool belt from which hung pouches and pockets as well as tools. He reminded Ellie of a mole, or maybe Moley in *The Wind in The Willows*; Joe even wore little round spectacles, too.

'Now then, Professor. I've forged the links this morning, so I'm all set to attach the items for the young ladies.' He nodded towards the four friends with a friendly smile.

'Excellent,' replied Titch. Turning his gaze to Ellie, he said, 'If you'd all care to remove your bracelets, Joe can attach the amulets for you.' Upon seeing Ellie's reticence, he added reassuringly, 'You are well protected here. It is safe to remove them.'

Ellie nodded at the other three, and they all removed their bracelets and laid them on the desk. Joe got to work attaching the amulets to the links of the bracelet chains with a gold loop of metal. Ellie couldn't quite see how he closed the loop, but there was a brief flash of green light before Joe handed each bracelet back to its owner. Examining hers upon its return, she saw no obvious join in the metal of the gold loop, but there were some tiny markings on the inside of it. She looked questioningly at Titch, who was watching her.

'Just a little extra something of my own,' he said with a smile.

'I don't suppose you're going to tell us what that is?' queried Jaz.

'Correct,' confirmed Titch with a grin. 'Just trust that it will help to keep you safe. Now, I have some other people who are wishing to speak with me today and to neglect them would be impolite, so I must bid you farewell and a safe journey home.'

Titch offered his hand to Flick, Jaz and Meg who all shook it with profuse thanks for his gift and his time, as well as renewed thanks for letting them stay at his splendid apartment.

Finally, Ellie stepped forwards and gave Titch a hug. 'Thank you,' she said.

Titch dropped his head to her ear and whispered, 'You know where I am, if you need me. But I have a hunch you have greater protection than I can give.'

Ellie blushed as she smiled. 'I do hope so,' she replied into the fabric of his lapel.

30

# Chapter 30

The four friends exited the British Museum in the same way they'd entered. Veronica accompanied them to the door leading to the Sainsbury's Africa exhibition. With final thanks and farewells to her, they entered the gallery, and the door in the panelling closed soundlessly behind them; it seemed the accompanying click and hiss were only audible from the corridor side.

The friends stood and looked at each other. Amazed smiles spread across their faces as the realisation of what they had just been made party to dawned upon them.

'Wow!' said Meg. 'I can't believe the last forty minutes have just happened.'

'I think,' Jaz butted in before any of them had chance to speak further, 'we should confine any discussion of our meeting to either the open air or somewhere more private.'

'Agreed,' said Flick. 'Let's get out of here.'

They trooped towards the stairs that led back up to the ground floor level, wending their way between the display cases, exhibits and fellow visitors. It was busy in the Africa

361

Gallery, although, curiously, there was one exhibit that was not being looked at much while the others were crowded with visitors. Ellie paused briefly and closed her eyes to summon an energy picture to see if her hunch was correct.

She was right; there was an unpleasant, oily brown-purple energy around the artefact. It made her want to move away from it, yet she couldn't stop herself from watching its energy; the greasy swirls of colour moving slowly in a viscous manner was mesmerising. A feeling of lethargy overcame her, and she felt her shoulders droop. She thought she'd better open her eyes, but the lids were so heavy and the energy patterns so hypnotising that she just stood there. Sickness rose inside her, and Ellie felt herself become even more drained.

Suddenly, she was knocked forwards from behind and she stumbled, opening her eyes. An apologetic tourist helped her to regain her balance, explaining that he'd swung his loaded backpack onto his shoulder without checking behind himself first.

Ellie staggered to her feet as Flick, Jaz and Meg came rushing back across the gallery.

'We didn't notice you'd fallen behind! Are you OK?' spluttered an anxious Meg.

'Yes. I'm OK; just a bump with a bag,' said Ellie.

'You don't look OK. You're pale—and look at your hands.'

Ellie held out a hand in front of herself; it was visibly shaking. 'I need some fresh air,' she said.

Jaz took the backpack from Ellie's shoulders, and Flick and Meg each took one of Ellie's arms.

'Come on,' said Flick. 'We're out of here.'

Out on the neatly mown lawn, they sat down.

'Right, out with it,' Jaz commanded, staring at Ellie.

'It was weird,' Ellie began. 'I looked at the energy of an exhibit no one was paying much attention to, kind of on a hunch, and there was this sort of gloopy energy around it. The more I looked at the swirling colours, the more I couldn't look away. I felt drained, like it was zapping my strength as I watched it move.'

'Negative energy, I'm guessing,' said Flick.

'What did it look like, Ellie?' asked Meg.

'Sort of oily, like the dark iridescent colours you get on a wet road splashed with diesel. Also, it looked thick and sort of slow-moving, like it was biding its time. It made me feel sick, but I couldn't stop looking.'

'And you were wearing your bracelet?' Flick asked.

'Yes.' Ellie raised her arm to show them the bracelet dangling from her wrist, its crystals sparkling in the sunlight.

'Hmm. It doesn't seem like an attack. If we were being attacked, the amulets and crystals should have warded off some of that, shouldn't they?' remarked Meg.

'I guess that's why Jill and Titch gave them to us,' said Jaz.

'In that case, it wasn't an attack. But it's good that you now know how negative energy can affect you, Ellie. My advice? Stay away from the stuff,' said Meg.

Ellie gave a wry grin. 'I intend to. I really do.'

'OK, we have just under an hour before we need to be at the station. What do you all want to do?'

'I'm going with Ellie,' said Flick. She gave Ellie a meaningful look and indicated the other two with a tilt of her head. Ellie understood: Flick was trying to give Jaz and Meg some alone time.

'Great,' said Ellie. 'We'll have a mooch around the shops while you get a coffee or whatever.'

363

They agreed to meet up at the station by the Paddington Bear statue.

With a wave to the other two, Ellie and Flick set off back towards Tottenham Court Road with the intention of wandering down it until they reached Goodge Street Underground.

'It's cool how quickly Meg feels like she's always been one of our friends,' Ellie remarked.

'Yes, she's one of the Scooby gang all right. And I think she even manages to keep our beloved Jaz in check. Have you noticed Jaz hasn't been smoking at all lately? Not even when she's been out on the lash?'

'Yes, I had. Meg's influence, you think?'

'Most definitely. And Jaz seems a lot more settled.'

'She's happy.'

'Yeah, it's great what love can do, ain't it?'

'It definitely seems so, if you, Meg and Jaz are anything to go by.'

'What about you and Mr. Very Dark and Handsome? Anything going on yet, or don't magical superheroes act like normal guys?'

Ellie blushed and laughed. 'I'll be sure to let you know if I ever find out,' she replied.

'You're saying you haven't done anything with him yet?'

'I wouldn't say that exactly,' smiled Ellie. 'We've ... I've definitely explored a few things. Kissing him is amazing. Sometimes, even when I can't see him, I can sense him and his lips on my skin.'

'Ooo, *kinky*. I like the sound of that.' Flick grinned. 'Or is it weird and you'd rather not?'

'No, it's not weird. Exciting and different, but not unwanted by any stretch of the imagination.'

'So, it's safe to say he's your man? Despite all the weird stuff?'

Ellie grinned again. 'Yep, I'm sold on him. The whole package.'

'His package is something I'd advise you prioritise investigating. Wouldn't want to commit to all this and then get a rather nasty small surprise ...'

'Flick! You're *terrible*! I'm sure, in time, at the right time, that will come up.'

'I'm sure it'll come up, too.' Flick gave Ellie a suggestive dig in the ribs and burst out laughing. Ellie joined in.

'Enough!' she giggled. 'A little decorum, please. We're shopping on Tottenham Court Road, after all. Raise your game, lady!'

Flick chortled. 'I can raise all sorts of stuff. Can you though? That's the question.' She glanced at Ellie's expression. 'OK, OK—consider it toned down, Mrs. Sensible Pants. Although now we're talking about it, judging by what I witnessed hanging out of your backpack this morning, you might need to upgrade those, too, if you're out to snare yourself an interdimensional mega-hunk. There might be a Victoria's Secret around here somewhere, if you're lucky.'

Chuckling, Ellie dug Flick in the ribs in return, and they sauntered on down the street. It felt good to be teased about Darkall, as Flick would do for any new boyfriend of Ellie's.

Ambling past the huge plate glass windows of a designer furniture shop, they paused to admire the tasteful white furniture display juxtaposed against warehouse-like bare brick walls and visible downpipes. No prices labels could be seen on the pieces, which tended to suggest they were likely to be jaw-droppingly expensive, in Ellie's experience.

Absorbed in her musings, Ellie didn't notice anything peculiar about the queue of people waiting at the bus stop behind them until a sudden burning on the back of her head made her start and turn around.

The queue looked perfectly normal until three heads turned in unison, blank eyes staring, mouths open.

Ellie grabbed Flick's arm. *'Move,'* she said urgently.

Flick didn't need to be told twice. They set off down the street at a speedy walk, dodging fellow pedestrians, telephone kiosks and litter bins. Glancing behind her, Ellie's fears were confirmed as three synchronised figures detached themselves from the queue of people and began marching after her and Flick, matching their pace.

'*Shit,*' Ellie said in a tense voice. 'We've got three of them after us! Keep moving, or they'll catch us up.'

Goodge Street Underground Station was on the other side of the street, but Ellie couldn't countenance going underground. Their best chance, she figured, was to lose the three zombies in the maze of London streets.

Hastily glancing left and right, Ellie and Flick charged across the road, causing a taxi to sound its horn angrily and a cyclist to swerve, yet they managed to reach the pavement on the other side without accident. Ellie part hoped that the zombies wouldn't be able to do the same, but, then again, she didn't really want the people injured, only their controlling force. The pair continued to speed-walk down the street and spun around the corner into a side road. Behind them, blaring horns and annoyed shouts indicated their pursuers had successfully crossed the road.

'Run!' commanded Ellie.

Accelerating to a flat-out run, they sped down a tree-lined one-way road, tore around a corner to the right into a wider street and raced across the road. On down the block they ran, to the next side road, then threw themselves into it. Reaching solid brick instead of the glass window of the office on the corner, they paused for a moment to catch their breath and to peer cautiously through the glass back the way they'd come. The three figures were halfway down the previous street.

'Christ! Come on!'

Ellie grabbed Flick's arm, and they set off again. Lungs burning, they made it to the end of the street and turned right to see the monumental BT Tower looming ahead of them. Onwards they ran, turning right again and dashing past a glass-fronted building stretching the length of the block.

'Ellie,' gasped Flick. 'Can't run ... anymore.'

'You've got to!' shouted Ellie, pulling her along by the arm, her own breath catching in painful heaves, the taste of blood in her mouth.

They turned left, following the reflective wall of the building along its side edge, at more of a trot now than a run. Flick was tripping periodically, exhaustion causing her feet to drag. They passed a row of scooters and turned into a narrow street. Halfway along, a small road led off to the right underneath the upper floors of a building and they fled into it, only to find it was a dead end.

Flick and Ellie had no more energy with which to run, so they hunched down in the corner of the mews with the deepest shadow, against a tall up-and-over warehouse door, and tried to regain their breath. Surely they'd given the zombies the slip by now?

The entrance to the mews was fairly discreet; it was little more than a service road into an alley where the backs of buildings with painted-out windows faced each other across pitted tarmac. If anyone looked in, all they would see was a row of parked vehicles and wheelie bins. But were the Others tracking them using vision or some other sense?

Ellie glanced at Flick, who had her phone in her hand and was frantically trying to text someone, but her hands were shaking so much that the words made no sense.

Despite their bodies being slumped in exhaustion, Ellie's mind was still racing: how was she going to get them safely out of this? Jill had said that Ellie could use her energy for protection. What was it that Jill had suggested doing? Imagine an energy egg with a miniature Ellie inside, create a wall of energy around her and then expand it to encompass others too?

God, why hadn't she practised that instead of falling asleep on Titch's sofa? OK, she had to focus now. She closed her eyes and tried to picture the energy inside her forming a shell around herself and Flick, but the picture wouldn't form; she was too tired from running, too desperate, and she didn't have the strength left to marshal her mental energy.

What else had they got? *The bracelets.* They were for protection, weren't they? Surely they could do something. Ellie wrenched her bracelet from her wrist and clenched her fist around it. She tried to imagine energy from the crystals flowing up her arm and feeding the energy shell.

There was a wail from Flick, and Ellie's eyes snapped open. The three figures were coming up the mews at their relentless, robotic pace.

'Get behind me!' insisted Ellie.

Flick cowered in the corner of the warehouse entrance while Ellie stood in front of her, her backpack held as a shield and her hand holding the bracelet raised in front of her. The possessed trio were metres away now. Ironically, they ought to have been harmless: a middle-aged woman, a suited office type and a young man in a hoodie. But they weren't.

They embodied the Others.

As they crossed the tarmac, the three zombies raised their arms, holding weapons ready to strike. The woman had a bottle of wine from her shopping bag, the man in the suit raised his briefcase, ready to batter, and, most scary of all, the youth held a short-bladed knife.

Ellie adjusted her backpack to afford what protection it could give in the direction of the knife and closed her eyes. The shell. She had to see it, had to make it happen, but she'd begin with what she knew she could do. She pictured the swirling spiral energy inside of her, then sped it up and set it free from the confines of her chest to fill her whole body. Intensifying it still further, her mind fully focussed, she unleashed it from her body in sweeping waves of fiery light.

'You're doing it, Ellie,' whispered Flick. 'They can't come any closer! The light's stopping them.'

Ellie could sense light passing her closed eyelids in strobing bands. Concentrating on the spinning and trying to maintain its ferocity, Ellie was completely unprepared for the glass bottle that came hurtling towards her head.

Flick had seen the woman's arm jerkily pull back for the throw and pushed Ellie out of the way just in time to save her from a serious head injury, but, in doing so, she broke

Ellie's concentration and the bands of gold light dissipated. The attackers advanced once more and, this time, Ellie and Flick had no escape.

Ellie held her backpack in front of them, and Flick raised hers above their heads; they didn't offer much protection, but it was all they had.

Just as they braced themselves for the first blows, tensing against the inevitable pain, there was a flash of blue light from behind them. The aggressors flew backwards, landing against the overflowing bins on the other side of the mews. Ellie felt an arm envelop her as her vision briefly blurred. When it cleared, she found herself standing disorientated and dizzy in the cellars of what smelt and sounded like a pub.

Darkall released Flick and waved his hand through the air in front of his face, as if snatching it into his fist. The noise ceased. In fact, *all* noise ceased, including Flick's voice in mid-scream.

Ellie looked at Flick. She stood motionless, her hair, frozen in time, flung out around her from the momentum of the turn she'd been executing when the sound had stopped.

'Flick! What have you done to her?' Ellie demanded, trying to pull away from Darkall's arms.

'Don't,' he said, resisting her attempts. 'If you leave me, you will be the same as she.'

'And what is that, exactly?' asked a frantic Ellie.

'To us, she is paused.'

'You froze her?' Ellie asked in disbelief.

'No. I merely extracted us from her time. But if you lose contact with me, you will be subject to your reality's timeline once again.'

'That makes no sense. How can anyone be outside of time?'

370

'It is not something that can be explained succinctly. Just accept you are currently not fully outside of time, just mostly. A better analogy would be you are in an accelerated time loop, separate, but not completely unlinked, to the time your friend is experiencing. Suffice to say, I am able to experience time in your reality as I so choose and that if you are touching me, then you can break the rules of your four-dimensional space-time universe. Don't try to touch your friend; you may unwittingly harm her.'

Ellie, midway through reaching out a hand towards Flick, sighed. 'I ... I don't know what's going on anymore. This is too much.'

Ellie's head sagged against his chest.

'You were brave, Eleanor. You attempted to fight them off.'

'I was trying to protect us, not fight. But I failed,' said Ellie.

'What good would that have been when you can't hold the protection barrier indefinitely? The best course of action would have been to attack and render them harmless.'

'But I can't. I don't know how to, and I didn't have the power to do that. I'm not strong enough.'

'You were strong enough to hold them back for a short while.'

'I couldn't harm them; they're just people once the Others relinquish control. Like Chris.'

'Then you need to discover how to force that controlling influence to relinquish them.'

'But how? No one can teach me this stuff!'

Ellie was getting irritated. The adrenaline, shock and fear were making her want to hit him, to scream at the unfairness of it all and cry, her face buried in his sweatshirt.

'You began to learn how today. Use what has worked and

371

develop your skill. Remember that you have other help.'

'I tried the bracelet; I tried to use its energy. But I don't think it worked.'

'Look at the bracelet, Eleanor.'

Ellie unclenched her fingers and peered at the crystals. To her surprise, they had all turned a dull grey. No matter which colour they'd been before, they now looked like a row of normal grey stones hanging on a tarnished chain. The coin which Titch had had Joe add to her bracelet just an hour ago was tarnished black and had twisted and shrivelled. Ellie gasped.

'Channelling that energy was what saved you, at first,' Darkall told her. 'It is something to bear in mind. Also, even though your healing energy is golden, your attack energies may well appear to be of another hue.'

Ellie was suddenly feeling very tired, and she slumped against Darkall. Her senses seemed disordered. The light was blurring around the edges of her vision, and she could no longer see clearly. She couldn't feel the extremities of her body or sense her arms and legs anymore. Every sense was shrinking, to the point she was left with just her mind; no connections with the outside world remained.

'I need to return you to your time,' Darkall said. 'Even when insulated by contact with me, you cannot tolerate experiencing time variance.'

Then all went dark. To Ellie, it felt like falling into her bed at home.

A fall into comfort.

\* \* \*

'Ellie. Ellie! Wake up!' Flick's voice urged. 'Ellie, come on! It's OK—they've gone.'

She was pulling at Ellie's arms, trying to get her to her feet. Ellie opened her eyes. They were alone in the alley.

'I've called Titch, and he's sending some guy called Norman to pick us up. We just have to wait here until he arrives to take us to the station,' Flick told her.

'We'll be safe here?'

Flick indicated over her shoulder, gesturing for Ellie to see for herself.

Looking up, Ellie saw a large spiral scored into the metal of the door. Reaching out her hand, she touched the edge of one spiral arm, and the metal was warm. She smiled.

'I guess so,' said Flick. 'Mind you, maybe we won't be so safe if the owner comes out and sees your boyfriend's tag defacing his door.' She slumped down onto the ground beside Ellie. 'We can just rest here for a bit. You must have hit your head when you went down or one of those zombies got a hit in on you. You were out cold.'

'I was? You saw what happened?'

'When the golden light bands you made stopped, those things came at us again. Just as they were about to beat the hell out of us, there was a flash, and they went flying backwards into the rubbish over there.

'Maybe I was a bit dazed, too, as I could have sworn I was in a dark place for just a few seconds, then I was back here.'

Ellie didn't comment, so Flick continued.

'The young guy was the first one to his feet. He looked around him and ran off. The suit got up next, looking confused as hell. The woman was coming to by then, so he helped her up and they left the alley together, not noticing us at all. They spoke to each other, and she bent down to pick up her dropped shopping while he dusted down his suit, so I guessed they were back to normal. I kept out of sight, crouched down here, just in case.'

The sound of a car pulling into the mews made them look up. It was a green Range Rover. A short man got out.

'It's OK, ladies. Titch sent me to look for you.'

Flick sighed in relief and pulled Ellie to her feet.

'Here, let me help you in,' Norman said as he opened the rear door nearest them.

Ellie and Flick clambered gratefully inside and settled comfortably against the cream leather upholstery.

'The professor informed me Paddington Station is your desired destination, is that correct?' Norman enquired in a friendly tone.

'Yes,' Flick answered. 'Please. We need to get to the Paddington Bear statue.'

Norman nodded and, skilfully turning the Range Rover in the narrow space, pulled out of the alley and into the street.

Ellie let her head flop back onto the headrest and closed her eyes. She hadn't hit her head. Nothing hurt. Surely a bang to the head severe enough to knock someone out would hurt like hell and leave a bump or bruise? She ran her hand over her head to check, but encountered no sore spots.

She had been with Darkall outside of normal time. How come Flick, who Ellie had seen frozen in time, could remember stuff that had happened while Ellie was apparently unconscious; stuff that Ellie herself had no knowledge of? She hadn't been unconscious, had she?

If so, then perhaps the effects of being outside of normal time had rendered her so. The sensation of falling into her

374

bed had been very similar to her one and only experience of fainting. She'd been at a concert and hadn't eaten any tea before going. She remembered standing there in the dense crowd near the stage, feeling very tired. She had wanted to sit down, but there wasn't anywhere to sit. She had remained standing but had suddenly become hot and shaky and felt sick.

The next thing she had been aware of was a sensation of falling into her bed at home: the bedside light had been on in her dark room, and her pillows had come up to meet her as her head fell towards them. But just before her head had actually touched the pillows, she had woken up and found herself sitting on a blanket at the side of the concert hall, being attended to by St John's Ambulance staff.

Ellie opened her eyes and looked across at Flick. She appeared to be asleep.

'There is time for you to have a quick snooze too, Miss,' said Norman, his eyes catching hers in the rearview mirror. 'You are safe here. Both this vehicle and I are heavily protected.'

Ellie relaxed a little and closed her eyes again, and very soon, the motion of the well-sprung vehicle swayed her to sleep.

# 31

# Chapter 31

Paddington Station was windy, noisy and overcrowded. Norman drove them right up to the entrance on Praed Street, stopped the car and helped Ellie and Flick out. He left the vehicle parked where it was and escorted them onto the concourse.

'Your friends will be over there,' he said, indicating the direction of the Paddington Bear statue. 'Do you wish me to stay with you?'

Ellie looked in the direction Norman had pointed. She could see Jaz and Meg talking together over by the small statue. Moreover, as she glanced at the dark, obscured glass window of a coffee shop, she saw a brief flare of two silver-purple eyes.

'No, thank you. We'll be fine from here,' she said confidently.

'Very well, then. I wish you both a safe journey home, and I hope you haven't been put off from visiting the capital again.'

Flick managed a rueful smile.

'Thanks for the rescue, Norman.'

Norman nodded in response, then, raising his hand in farewell, walked back to his most probably illegally parked vehicle.

'Hey! Over here!' Meg's voice called from across the concourse.

They turned to see her waving and smiling at them.

'You've just about made it. We need to get onto the platform right away, though. It's over here.'

Meg shouldered her backpack and headed off with Jaz in tow towards the gate for Platform One.

'No time for the loo, then,' Flick grumbled.

'You'll just have to go on the train. Rather you than me, though,' Ellie said with a forced smile.

Flick gave her shoulder a squeeze, recognising her attempt to lighten the awfulness of their recent experience. 'Bet you'll be following my lead before Reading, though.'

'You're on,' Ellie grinned, this time with genuine amusement.

When they walked onto the platform, the guards were closing carriage doors, and there were only a few other people left hurrying towards the train.

'Over here!' shouted Jaz from the train, drawing their attention towards a door that was still open at the concourse end of the platform.

'But that's First Class,' objected Ellie.

'Titch upgraded us!' replied Jaz.

Flick and Ellie trotted towards the door and bundled themselves and their bags on board. Behind them, the door slammed shut, and a whistle sounded.

'You could have moved a bit faster,' complained Jaz.

'No, we couldn't,' replied an unsmiling Flick, turning away

from Jaz to make her way down the carriage.

'I'll explain in a while,' murmured Ellie as she passed a confused-looking Jaz and followed Flick.

Right at the end of the carriage, Meg was sitting against the window on a set of table seats. Jaz slid in beside her. Ellie and Flick took the opposite double seat and stowed their backpacks under the table. There was no one in the seats opposite, and the guy at the table behind them had headphones on and was typing on his laptop.

As the train pulled out of the station, Ellie felt a tremor reverberating through the band of her ring and knew they were safe.

'This is very nice,' smiled Meg, wriggling in the comfortable seat. 'I've not travelled First Class on a train before.'

She looked happily at the others, then her smile faltered as it met Ellie and Flick's unsmiling, strained faces. 'What is it?' she asked, leaning towards them in concern.

'Another attack,' Ellie answered her. 'And they really meant business this time. Three possessed people chased us around for a quarter of an hour before attempting to bludgeon and stab us to death in an alleyway.'

'Christ, no!' exclaimed Jaz.

'Afraid so,' confirmed Flick, an ironic cheer to her voice. 'If it hadn't been for Ellie holding them off and then her fella blasting them, we'd most likely be in the morgue right now.'

Ellie and Flick recounted their ordeal to the obvious dismay of the other two.

'Jeez! This is getting heavy now,' Jaz exclaimed. 'What's to say we're not going to get a crazed ticket collector gunning for us next?'

'You won't on here. It's safe. He's around,' Ellie reassured

378

them.

'Darkall?' clarified Meg.

'Yes.'

'How do you know?' asked Jaz.

'Three ways.' Ellie counted them off on her fingers. 'One: he gives me subtle hints, like a quick flash of his strange eyes in a dark reflective surface. Two: I've noticed that the ring tremors or vibrates slightly when he is or has been around. And three—I just feel safe.'

'Well, I can't comment on his presence, as only you can detect those hints, but your feelings about danger have been pretty accurate so far. So I'm happy to trust we're in no immediate danger if you say you feel safe,' Meg reasoned.

'Wait until *you're* chased over half of bloody London,' said Flick in a dour voice.

Ellie turned to her. 'I'm sorry Flick. I'm sorry you were in danger once again because of me.' She turned to face the other two. 'And I'm sorry to the both of you, too. I hate not being able to guarantee your safety.'

'You fought them off as best you could, Ellie,' said a mollified Flick. 'You told me to get behind you and were willing to shield me with your body—and I won't forget that. It's just ... you didn't have the power to get rid of them like Darkall did. I think you urgently need to work on developing your powers. One of these times, Mr All Powerful is going to slip up and then it's curtains for the lot of us. You're the one with the magical weapons at your fingertips. You're the only one who can fight them.'

'That's just the problem—I don't know what I *can* do.' Ellie hung her head. 'I can't control it. I couldn't even summon it at first.' She held up her wrist to show them the energy-drained bracelet. 'I even had to take the energy from these to kickstart anything inside of me.'

Her three friends looked at the tarnished, twisted, dead bracelet. None spoke for a while; they just stared at it and looked at each other's faces.

Jaz cleared her throat. 'You took the energy from the crystals and Titch's amulet? You can do that? Move it around or suck it out of something else?'

Ellie thought for a moment; she hadn't really looked at it like that. In fact, she hadn't *thought* of it at all. She'd only intended to somehow tap into the protection power of the crystals and amulet. 'Err … yes. I suppose I can.'

Flick exhaled. 'Then you can definitely do more than you're giving yourself credit for, Ellie.'

'Do you think you could extract the power from other things, too? Like that jade statue your dad sent to Titch?' Jaz asked Ellie.

'I suppose so.'

'What about living things? Everything that's alive must have energy. Could you tap into the energy of a tree, for example, and take it to use? What about a creature?'

Flick asked the inevitable question. 'What about a *person*?'

'No! At least, I don't know—and I wouldn't. I couldn't risk turning a person into this.'

She shook her wrist, jangling the lifeless grey stones together. There was another pregnant pause as the enormity of what they represented sunk in.

'Shame.' Flick broke the silence. 'We could've used a few of my ex-boyfriends,' she quipped.

Jaz smiled and joined in. 'And some former members of my year group at Turrell's.' Coming back to the point, she chose her next words carefully. 'But seriously, harnessing energy from those around you could be a really powerful weapon.'

Ellie was about to refute Jaz's statement, to explain that there was no way she'd ever drain human energy, but she stopped herself. If she was truly honest with herself, if it came down to her friend's life or that of an attacker, what wouldn't she countenance to save her friend? Ellie looked at Jaz and gave a slight nod to show she'd recognised her point: Ellie might well have the ability to kill.

'Do you have any idea how you can learn about your powers, Ellie, or who could help you learn to control them?' Meg asked, her mind already working on how to solve the most pressing problem.

'Not really. The only person I can think of is Jill. She's already tried to help me. She suggested a protection energy method I could try.'

'Well, that's a start, at least. You can practice that until you talk to her again. Jill might even recommend someone else you could learn from. Like a mystic teacher or something.'

'Maybe,' Ellie answered, chewing her lip.

Sensing her hesitation, Meg tried another tack. 'There's always my Auntie Zara. She's kind of a white witch and has more understanding of mystical things than I do. We could go and see her in Wales. She has a place there. It's beautifully remote,' she suggested enthusiastically. 'Maybe a few days away from it all, somewhere without many people around, is just what we all need right now.'

Jaz smiled affectionately at Meg and brought their clasped hands up from under the table. She planted a kiss on Meg's folded fingers before laying their joined hands onto the tabletop.

'It was Zara who gave me the recipe for the banner,' said Meg, further promoting her scheme.

Lost in thought, Ellie surfaced with a frown. 'Sorry? You were given a recipe for your banner? The one on the march? Why did it need a recipe?'

'Yes, well not the banner itself. Zara gave me a recipe for the protection spell and warding herbs that I sewed into it. I put them in the handles and around the hem at the edge of the sheet. That's why when a surge of protesters startled us from the right, we wrapped it around you in case you were under attack.'

Ellie recalled a strong waft of floral scent from when she'd first held the banner. At the time, she had thought it was fabric conditioner.

'Lavender?' she asked.

'Yes, and a few other things. Lavender has been used for protection for centuries. It safeguards against attack from the Evil Eye, ill wishes and psychic attack. It also drives off demons and evil spirits. In fact, people used to be put it in bathwater to drive away spirits thought to be making children testy and draining the strength of adults,' Meg added, unable to resist the opportunity to enlighten her friends. 'Rosemary, too. It's a powerful guardian and specifically gives power to women. Many people use it to ward off evil.'

Ellie looked around at her friends. 'You all knew about this?' she asked.

'Yes. We had it all planned,' Flick answered her.

Ellie thought for a moment.

'So, when I saw the banner laid over your bed at Titch's … ?'

'Ah, well, we were a bit shaken up that night. We thought

382

any extra protection while we slept couldn't do any harm,' explained Jaz.

'You had all this prepared to protect me?'

The others nodded.

Ellie was overwhelmed. All the while she had been blaming herself for not being able to protect her friends and keep them out of danger, they had actually been trying to keep *her* safe. She reached across the table and squeezed Meg's and Jaz's interlocked fingers, then did the same to Flick's arm. A tear ran down her cheek.

'I don't know what to say,' Ellie said in a choked voice. 'Thank you.'

Meg squeezed her hand in response, and Flick tucked Ellie's arm through hers.

'We meant what we said back at Bertie's. We have your back,' Jaz reminded Ellie.

'Well, I'm definitely going to have a chat with Zara,' Meg said in a decisive tone. 'I'm sure she can teach us more methods of keeping each other safe.'

'Good idea,' agreed Ellie, feeling she had underestimated her friends once again. After a moment's thought, she said, 'There was one other thing that I wanted to run past you ....'

'Hmm,' said Flick, her index finger pressed to her lips, pretending to consider the question. 'That could literally be *anything*, considering how far we are now into the world of weird, but fire away.'

Ellie cleared her throat.

'Straight after Darkall fired his energy bolt at the zombies, he took us both to a cellar.' Flick frowned and was about to speak, but Ellie continued before she could. 'It was only for the briefest of moments before returning us to the alley.

383

Maybe I should have said "transported" rather than "took.""

Flick's face cleared as she recalled the brief sense of darkness she'd previously attributed to having passed out, but then she frowned again. 'What was the point of that? It gave you no time to talk to him or anything,' she asked.

'We did talk,' Ellie replied.

'Sorry, I don't understand.'

Ellie rubbed her head, knowing the next bit was going to sound the craziest yet. 'He took us both to a cellar and removed me from real time. He and I talked while everything else around us was frozen.'

Her statement was met with silence and confused, stunned faces.

'How can you be outside of time when you're a creature of it?' Flick objected. 'We all are. Without time, we'd be all frozen in one moment, unable to move forwards.'

'That's exactly what you were,' Ellie said, speaking directly to Flick. 'Frozen like a statue. Although I suppose you'd really have been moving, but just incredibly slowly, from my perspective. Darkall is able to take me out of my ... *timeline*, I think he said ... but I have to remain in contact with him, otherwise I'd just be a statue, too, and unable to communicate. I can't stay like that for long; I started to lose all my senses, and just before we left, all I felt was my mind, with no body attached.'

'Sorry, but I just can't get my head around that,' said Flick, shaking her head. 'You were *unconscious* on the ground in the alley. I had to wake you up.'

'Yes, I was out cold. I think being outside my normal time caused me to lose consciousness,' clarified Ellie.

A few moments passed while they considered this and then

Jaz started to speak slowly, as if warming up her thoughts.

'We live in a four-dimensional universe. There are the three space dimensions of height, width and depth and then time is the fourth dimension. Except time is different from the others, as it is a single-direction dimension. Interestingly, scientists have identified other dimensions—about twenty-six, I think the count is up to— but they're so small as to be insignificant because they didn't get themselves sorted out properly way back during the Big Bang, when height, width, depth and time stole the show. Anyway, coming back to time, we need time to move forwards, but we can't go backwards or sideways through it. Our four-dimensional space-time picture of our lives would be like a long snake; starting at one end when we're born, then morphing into adulthood and old age along the length of the snake's body before ceasing at our death. This 4D object, or snake, twists around in three-dimensional space, but its curves only go forwards and don't loop backwards because time doesn't go backwards. Although *we* can only move forwards in time, we have to allow that it's possible for something else—something that can exist in more dimensions than we can—to be able to move through time in different directions, like we can in our three space dimensions.'

'Einstein said time was relative,' added Meg. 'He formulated that speed equals distance divided by time, which works for most things, but he also worked out that for an object travelling at near light speed, the parameters change. The object will see distances around it as shortened—it's called Lorentz contraction—and the time experienced by the object is reduced. Or at least, I think I've got that right. It's called time dilation.'

'Spot on,' agreed Jaz. 'Time can vary. It's not as fixed as we think it is—or at least as fixed as we experience it to be. For example, time goes slower if you're moving faster because you experience less of it compared to the time of someone at rest. Someone worked out that an astronaut who spent a year whizzing around the planet in a space station had actually aged ten milliseconds less than his twin back on Earth.'

Flick looked amazed, if somewhat disbelieving.

'It's a fact,' said Jaz, grinning. 'Huge masses warp space-time, too, like bowling balls on a stretched rubber sheet. Time is slower near these masses than further away from them, where their gravitational effect is stronger: it's called gravitational time dilation. Black holes—being super dense matter and so *super masses*—slow time around them, too. Time is not as set in stone as we might think.'

Jaz paused to marshal the words for her next point.

'Coming back to what you've said, Ellie, I really have no idea. But I suppose what I'm running through in my mind is that because we only move forwards in time, we don't really know how other things might move through it—or even in and out of it. Even quantum physics hasn't got that one properly worked out yet. Logically, if you're not bound by the rules of our four dimensions, I suppose anything is possible when it comes to time.'

Ellie nodded, impressed as always with the recall ability of Jaz's mind and all the knowledge and understanding she managed to cram in there.

'I reckon I could have come up with "We just don't know. Anything is possible" without the long-winded lecture,' said Flick, before adding, 'It was pretty interesting, though.'

Jaz smiled at the unexpected compliment and raised her

eyebrows at Flick in surprise.

'Well,' Flick blustered, caught out at being pleasant to her arch-rival. 'If we're living on a knife edge, not knowing who might get attacked next or whether we'll survive it, then I suppose it's OK to let you guys know how important you are to me.'

'Why thank you, Felicity,' responded Jaz.

Ellie grinned. 'Is that because I'm a gold bucket?' she asked.

'Excuse me?' said Meg.

'It's something a child said to their mum about me in one of the museum galleries.'

'That you were a gold bucket? That's pretty *specific*,' queried Jaz in disbelief.

'Something about me being sparkly like the gold bucket. They were in the Sutton Hoo gallery.'

'What was in the gallery where you first saw the child? Anything unusual?' Meg asked.

'I was looking at the Oxus Treasure. An armlet caught my attention, and when I looked for energy around it, I saw it was pulsing with a purple-red energy. There was another exhibit further on that was swirling with gold energy.' Ellie paused as realisation dawned. '*Oh.*'

'What?'

'The thing swirling with gold sparkles—it was a gold *buckle* in the Sutton Hoo gallery.'

'Would this happen to be the same gallery where the hoard that contained Titch's amulets is on display?' asked Jaz in a suspicious tone. 'Could it be that the buckle is from that very same hoard that blew the metal detectorist into a tree just for unearthing it? And you're apparently sparkling with the same energy as this clearly very powerful and ancient artefact, are you? *Wow.*'

Jaz sat back in her seat with an air of a barrister resting their case.

'It didn't say that on the card. It said that the buckle was found in the ship burial,' Ellie objected, in defence of her consistent underestimation of her own abilities.

'Well, it was hardly likely to say "found by traumatised metal detectorist and speedily hushed up", was it? So, my point still stands,' argued Jaz.

Meg leant forwards. 'Ellie, the child could see your energy, just as it could see the energy emitted by the gold buckle. You share the same power!'

'How weird that the child could see the energy,' remarked Ellie.

'I'm finding it even more weird that you're leaking gold sparkles,' replied Flick. 'I'm seriously hoping none of them rub off onto me! Eugh! And I'm the one sitting next to you for the next couple of hours! Roll on Laneway Station; the end of the line ain't coming soon enough for me!'

With a feigned look of disgust and pretending to brush things from the sleeve of her top, Flick turned towards the window, used her jacket as a pillow and settled as comfortably as she could to try and get some sleep. 'Night-night, chicks,' she said.

'Good idea,' said Meg with a tired smile. 'It definitely feels like our trip's been longer than one night. I'm not sure my brain can take any more revelations at the moment.'

With a yawn, she leaned her head against Jaz's shoulder and closed her eyes. Ellie and Jaz soon followed suit, balling up their jumpers as pillows. Consequently, as the train journeyed across the vast green waistband of England, all four friends slept soundly in their First Class compartment.

# 32

# Chapter 32

Ellie was pleased to be back at home. Chris had met them at Lowford Station and driven them back to the college car park to collect their own vehicles. The train journey had been thankfully uneventful, and they hugged one another before parting ways. Yet Ellie couldn't help but feel that her friends must be relieved to be getting away from her and the ever-present danger which stalked her.

By the time she arrived at Owl's Ridge, it was getting dark outside. A few birds flew over her head on their way to roost as she got out of her car and crunched across the gravel to the front door. Glancing at the lit window, she noted that her mother had replaced the broken bottle charm that had hung from the lintel.

Thinking back to when she'd cut her finger on the broken glass, Ellie marvelled at how naive she'd been back then in trying to find a plausible, rational explanation for why it had broken. Indeed, what would she think if she'd found the broken bottle now instead of then? An attack on her home could be either psychic, physical or magical. Was that, in fact, what had happened to the original bottle? Alarms bells rang in her mind, and she hurriedly opened the front door and, once inside, bolted it securely behind her. Leaning against the back of the door, Ellie took several deep breaths.

'Ellie, is that you?' her mother's voice called from the kitchen.

Ellie hung her jacket on the hooks by the door and dumped her backpack at the bottom of the stairs. 'Yes, Mum.'

Taking a few more calming breaths, Ellie steadied herself to face her parents. Her mum came out of the kitchen door, tea towel in hand, and, walking forwards, enveloped Ellie in a hug. 'Good to have you home, sweetheart,' Grace said warmly.

Ellie's stiff shoulders sagged onto her mother's, and she sobbed a great breath born of tension, fear, anxiety and relief to be home.

'Hey, hey, sweetheart. Shh,' her mother said, stroking the back of Ellie's head and holding it against her shoulder like she'd done since Ellie was a small child. 'It's OK. We can sort it out, whatever it is.'

Ellie pulled herself together and straightened up with a watery smile. 'It's OK, Mum. I'm just glad to be back, that's all.'

'Oh, honey. Come on in and see your dad.'

Andy was sat at the kitchen table, reading a book. Sprawled on their communal bed in front of the Aga, Raff and Chipper's paws twitched occasionally as they dreamed of chasing pheasants. Andy looked up and pushed his rectangular steel-framed glasses back up his nose.

'Hey, Wellie. Glad to have you home.' He smiled. 'Did you have a good trip?'

'Yes and no, Dad. Some bits were better than others.'

'Do you want to tell us about it?' he offered.

This was it. This was the perfect moment to tell her parents about everything that had been going on—all the weird stuff, the terror, the attacks, her abilities. All of it.

Ellie baulked. How could she do it to them? How could she destroy their comfortable world of New Age beliefs and pseudo-science which they'd blended so snugly together over the last twenty years?

Ellie swallowed nervously as the moment stretched out awkwardly before her. Both Grace and Andy were looking at her with loving concern etched on their faces.

'No, it's fine. I'm OK,' she said, chickening out. 'I think I just need to get some sleep. It's been a very busy couple of days.'

'OK, well … if you're sure,' said Grace. 'Maybe you can tell us about it tomorrow if it's still bothering you.'

'Thanks, Mum.'

Ellie hugged her mother and gave her father a kiss on the cheek before heading out of the kitchen. Scooping up her backpack, she slowly made her way upstairs to her bedroom. She could hear her parents quietly discussing her in concerned voices, and she paused at the top of the stairs to listen. Her mother was suggesting phoning Titch to find out what had happened, but her father said it would be better to wait and let Ellie tell them about whatever it was that had gone wrong with the trip; it had obviously upset her, but maybe it was a friendship thing and nothing that Titch would know about. Her mother finally agreed, but vowed to phone him this time tomorrow if Ellie was still upset and uncommunicative.

Realising she was earwigging on her parents, Ellie moved on to her room. Shutting the door, she collapsed onto her bed. Lying on her side, she curled herself into a ball, still fully clothed.

'Are you there?' she asked the darkness. 'Can you just hold me?'

Darkall's arms curled around her body and Ellie relaxed against him, feeling cosseted, cherished and guarded. She sighed. No words were needed nor wanted; she didn't want to discuss anything or question him. She just wanted to feel safe and secure, defended against all the terror and bizarre abnormality of recent days by the only being that could safeguard her completely.

As if sensing her thoughts, Darkall had not apparated to avoid being visible to either of her parents should they check in on Ellie later. But he was here with her, holding her, and because of that, she was finally able to relax fully into an exhausted, dreamless sleep.

* * *

Ellie slept until the middle of the next morning and woke alone. Neither of her parents worried about her missing college that day, and nor did Ellie. Sometimes, you just had to deal with what was in front of you and put the other stuff on hold.

After showering and dressing in fresh clothes, Ellie went downstairs to find some brunch. In the kitchen, she found fresh bread and, cutting a thick slice, slathered it with butter and honey before making herself a cup of coffee. Perfect.

She peered out of the kitchen window while munching on

her bread and saw Grace in the garden. Not yet ready to have the inevitable conversation, Ellie chose not to join her and instead took herself into the study to sit in her father's chair.

As much as the vegetable patch was Andy's domain outside of the house, so, too, was the study his interior kingdom. There were built-in bookshelves all along one side of the room, a window to the front garden and Andy's desk along the wall underneath it. It was one of those vintage desks with a green leather top. Andy kept a traditional blotter on it, more for putting coffee cups down on and jotting phone messages than for blotting ink pens, as he worked mostly via computer.

Ellie thought about phoning Jill, but should she tell her parents all that had happened in London first? No, maybe not. Jill, at least, knew some of the story, whereas telling her parents would involve having to begin back at square one.

The phone rang eight times before Jill picked up. She immediately began speaking in a grave tone.

'I have spoken to Titch, and he's informed me of what happened in London. This is very serious, Ellie. The cards say that you are in great danger.'

Ellie felt this to be rather a moot point and certainly not one she needed pointing out to her.

'Have you spoken to your parents yet? Are they up-to-date with all that has occurred?'

'No, not yet. I'm planning on telling them today.'

'I urge you to do it right away.'

'I'll tell them today,' Ellie said more firmly.

'I'm glad to hear it. If you don't, I will be forced to tell them myself. This is now an issue of your personal safety.'

'It's for *their* safety I haven't soiled their lives with all this eerie stuff.'

'You continue to underestimate them. They will surprise you. Tell them, Ellie.'

'*I will*,' Ellie almost snapped.

'Good. Now, have you been practising that protection energy visualisation technique I suggested?'

Ellie hadn't, and she felt like a guilty schoolgirl in front of the headmistress. 'No. I did try to use it to save Flick and me from the three possessed people attacking us, but it didn't work.'

'You can't expect it to work without you taking the trouble to practise it.'

The feeling that she was being told off grew even stronger. 'I *will* work on it, I promise.'

'Make sure you do. It is not just your safety at stake here. If your friends are to be safe, you must put more effort into developing your skills.'

Ellie felt the guilt rising uncomfortably again; an ever-present guilt that she was putting those she loved in danger. It soured her stomach to acid.

'Ellie, this is not your fault,' Jill said with remarkable perspicacity, 'But it *is* your responsibility to deal with and to find a safe route through to the end. You are the only one who can. Remember your first reading? The Tarot foretold that you had to face the change that was coming because to ignore it would be to endanger those you loved. And you are in danger of doing just that, Ellie: you are hiding information from your parents that could help them to be safe. In underestimating your abilities, by hiding from them and denying them instead of embracing, exploring and developing them, you put yourself and those around you at great risk.'

Ellie felt her anger at Jill's censure drain out of her. Jill was right. She was letting everyone down and putting them in danger when they needn't be. She was the only one who could deal with the Others, and that was what she had to do.

But how was she meant to accomplish that? Who could show her what to do?

'It might be something you are going to have to work out for yourself, Ellie. I can only help so far; your abilities are reaching beyond my understanding.'

Ellie sighed. She might as well fill Jill in on the whole picture.

'I've discovered something else I appear to be able to do. I can move energy.'

'I would have thought that was obvious, Ellie, or you wouldn't have been able to transfer your energy to another creature to heal it.'

'Not just that. I seem to be able to drain things of their energy and use it for myself. To enhance my own power.'

'A Syphon? Are you sure? That is extremely rare—unheard of, in fact! I have only read about the ability as speculation.'

Ellie recounted to Jill the fate of her bracelet.

'Well, well. That is potentially a very valuable skill. But you must be extremely careful if you were ever to use it on a living being. You could inadvertently drain too much energy and kill them.'

'I'd already thought of that,' Ellie replied.

'Your abilities are already evident: healing, protecting, being a Syphon. Even boiling your coffee demonstrates what a vast amount of energy is yours to control. You have to learn to utilise effectively what you can already do, while at the same time push yourself to find out what else has been gifted to you. There is not time for you to wait about in the hope that your abilities will simply reveal themselves.'

Ellie felt a hollow pit of worry forming in her stomach and her confidence slipping into it. How was she supposed to find what she could do without even a hint of what to look for? It felt like she'd be searching for a needle in a haystack, and it was even more daunting to know that the haystack hiding the needle was *herself*.

'Don't beat about the bush. Ask for help. Ask *him* for help. Lives may well depend upon you embracing this next stage of your evolution.'

Ellie sighed. 'I will, I promise.'

Seemingly satisfied with Ellie's response, Jill said goodbye and hung up.

Ellie sat staring out of the study window, seeing nothing. She felt alone. All this had been thrust on her shoulders, and she didn't know how to carry the burden. She dropped her head onto her hands and looked down at the desk.

Over the years, her father had scribbled over the entire surface of the blotting paper, making notes and turning coffee cup rings into designs and circular travelling caterpillars. Inside one of the coffee circles, a particular doodle caught her eye. It was a spiral; not just concentric to the ring mark, but offset and oval in form, like the one on her ring. Another odd coincidence?

She couldn't believe in coincidence anymore. She had to speak to her parents.

Ellie went into the kitchen. Her mother had come in from the garden and was washing her hands in the sink, a bunch of cut flowers lay on the draining board.

'Mum, can we have a talk, please?' Ellie asked.

Stock-still for just a moment, Grace turned around and gave Ellie an encouraging smile. 'Yes, of course we can, darling. You can tell me anything, you know that.'

'With Dad, too. What I have to tell concerns both of you.'

Grace's expression faltered, concern briefly flickering in her eyes, although she kept a reassuring smile plastered across her face. 'Of course,' she said, going to the kitchen door and calling for Andy, who was in his usual retreat of the vegetable garden. 'I'll put the kettle on, shall I?'

Leaving his muddy boots outside the door, Andy walked into the kitchen in his thick stripy socks.

'Ellie has something she wants to talk to us about,' Grace explained to him.

'Oh, right,' he responded in an overly positive voice, like his wife had just announced she'd made his favourite chocolate trifle for tea and it was imperative he came in and ate the lot right away.

Ellie got the feeling that her parents had discussed how to behave if she decided to explain what was bothering her, and that enthusiastic positivity was their chosen format for the big reveal.

Andy briefly washed his muddy hands and, drying them on the tea towel, sat down at the table. It was a mark of how determined they were to keep the atmosphere positive and encouraging that Grace made no comment: him using the dish-drying towel as a hand towel was one of her pet hates.

Grace set mugs of tea down on the scrubbed pine tabletop. The table had been in the kitchen for as long as Ellie could remember. It displayed evidence of her painting attempts as a young child and her cursive writing practise as a heavy-handed eight-year-old, all the way through to thoughtless teenage doodles and gum collections on the underside. It was their family meeting point. It had bore witness to remonstrations and talks delivered on misbehaviour, meals with friends that stretched late into the night as conversation flowed back and forth, celebrations and daily family life for over two decades. Grace pulled out a chair and sat down beside Andy. They both looked up at Ellie expectantly.

Taking a deep breath, Ellie pushed herself away from the pine dresser and stepped around to the other side of the table. Twisting the ring from her finger, she sat down and placed it in the middle of the table. The audible tap of metal on wood in the expectant silence drew their attention to it.

'A while ago, I bought this ring,' Ellie began.

* * *

Some considerable time later—well over an hour, Ellie would have thought—she came to the end of her account. Her parents had sat and listened in near silence for the whole of her tale. They sensed that to interrupt at any point would be to break the flow and possibly prevent their daughter from fully unburdening herself. Grace had gasped in shock when hearing of the attacks and smiled slightly when hearing of Ellie's burgeoning powers, then more fully when she had heard of the support of Ellie's friends. Yet, most unexpectedly, neither of her parents had looked disbelieving or incredulous at any point during their daughter's account.

Ellie rubbed her eyes as she finished recounting her recent conversation with Jill and that she, Ellie, had apparently now developed the abilities of a Syphon. Andy raised his eyebrows in surprise, but not disbelief.

Ellie sat silently waiting for them to speak; to question or challenge what was clearly impossible from their rational, parental point of view. But they didn't. Eventually, Andy looked at Grace, a question in his eyes.

Grace raised her eyebrows at him, but then changed her mind and gave a slight shake of her head. 'Later. She's tired,' she said quietly to him.

Andy turned to Ellie and reached across the table to take one of her hands. Her ring, which he'd been turning around in his fingers for the last half an hour, he slid back onto her finger. Ellie felt relieved, as the heavy, cool metal was once again against her skin.

'You have been very brave, Wellie.' Her father spoke the words in a rather croaky voice; they were not what Ellie had been expecting at all. Clearing his throat, he continued. 'When you were fourteen, you tripped over one of the spaniels and were saved from a bad head injury by a pile of sofa cushions that hadn't been there moments before.'

'Yes, I remember,' Ellie said quietly.

'When you were small, you fell off the fence by the barn ruins and instead of landing on the piles of granite below, you landed feet away on the compost heap,' Grace added. 'Further back, when you were only about three years old, you escaped from the garden and wandered into the middle of the field where there was a herd of steers. A shot sounded in the field on the other side of the lane—either a bird scarer or the farmer shooting crows—and we looked up to see you standing in the middle of the field with twenty huge, spooked cattle rushing towards you. I just froze, but your father ran to the gate, vaulted it and tore across the grass to get to you.'

400

Grace's voice faltered at the painful memory.

'However, we could both clearly see that there was no way he was going to reach you in time. I have never been so scared. I remember hearing this keening wail and realising it was coming from my own throat. There you were, a tiny three-year-old just standing blissfully pulling at grass heads directly in the path of tons of frightened, stampeding cattle. Then, within just metres of you, the charging cattle suddenly diverted from their course, like there was an invisible wall between you and them. Once the shock had worn off, and we were sure that you were fine, I remember joking that you must have a friendly ghost watching out for you or your own personal guardian spirit. I suppose we didn't know how right we were. But we've always known there was something special about you, Ellie, and that, because of it, you may be facing a destiny greater than most.'

Ellie didn't answer; she just sat there, turning the ring around her finger and staring at it as she did so.

'Your ring has an inscription on the inside,' Andy said. 'The first part is Latin. The rest I can't read—one of the ancient languages that don't use the European alphabet, maybe.'

Ellie frowned; she recalled the inscription being written *entirely* in a language she couldn't read, otherwise she would have worked out the meaning herself. She took the ring off her finger and peered inside the shank.

Andy was right; the first three words could now be read. She looked at her father while sliding it back on.

'*Luceu inventi tenebras,*' said Andy. 'It means "the light from darkness found" or, to put it more clearly, "light found darkness". It's you and him, Wellie; you're the light and he is darkness. Whatever else he is, he is part of your future now.'

'May I see the ring again, please?' Grace asked.

Ellie slipped it from her finger again, now used to the pang of regret each time she did so, and passed it to her mother.

'Have you really looked at the design of this ring, Ellie?' Grace asked. 'Five white crystals leading to the spiral centre stone. By my count, you met Darkall five times before you kissed him: the Spring Thing, on the terrace at Baubles, by the river, when you ran out of petrol and here, in the garden. Five meetings and then you were together; five crystal chips on the ring. The ring has accurately predicted the timing of you and him meeting, but there is more. Five is the number of Man, who is a mortal. Five mortal steps you took towards him and now you are at the centre point of the spiral, where the purple stone sits. You have taken the sixth step, and you have stepped beyond mortal. You have evolved these incredible powers; you are now more than just a mere mortal.'

Ellie looked shocked. She hadn't considered for a moment that developing abilities beyond normal human parameters meant she was becoming something *other* than human; other than mortal, even.

Seeing her expression, Grace continued. 'If I'm right, Ellie, you've been wearing a symbol of your destiny the whole time.' Seeing Ellie's perturbed expression, she added, 'You are with him now. Trust that.'

Grace smiled a gentle smile and handed the spiral ring back to Ellie. 'And here is something from me to you,' she added, forcefully twisting one of her own "pebble rings" from her hand and passing it to Ellie. 'It's a moss agate. Not like your ring at all, but still beautiful and helpful in connecting you to the Earth and nature as you journey further from it. It is also an aid to healing and clear thinking and was once thought to make warriors strong. Wear it on your middle finger, Ellie, so that its halfway between your five digits; grounding Man from within.'

Ellie took the ring and slid it onto the middle finger of her left hand. Her mother's hands were the same size as hers, although Grace's fingers were slightly thicker from work and age. It slid easily onto Ellie's finger and sat comfortably between her index and ring fingers.

Pushing back her chair, she stood up and took several paces back and forth across the kitchen to stretch her leg muscles. Ellie linked her hands on the top of her head and took a deep breath, then blew it out slowly. She turned to her parents.

'I thought you would be different about this,' she said. 'Shocked or disbelieving or angry or something. Everyone's been urging me to talk to you; Jill even threatened to do it today if I didn't. I should have given you more credit, and I'm sorry. But I was trying to protect you from all this. Once people get involved in what's going on around me, they get thrust into dangerous situations.'

Andy smiled and came to stand in front of her, as did Grace. 'I have to say, I'm not totally surprised by what you've told us. It's not utterly unexpected, considering you are our daughter,' he said.

'We knew there was something going on following the Tarot reading Jill did for you. But we didn't understand how deeply it was connected to you. We are here for you one hundred percent; we're your parents. We've always loved you and always will.'

Grace smiled and stepped forwards to hug Ellie, then Andy reached out and wrapped his arms around them both. He rested his chin on top of Ellie's head.

'There are more things that we need to talk about; things we should explain to you,' he said. 'But not today; they will keep for tomorrow. Today, I think we just need to digest everything you've told us and, more importantly, savour the fact we're all here together, all safe and loved. We should take a little while to really appreciate that fact and relish it.'

He gave them both an extra squeeze before releasing them. 'Now, who's for lunch? I'm starving,' he said with a smile.

# 33

# Chapter 33

After a surprisingly lighthearted family lunch, Ellie wandered back up to her room. She picked up a book at random from her bookshelf and lay on her bed, determined to lose herself in the story and not to think about anything else. She must have dozed off, as she woke suddenly, feeling as though something was badly wrong.

Scrambling quickly off her bed, she didn't know in which direction to dash to confirm her fears. Closing her eyes for a moment, she felt a tug towards the bedroom window. Crossing the room in three strides, Ellie looked out to see the rear of a grey four-by-four idling at the driveway gate. She couldn't see much from where she stood and opened the casement to stretch out and see more. Holding the frame, she leaned right out of the window before freezing in horror at the sight of her father standing at the driveway gate, talking to the occupants of the vehicle.

It was them.

The Others.

She caught a whiff of their reek, even at her elevated

405

position, and a wave of dizziness washed over her. She grabbed at the windowsill to steady herself, and, in doing so, her hand unintentionally grasped one of the amethyst crystals her mother had placed there. It was hot. She looked down at the windowsill and saw that the dried leaves in one of Grace's charm bottles were smouldering: the protection crystals and charms had all been triggered.

Ellie rushed from her room and hurtled down the staircase. She had to get to her father before the Others hurt him in their search for her. She slammed the front door back against the wall and raced through, skidding abruptly to a halt as the stench hit her full force. It was reminiscent of something dead and decaying, but the sheer potency was like rotting meat festering and suppurating in a sealed container that had just been opened. Ellie retched and held her sleeve over her mouth to breathe, the repugnant smell so strong that her eyes were watering.

'Very generous, and far more than it's worth, I'm sure.'

Andy's voice floated over to her. How was her dad not noticing this? He just stood there, talking to them like they were normal. Could he not sense them? Could he not *smell* them?

Her vision blurred. Blinking and rubbing her eyes, she saw clearly, for the first time, what was really inside the car. The Others were wearing human clothes—dark grey suits, and by the look of it, one of them was wearing what remained of the suit's previous owner, too. Waxy, yellowed skin sagging and eyeless sockets staring, the cadaver's head turned towards her, its mouth open and hissing. The other occupant of the vehicle didn't share the same state of decay. Maybe it was a still living person, but if so, clearly one being possessed. He also turned to stare at Ellie, a hissing noise emanating from his partly opened mouth.

Ellie looked at her father. He was casually leaning with one hand on the wooden five-bar gate, the other on his hip in a relaxed pose. He was talking to the Others as if they were conversing normally, although, clearly, they were doing no such thing.

At any moment, they could reach out of the vehicle and attack him; she had to get her dad away from the disgusting, stinking abominations. But what could she do? Ellie felt the familiar panic rising in her chest. She had no skills, no mastery of her power with which to protect her father. She just stood there, putting his life in greater danger with every passing second. What use was she?

None. She was nothing.

Tears rolled down her cheeks as she stood there, flaccid and impotent. She closed her eyes in shame.

'*Eleanor.*' Darkall's voice drifted across her mind.

She felt the slightest pressure of his touch mid-forehead; just a suggestion of his hand against her skin. Her eyes snapped open.

No. She was *not* nothing. She had more than anyone else did; she had a power drawn from her energy, and she could use it. How dare these detestable things come here, to her home, and threaten her family! How dare they be here in all their repulsiveness, choking the air with their rank foulness, sucking the will out of her! She would not tolerate such an outrage. She would not allow them to be here. This was her family home—and she would fight them for it.

Anger rose in Ellie like a tide. She straightened her spine and squared her shoulders, then planted her feet firmly on the ground and clasped her hands in front of her, as Darkall had shown her.

Touching the hand spiral briefly to her forehead, she then dropped it and punched it to her sternum. She closed her eyes. She could see a line of silver energy connecting her head to her chest, dancing with the ragged power of a lightning bolt. Ellie cleared her mind and filled the space behind her eyelids with silver-white light. Keeping all thoughts at bay for over ten seconds, she felt the tingling rising at the back of her head. She let it build; let it burn behind her eyelids until it was almost unbearable.

At the point at which she could hold it no more, she opened her eyes and released the energy, pushing it from her head and down into her spiralled hands. Simultaneously, she thrust her hands forwards and blasted the energy out of her, sending it streaming towards the four-by-four, her will burning as brightly as the blue-white light shooting from her hands.

*GO.*

There was a flash of light. Andy staggered, fell to his knees and then began to vomit. The vehicle, which had been sat with its engine idling, shot forwards. Its left front wheel climbed the verge and half the height of the hedge before it swerved the other way and dropped back onto the road. Careering madly from hedge to hedge, it finally righted itself and sped on down the lane, disappearing around the corner.

Ellie rushed to her dad and knelt down beside him, avoiding the pool of dark mucus on the ground. 'Dad! Are you OK?'

'I'm … I don't know. What's that god-awful smell?'

'It's them!' replied Ellie. 'You were standing there, casually talking to people being controlled by the Others!'

'I was talking to a couple of guys searching for a home in the area for a client. They offered to buy this place, but I told them it wasn't for sale.'

'No, Dad. You were being mind-controlled to see only what they wanted you to. It was *them*,' she said, shuddering at the memory of the gawping cadaver.

As he took the handkerchief from his shirt pocket, she noticed two pale stripes encircling his fingers that contrasted sharply with his tanned skin. Her father was not wearing his usual rings. The incongruity struck her; she'd never seen him without his rings. To her, it was as peculiar as if he'd been standing at the gate naked.

'Dad, where's your ring? The one your old professor gave you. And where's your wedding ring?'

'They're on the kitchen table; I took them off just before I came out here. I was thinking about your ring and how it chose you—or you chose it— how, either way, it had mapped and shaped your recent past. I guess I was just following a hunch; I thought I'd see what life was like without them, just in case anything felt different, you know.'

She helped him to his feet.

'I'm OK, Ellie,' he said. 'I'll just go in for a glass of water and sit down for five minutes, then I'll be right as rain.'

She knew he hated being ill in front of her, that he wanted to maintain the strong father figure for his little girl, so she didn't offer to help him any further and merely watched him walk into the house.

Ellie leant on the gate, the end furthest away from the vomit, and looked down the lane. She turned slightly to see further, then snatched her bare arm away from the gatepost, peering at the reddened skin. The granite was hot—not just warmed-in-the-sun-type hot, but painful heat. She gingerly grazed her fingertips against the rough surface to find the hottest point. Climbing the first two bars of the gate, she leant over to examine the outward face of the post where the stone was too hot to touch.

There it was: a spiral. Another ward of Darkall's making. But this one wasn't freshly carved or scored through like the one on the stile that she'd mistaken for a knot in the wood. This one appeared as ancient as the gatepost, weathered and covered with lichen like old headstones. Just how long ago had it been carved?

Little plinks sounded from the cooling stone as the quartz crystals from which the granite was formed let go of their charge. Some had shattered, and tiny pieces of crystal fired off as the stone cooled. Ellie straightened up to protect her eyes, then stepped back down to the ground.

What if the ward hadn't been there? The Others would likely have been able to enter Owl's Ridge. She wrapped her arms around herself as she began to shake. Her intense anger had left with the energy blast and now she felt empty and scared for her parents' safety.

She walked around the house to the back garden, then down the path to her favourite tree. This spot always gave her solace; this was her place. But this time, no relief from her agitation was forthcoming. Leaning against the tree, usually such a source of comfort, just made her feel fidgety and unable to be still. She needed to move.

Marching back up to the house, she looked in through the kitchen window. Her mother stood with a comforting hand on her father's shoulder as he sat at the table, his head resting on his folded arms.

These two people who she loved most in all the world were not superhuman like she was supposedly becoming. They had no chance of standing up to creatures like the Others. They had no way of seeing the things that were really out there, ready to feed from humanity and use it for their own purposes.

She couldn't allow her parents to become embroiled any further in what was happening to her. Nor her friends. No one she loved was going to be made to suffer like Chris had—or worse, be killed because of her.

But what could she do?

Returning to the house, she grabbed her coat and car keys before shouting down the hall to her parents that she loved them and was going out. She couldn't bring herself to actually go into the kitchen and face them; she couldn't bear to see their beloved faces and give them the hugs she so badly needed. Guilt prevented her from doing so; she felt ashamed that she'd put everyone in this situation.

Leaving quickly, Ellie shut the front door behind her and opened the driveway gate before scrambling into Dolly and sending gravel flying in her haste to get away.

One thought was fixed in her mind. If she wasn't there, they wouldn't be harmed.

# Chapter 34

**The End of the Beginning ...**

Ellie drove on autopilot, her mind a whirlpool of unsolicited experience and fear: fear for her parents and friends; fear of the Others; fear of what was yet to be faced; fear of all she didn't yet know; and fear of her own inadequacy.

She needed to escape; to find sanctuary from the insane, impossible alternate reality in which she had become embroiled. To find peace and space in which to think.

How on earth had she thought she could possibly handle getting involved in all of this? She had been totally deluding herself; this was far too huge and strange and terrifying to even begin to adjust to and cope with. Her home, her friends, her parents—everything she had ever known was under attack because of her. She was the danger to them, and in that way, she was just as bad as the Others. She had to get away from anything she loved before she brought about its destruction.

Ellie drove to the moors, heading for the specific place

she'd always found had grounded her. It was her mental harbourage; a place where she could anchor her tumultuous thoughts, just as the granite tors anchored the moorland. Ellie's ancestors on her mother's side of the family had been hill farmers who had eked out an existence on the fringes of those moors. This place was Ellie's ancestral home; her roots; in her blood.

Her grandmother had told Ellie many tales of their forefathers and had always remarked during these accounts that "they were hard men, the moor farmers", meaning that they had to be very tough to draw a livelihood from the unforgiving, granite-strewn ground at the edges of the moors. Creating fields on the moors had meant moving many tons of granite boulders and rocks from the peaty soil, then using these to build stock proof walls which enclosed the acres and declared them as now tamed and separate from the wild moorland. The walls still demarcated the ancient fields at the edges of the steep land, although many of these boundaries had fallen into disrepair as generations passed and there were no longer men hardy enough to cultivate such wilful territory.

Man had survived on the moor since prehistoric times. Bronze Age hut circles could be found in many places, as well as other prehistoric markers such as monoliths and groups of huge stones marking the sites of ancient burial chambers. Naturally, there were local legends attached to many of these ancient monuments, and they were still recognised as places of mystery. One such single chamber tomb, consisting of three large, upright stones with a fourth stone balanced on top was called Spinsters' Grotto. Legend told that if an unmarried female were to stand under the stone ceiling on midsummer's eve from dusk until she could no longer see a black thread held in front of her eyes, then she would find herself a husband before the end of the year. Ellie loved the ghost stories and legends attributed to the moor; they added to its mystery and, hence, its allure for her.

She, too, knew of family legends relating to the moors where her ancestors had lived, worked and died. Her grandmother's family name had been Rice, and the stories were all of that long-lived family tree.

One such tale was of an irreverent forebear of Ellie's called Jack. Out on the moor late one night, he had seen a ghostly funeral procession making its way from the chapel in one village to the graveyard in the next, as was the custom in that district. Instead of showing due respect or fear, Jack had followed the procession, and from the moment it vanished at the lychgate of the graveyard, the fortunes of the Rice family took a turn for the worse. It was said that until a member of the family follows the ghostly procession back to the chapel, they will never be wealthy again. Grace usually joked, whenever the story was told, that she had often considered changing her name to Rice and doing exactly that.

The tales of her ancestors made Ellie feel that the moors were part of her soul; that she belonged there. Going to the moors felt like coming home.

* * *

Dolly climbed the twisting road that led to the high moors, and as her wheels trundled over a cattle grid marking the entrance to the wild land, a drop of calmness fell into the back of Ellie's mind, the first in a long while.

414

Trees now gave way to gorse, heather and tufted grass kept close-cropped by the hardy local sheep. Granite boulders were strewn indiscriminately across the open expanse of moorland spread before her, and behind her lay the shadowy vista of the low land. Ellie drove on towards her favourite place.

Tors capped the highest points of the moor here; evidence that the land had once been even higher. The enormous granite piles seemed to Ellie like the ancient teeth of that lost land. She'd read that some geologists thought the moor to have once been an enormous mountain and that today's high places are merely the ground-down stumps of that long-vanished leviathan landscape.

Climbing still further as the light slipped from the day, the austere beauty of the scenery began to soothe her. She felt her shoulders relax downwards and her hands unclench from around the steering wheel.

\* \* \*

Reaching her destination, Ellie pulled over and turned off Dolly's engine. She got out of the car, closed the door and, leaning against it, cast her eyes skywards. The sun was now setting, and night would soon descend softly across the countryside. Ellie thought that if she waited here long enough, it would be the perfect place to stargaze—maybe she might even see the Milky Way more clearly up here, where there was no light pollution. Ellie could recognise Orion's Belt and The Plough and, from that, work out the Pole Star around which the night's sky rotated; a further example of ceaseless rotational motion.

She sighed wearily. Ellie felt that she was in a constant state of motion herself, spinning from one bizarre event to the next, finding no time to stop and process these strange experiences, nor attempt to rationalize them. But, then again, could they actually be rationalised? Everything was pointing to the conclusion they could not. Was this perverse, secret world her reality now? And if so, could she accept it, or would she forever be trying to deny what she saw, heard and felt to explain away strange circumstance with thinly-spread excuses as she clung to the tatters of normality?

'There are more things in Heaven and earth, Horatio.'

Ellie sighed the famous lines from Shakespeare's Hamlet, the ones quoted to her by her father at a time that now felt so long ago. The words had stuck in her mind back then and now repeated themselves ceaselessly as she struggled to come to terms with all that was happening.

She yearned to be with Darkall, but then, what actually was he? Certainly not human. Could she, a mere mortal, really be with something like him? Had this ever happened before? It was not even as if she could go to Flick and Jaz for relationship advice. But then, according to her mother, she was becoming more than a mere mortal herself.

She leaned back against Dolly's roof and banged her head against it several times, as if she could knock her thoughts into some kind of order, or at least to stop their cyclonic raging.

Ellie prised herself away from the car and walked the short distance to her favoured granite boulder. It was a couple of metres square and flat, most of it underground. Slipping her feet from her shoes, she stepped onto the boulder.

The rock was cool but not cold against her skin, having not

yet relinquished the warmth drawn from the sun during the day. The surface felt like fused grit—the tiny, sharp crystals within the granite resolutely defiant of the weathering elements for millennia. Ellie knew granite to be one of the hardest of rocks, that was why the massive promontories of the tors still stood. She felt the age and gravity of the stone; eons had passed without it changing. Time stood still here.

Ellie cleared her mind of the spiralling questions. *Breathe: inhale, exhale. Blow out all the breath. Again, breathe.*

Feeling more centred, Ellie imagined all her confusion flowing out of her like water down a sink, whirlpooling into the rock below. She closed her eyes and inhaled the night air. A long moment passed. Finally, she was ready.

She spoke aloud into the lonely night, half dreading a reply, half fearing silence. 'Are you there?'

'Yes, Eleanor. I am here,' he answered her, his voice as close as an embrace.

'If I open my eyes, will I see you?' she asked.

'I am in front of you.'

Ellie kept her eyes closed. If she opened them now, then she would have to commit to going with him; to being with him. Everything she knew, everything from that point on, would be new and fantastically, horrendously unfamiliar and outlandish to her. All would change; her reality forever and irrevocably shifted.

Ellie felt scared to take that last step; to make all the strangeness real. She felt herself trembling despite the grounding granite beneath her feet. She pushed her toes against the hard, crystalline surface as if bracing for a leap from a diving board, and, taking one final, deep breath of her old life, Ellie opened her eyes and found herself looking directly into his.

Silver lights dancing against deepest purple were the first things she saw with her newly-unveiled eyes. Darkall cupped her face in his hands, his own face close enough to hers that the blue glow of his palm sigils illuminated it from beneath; making his strong features even more arresting.

'You are brave, Eleanor,' he said. 'You have chosen to see what most mortals refuse to: the truth of that which exists around them, that orders their lives and influences their destinies.'

Lowering his head while still keeping their gazes locked, Darkall pressed a kiss to her lips. A fizz of electricity instantly burned on Ellie's lips and she returned his kiss, crushing the tingle. Deepening the kiss and closing her eyes, Ellie put her arms around him, drawing the otherworldly being to her.

Reluctantly pulling back, Darkall stared into her eyes once more. 'You will not find this path easy,' he warned. 'There will be many things that you find strange and much that you will need to learn. But I will be there to help you, I promise you that.'

'Show me,' said Ellie.

# Epilogue

The next morning, the Johnstones knew that Ellie had gone. Her car had been returned without them hearing any engine noise or, indeed, without a single alarmed bark from the spaniels.

Then, of course, there was the note. It had been left on the kitchen table, propped up against a vase of white lilies. Beside it sat the box Titch had sent back with Ellie.

A piece of white paper had been folded into four, with *Mum & Dad* written by Ellie's hand across the outer leaf. When Grace had seen it upon first entering the kitchen, she'd let out a wail of anguish. Andy had run downstairs to find his wife crumpled on the quarry tiles, the opened letter clutched in her fist.

Andy took it from her and read the brief lines. Ellie assured them that she was OK and asked that they try not to worry about her: she was with Darkall and might be away for a while. At the bottom of the page was a spliced quote in Andy's own well-known style.

"'I cannot be whole without my shadow; the dark and the light dwells within all. To gain the stars, one traverses the dark, but to lighten that darkness, one must open one's eyes.'" Andy read aloud.

'She's gone with him,' said Grace flatly.

'Sounds like the essence of Jung.' Andy focussed on the

words to keep his tears in check. 'Our girl studied her psychology well,' he added.

'*Studies*,' corrected Grace, tears running down her cheeks. 'She *is* coming back.'

'Yes, of course she is,' Andy soothed, easing Grace up and onto a chair, then sitting down beside her. 'Our girl is a smart cookie. You've taught her well.'

Grace nodded but still sagged against his side, her loss overwhelming. 'Why her? Why any of us?' she sobbed. 'Couldn't we just have had a normal family life? Just be a normal family?'

Andy rubbed her back in an effort to comfort her, but forbore to answer her question as there was no reply he could give right now that would help her. He knew all too well the confusion and turmoil of having had the burden of being the Keeper thrust upon him when he was just a couple of years older than Ellie. Because of that, Andy understood some of what Ellie had been going through—and because of the Duty, so did his wife.

Andy ran his hand through his hair. He feared Ellie's trials were really only just beginning if she seriously intended to be with Darkall. There were others who would not be pleased with their union. Andy was worried for Ellie; she would have a seriously steep learning curve to tackle if she was going to keep ahead of Them.

'Let resolve steer your path,' murmured Andy, before lapsing into silence for several minutes. Absentmindedly fussing the ear of a spaniel, he sat staring directly ahead, looking without seeing, and listening to the sounds of his wife crying.

Eventually, Andy spoke, decisively reaching for his phone.

'I'll call Bertie, darling. And you must phone Jill. Titch will know already, as will Dorrin.

'We all need to meet.'

THE END.

# Acknowledgments

As ever with creative endeavour, feedback is key to producing the best outcome. Without my patient readers Christine, Sarah, Angie, Susan, Rachel and Christine, this book may never have gone further than the first draft. Thank you, ladies, for your observations and suggestions, and thank you to Ruth who told me to just sit down and start writing.

Thanks, also, to my editor Pete Smith of Novel Approach Manuscript Services Ltd., for his invaluable input and freely given support.

Lastly, special mention must be made of the efforts of my spaniels whose loving (yet inappropriately placed) paws sprinkled typos bountifully across the many drafts of this book. If you're very lucky, you may still find a few.

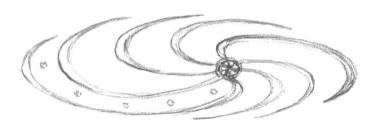

# Author's Note

If you've enjoyed reading Pivotal Darkness, please do leave a review on Amazon. Positive reader reviews are vital to self-published authors as they provide proof that our work is worth a read. Sales of self-published books are mostly online, and Amazon reviews can make or break a book. As most of us are filled with self-doubt to begin with, your thoughts can make our day...week...month, or even year. A little encouragement goes a long way!

Find out more about The Darkness Journals (and the next book in the sequence) on the EB Janes Writes Facebook page.

Printed in Great Britain
by Amazon